Copyright © 2024 by Melody Tyden

All rights reserved.

The characters and events portrayed in this book are fictitious. Any similarity to real persons, living or dead, is coincidental and not intended by the author.

No part of this book may be reproduced, or stored in a retrieval system, or transmitted in any form or by any means, electronic, mechanical, photocopying, recording, or otherwise, without express written permission of the publisher.

Cover design by: GetCovers

MELODY TYDEN

For all the Supernatural fans!
And for Kath, who asked me to write this book.

Contents

1. Prologue   1

2. Chapter One   7

3. Chapter Two   15

4. Chapter Three   21

5. Chapter Four   27

6. Chapter Five   33

7. Chapter Six   39

8. Chapter Seven   45

9. Chapter Eight   51

10. Chapter Nine   57

11. Chapter Ten   63

12. Chapter Eleven   69

13. Chapter Twelve   77

14. Chapter Thirteen   83

15. Chapter Fourteen   91

16. Chapter Fifteen   97

17. Chapter Sixteen   103

18. Chapter Seventeen   109

19. Chapter Eighteen   115

20. Chapter Nineteen   121

21.	Chapter Twenty	127
22.	Chapter Twenty-One	133
23.	Chapter Twenty-Two	139
24.	Chapter Twenty-Three	145
25.	Chapter Twenty-Four	151
26.	Chapter Twenty-Five	159
27.	Chapter Twenty-Six	165
28.	Chapter Twenty-Seven	171
29.	Chapter Twenty-Eight	177
30.	Chapter Twenty-Nine	183
31.	Chapter Thirty	189
32.	Chapter Thirty-One	195
33.	Chapter Thirty-Two	201
34.	Chapter Thirty-Three	207
35.	Chapter Thirty-Four	213
36.	Chapter Thirty-Five	219
37.	Chapter Thirty-Six	225
38.	Chapter Thirty-Seven	231
39.	Chapter Thirty-Eight	237
40.	Chapter Thirty-Nine	243
41.	Chapter Forty	249
42.	Chapter Forty-One	255
43.	Chapter Forty-Two	261
44.	Chapter Forty-Three	267
45.	Chapter Forty-Four	271
46.	Chapter Forty-Five	277

47. Chapter Forty-Six   283

48. Chapter Forty-Seven   289

49. Chapter Forty-Eight   297

50. Chapter Forty-Nine   301

51. Chapter Fifty   307

52. Chapter Fifty-One   313

53. Chapter Fifty-Two   319

54. Chapter Fifty-Three   325

55. Chapter Fifty-Four   331

56. Chapter Fifty-Five   337

57. Chapter Fifty-Six   341

58. Chapter Fifty-Seven   347

59. Epilogue   353

The Story Continues   357

Keep in Touch   359

Prologue

In the moonlight that streamed through the window, unshed tears shimmered in the little girl's eyes. Her chin wobbled as she peered up at her father sitting next to her on the bed.

"I told you, sweetheart, it was just a bad dream."

Despite his intimidating size, the man's voice sounded soft and soothing in the still air of the dimly-lit room. No matter how scary he might seem to others, he never scared her.

"It felt real, but it only happened in your head. Your mom's fine, your brothers are fine and I'm fine too. Everyone else is asleep and you should be too. Tomorrow is a big day."

The next day marked her first day of school, and her father suspected that uncertainty over the new experience lay behind whatever unhappy thoughts haunted her sleep. Any kind of big change in life could be scary, but once she settled in at the neighbouring pack's school, she would see she had nothing to fear. He couldn't wait, not just for the sake of his own sleep but because the terror in her eyes clawed at his heart.

He never wanted her to feel afraid, not as long as he could do anything about it, and he *would* do everything he could to protect her, to his dying breath.

Leaning down to kiss her smooth, soft forehead, he paused to let her inhale his scent, knowing it would help to calm her. Werewolves communicated in many different ways, and scent held special meaning, especially among mate pairs and families. Their sense of smell far stronger than a human's, pups would recognize their parents by scent long before their faces or voices became familiar.

As the little girl breathed in, nestling her face into the crook of her father's neck, her eyes began to close. By the time he pulled back, she had already fallen asleep. With a tender smile, he tucked the covers tightly around her, knowing it would take him much longer to get back to sleep, even with his mate beside him. The nightlight plugged into the wall cast a canopy of stars over the ceiling, and he left it on as he slipped out of the room, just in case she woke up again.

"The same dream again?" his mate mumbled as he climbed back into bed beside her. She had offered to get up, but he told her to stay; the new baby would be arriving any day and she needed all the sleep she could get. It would be another girl, a little sister for their daughter and her two older brothers. Their family continued to grow, and he couldn't be happier about it. Despite the occasional worry like their daughter's nightmares, life had never been sweeter. "You don't think it means anything, do you?"

"Of course not. We're completely safe here on the pack land..."

He didn't even get to finish the sentence before their window blew inwards, the crash shattering the stillness of the night. Shards of jagged glass flew in every direction as the projectile broke through, exploding on impact and silencing his voice forever.

The little girl's eyes, so recently closed, sprang open again as the bed shook beneath her. Just like in her dream, something buzzing overhead, followed by the shouts of people outside her window. The stars on her ceiling flickered and went out as the house lost power. Beneath her bedroom door, the orange glow of a fire licked its way towards her, and she knew in her heart that this time, she wasn't dreaming. If she stayed in her bed, the flames would swallow her, just like they had the first time the dream came.

Each time the nightmare returned, she tried something different to escape the flying bombs. Each time, they found her.

Only in the very last dream, the one her father had just comforted her from, had she managed to get away. Instinctively, she followed those same actions, her body already knowing exactly what to do even as fear gripped her.

It took a couple of tries to pull her window open with her tiny arms, but eventually, it gave, and the cool night air flooded in, adding to the icy chill inside her veins. The late-September Montana evening felt crisp and clear, not quite cold enough for frost in the morning but not far off either. The bare skin of her arms and legs, all the parts not covered by her pajamas, puckered into goosebumps.

Pulling herself up onto the windowsill, she looked down at the drop, her heart pounding in fear. It seemed impossible that she could survive the fall without being hurt, but in the dream, she did. So, whimpering her parents' names, she let go just as the explosive device flew in through her open window. A second later, it detonated and the explosion destroyed the bed she had just been in, just as it always did in her dream.

The blast created a wave of hot air behind her that pushed her away from the house, changing her trajectory from a straight fall to a rolling one in the soft, tall grass that grew around the pack house. Maybe that explained her survival, how she managed to stand up with barely a scratch on her. Turning back, her wide, helpless eyes reflected the burning house, the windows of her parents' and brothers' rooms already engulfed in flames.

From the woods around her, wolves appeared, and on the road, a large vehicle barrelled towards her, men jumping out of it with weapons to fire on the wolves that ran past her to attack them.

Shouts, screams, growls and gunfire filled the night air. Numb with shock, she ran further away, into the woods. Looking back over her shoulder as darkness closed in, she didn't see the woman ahead of her until she ran straight into her. When her head jerked up to take in the unfamiliar face and her nose sniffed out the woman's strange scent, the little girl shrank back in horror. In her desperation, she lost control of her bladder, and the warm trickle down her leg making her whimper again in embarrassment.

"Shh, it's alright, sweetheart." The woman sounded surprisingly kind, given the circumstances. "Don't be afraid. I can help you."

From her pocket, she pulled out a large needle like the ones the doctor used, and the little girl's eyes went even wider.

"Mommy, help!," she wailed. "Daddy!"

She looked back towards the house as she cried out his name, and with her back turned, the woman gripped onto her tightly from behind.

"No! Let me go!"

Her small body struggled as hard as she could, but she was no match for the grown woman's strength. The needle pierced her neck. She called for her parents one more time before her vision went black, her body falling limp in the woman's arms.

Picking up the girl's unconscious frame, the woman headed back to the truck where her husband sat, supervising the entire operation. His lips tightened in disapproval as he looked down at the child in his wife's arms.

"I hope you're not thinking what I think you're thinking."

She ignored him as she opened the door and placed the child on the seat before climbing up herself. "She's just a baby. She's not dangerous."

"She's gonna grow. Would you bring a lion cub into your house?" He glanced down at the child warily, as if it might bite him right then and there, despite being unconscious.

"Lions can be tamed. Maybe she can be too. It'll give us a chance to try."

He shook his head. "I didn't bring you along so you could find a subject for your experiments."

"She ran right into me. It's got to be a sign. After everything that happened, maybe it's meant to be."

He could tell by the set of his wife's jaw that he wouldn't win this argument, so he gave in, turning his attention back to the destruction and devastation ahead of them. Wolf bodies numbering in their dozens lay strewn across the lawn in front of the burning house, illuminated by the spotlight of the truck's headlights.

"Looks like we got 'em all, other than that one. Shame it had to come to this."

His wife sounded less sympathetic. "They knew the rules, and they knew the consequences of breaking them."

When the echo of the last gunshot died out, the men checked in with each other. It looked like they hadn't lost anyone, which he counted as a miracle up against a werewolf pack, even a smaller one like this. The new projectile explosives might have been expensive, but if they saved lives, they were worth every penny.

"Let's move out," he announced into his radio. "Hop in the back."

A dozen men all pulled themselves into the open truck bed, and with the former pack house still ablaze behind them, they drove back down the mountain road and into the forest as clouds began to gather. The heavy rain that had been forecast for the next few days would put the fire out before it could spread.

Violence never brought him joy, but it did leave him with a sense of achievement. With the bloodshed, they'd made the world a little safer for all humans, especially the ones who never had a clue that werewolves existed at all.

Chapter One

Sixteen years later

~Calista~

My father's voice spoke in my ear through the earpiece I wore, quiet but as authoritative as always. "He's coming your way, Calista. Everyone else, keep your position. I'm going silent now so I won't give your position away. You've got this."

I sure as hell hoped so as my grip tightened on the rifle in my hands, loaded with silver bullets. Some creatures, I could hunt without a second thought, comfortable in their familiarity and predictability, but others still sent a spike of adrenaline and fear through me, making my heart pound and my palms sweat despite the cool night air surrounding me.

Wendigos fell into the second category. In the five years I'd been hunting full-time, ever since I turned sixteen, we'd only encountered one before and that encounter didn't go well. In that case, we were called up to Alberta to deal with a wendigo who killed two hikers in one of the national parks there. Officially, their deaths were recorded as bear attacks, but we knew better. Wendigos were tall, humanoid creatures who fed on humans. Their claws might make an attack look like a bear hunt, but bears didn't suck all the marrow out of the bones like a wendigo would.

Some hunters thought all wendigos were ancient, existing for thousands of years and hibernating until their hunger became too great, at which point they awoke to kill and feed again before returning to their slumber. Others believed humans could be turned to wendigos through the ritualistic eating of human flesh. Either way, everyone knew that wendigos couldn't be reasoned with. They had no soul or conscience left, meaning death was the only option for dealing with them.

However, just because we couldn't talk to them didn't mean they weren't smart.

Realizing we were hunting it, the wendigo three years earlier turned to tricks and traps, managing to kill two of our men before it found me. Using its power of mimicry, it called out to me with my mother's voice, begging for help. In my inexperience and the sheer panic of thinking someone I loved was in danger, I fell for it, abandoning my post as I ran to help her, and fell right into its trap, quite literally, when the ground gave way beneath me.

Stuck in the hole it had dug, I only got a glimpse of the creature's skeletal appearance, its paper-thin skin pulled tight across its face, its bones straining against their covering as if they might poke through at any second. Black, hollow-looking eyes stared down at me while the creature licked its thin, white lips. Shivering in terror, I prepared to fight, knowing I probably wouldn't succeed.

I survived only because my father also deviated from his plan, coming to my rescue. They struggled above me while I could do nothing but listen to the horrible howls and shrieks of the creature and my father's anguished cries.

He killed it, but not before the creature pulled his leg off.

Since then, my father stayed in his truck during all of our hunts, using drones with night-vision cameras to track our prey and the earpieces we wore to direct our movements, but his days of hunting himself were over. Now, I acted as his legs, and though he never once blamed me for what happened, I was determined to prove to him that I'd learned my lesson.

This time, I would kill the wendigo myself.

"Help!" The faint cry came from ahead of me, sounding for all the world like Darryl, one of my father's regular freelancers who had joined us on the hunt that night. "Calista, help!"

My heart beat even faster as the sound of my name drifted to me through the air. How would the creature know my name? What if Darryl actually *was* in trouble? Doubts clouded the edges of my thoughts, but I stuck to the plan, waiting in my hiding spot for the creature to show itself. Wendigos had an excellent sense of smell, so it would find me no matter how well I hid myself. I counted on that, and I counted on the fact that as long as I didn't move, I would have a chance to see it before it saw me.

The cries grew louder and more panic-stricken until, suddenly, they stopped. The echo of them in the stillness of the night seemed even more disturbing than the screams had been, and I swallowed down the nausea that threatened to take over at the thought that it might have been Darryl after all. What if the creature killed him? What if I could have saved him but didn't?

With my finger resting on the trigger, I waited, my ears tuned to each rustle of the leaves or stirring in the trees that might give the creature away. I barely blinked as my eyes scanned the small opening in front of me in the direction that the screams had been coming from.

I didn't hear it until a twig on the ground snapped, not in front of me, but behind me.

It might have been one of my own group. It might have been a bear or a deer or anything else, but I couldn't take any chances. Spinning around, I fired before I even laid eyes on it, and this time, luck was on my side.

The bullet caught the creature in the stomach, slowing it down enough that I could take aim properly. At least eight feet tall, it lumbered towards me, its skin almost translucent in the moonlight as it let out an ear-piercing shriek. I kept focused on its chest until I could make out the shape of its icy heart beneath its skin. With steady hands and grim determination, I fired the bullet straight into the heart, shattering it on impact.

The wendigo's cry died out as it flopped over, stumbling a few times before collapsing on the forest floor. My heart continued to thud as I watched it, just to make sure I'd actually killed it before moving any closer. I would still cut out its heart, just to be sure, and bury it in several different places. Regeneration wasn't unheard of for wendigos. Some creatures clung to life more than others.

Usually, the less human they were, the harder time they had dying.

"Nice shot."

The unfamiliar voice came from my left, and I pivoted in that direction, my gun still raised. Through the sight, a young man appeared, not much older than me, his hands raised to show me he was unarmed.

I kept the gun up anyway. "Who are you?"

He wasn't one of our group, and no one else should have been crazy enough to be out in the forest at this time of night with a wendigo on the loose or not. The Montana backwoods held enough dangerous creatures besides the dead one in front of me.

The man kept his hands up, not moving. "Take it easy. I'm an ally. I've been tracking the wendigo but you got to him first. A lot cleaner than I would have too. Like I said, nice job."

"Tracking? Without a weapon?" Besides having nothing in his hands, I couldn't see anything attached to his body either. His wide, strong body, I couldn't help noticing, the muscles well-defined beneath his tight t-shirt. I might have been a hunter, but I still had a woman's eyes, and it had been a long time since I'd seen any eye candy quite like him.

"I have my own methods. Like I said, they would have been messier. You're a great shot, but you could listen better."

His teasing felt completely out of place. "I would have shot *you* if I saw you first. You're lucky I didn't."

"Was it luck?" It almost looked like he winked at me beneath the moonlight. "Or did you not see me because I didn't want you to?"

"Calista?" My father's voice crackled in my ear. "I heard the shots. Did you get him?"

I glanced down again at the creature on the ground, still motionless. "Yeah, I got him. I'm going to get the heart now and I'll make my way back. Is everyone else okay?"

"Everyone's checked in," he confirmed, and I breathed a sigh of relief. The wendigo hadn't got Darryl after all, then. It had been a trick, just like I hoped. "Good work, honey."

Turning back to where the stranger stood, I started in surprise. He had completely disappeared. My eyes darted left and right, searching the moonlit trees, but no sign of him remained.

Could my mind have been playing tricks on me? I'd heard of wendigo psychosis, a condition caused by exposure to the wendigo that could cause hallucinations and ultimately make people turn to cannibalism themselves, but those few seconds in his presence shouldn't have done it. My dad had fought the other one longer and never shown any signs of it.

I didn't think I'd made the man up. Something about him felt almost... familiar, though I couldn't explain why.

Putting my rifle down, I pulled out the hunting knife I kept strapped to my leg, and gave the wendigo a kick to roll it over. Its features had shrunken into its face even further, making it look even more like a skeleton, but I didn't look at it too closely as I dug into its chest to retrieve the pieces of its heart. I buried one of them there and took the others with me, to be disposed of as far and wide as possible.

My dad had the truck running when I got back, the others already having left, and we headed out down the dirt trail we'd come up on, barely a road through the trees.

"You okay?" he asked, glancing over at me for just a second before turning his gaze back to the road. In his fifties, Frank Johnson had seen more than enough in his lifetime to account for his hair's steely shade of grey. His eyebrows, however, remained stubbornly black and his eyes, a deep brown, had a way of looking past what most people saw. They looked just as sharp now as the night I first remembered seeing him.

"I'm fine, but there was someone else out there, Dad. A man who came out of the woods after I killed the wendigo. He said he'd been tracking the creature too, but he didn't have any weapons with him. I didn't recognize him."

We weren't the only hunters in the area, and sometimes, if a big job came up, others would come in from across the country. But we knew most of the usual suspects. Coming across one I'd never seen before, especially in the middle of a job, rarely happened.

My dad's jaw tightened as he kept his eyes ahead. "A big man? Tall, broad?"

I nodded in confirmation. "Yeah. Did you see him too?"

"Not with my eyes, but I saw someone else in the area with the drones. I didn't realize he'd gotten that close to you."

Something in my dad's tone told me he knew more than he was sharing with me. "Who is he?"

"I don't know *who* he is, but I know *what* he is. A werewolf."

His eyes darted to me again, to check my reaction, but my surprise startled me so much that I didn't really react at all. *That* was a werewolf? I'd never been face-to-face with one before but in my mind, they were snarling, aggressive, mean humans that turned into even more snarling, aggressive and mean wolves.

Most of the time, they stuck to the agreed rules that governed hunter/creature relations; they didn't trouble us so we didn't trouble them. I'd never had reason to hunt one, but I knew what they were capable of.

Of all the creatures in the world, every species I knew, they were the only ones I truly hated.

Wendigos had no sense of right or wrong; they hunted and fed because instinct drove them to it; they existed only to survive. They couldn't control it any more than a tiger or a snake could.

Werewolves, however, could choose to be human and civilized, but they didn't. They *let* their baser animal instincts control them; they *chose* to give up that control.

They chose to kill my family.

I didn't remember anything about that night other than vague flashes of wolves and flames, but my adoptive parents told me the story about how werewolves attacked my home. We weren't the only ones; there had been four other attacks, four other families wiped out, and my new family, my hunting family, had been tracking the pack because of it. That night, they took them out, but got there too late to save my family. Only I survived, and I had no memories of my biological parents other than a feeling of belonging, of being loved and cared for.

My new parents, my mom and dad, took me in and raised me as their own. They provided for me and taught me to survive in this world. I could never adequately repay them for that, but I also never forgot what the werewolves took from me. The idea that the handsome, teasing man I'd encountered had been one of them made my skin crawl.

"How do you know?" I asked my dad, my voice sounding flat as I tried to push down all the emotions the mere word 'werewolf' caused to bubble up inside me.

"The heat cameras on the drone picked up the difference in his body temperature. I know there's a pack nearby, a big one, and if he says he was hunting the thing, well, it makes sense. They wouldn't want a wendigo around any more than we do."

I supposed the wendigo would probably feed on them too, mistaking them for humans. They looked the same in their human forms, close enough that I'd been fooled. How many other times had I spoken to a werewolf and not even known it? I shuddered at the thought.

My dad glanced over at me once more, this time in concern. "You alright? You taken your meds yet today?"

"Just cold. The temperature's dropping." My dad was always paranoid about me forgetting to take my epilepsy medication, especially when we were hunting, but I never forgot. I always carried a few extra vials on me, just in case. On the job, I needed to be at the top of my game, and having a seizure on top of everything else wouldn't help anything. "I'll take them when we get home, before I go to bed."

Another instance of sleeping all day after being out all night, but it would be worth it knowing that the wendigo had been taken care of. Hopefully, fewer families out there would have to go through the pain of losing their loved ones, a pain I knew all too well.

CHAPTER TWO

~Vaughan~

In the light of the fire's glow, I reread the terms of the alliance contract, even though by that point, I practically knew the words by heart. Only two pages long, the agreement represented months of work and diplomacy by me and my team. Nothing in the final version of the document took me by surprise, so why the thought of signing it should be keeping me up at night, I had no idea.

The fire cracked and snapped within the stone fireplace in my office, one of the many administrative spaces that made up the ground floor of the pack house. The large log cabin blended into the surrounding wilderness as much as any building could. In my travels as Alpha of the Crimsontooth Pack, the largest pack in the northwest of the country, I'd seen many pack houses of various styles and sizes, but none felt like home in the way that ours did.

A home that I'd soon be sharing with a new mate if I signed the document in my hands. At twenty-seven, I'd already waited for my mate longer than most Alphas would. I could still hear the words my mother used to explain the ways of the world to me: a mate was the greatest blessing of a werewolf's life, a perfect partner chosen by the Moon Goddess herself to provide balance and love and, of course, children. When we met our mates, we recognized them instantly, feeling the special bond that existed between us from birth in the same way that our wolves were assigned to us. A fated mate was nothing short of a miracle, one of the few truly miraculous things in life, and no matter how unlikely the odds, most wolves found their mates, even if some had to wait longer than others.

In times of peace, I would have waited even longer, but peace had been in short supply lately. Wolves were howling at our door, quite literally, with several upstart packs trying to make incursions into our territory as humans pushed them further out of their traditional lands. No matter how much I sympathized, I couldn't give them land out of our territory; if I were to start, where would it end?

If the pack was large, I rebuffed them by force, making them move on, but if they were small enough and willing, I would invite them to join us as full members of the Crimsontooth Pack, living on our land under my own authority, providing them security and protection in exchange for their loyalty. In that way, we'd gained more than a thousand new pack members in the last few years alone. Our once-small settlement in the deep forest had started to resemble a human town, and we'd even had the occasional human tourist show up, curious about the remote town they could see on their satellite map.

The bigger problem caused by our expansion was that other powerful packs in the area had started to accuse us of trying to swell our numbers for our own benefit. They saw it as a power grab, and I knew from my allies that our enemies were growing more vocal. Among the untrue claims they made about us, one that kept coming up was that I must have been cursed not to have a mate or heir yet. After taking over from my father at such a young age, they argued my lack of a mate proved that the Moon Goddess didn't favour me, and they took it as an invitation to claim ownership over my pack.

The arguments were ridiculous, but desperate people would believe ridiculous things if it meant improving their own situation. Even some factions within my own pack were spooked, and several of my father's old advisors believed getting myself an heir as soon as possible would not only be advisable, but necessary.

Not least because any kind of violence between packs ran the risk of attracting the attention of hunters, and that meant danger for all of us.

My father taught me that the pack's safety took priority over everything, and though he never said so explicitly, I knew that he would include my fated mate in that equation.

And so, to keep the vultures at bay, I invited the Alpha of the Ravenstone Pack, a large pack from just over the border in Canada, to enter into an alliance with us. Not only would we agree to defend each in the event of an unprovoked attack, but I would take his daughter, Amanda, as my chosen mate.

At twenty-five, she hadn't found her fated mate yet either, a situation even more unusual for a female wolf of Alpha blood than a male one. As any loving father would, Amanda's father wanted to see her settled and provided for. Amanda and I met once, a few months earlier, and she came across as smart, well-spoken and pretty. I couldn't find any fault with her.

On my side, it would help quell the grumbling within my own pack and weaken any external claims to our territory. There really weren't any downsides, so my hesitation as I stared at the papers in my hand frustrated me.

What was I waiting for?

Rather than sending me an answer, the Goddess sent me my Beta, Felix.

"Were you waiting up for me?" he teased as he blew into the room, full of far too much energy for three o'clock in the morning. A rosy hue tinted his cheeks from the cold air outside, the wind had tousled his short blond hair, and excitement sparked in his blue eyes. "I'm touched that you care so much, Vaughan."

Putting the papers in my hand down, I picked up my glass of whiskey instead, brushing my darker, longer hair back from my face as I took a drink. "I stopped worrying about you a long time ago. If you want to go get yourself torn apart, that's your own problem. I see that you're still in one piece, though."

Ever since we were kids, Felix had a fascination with other species of supernatural beings, and it often got him into trouble. He'd nearly been bitten by a vampire, eaten by an ogre and turned into kindling by a dragon, but somehow, he always managed to come back unscathed. He kept a close eye on the online message boards that tracked and documented all kinds of creatures, and when he told me that night that he planned to try to track down the wendigo that rumours had placed just south of our territory, I barely even batted an eye.

"I'm assuming you didn't find it?" Without a drop of blood on him and his clothes intact, it seemed unlikely that he engaged in any kind of skirmish.

Felix helped himself to a glass of his own from the whiskey bottle on my desk and sat down in the armchair next to me in front of the fire. "Actually, I did find him, but only in time to watch him die. A hunter beat me to him."

Instantly, the hairs on the back of my neck stood up. Other supernatural creatures, I didn't mind him messing around with, but hunters, despite being human, were a different story. While wendigos only wanted to eat, hunters' motivations were far more complicated, and that made them unpredictable. "You got away before he saw you?"

"Nah, I talked to her for a little while. She had great reflexes but no sense of humour at all."

Her? Female hunters weren't unheard of, but they were rarer. "Did she know you're a wolf?"

He snorted into his drink. "I wasn't wearing a big sign around my neck or anything. She looked familiar, though. Pretty, too: blonde, blue-eyed and deadly serious. Just your type."

"I don't have a type." I'd dated a little, but never seriously, and the woman he described didn't match Amanda at all. A dark-eyed brunette, quick with a smile, she would be the perfect Luna for a large pack like mine, a role she'd been training for all her life.

All I had to do was sign the piece of paper to make it official.

"What do you mean she looked familiar?"

One shoulder lifted as he took another drink. "Not like we'd met before, but like she's related to someone I know. Something about her features. I can't put my finger on it and it's bugging the hell out of me."

Felix had a great knack of never forgetting a face, and it made him invaluable at meetings with other packs when he would recognize everyone on sight and mind-link me with their names and positions before I made a fool of myself. I could quote werewolf laws and remember the details of treaties signed between packs and the old feuds that led to them, but for some reason, remembering faces had always been a weakness of mine.

A Luna might help with that, but since I didn't have one yet, Felix had my back instead.

As if he were aboard my train of thought, Felix gestured to the papers I'd put down. "You still haven't signed it yet."

Felix hadn't found his mate yet either, but he was three years younger than me and not the Alpha. He didn't feel the urgency like I did. "I will."

"Then why haven't you?" He leaned forward, resting his elbows on his knees. "It's not like you to put something off, Vaughan. If your gut is saying no, maybe there's a reason for it."

I'd wondered the same thing, but no matter how hard I tried, I couldn't see an alternative. Without a fated mate, I'd have to take a chosen one. On paper, no one made a better choice than Amanda. Some might even call her perfect.

Not perfect for you, though. No one is, other than our mate. My wolf, Atlas, rarely chimed in uninvited, but even though I hadn't asked his opinion, he offered it anyway. *You'd be giving that up forever.*

I knew that. As soon as I mated and marked Amanda, my bond with my fated mate would sever, so even if I met her afterwards, I would never feel it the way I would have. I might feel attracted to her, might even fall in love with her if we spent enough time together, but I'd never know for sure that she had been the one meant for me.

So I should keep waiting and keep giving people an excuse to plot against me?

*I never said that. I'm just telling you **why** you don't want to sign. It's your call, Vaughan. I'll support you either way.*

I didn't doubt it. Atlas had always been the best wolf and the best companion I could ask for, especially when he had to step up at such a young age, just like I did. By making the call, I'd be denying him his fated mate too; it had never been only about me, and yet, he trusted me to make the right decision for both of us and for the pack too.

"I've been waiting nine years for my mate," I pointed out, speaking out loud so both Atlas and Felix could hear me. "It seems pretty unlikely she's going to show up right now. I have to stop fooling myself and make the smart choice."

Gulping down the remains of the alcohol in my glass, I reached for my pen and signed my name across the bottom of the agreement.

"There. It's done."

I didn't know what I expected to happen, but the world didn't shift. Nothing happened at all, no reaction to my proclamation other than the quiet ticking of the clock, telling me to get to bed before the next day began.

In the morning, I'd send the signed document over to the Ravenstone pack and make arrangements to go and pick Amanda up to bring her to her new home. We'd have to plan a huge celebration, to make it clear that this happy occasion meant our pack would be more stable and secure than ever before. It would take a few weeks to put all the arrangements in place, time that I could use to get myself used to the idea.

Hopefully, when the day came, I could force myself to feel happy about it, because at that moment, as I looked down at my name in black ink, all I felt was loss.

Chapter Three

~**Calista**~

A week after the wendigo hunt, breakfast with my parents was interrupted by the kind of call we all hated.

"Johnson," my dad announced in greeting, wiping his mouth with a napkin before stepping away from the table.

While my dad spoke tersely into the phone, my mom and I shovelled the last of our cereal into our mouths, anticipating that we'd need to leave soon. Carol Johnson and I had very little in common on the outside, which made sense given that she and my dad adopted me. Where I had blonde hair and blue eyes, her hair had once been jet black before the silver strands began to appear. Her slim, athletic build contrasted with my curves, and where my nose spread wider, hers formed a thin, narrow line down the centre of her face.

"Put the dishes in the sink," she ordered when we finished, pointing to the stained basin. "We'll clean them later."

The simple, two-storey house in the woods where we lived might have been run down, but spending time and money on home improvements didn't make sense. We all knew the dangers of getting too attached to a building. This wasn't the first house we lived in since my parents took me in. It wasn't even the fifth. Somewhere along the way, I'd lost count. We moved regularly, whenever any of the creatures we hunted managed to track us down, and we kept everything inside as portable as possible in case we needed to leave in a hurry. We never went too far, though. Montana was home, and it had more than enough supernatural happenings to keep us busy.

The house had been abandoned several years before we moved in. My dad hooked up the electricity to our portable generators, ensuring we had a fridge and oven and our own personal electronics. For furniture, we had a kitchen table, a couch in the living room and two beds in the bedrooms upstairs, one for me and one for my parents, though more often than not, my dad slept on the couch downstairs rather than navigating the narrow stairs on his prosthetic leg.

The wallpaper on the walls peeled in long, uneven strips, dark stains dotted the carpets, and any curtains that might have once covered the windows had disappeared. At night, the darkness of the woods outside and all the night noises would have frightened a lot of people, but I had grown used to it a long time ago. A salt perimeter warned of any kinds of ghosts or demons approaching and the rifle beneath my pillow acted as defense against everything else. If anything came for me during the night, I wouldn't go down without a fight.

A bedroom filled with fluffy stuffed toys as a child or posters of actors and rock stars on the wall as a teenager had never been part of my life. All my belongings in the world could be packed into two suitcases at short notice. Sometimes, in the years when I actually attended school, I visited other kids from my classes and marvelled at their homes and all the *things* they had. It felt almost familiar, as if I must have had that kind of life at some point, but when I made an off-hand envious remark to my mother, she quickly set me straight.

"They can only live that way because people like us keep the monsters at bay. Someone has to protect humankind."

Why that someone had to be us, she never explained. Some things were just the way they were. My father's parents had been hunters before him and my mom took it up after a run-in with vampires as a teenager. Together, they made a formidable team, and if they ever regretted their lifestyle, they never showed it.

From them, I learned how to exist on the fringes of society, fend for myself and keep all my cards close to my chest. We didn't get close to anyone and we didn't let anyone close to us.

Despite all their creature comforts, other people weren't so well prepared, and the phone call we received that morning provided one more sad example.

"Let's move out," my dad announced as he hung up his phone, quickly shoving the last of his toast into his mouth. "That was Steve."

'Steve' meant Steven Haddon, a police officer and one of my dad's few friends outside the hunting community. Normally, we tried to stay out of the way of law enforcement, but after a run-in with a particularly nasty poltergeist a few years earlier, Steve became a believer in the supernatural and a fan of my dad's when he saved him. One of only a handful of civilians who knew what we did, he gave us a call whenever he came across anything that looked suspiciously inhuman.

"What are we looking at?" my mom asked as she climbed into the truck next to my dad. Despite his injury, he always insisted on driving and had adapted his truck to make it easier for him. We didn't argue.

"A farmhouse off the highway, not far from Helena. The police went out to check when the kids didn't show up to school. The whole family's dead and their pets too. He said it looked like a wild animal attack except it happened indoors. No signs of forced entry."

That definitely sounded like something we should be checking out, but I didn't miss the look my parents exchanged when they thought I couldn't see them. "What is it? Do you know something else?"

My mom shrugged. "Not for sure. We'll see when we get there, but it sounds similar to a situation we've dealt with before."

"What situation?" I pressed, but she kept her answer vague.

"Before you would remember."

The drive took us just over an hour but the police were still there when we arrived, along with the medical examiners. Steve came over to meet us as we got out of the truck. He greeted us all but addressed me in particular. "I'm not sure you want to see this, Calista. It's pretty brutal."

He had no idea the kinds of things I'd seen. "I'll be alright. Thanks, though."

"Your call." With a shrug, he looked back at the house and the cars surrounding it. "I've told the others that you're animal experts. Stay out of their way, okay?"

Taking us in the back door, he brought us to the kitchen first. A cozy, tidy space with gingham curtains and towels, it would have looked idyllic if not for the bloody footprints on the floor, both human and animal. Blood smeared across the fridge handle and the countertops, like someone had made themselves a snack while bleeding to death, or more likely, after they caused a death.

Steve immediately backed up that assessment. "The deaths took place upstairs, mostly in the bedrooms, although at least one of the kids made it part way down the stairs. It almost looks like the killers stopped to feed themselves before leaving. They weren't in any kind of hurry."

While my mom and dad went to look at the fridge more closely, I knelt down to take a closer look at the animal prints on the ground. If I were looking for a non-supernatural explanation, I would say that humans had broken in and brought some vicious, trained dogs with them. That would explain the two types of footprints, the fact that they got in and out by using the door, and the types of injuries Steve had described.

Through a hunter's lens, though, it seemed far more likely to be a creature who could change between human and animal form. Different kinds of shifters existed, but the prints were clearly canine.

Just a week after speaking to one in the forest, it looked like I might get a chance to hunt my first werewolves. Slaughtering a human family in their home definitely breached the agreed-upon rules of conduct.

My dad seemed to have reached the same conclusion. "Has your team found any fur near the bodies?"

Steve reached into his pocket and pulled out a Ziploc bag. "When I noticed it there, I had a feeling you were going to ask."

My mom took it from him while my dad pulled out his phone and took some pictures to document everything. Steve took him to see the bodies and take more photos there, while my mom and I stayed in the kitchen.

"You said you've encountered something like this before," I reminded her, my stomach turning over as I connected the dots in my head. "Did you mean my family?"

If we were dealing with werewolves, it would make sense. We so rarely had a reason to hunt them.

Her lips tightened as she looked around but she answered more forthrightly than before. "I'm afraid so. There were several attacks, a lot like this one: brutal, random, and callous. Right down to helping themselves to food after killing the family..." She shook her head in thinly-disguised loathing. "It's almost exactly the same."

Of course I agreed the whole situation was reprehensible, but I had more questions. "You hunted the pack that carried out those attacks though, right? You killed them all?"

I'd always been told that, and she nodded in confirmation. "Yes, and that put an end to the attacks immediately."

In that case, it seemed pretty clear that they'd tracked the right pack, but something still felt a bit off. "If that's the case, why would this attack be *so* similar? Is this typical werewolf behaviour, or is it some kind of copycat?"

Her frown made it clear she hadn't considered it in those terms yet, and she had no ready answer. "I'm not sure. We'll have to do some research when we get home."

While planning and strategizing our jobs was my dad's strength, my mom excelled at research. A scientist by training, she could see patterns other people couldn't. My brain would never work like hers, but I learned a lot by watching her and I always felt a sense of pride when I thought of something she hadn't.

"What's the fur for?" I asked next. I assumed my dad would have a good reason for asking for it.

"Wolf packs have distinctive biomarkers in their fur that help them identify one another. They recognize each other by scent. We won't be able to smell it but we can analyze it chemically. It'll be the quickest way to determine which pack is responsible for this. It's how we tracked down the other pack all those years ago."

In that case, finding the culprits should be easy enough but bringing them to justice could be a lot trickier, depending on the size of the pack. We'd need more information before we could proceed, and as we drove home with our evidence to begin the task of putting it all together, it felt like this job would not only be a big one, but an important one too, at least on a personal level.

Ever since werewolves slaughtered my family, something in my life had always felt slightly off. Something didn't quite make sense. By confronting these new werewolf killers, maybe I could find a way to put the ghosts of my past to rest too.

Chapter Four

~Vaughan~

"Vaughan, are you listening?"

My Gamma's words pierced through my distracted thoughts and I blinked across my desk at him, forcing myself to focus. The afternoon sun shone brightly through the large windows, bathing my office in light, and I would much rather be outside in it than stuck indoors. "Yes?"

The fact that I phrased my answer as a question made it clear I hadn't been listening, and Leo's lips pursed into an unimpressed grimace as his fingers tapped against the checklist in his hands. "Honestly, Alpha. This is important! You want your mate to feel valued when she gets here, don't you?"

His admonishment made me bristle. "Of course I do, but I don't understand how picking out the flowers for our mating ceremony accomplishes that. Just pick them for me. She'll never know the difference."

When I put Leo in charge of the arrangements for the mating ceremony and Amanda's Luna ceremony, I thought I could leave it all to him. Out of all my team, he knew the most about our pack's traditions and cared the most about appearances. I gave him a generous budget to create a memorable event and celebration for the pack, and carte blanche to plan it however he wanted. He should have been thrilled.

Instead, he kept coming to me to approve every minor decision when I honestly couldn't care less. I would rather forget the impending celebrations while I still could.

"It'll mean more if it comes from the heart," he argued. "What would you say if she asked you *why* you chose calla lilies?"

I had no idea what a calla lily was, but since he'd probably just been talking to me about them, I pretended I did. "I'd say it's because they're pretty, just like her."

He rolled his eyes so hard, he nearly fell out of his chair. "Can you try to think like a woman, just this once?"

I had no idea how I was meant to do that, but luckily, I didn't have to try. Felix came bursting through my office door instead, and I had never been so glad to see him.

"Do you need me?" I asked hopefully.

"I just heard from my friend, Patrick, about an investigation he's involved in. I think you're going to be interested."

Thank the Goddess. I couldn't remember exactly who Patrick was, but whatever he wanted, it had to be better than picking out flowers. "You want me to talk to him?"

"We should go take a look ourselves. I'll fill you in on the way."

"Sorry, Leo." I got to my feet, trying to look sincere in my apology. "I know you've got to get these orders in, so why don't you just go ahead and make the call?"

With that off my plate, I headed out the door with Felix. The staff all bowed their heads and greeted me as we walked through the wide hallways, and outside, on the communal open field across from the pack house, a group of young men played an informal game of football. They called over to me and Felix to join them, both sides already arguing over whose team would get whom, but we had to turn them down.

Climbing into Felix's truck instead, we headed off pack land while he laid out the situation, waving at the guards manning the checkpoint that straddled the road in and out of our territory. "Since I know you don't remember, Patrick's a medical examiner. Human."

That helped. Felix had made several human friends in his online hobbies and he took great pleasure in going to gatherings with people interested in supernatural beings to see if anyone outed him as a were-wolf.

So far, no one had, and I tried not to think about what would happen if they did.

"I asked around on some of the message boards about that blonde hunter I met to see if anyone knew her, and today, he sent me a message."

"This is about a woman? A *hunter*?"

Maybe I should have stayed in my office and picked out the flowers. With my departure to the Ravenstone pack scheduled in just a few days, I had too much to do to get caught up in Felix's search for some random female he met for a few minutes. My Beta had always been a sucker for a pretty face but he could usually find enough women to keep him occupied within our own pack, especially when we kept taking on new members.

"Hold on, let me finish. I told you it's been bugging me that I can't place her face. That's the only reason I asked and I didn't tell anyone she's a hunter. I just said I thought she had an interest in the supernatural. No one knew anything when I asked, but today, Patrick messaged me to say he was working at a crime site earlier today and saw a woman who fit her description, along with two other people. The guy in charge told him they were 'animal experts.'"

"I'm still not seeing what this has to do with us, Felix." His hobbies didn't bother me as long as they didn't interfere with his work for the pack, but we seemed to be crossing that line.

"I'm getting to the point. He said he wouldn't have necessarily made the connection to the woman I asked about if it weren't for the nature of the crime scene itself: a whole family murdered by what he said seemed like 'wild dogs.'"

Instantly, my body tensed. "Werewolves?"

"He didn't use the word but it sounded possible to me. It's not far from our territory, so I thought we better check it out."

Put that way, I completely agreed. If wolves were causing problems with humans near us, we needed to put a stop to it, immediately, both for the humans' sake and for ours. If they were rogues, we should know about it. If another pack decided to cause trouble, we should put a stop to it.

Nobody wanted a repeat of the Deep Valley massacre.

When we arrived at the farmhouse, the police tape was still up but the humans themselves had left.

"Where is everyone?" My eyes searched the remote farmland where nothing stirred. The crops had all been harvested, the fields laid bare.

"Police cutbacks," Felix said with a shrug. "Or maybe they assumed no one else would be out this way. Works for us, at least."

Always prepared, Felix had brought some gloves for us so we didn't leave fingerprints lying around anywhere, and we ducked beneath the tape to go in the front door.

The scent of blood hit me first, strong and persistent, permeating everything. Grimly, we headed up the stairs, stepping over a large pool of blood on the stairs itself, past the bloody footprints, both human and canine, and into the master bedroom. The bodies had been removed but we could clearly see where they had been.

Once my nose got used to the smell of blood, another scent began to creep in, one that made my stomach turn.

"That's *our* pack scent."

It shouldn't have been possible. My pack was like my family; a very large family, but a family all the same. Discipline and loyalty were every-thing, and the idea that some of my own could have done something like this truly sickened me.

However, we *had* been taking in a lot of new pack members lately and maybe we hadn't screened them as thoroughly as we could have. Once they joined the pack, connecting with the Alpha blood that ran through my veins, they took on our pack scent the same as someone who had been born into it.

The thought of the innocent humans slaughtered turned my stomach, but I had other concerns too. If hunters had already been there, as Felix's friend suggested, they might also make the connection to our pack, and that could put all of us in danger.

"I want a report of everyone who was off pack land at any time over the last 36 hours. I want to know where they went and what they did. I want every minute accounted for."

Felix nodded, already typing on his phone. "It'll be waiting for us when we get back."

We looked around a little more, noting the claw marks on the bed and the way the carpet had torn beneath the wolves' feet. Heading back down the stairs, we followed the trail of bloody footprints into the kitchen, and there, a new scent joined the others. Although faint, it smelled like salted caramel, sweet and a tiny bit sharp at the same time, and if it weren't for the smell of blood mingling with it, it would have made my mouth water. When I looked around for the source of it, though, I couldn't see one.

"Where is that sweet scent coming from?" I asked Felix as he walked over to the fridge, looking at the blood on the fridge door.

"Sweet?" He glanced back at me in confusion. "I don't smell anything sweet."

Maybe my imagination conjured the smell because of the country kitchen setting, but I didn't think so. My sense of smell didn't usually let me down, but if Felix didn't smell it, it didn't seem worth dwelling on. We'd seen what we went there to see, and now, we had to get back to the pack, figure out who could be behind such a horrific attack, and punish them ourselves before any hunters showed up to do it for us.

CHAPTER FIVE

~Calista~

The research into the werewolf fur we collected didn't turn out to be as straightforward as I hoped it would be. When my mom said she could analyze the chemicals in the fur to determine which pack it belonged to, I imagined that there must be some kind of database, similar to human DNA or fingerprints, that would help us match it once we had the results. Unfortunately, that wasn't the case.

"We're relying on other hunters sharing their information, and not all of them do these kinds of analyses," she explained as I leaned over her shoulder to examine the computer screens set up in her makeshift laboratory. "I'd love it if we had a database, but we're not there yet."

The fur didn't turn up any immediate hits against her own records, and she had two possible explanations.

"Either they're a newly formed pack or they usually stay out of trouble so we haven't had reason to investigate them before. I'll just have to dig a little deeper."

While she worked on that, I went back to my room and pulled out my laptop to look up information about how frequently werewolves were involved in the kind of attack that had just taken place.

It didn't seem to be common at all.

Besides the attacks sixteen years ago, the ones in which my own family perished, large-scale attacks on humans were rare. Usually, they spent their time attacking each other and sometimes, humans got caught in the crossfire. Occasionally, there were what they called 'rogues', wolves without a pack, who killed people and stole from them in order to survive, and there were even a couple of cases of werewolf serial killers, but no more than there were human ones.

All in all, at least in Montana, it didn't seem like werewolves were much of a problem. Something happened sixteen years ago to change that, and whatever it was seemed to be happening again. This attack didn't seem to be about survival; although they'd taken food from the fridge, they left much more of it behind. They attacked in their wolf forms, making it as bloody as possible, when in their human forms, they could have used guns or any other kind of weapon to make it less messy. It felt like they *wanted* it to be brutal, like they took some kind of enjoyment from it, and stopping for a snack afterwards seemed to back that up.

The more I read, the more I wanted to know about the wolves from all those years ago who killed my family. Although my parents had never hidden it from me, they never went into detail about it either, and now that we might be dealing with a copycat attack, it seemed prudent to know exactly what happened back then.

Knowing my mom would still be busy with her analyses, I went to ask my dad about it instead.

"That was one of the biggest jobs we ever did," he told me out in his trailer, which served as his portable workshop. It held our largest cache of weapons and all his tech equipment, including his drones. Whenever we weren't hunting, he would be out there, making sure everything stayed in working order, ready for when we needed it.

Although he called it a 'job', no one hired people like us. Hunters were called to their vocation in some way, usually from losing a loved one to a supernatural force, just as I had. My dad had never known any other life. A natural leader, others would come to him to organize attacks when a problem arose. He had a network of acquaintances he could call upon to help him when the situation called for it, but most of the time, we were on our own.

It could be a lonely life, and hunters were often, of necessity, not the friendliest people. That had been another thing I envied about the kids

I used to attend school with: how they belonged to extended families and social groups, a whole community of people who loved and cared for them.

I honestly didn't know what that felt like.

"Like your mom said, the attacks were a lot like this one, at least at first, and they were only getting worse. It started with one family, then another one. After that, they got bolder, taking out two neighbouring homes in the same night. Next, they attacked a trailer park and got through five homes."

"Is that when they killed my family?"

My father's gaze remained fixed on the weapon in his hands, carrying on with his story as if he hadn't heard my question. "The attacks were a week or so apart at first, but getting closer together. There were only two days between the last two. It felt like if we didn't move immediately, things would get even worse. Based on the evidence, we identified the pack it had to be."

"What evidence did you have?" I interjected.

That question, he answered. "We found fur, same as this time. That suggested we were looking at werewolves, and based on the location of the attacks, we narrowed it down to three different packs. We went to the areas surrounding their lands, not on their territory where they could find us, but close by, and searched for hours until we found fur samples we could compare. Often, in their wolf forms, they'll rub up against trees or snag their fur on bushes when they pass by, so with a bit of patience, we were able to find some from each of the packs. Only one pack matched the fur we'd found at the crime scenes. We identified them after the second attack."

Although that would have been a step in the right direction, it didn't sound conclusive to me. My father always taught me to question everything. "Then what?"

"With only one main road in and out of their territory, I set up a sensor to capture traffic along it. The night of the third attack, a vehicle left their territory before the attack and returned after it."

Again, that looked bad, but it still didn't prove anything. "Did you try talking to them?"

Talking to a wendigo would be pointless and likely to get a hunter eaten, but with creatures such as werewolves, where we had established rules of coexistence, we usually gave them a chance to make their case in person before we turned to extermination. Killing them would be the very last resort.

"Of course I tried, but their Alpha refused to see me. Despite being unarmed and following all the rules of protocol, I got chased off their land and threatened if I tried to come back. When the fourth attack happened, leaving more of their fur behind and another vehicle caught on my sensors, it didn't leave us much choice. We couldn't let them carry on slaughtering people like that. In fact, I wish we'd acted sooner. We could have saved the lives of those other people..."

His jaw tightened and loss stung at my chest. Though he hadn't said the words, I knew what he meant: they could have saved my family.

As much as their absence still pained me, even after all these years, I did my best to ignore my emotions and focus on the problem, just as I'd been taught.

"Do you think they were ill in some way? It doesn't sound like this is typical werewolf behaviour, and if they don't normally behave this way, maybe something infected them?"

My dad's lips pursed thoughtfully. "I suppose that's possible. Like wendigo psychosis, you mean?"

That was exactly what I meant, though I hadn't thought of the wendigo specifically. As soon as I did, I remembered the werewolf I'd spoken to that night. He said he'd been tracking it; had he spent too much time in its presence? Or maybe some of the other pack members had?

It made sense to me, and at least gave us a place to start. "Maybe that's exactly what it is. You said the place we hunted the wendigo was close to a werewolf pack, right? Maybe we should go back there and see if we can find some fur, like you did before. We could at least see if it matches the fur from the farmhouse?"

"That's a great idea, honey. I'll head out now."

That sounded like a dismissal, and I didn't like the idea of being excluded. "I can go with you, Dad. It'll be faster with the two of us."

My father gave me a look tinged with concern. "I know, but I think maybe you should sit this one out. I understand it might feel personal to you and we all know that emotions are our enemies on the job."

I knew that, but I also didn't plan to hide from my past. If we had a job to do, I would do it, and do my best to keep any personal feelings I might have out of it.

"I can handle it. I want to help. Let's go and get started."

Chapter Six

~**Vaughan**~

When the Canadian border security officer asked me the reason for my visit, I answered *almost* entirely honestly. "I'm going to pick up the woman I'm going to marry."

We weren't getting married, but close enough. As a human equivalent, I used the word he would understand.

To my surprise, he laughed. "From the look on your face, I would have guessed you were heading to a funeral. It can't be that bad, can it?"

"Of course not." I tried to smile, though it didn't come easily. "I've just got a few other things on my mind."

It had been four days since Felix and I visited the farmhouse crime scene and we were no closer to figuring out how our pack scent ended up there than we had been at the time. Everyone who'd left pack land during the time leading up to the attack had been accounted for. I knew them all and trusted the alibis they gave me, but I followed up on them anyway and they all checked out. So far, we'd found nothing to indicate anyone was lying.

My nose didn't lie either, though. I knew what I smelled, but with no explanation and no other leads for the time being, I had no excuse to put off my trip to pick up Amanda. I left strict instructions for no one to leave pack land during my absence, and I left first thing in the morning, hoping to get there and back all in the same day, even though it would mean fourteen hours of driving in total. I would rather not be gone any longer than I had to be.

The officer handed my passport back to me, still smiling. "Good luck."

"Thanks." At that point, I felt like I would need it.

Atlas had been growing more and more restless as the day to make the trip grew closer. At first, I thought it had to do with the attack and our pack's security, but eventually, my wolf confided a more personal reason for his unease.

I think it has something to do with our mate, Vaughan. Our real one, our fated one. I feel like she's close.

He had to be kidding me. *Do you have any actual proof of that, or is this just cold feet about Amanda?*

It's just a feeling. An instinct.

As much as the idea of finding her after all this time appealed to me, I had to be realistic: I'd already signed the agreement. With things as tense as they were in general, I couldn't risk upsetting the Ravenstone Alpha by delaying my trip without a good excuse, and my wolf having a 'feeling' didn't count as a valid reason.

The beautiful drive to the Ravenstone land should have distracted me, with snow-peaked mountains to my left and gently rolling fields to the right, the sky clear and blue overhead, but I barely saw it. My body might have been there in my truck, but my thoughts remained back with the pack, wishing I hadn't left. Just as Atlas felt restless about our mate, the attack on the humans unsettled me. As much as I hoped nothing would come of it, I had a feeling too, one that told me it wouldn't be that simple.

Eventually, I reached the unmarked road that would lead into the foothills and the entrance to the Ravenstone territory. The paving gave way to a dirt track which ended entirely at a dirt parking lot big enough for three cars. Next to the lot stood a small cabin, the door of which opened to reveal a couple of large, broad-chested men as I drove up and parked.

Signs warned me that I'd entered private land and that dangerous wild animals roamed freely, trying to discourage any humans from thinking they could go for a leisurely hike. I was no human though, and a quick sniff of the air told the approaching men so. They greeted me politely, asking for my name and business there.

"Vaughan, Alpha of the Crimsontooth pack. Alpha Warren and his daughter are expecting me."

My ID verified my story, and their already polite demeanour turned even more friendly. "Welcome to the Ravenstone, Alpha Vaughan. The pack house is about ten kilometres to the west, but there are no roads so you'll have to go by foot. We've got a satchel for you to put your clothes in when you shift."

I appreciated the thoughtful gesture, but the distance made me grimace. It would take just over an hour to get there in wolf form, and added to the return journey and the drive home, it seemed unlikely I'd be able to get home that evening.

Nothing could be done about it at that point, though, so I undressed, put my clothes in the satchel they provided and shifted to my wolf. The chance to get out and run delighted Atlas after the long drive, and with the satchel attached to me, I followed one of the men who led me through the forest and over the hills through the wilderness. The fresh scents of pine and earth and wildflowers made it feel almost like home, but the pack scent of the wolf with me served as a reminder that the territory didn't belong to me.

With no signs of civilization since leaving the parking lot, the Ravenstone pack house appeared like a mirage out of the forest. Situated on the shore of a clear, ice-blue lake with the mountains looming just beyond, the two-storey Alpine-style house couldn't look more inviting. Smaller cabins spread out along the shore for the other pack members, and people crowded along the shoreline beach, a large bonfire already burning despite it still being mid-afternoon.

My companion must have already linked the Alpha's team to let them know we were on the way because as soon as I shifted back and redressed, a small delegation stood ready to meet me. Felix had drilled me on the names of the pack's leaders, so I recognized them all as they introduced themselves. After exchanging pleasantries and asking me about my journey, they led me to the pack house where the Alpha and his daughter themselves were waiting.

"Alpha Vaughan." The older man held out his hand to me and I gripped it firmly. He had the same dark eyes as his daughter, some grey threaded through his dark hair. "Welcome to the Ravenstone."

"Thank you, Alpha Warren. You have a beautiful territory and an even more beautiful home."

He smiled in acknowledgement of the compliment, recognizing its sincerity. "I didn't expect you to come alone. Where's your Beta?"

Normally, Felix would have accompanied me on an important trip like this, but given the situation at home, I thought it better that he stay behind, just in case anything happened requiring an immediate response. Since I didn't want to share anything with the Alpha that might give him concern about sending his daughter with me, I kept my response vague. "He had other duties to attend to, and I thought the time alone might give Amanda and I a chance to get to know each other better."

I turned my gaze to my future mate, offering her what I hoped looked like a genuine smile. She had obviously made an effort for my visit, wearing a pretty pink dress that showed off her undeniably appealing curves. Her dark brown hair curled over her shoulders and false eyelashes drew attention to her deep brown eyes, but I felt nothing in particular when I looked at her.

Nothing except Atlas' uneasiness.

"I'm looking forward to making the trip," she told me, smiling confidently in return. "But first, the pack wanted to celebrate our impending mating. They've prepared a feast for tonight."

That explained the gathering on the beach, and dashed any final hopes I had of returning to my own land that evening. Duty came first, unfortunately; it always had.

After sending a quick message to Felix to let him know of my change of plans, I headed outside with Amanda where she introduced me to what felt like the entire pack. She stood close to me as we made small talk, her hand sometimes going to my arm, and I had to force myself not to take a step back. Atlas felt the same, almost growling in my head at times when she touched us.

We're not being fair to her, I admonished him. Though I had to assume she felt nothing more for me than I did for her, she made an effort.

Having accepted the arrangement, I owed it to her to give her the same chance.

One man in particular kept catching my eye; every time I looked up, he seemed to be glaring at me. I didn't think Amanda had introduced me to him, but I couldn't be sure since I'd lost track by that point. "Who's that guy?" I had to ask her when I caught him yet again looking at me over his beer.

When she glanced over in the direction of my gaze, her lips tightened. "That's Troy. He's not happy about this alliance and he can't use his words properly, so he'll just stand there and glower at us instead. Pay him no attention."

That answer sounded rather more personal than I expected. "An ex?"

"A mistake," she corrected me. "Trust me, there are no lingering feelings on my side."

I wouldn't put money on the same being true of him, but she seemed to have it under control, so I wouldn't interfere unless she asked me to.

When the night drew to an end, the sun setting in a glorious orange blaze over the tops of the mountains, I pled fatigue from my long drive and asked to be shown to a room. Amanda took me herself, leading me to a comfortable and clean guest room with a king-sized bed and an ensuite bathroom. "Since you didn't bring a change of clothes, just put your clothes in this hamper outside the door and the staff will wash them for you. They'll be ready in the morning."

"Thank you."

She lingered in the doorway as if she might be expecting me to invite her in, but I had no intention of it. Even if I felt any arousal at the idea, which I didn't, it had been a long day and the next day wouldn't be a short one either.

"I'd like to leave as soon as possible in the morning," I told her. "Will you have someone wake me up by six?"

That should make it clear that I didn't see her staying with me, and thankfully, she took the hint. "Of course. Goodnight, Vaughan."

She left me on my own and after placing my clothes in the hamper as she suggested, I sank down into the comfortable, warm bed, still trying to ignore the disquiet that had been plaguing me all day. It would get better, I told myself. It would have to.

I just wished I understood why doing the right thing felt so wrong.

Chapter Seven

~Calista~

It took a few days of searching along the edge of the werewolf territory before we found enough fur to make a representative sample. At the same time, my dad preemptively set up some sensors to monitor traffic along the main road in and out of their territory, just as he'd done the last time.

My mom came out of her makeshift lab as I finished putting lunch together for the three of us the day after we'd returned with the samples. "It's a match. The fur we got from the scene matches 83% of the fur you picked up."

That should have made my dad happy, but I saw the look of concern on his face instead. "What is it?"

His lips pulled down, deepening the lines on his weathered face. "This is a big pack, a *lot* bigger than the last one we dealt with. They've got a whole town; we're talking about thousands of people. An operation like the last one is out of the question."

"How exactly did you deal with the last one?"

I'd asked that question before and my parents always refused to share any details. This time was no different, both of them carrying on as if I hadn't spoken.

"Maybe you could do some recon with the drones," my mom suggested to my dad. "That way, we can see for ourselves what we're dealing with."

"I should try to speak with their Alpha first," my dad countered. "The drones might upset them, and there's no point getting on their bad side right off the bat. These attacks aren't likely to involve the whole pack anyway, not with a pack this size."

"The whole pack is still responsible," she argued back. "That's the way it works."

Although my parents generally avoided talking to me about werewolves unless necessary, I knew about the pack structure from the research I'd done on my own. An Alpha wolf led the pack, almost always a man. The position usually passed down by bloodline, like a royal family, but unlike a human royal, werewolves' loyalty to their Alpha was embedded in their instinct, built into their DNA. The Alpha's authority exercised an almost physical force over them that most were unable to resist.

Just one example of where their animal side outweighed any kind of human reasoning.

Due to this patriarchal relationship between the members of the pack, the Alpha bore responsibility for the entire pack, and a rotten Alpha usually meant a rotten pack. Hunting rules dictated that if a hunter had a problem with a pack, they should go to the Alpha first to try to resolve it. In some cases, Alphas actually worked with the hunter to solve the issue, though that didn't happen often. More frequently, they closed ranks, defending their own, just like the Alpha had when my parents investigated the last series of attacks.

The insularity left hunters with little choice. Sanctions would be issued, depending on the severity of the offense, and in serious enough situations, like the one with the pack that killed my family, the hunters might have to destroy the entire pack.

Usually, packs weren't thousands of members strong, though. Obviously, we would need to tread carefully, and if force turned out to be necessary, we'd need to call in a lot of backup, even more than my dad's usual freelancers.

That would be a final resort.

"We try to talk to him first," my dad said firmly, putting his foot down. He rarely insisted on getting his way, more often than not deferring to my mom, so when he did draw a line in the sand, she paid attention. "Once we know where he stands, we can decide what to do from there."

Over lunch, we discussed the logistics of the visit, and as soon as we finished, I stood up to get ready to leave.

My mom stopped me. "Calista, you can stay here and man the comms. We should leave our phones behind if we don't want them taken from us."

Once again, they were trying to shut me out. They never did this with other hunts, so it must have been because we were dealing with werewolves, but I wasn't as fragile as they seemed to think. They'd trained me better than that. "I'm just as much a part of this as you are. You always say that the more eyes we have on a situation, the better. I might see things that you miss."

Unfortunately, on that point, my dad had my mom's back. "We don't need all of us just to have a conversation with the guy. I agree with your mom: you stay here and we'll fill you in on what we learn when we get back."

Simmering with frustration, I watched them go out to my dad's truck, remove all the weapons and anything else that might seem aggressive, and set off to the werewolf territory. After cleaning up the dishes from lunch, I tried to distract myself by checking through the hunting message boards but my mind kept returning to the werewolves.

My mom had a point about the drones helping us to determine the pack's size and scale, but with the wolves' sensitive hearing, it would be difficult to get drones in unnoticed. They'd know someone was checking up on them.

In which case, it might actually be better to send the drones in during my parents' visit. It should help to deflect suspicion that the drones belonged to them; why would they need to send the drones in if they were already allowed onto the land?

It made sense to me, and it would save us time if we ended up needing to do some recon later on.

Making up my mind, I went to my dad's workshop and grabbed a couple of his camera-equipped drones. Hopping in my own truck, I headed out towards the pack territory, to the same place my dad and I had gone to find the fur and not far from where we hunted the wendigo not quite two weeks earlier.

Werewolves could tell when people came onto their land uninvited. Although I didn't fully understand how it worked, from my research I knew it had to do with their relationships to each other and a primal connection to the earth beneath their feet. Wanting to be sure I didn't accidentally alert them to my presence there, I made sure to stop a mile before where my dad had marked the border of their territory. Trees surrounded the dirt track I'd driven down, providing me plenty of cover, and I took the drones and headed a few hundred feet into the woods to a small glade that opened up to the sky. After testing the drones and their controls, I flew the first one up through the opening in the trees and north into the wolves' territory.

For quite a while, I could only see wilderness through the camera, but gradually, the trees began to give way to 'civilization'. As my dad suggested, they'd built a whole town in the forest, looking like any other town in the area, at least on the surface. I skirted the edges of it with the drone, taking a few long-distance photos, not wanting to attract too much attention, and followed a dirt road that led even further north into the forest. At the end of the road sat a cleared field and a smaller group of buildings, including a large two-storey log cabin that, based on my research into wolf packs in general, seemed likely to be the pack house.

Each pack had one: a communal building that served as both a home for the Alpha and a centre for pack gatherings and business. Like a medieval king's castle or the White House, it played a key role in the pack's life, and if it became necessary for us to attack, getting to the Alpha would be the key priority. The Alpha would likely be in the pack house. Knowing as much about it as possible would only help us.

Bringing the drone closer to the ground, I took some pictures of the layout of the buildings and the approaches to it. My parents' truck was parked outside it, which suggested the Alpha had let them in. That was a good sign. Maybe my efforts wouldn't be necessary, but it never hurt to be prepared. On the other side of the parking lot, a group of young men seemed to be taking part in some kind of training activity on the cleared field, and several of them looked up in the drone's direction as it passed over. With their stares turned towards the camera, I quickly pulled it back over the trees and out of sight.

Following the road in the other direction, I found what seemed to be some kind of power station, likely providing all the power the pack needed to make them self-sufficient. That could also be useful if we needed to attack, so I took a few more photos there before returning back around the town and bringing the drone back to me.

Overall, the images should prove very useful, and I uploaded them to our shared drive once the drone returned. With that finished, I sent the second one up, equipped with a heat camera that would give us an idea of just how many wolves we were dealing with.

It quickly became apparent that my dad hadn't been exaggerating. In the pack house alone, it picked up almost a hundred heat signatures, and thousands in the town. Not good news, but information we should have, so I uploaded those details to the drive too. When the second drone landed, I gathered all my things and headed back towards my truck.

"Going somewhere?"

The man came out of nowhere. Tall and broad and blocking my path as he stepped out of the trees, his eyes went to the drones in my hand in disapproval.

My heart rate spiked even as I did my best to stay calm. "I'm going home, actually. Thanks for asking."

I tried to move around him, but he quickly stepped to the side, his girth easily cutting off my escape route. With his buzz cut and muscled bulk, he reminded me of a college football player from the 50s, the kind that showed up in the old movies or TV shows my parents favoured. "Actually, you're coming with me."

"I don't think so," I scoffed, trying not to panic. Stupidly, I had left my gun in the truck and I felt naked without it. "You're not my type."

Nothing about the smile he gave me felt friendly. "You should be so lucky. That would be better for you than having to explain why you're spying on us."

Shit. That seemed to confirm he was a werewolf, but how did he find me?

"This is public land," I pointed out, eyeing the distance to my truck and making the mental calculations in my head. "I was taking nature pictures of the forest, not 'spying' on anyone."

"In that case, you won't mind showing my boss the photos you took?"

His 'boss' must be the Alpha, and that sounded like a conversation I would rather avoid. "Sure. In fact, you can take them all."

I shoved the drones at him, taking him by surprise, and a well-placed kick to his groin brought him to his knees. That one always worked, man or werewolf.

With my path free, I sprinted to my truck, throwing the door open and grabbing my rifle off the seat. By the time he got back on his feet and lumbered out of the trees after me, I had it pointed at him.

"There are silver bullets in here. Don't do anything stupid. Let me leave and no one has to get hurt."

"It's not quite that simple," he stated, wincing as he adjusted his stance. "I'm not here on my own."

From the surrounding trees, five other men all appeared, all equally large and all looking equally unimpressed.

"How about you put the gun down and come with us, and *you* don't have to get hurt."

Again, I calculated the odds, figuring how quickly I could get the shots off versus how quickly they could reach me, and unfortunately, things weren't in my favour. With little choice, I placed the gun back down.

It seemed I would get a chance to speak with the Alpha that day after all.

Chapter Eight

~Calista~

The man I kicked got in the truck with me while the others all hopped in the back. From the passenger seat, he directed me deeper into the woods, into the werewolves' territory. Other than grunting directions at me, he didn't say anything and neither did I. My mind raced with calculations about how I could talk myself out of the whole situation.

The photos had already been uploaded, so as long as I could delete them off the drones' internal drives before anyone had a chance to look at them, they would have no proof of what I'd been doing. The phone in my pocket had two profiles so I could log into the 'clean' one and let them look around while concealing all of the hunting-related activity in the second profile. My dad had trained me well.

The only slip-up I made was mentioning the silver bullets in my gun. If he caught that, he must have figured out I knew *what* he was, so claiming I had just been exploring the forest with my drones would take more convincing. With a little time, though, I could come up with an excuse for that too. I had no plans to give in easily.

We reached the town I'd seen from the air, and as I suspected he would, the man directed me along the path that led to the pack house. It looked even more impressive from the ground than it had from the air, appearing both majestic and humble at the same time, like it belonged there but still felt like something special. Something tugged in my chest, almost like nostalgia. Based on my experience of moving around all the time and not getting too attached to buildings, that reaction made no sense and I pushed it down to focus on my current predicament.

My parents' truck had disappeared from the parking lot where I'd seen it before and I couldn't decide whether that disappointed or relieved me. I wouldn't have them as backup, but I wouldn't have to explain to them how I got myself caught either. Hopefully, I could talk my way out of this and be back home before they got worried.

"Come with me and bring the drones," the man beside me barked as he opened the door and got out, giving me exactly the opportunity I'd been waiting for. Picking them up from the floor where he'd left them, I placed my thumbs on the reset buttons, clearing the hard drives before following the man into the house.

Inside, the pack house impressed me just as much as the outside had. The large entrance hall felt warm and inviting with a large, winding wooden staircase leading up to the second floor. The decoration was rustic but refined and everything looked spotless and in good repair, nothing at all like my own home. My eyes drifted curiously to the top of the staircase as I wondered what the rooms up there would be like, but the stairs weren't our destination, and neither were the large, comfortable sitting room I could see to one side or the more formal dining room to the other. Instead, my escort led me down a hallway in front of us, to the side of the staircase, past several closed doors until he stopped at one and knocked on it.

"Come in," a voice called out from the other side, a voice that sounded vaguely familiar.

The man with me pushed the door open and gestured for me to go in first. Swallowing my nerves, I walked into another large, impressive room, this one some kind of private office or study built into the corner of the house. To my right, a stone fireplace dominated the wall with a couple of comfortable-looking armchairs in front of it, and to the left, a large window looked out into the forest, almost making the room feel like an extension of the natural landscape. At the far end of the room sat a solid wood desk in front of another window, and behind it, a chair faced the window, its occupant hidden from me. Two chairs sat in front of the desk and I had to assume my parents had been sitting in those very chairs not very long ago.

"Here's the woman I told you about," the man who had brought me there said, coming to stand beside me. "Do you want me to stay?"

How had he told him about me? I'd been with him the entire time since he found me and he hadn't communicated with anyone.

"No, you can go." The man who I assumed must be the Alpha stayed facing the window. "Thanks, Darius."

Darius withdrew, closing the door behind him and leaving me alone with his 'boss'. Quickly, I surveyed the room for anything that could be of use. The large windows were a benefit; if I needed to, I could break my way out through them rather than returning through the house. A ceremonial sword of some kind mounted on the wall above the fireplace might serve as a weapon in an emergency if I could pull it down. Plenty of heavy things on the Alpha's desk could be used as blunt weapons in a pinch.

I wasn't quite as defenseless as I might have appeared.

"Come and sit down," the voice from the other side of the desk invited, and as I stepped forward, he finally turned. His eyes widened in surprise as he saw me and mine did the same.

"You?" we both exclaimed at the same time.

The man at the desk was none other than the man I'd spoken to the night I killed the wendigo. *Shit.* So much for hiding the fact I was a hunter.

I could see him a lot better than I could the first time we met, his features clearer now but still unmistakably the man from that night. Short, sandy blond hair gave way to blue eyes, dimples, and the wide, strong chest I'd noticed that night in the woods. In another circumstance, I might have found him handsome, but in our present situation, attraction was the last thing on my mind.

He spoke again first. "Well, this is a lucky coincidence. I've been trying to track you down and here you are."

The idea that he'd been trying to find me put me even more on edge as I stepped forward and placed the drones on his desk, trying to get this over with as quickly as possible. "Your men seem to think I was spying on you, but you can check the drones if you like. There's nothing saved."

"Of course there isn't," he agreed, not even glancing at the electronics. "You must have deleted it all already. Please, sit down."

My expression never wavered, giving nothing away. "There's nothing for us to discuss, Alpha. You have no proof that I did anything wrong and you can't hold me here against my will."

"I'm not the Alpha," he countered. "I'm the pack Beta, but you can call me Felix. As for 'holding you', I certainly can if I think you're a danger to us. What's your name?"

What did that matter?

"It's none of your business. I haven't hurt anyone and I'm leaving now. You can instruct your men to let me go."

I hoped my confidence would convince him, but of course, it wouldn't be that easy.

"You're not leaving yet, Ms Hunter."

My lips pursed. "That's not my name."

"No, but since you won't tell me your name, it will have to do." His eyes twinkled with humour above his serious mouth, the same as they had the first night we spoke. "Now, sit down before I call Darius back and have him sit on you to stop you from leaving."

I felt pretty certain he didn't mean that seriously, but I didn't want anyone else joining us. My odds were better one-on-one, so I reluctantly took a seat. "Why are you seeing me and not the Alpha?"

"Am I not good enough for you?" he teased, despite me giving him no indication that I found him funny. When I didn't crack a smile, he turned more serious too, leaning forward across the desk. "The Alpha's away at the moment. He'll be back later this evening, and you'll get a chance to meet him then if you don't start giving me some information. What were you looking for with the drones?"

Since he already knew about my hunting, I used that as an excuse. "I wanted to be sure the wendigo didn't have any friends. I didn't realize this was your territory. I'll avoid it in the future."

"You told Darius you were taking nature photos," he reminded me, though how he knew that, I had no idea. I hadn't heard Darius speaking to anyone.

"I didn't know if Darius knew what a wendigo is," I countered. "If I go around talking about them to most people, they think I'm crazy."

His lips twitched again, even as he tried to intimidate me. "Look, you obviously want to get out of here and I want that too. It would go a lot faster if you just told me the truth. Or I could guess and you could tell me how close I am?"

The offer intrigued me. How much did he know?

"Go ahead."

He leaned back again, sizing me up. "I think you're with the two hunters who came to speak to me earlier, or at least investigating the same thing they are. You want to know if we're connected to those awful murders that took place a few days ago. You want to know about our pack. I'll tell you the same thing I told them: we don't know anything about the killings, but I'll let the Alpha know about it when he gets back and he'll reach out to them if he gets any further information. How'd I do?"

Of course he had it exactly right, but I didn't want to get my parents into any trouble because of my decisions so I stuck to my denial. "I don't know any other hunters or anything about any murders."

My phone rang before he could respond to me, with my dad's custom ringtone, and Felix leaned forward again. "Answer it."

"No, that's alright. I'll call them back later." With his wolf-like hearing, he would hear every word that was said, and my dad could very well be calling to tell me about their meeting.

"It wasn't a request." His good humour had completely vanished. "Answer it."

Weighing my options, I decided to give in. My parents and I had a code to use for when we weren't free to talk, so if I employed that, he shouldn't give away anything important, and if he was just calling to check up on me, I could assure him I was okay.

Pulling out my phone, I held it to my ear. "Hey, Dad, it's…"

I was about to say 'it's too early for dinner', our code for this type of situation, but he didn't let me get the words out, which wasn't like him at all. Something big must have happened.

"Where are you, Calista? There's been another murder, just like the first one. We're going to check it out now, I'll send you the coordinates. Get there as soon as you can, okay?"

He didn't even wait for a response, hanging up as my eyes met the Beta's unimpressed ones.

"Funny, that sounded an awful lot like the man I spoke to earlier today, talking about the very murder you know nothing about. Either you start telling me the truth, Calista, or you can make yourself comfortable in our holding cell while we wait for the Alpha to return. What's it going to be?"

Chapter Nine

~Vaughan~

Before we left in the morning, I took a moment to speak to Alpha Warren alone. It came to me during the night that perhaps the reason I felt so uneasy about the whole situation with Amanda had to do with taking her back to my pack when things felt so uncertain there. As her father, he wouldn't want me to put her in any kind of danger, so I was completely up front with him about the attack we'd learned about and what happened to the Deep Valley pack.

I laid it all out and part of me hoped that he would tell me the danger was too great, the situation too uncertain, and we should postpone the mating ceremony and having Amanda join the pack until I figured out how our pack scent ended up at the murder scene and ensured that no hunters were going to blame us for it.

Unfortunately, his response went in the opposite direction. "Amanda will be a great help to you with this. She has a way of getting people to open up to her and being able to tell when people are lying or holding something back. Honestly, she's been a huge help to me around here. I'm going to miss being able to ask her opinion on things. And if you feel there's a real danger from the hunters, let me know and I can send you back-up. That's the point of our alliance, isn't it?"

To my chagrin, I couldn't argue with any of that, so as soon as we'd eaten breakfast, Amanda said goodbye to her family and we shifted together for the run back to my car. Once we marked each other, we'd be able to communicate telepathically through our mind-link, but until then, we had no way to talk in our wolf forms, so we simply ran silently together back through the wilderness.

She's got a good, strong wolf, I pointed out to Atlas, trying to make him feel better. He'd been silent all through the reception the night before, retreating into my mind even more than usual. Though I couldn't say I found any wolves particularly attractive, he had a different perspective.

There's nothing wrong with her, he agreed, which was exactly what I kept thinking too. It couldn't really be called an enthusiastic endorsement, but I couldn't find any reason to call off our agreement.

When we reached the small cabin where I'd left my truck, Amanda's suitcases were already waiting, having been brought there earlier by some of the other pack members. The rest of her things would be shipped separately. As I loaded everything into the car, I tried to remember that no matter my own feelings on the subject, she made the bigger sacrifice, leaving behind her pack and the whole life she knew to live with a total stranger. I owed it to her to make that transition as easy as possible.

So, when she asked me about the pack as we set out along the highway back to the American border, I told her about all the key people she'd need to know. "My Beta is Felix. He's a joker but knows when to be serious. I trust him completely. My Gamma, Leo, is the one who keeps us all in line when it comes to following traditions and protocols, and he's very excited to have a Luna to serve. I have a team of Deltas who oversee different aspects of running the pack. Ethan looks after health care and education, Darius is in charge of security, Matthias trains all our warriors and Luke handles the finances."

"Those are all men's names," Amanda pointed out. "You don't have any women on your team?"

I didn't, and it had never seemed like a problem to me but I tried to guess why she would think it might be. "We're not a backward, sexist pack, if that's what you're worried about. The hospital, the college, and our investment program are all run by women."

"Who all report to men. So, it's not that you don't think women are smart, you're just not comfortable working with them?"

She smiled as she asked the question but it didn't feel like much of a joke. "I didn't set out to exclude anyone. I suppose it's just that these are the guys I grew up with and feel comfortable with. A pack is rarely a meritocracy; positions are inherited and assigned based on relationships. I suppose that's something I could be more aware of going forward but I don't think it negatively impacts the way the pack is run. And besides, my Luna will be on the team too."

I gave her what I hoped passed for an encouraging smile, though to be honest, I didn't feel entirely comfortable at the idea of involving Amanda in my team's meetings. I supposed that trust and comfort level would have to be built over time.

"What about other people in the pack I should be aware of?" she asked. "Anyone challenging your authority? Any rival factions?"

"There has been some grumbling," I told her honestly. "But most of it seemed to come from worry over me not being mated or having an heir. Since I'm addressing that now, that opposition should fade."

"Maybe. Or maybe they were just using that as an excuse to rally other people. No matter how loyal people look on the outside, you can never know what's going on in their hearts."

That seemed like a rather cynical view, but it also sounded like she might be speaking from experience, so I didn't contradict her. "Felix is the one who knows everyone's names and connections. If you want the low-down on who to watch out for, he'll be the one to talk to."

She nodded as if making a mental note of it. "What about rivals for your attention? Any jealous exes I need to be aware of?"

Again, her tone was not-quite-joking, and I wondered how much her relationship with Troy, the man who'd been watching us the night before, played into any concerns she might have. On that point, though, I could reassure her fully.

"I've dated women in the pack before, but always on a casual basis, and it always ended by mutual agreement. I made it clear from the start that I intended to wait for my fated mate to make any kind of commitment, so no one ever had any other expectations."

Amanda's eyes widened in surprise, and I cursed myself as I realized exactly what I'd just said.

"Obviously, my decision to wait for my fated mate changed once I realized she wouldn't be turning up. Our agreement takes precedence now. I'm committed to making this work."

Not exactly romantic, but my words seemed to reassure her, and we talked easily for the rest of the trip. She had no trouble keeping a conversation going, and though I would have been happy to have a bit of silence, I didn't mind her chatter either. It felt like we *could* make this work, which relieved me since, by this point, we didn't have much other choice.

Felix called when we were still two hours away to see how much longer we'd be, and I took the call through the car's speakers.

"Is something going on?" I asked him. He didn't usually check up on me.

"It's not urgent, but I'll need you when you get back," was all he would say. "Don't worry about it. I'll see you when you get here."

Of course that only made me worried and the closer we got to home, the tighter the tension in my shoulders got. Atlas felt it too, growing more restless than ever as soon as we got onto our land.

I turned to Amanda as we drove into town. "I'd planned to give you a bit of a tour when we arrived, but if you don't mind, I'd like to go and see what's happening with Felix."

"That's fine with me," Amanda assured me. "It's been a long drive. I wouldn't mind freshening up anyway."

I mind-linked both Leo and Felix to let them know we were almost there, and they both met us in the pack house parking lot. After making a quick introduction, I left Amanda in Leo's capable care while I followed Felix into the house.

"So, it's been a day," he started in his usual understated way. "Apparently, there's been another attack. The police are still on the scene so we won't be able to check it out until tomorrow at the earliest, but..."

He kept talking but I stopped listening as I sniffed the air of the entrance hall. Something new lingered there, something like that sweet, tempting salted caramel scent I'd noticed at the first crime scene. Why would I smell it in the pack house? Was it a clue?

"Vaughan?" Felix turned to me curiously, making me realize I'd stopped moving. "What's wrong?"

"Do you remember that sweet smell I mentioned in the kitchen of the farmhouse? I can smell it again here."

My Beta immediately understood the significance. "If someone from our pack *was* there, they might have been here in the house today too."

"That's what I'm thinking." Unfortunately, it didn't narrow things down very much. We kept the pack house open so people could come and go as they pleased. It could literally have been anyone, but it did seem to support the possibility that someone from our pack had been involved in the murders, as much as I didn't want to believe it.

Felix sniffed deeply, his nose twitching. "I still don't smell it though."

Strange. My nose was good, but not that much better than his.

"Let's come back to that," he suggested, starting down the hall again. "The bigger news is that two hunters came to visit us today."

He had my full attention again. "Why?"

"They're also investigating the murders and they told me they found fur that matched our pack signature. I don't know how they knew and they wouldn't explain it, but they just wanted to make us aware of it and ask if we had any information."

I'd been afraid of exactly that. "I hope you said we'd work with them."

"Of course. I told them if we found any information, we'd share it. I also told them you were away, though."

I didn't immediately see the problem with that, but a moment later, it hit me. "So, from their point of view, I was off pack land when the second attack occurred."

He nodded as he pulled the basement door open. "Exactly. And that's not all. We had another visitor after they'd left, though this one's not quite as forthcoming."

I didn't know why we were going to the basement, but as soon as he opened the door, the caramel scent got a lot stronger. "Felix, are you seriously telling me you don't smell that?"

"Smell what?" He looked genuinely confused. "Listen, I don't know if I did the right thing in keeping her here but she wouldn't talk and I know how quickly this could spiral out of control. I hoped she would talk to you."

Her? He'd lost me, and the scent made it hard to focus. It seemed to be pulling me down the stairs, though I still didn't know who or what waited for me down there.

Without waiting for an explanation, I followed my nose down the stairs, past the storage rooms to the small holding cell we hardly ever used. The silver-plated bars prevented anyone from breaking out, but the person inside wasn't making any attempt to escape.

She sat at the table in the room, her head down with her long, blonde hair hanging down over her shoulders and her hands folded in front of her. My footsteps must have warned her of my approach because she looked up right as I got there. Crystal-clear blue eyes met mine, sitting in a delicate oval face above pink cheeks and pink lips, all bathed in a defiant expression that spoke of conviction and passion and a whole lot of trouble.

I knew it as soon as I laid eyes on her. I knew it before Atlas even said the word in my head.

Mate.

Chapter Ten

~Calista~

Overall, I couldn't complain that the werewolves treated me unkindly. When I refused to answer his questions, Felix let me send a message to my dad so that my parents wouldn't worry before he took my phone and my other personal belongings away from me. I simply said that I'd got caught up in something and wouldn't be able to meet them at the crime scene but to go ahead without me. I still hoped that I could talk my way out of this, but I wanted to speak to the Alpha before I left, for a few reasons.

First, my parents hadn't met with him. They spoke to Felix instead, and while he could give them all the promises he liked, it wasn't the same as hearing it from the Alpha's mouth. I wanted to get a feel for the man we were dealing with and how committed he actually seemed to cooperating with our investigation.

Second, I didn't miss the fact that the Alpha just 'happened' to be away when another murder took place. If he had anything to do with the attacks, he might agree to help us on the surface, all the while covering his own tracks. I wanted to be able to look him in the eye while discussing it, to see his reactions and judge for myself how sincere he seemed to be.

And third, I had to confess to being simply curious about what the Alpha of this large park would be like. Felix didn't fit my idea of a typical werewolf at all. Darius had been closer, but even then, he hadn't treated me too roughly considering that he pretty much caught me red-handed spying on their territory.

My preconceptions of werewolves were tested even further when a young woman my own age appeared at the door of the holding cell Felix had taken me to when I refused to talk. Her tight brown curls bounced as she walked over to the cell door, her eye a matching shade of brown that peered over at me with both friendliness and curiosity. Above average height for a woman and with a solid build, she held a plate of warm lasagna and garlic bread in her hands. The smell of spiced tomato sauce and garlic butter that made its way through the bars made my stomach growl in a very unflattering way.

"You must be starving!" she exclaimed, though ignoring the sound would have been the more polite thing to do. "Here, come and take it."

I didn't particularly want to accept anything from these creatures, especially since I had no idea what might be in it. They could poison me or drug me, or God knows what else. No one knew my situation or location. No matter how good it smelled, or the fact that I hadn't eaten in seven hours, I had to think with my head and not my stomach.

When I didn't move from my spot at the table, the woman sighed. "Oh come on, now, don't be like that. What are you afraid of? Look, you want me to try it first?"

She picked up the fork on the plate and cut off a piece of the lasagna, her eyes rolling back in her head as she put it in her mouth.

"Oh, fuck, that's practically orgasmic."

Despite myself, I cracked a smile. "I've never had pasta *that* good."

"You don't know what you're missing, then." She took another bite, moaning with pleasure. "I swear, I'm ready to call this lasagna Daddy and take it to bed."

A completely unintentional snort slipped out of me. Since she didn't seem to be suffering any ill effects, I gave in to the demands of my stomach. "Alright, you've sold me."

Getting to my feet, I walked over to the cell door while she slid open the slot to pass the plate to me. "I'll get you a new fork if you want."

"Don't worry about it." I ate with twigs in the forest when I had to. I ate live insects on the job to survive. Experiences like those were why

I didn't have any friends who weren't hunters; our lives were just too different for us to find common ground, but for some strange reason, this woman put me at ease.

"I love your hair," she said wistfully as I took the plate back to the table and took a bite of the warm, buttery bread. Although I didn't moan as the salty sweetness hit my tongue, I came close. It really did taste as good as it smelled. "I wish mine would stay straight. As soon as there's even a bit of moisture in the air, it kinks back up again."

"I think it looks great as it is," I told her honestly. "Does your wolf have curly hair when you shift, too?"

I threw the question in casually, like I spoke to werewolves every day, and she answered me without hesitation. "No, thank the Goddess! Can you imagine? I'd look like a poodle!"

The visual made me laugh as I took a bite of the lasagna. I hadn't had food this good in a long time. My own cooking skills left a lot to be desired and my parents weren't any better. We always had more important things to be doing.

"My brother would be just as bad," she snickered, obviously finding the idea of curly werewolves as funny as I did. "It might undercut his Alpha authority."

Instantly, my guard went back up. "Your brother is the Alpha?"

Her expression turned to dismay as she nodded. "Yes, but please, don't get weird about it. Everyone always treats me differently. I can't even get a decent fuck around here since everyone's afraid Vaughan'll tear their balls off if they're not my mate."

I'd never met anyone quite so blunt and open with a total stranger before, but I could see an opportunity there. If she had no filter, she might be able to give me some more details about the pack. "What's your name?"

"Savannah. You're Calista, right?"

Word seemed to be spreading. "That's right. You must be able to find someone who isn't terrified of your brother, though. The pack must have, what, three thousand members?"

"Over four thousand," she corrected me while I made a mental note of it. "We've taken in some smaller packs lately. And you'd *think* there would be some with a backbone, but you'd be wrong. No one wants to get on Vaughan's bad side."

So, the pack wouldn't disobey their Alpha, even on something as relatively minor as consensual sex with his sister. What were the odds, then, that they'd be off committing murder without him being aware of it?

"Are you single too?" she asked eagerly. "Do you know any good places to pick up men? I would love to meet some new people, but Vaughan doesn't like us hooking up with humans."

He sounded more controlling with every word out of her mouth, and I kept my own reply short. "I don't get out much."

The few hook-ups I'd had were always with other hunters brought in to work a job with us. We helped each other out when we wanted a physical release. It had never been more than that, and I had a hard time imagining how it ever could be. My parents had found each other, yes, but they were an anomaly in the hunting community. Most hunters were solitary beings, and I'd never felt anything beyond lust for any of the men I'd been with. Given the life I had, getting attached to anyone seemed dangerous, and I didn't know how to live any other kind of life. Where would I even start?

Several more questions for Savannah were on the tip of my tongue, but before I could ask them, someone called down the hall. "Sav, get out of there. You were supposed to drop the food off and not say anything."

"Since when are there rules against being friendly?" she yelled back, crossing her arms, and a moment later, another large man appeared, looking like an Italian mobster with his slicked-back black hair, glaring at her while ignoring me.

"You're going to get me in trouble," he muttered, taking her by the arm. "Can't you ever just do what you're told?"

"Maybe if you gave me some instructions that were reasonable," she shot back, but when he went to pull her away, she didn't resist. She

threw me an apologetic look over her shoulder before being dragged back down the hall. "Enjoy your supper."

"Thanks." The interesting and unexpected conversation taught me the pack's size along with the Alpha's name, but with her gone, I could focus even more on the excellent food. It soon disappeared, and shortly afterwards, someone else came to collect the empty plate. Apparently, they didn't trust Savannah with me a second time. The new woman kept her eyes down, saying nothing to me.

Another hour passed as I sat at the table, reviewing all the information I had and the questions I wanted to ask the Alpha when he could be bothered to arrive. I half-wondered if he'd turn up with blood beneath his fingernails. If he really was behind these attacks, would I be in danger? I had the chair I sat on to defend myself, and they hadn't bolted the table down either. I made a note of everything in the cell that could be used, just in case the need arose.

Lost in my thoughts, I didn't hear the approaching footsteps until I noticed a movement in my peripheral vision, glancing up just in time to see a man walk up to the cell door.

Tall and well-built, just like all the other men I'd encountered here, his t-shirt stretched over his chest in a way that felt almost indecent. Stubble drew a firm line down his jaw, accentuating its sharpness, and intelligent, brown eyes stared back at me from beneath a rather unruly mop of curly brown hair that rested on his shoulders. Untamed and a bit wild, it still looked powerful and sexy, rather like him.

Where the hell did that thought come from?

The instant zing of attraction that shot through me, settling straight between my legs, took me completely by surprise as I stared at him openly, unable to look away. My unwavering gaze might have been considered rude were he not looking back at me in equal openness and what almost looked like disbelief.

For a long moment, neither of us spoke. Neither of us looked away. We just stared, caught in some kind of iron grip locking our eyes together, but eventually, I cleared my throat, trying to regain some semblance of control over the situation. "Alpha Vaughan?"

It had to be. The resemblance to Savannah didn't escape my notice, though where she was feisty, he seemed intense. An ingrained power and authority imbued his movements. Combined with the fact that I expected the Alpha's arrival at any moment, reason dictated that he must be the man I'd been waiting for.

"Who are you?"

His deep voice seemed to vibrate through my whole body, making my stomach flutter. It actually freaking *fluttered*. What in the world?

I would *not* let myself be distracted by a pretty face, no matter how appealing it might be.

Felix caught up to him a moment later, looking between the two of us curiously, almost like he could feel the same tension and heat between us that I did. "This is Calista, Alpha. Beyond that, she hasn't told me anything about herself. Hopefully, she'll be a little more forthcoming with you."

Vaughan stared at me a moment longer before turning to his Beta. "Bring her to my office. I'll be there in just a minute."

He walked away without a backward glance, and a pang of longing tugged at me as he disappeared from my sight.

What the actual hell? I'd never reacted to *any* man like that, and certainly not a supernatural one.

As Felix opened the cell door to take me back upstairs, I inhaled deeply through my nose and let out a long breath through my mouth, trying to calm my racing heart. *Focus on the job.* I had to determine whether Alpha Vaughan knew anything about the attacks. People had died, I reminded myself. That took precedence over anything else I might be feeling, especially when I remembered who he... *what* he was.

The one kind of creature I could never trust.

Chapter Eleven

~Vaughan~

I needed some air.

The sweet scent of my mate overwhelmed me, making it impossible to focus. A million different thoughts tried to form in my head, important things, but none of them made sense next to the smell of her.

Or the sight of her, for that matter. Beautiful didn't begin to cover it. Her hair flowed over her shoulders like molten gold, her eyes the blue of the brightest mountain lake, and despite her utilitarian jeans and button-up checked shirt, no woman's body had ever looked quite so enticingly strong and delicate at the same time.

Instinct instructed me to fall to my knees and thank the Moon Goddess for blessing me.

Things weren't quite that simple, though. Nothing could ever be that easy.

First and foremost, she was human. I could tell that both by the scent of her, the underlying smell when I pushed past the overpowering scent of our bond, and the lack of recognition in her eyes. As a werewolf, my mate should have recognized me as hers, but I saw none of that in her reaction to me. She seemed curious, certainly, but not possessive or excited. I'd witnessed enough mates meeting each other to know how she-wolves usually reacted to finding their mates, and Calista showed none of that. Maybe she hid it, but I didn't think so. My gut told me she simply didn't feel it.

Calista, Atlas sighed in my mind as I pushed my way out the back door of the pack house, gulping the fresh air in to try to clear my head. *It's a beautiful name. It suits her.*

I supposed it did, but he'd missed the point. *She's human. She doesn't have a wolf.*

Mates were important not just for a werewolf's human side but for the wolves as well. Atlas needed a partner as much as I did.

And she's a hunter, I added, that problem just as big as the first. Maybe even bigger. Being mated to a human would be challenging enough, but to be mated to one who dedicated her life, by choice, to controlling and eradicating creatures just like me? Rather than a blessing, it felt more like a curse.

Felix hadn't told me much about why she came or why he put her in the holding cell, but based on the fact that he'd lumped her in with news about the new murders and the hunters' visit, I had to assume those things were related. Hunters were our enemies. My father raised me to be wary of them, and I only had to remember the brutality of the Deep Valley massacre to know why. They saw us as less than human, unnatural, and their behaviour towards us backed it up. I'd never known one to change their mind, their beliefs and mistrust as deeply ingrained as my own werewolf instincts.

And lastly, the fact remained that I had just brought my chosen mate home with me that very day. The agreement had been signed, the alliance set. Pulling out of it would be an insult to Amanda, to Alpha Warren, and the entire Ravenstone pack, and the last thing I needed would be to turn my powerful new ally into another threat.

Weighing all those considerations in my head, the answer seemed clear: I had to reject her. At the very least, I had to send her away. Simply ignoring her and going ahead with the mating ceremony with Amanda would sever the bond between me and Calista, a bond she didn't even know existed.

It should be straightforward, but as soon as I pictured her beautiful face again or remembered her sweet scent, I had to admit it felt anything but simple. Nine years. Nine years I'd waited to feel the mate bond, and it lived up to every expectation I could have had of it: the instant connection, the pull, the yearning, the desire to protect and possess, to give everything I had and accept all of her in return.

The idea that I should turn my back on it felt almost inconceivable, just as impossible as being mated to a hunter in the first place.

What the fuck was I supposed to do?

In the long run, I had no idea, but right at that moment, I had to go and speak to her. Maybe that would help to make things clearer. Maybe she'd be shrill and obnoxious and make the decision easier for me. I almost hoped she would.

Whatever happened, I had to focus on the reason she'd come here, for the sake of my pack.

To be blunt, I had to pull myself together.

Felix stood outside my closed office door when I walked back into the house, waiting for me. "She's inside," he confirmed, but when I went to reach for the door handle, he stopped me. "Did you recognize her?"

I whipped around to face him, my heart rate spiking, completely taken aback by the question. How could he possibly know about our connection? Had he figured it out from me mentioning a scent he couldn't smell?

"What?" I managed to stammer.

He seemed surprised by my surprise. "She's the woman I met a couple of weeks ago while hunting the wendigo. I told you she looks familiar to me, remember? Does she seem familiar to you too?"

Slowly, my heart began to regulate its rhythm again. He *didn't* know she was my mate, but if I kept freaking out over innocent questions, he might figure it out.

With that in mind, I tried to answer him in my normal tone of voice. "No, I don't recognize her, but you're better with faces than I am."

He grimaced in acknowledgement. "It's driving me absolutely crazy. I *know* I know her from somewhere."

Atlas growled in my head at the idea that Felix would have any kind of connection to our mate, and I did my best to calm him. *He doesn't know her like that, buddy. I'm sure he would remember if he slept with her.*

I certainly would. I could imagine it would be memorable.

Fuck, Vaughan, focus.

Felix kept talking. "Darius caught her just outside our territory this afternoon. She'd been flying drones over our land, but what she's looking for, she won't say. One of the hunters who visited earlier phoned to tell her about the new murders and she called him 'dad', but I don't know if that's a code name or if they're actually related. That's how I found out there had been another incident. Do you want me to come in and question her with you?"

Having Felix there to help keep me on track and keep my distance would be the smart thing to do. I did the opposite anyway. "No, I'll speak to her alone. Will you go and check on Leo and make sure Amanda's taken care of?"

"Of course. Call me if you need me." He took a step away before circling back, reaching into his pocket. "Oh, and here: this is the stuff I took off her before leaving her in the cell: just her phone and some small vials of liquid, it looks like. She wouldn't tell me what they were for either. Aside from the drones, that's all she had on her. No wallet, no ID, nothing else."

He handed me the Ziploc bag with the items in it and walked away while I took a deep breath, trying to steel myself against the scent I knew would be waiting on the other side of the door. When I felt as ready as I could, I stepped inside.

Calista sat opposite my desk, her back to me as I walked in the door, and her long, blonde hair looked somehow even more enticing from this angle, like a curtain of silk down her back.

When did you get so poetic? Atlas asked me wryly, even though I knew he felt the pull just as much as I did.

I have no idea. I'm going to need your help here, okay? We need to keep our wits about us.

That would be easier said than done when she turned to watch me approaching, her blue eyes fixed on me with the same frank curiosity as before. I did my best not to look at her as I walked around my desk and took a seat across from her, the wooden desk that had belonged to my father and his father before him providing a useful buffer to keep me from reaching out and touching her hair to see if it felt just as soft as it looked.

Her eyes fell to the bag that Felix had handed me, the one containing her few belongings. "If you're going to keep me here much longer, I'll need to take my medication."

My chest tightened at both the word and the idea that she might be ill in any way, but I forced myself to answer calmly. "Medication for what?"

"That's not really any of your business."

True, but I needed to know anyway. "It's my business when you might try to use it on me instead. For all I know, it's some kind of poison."

The corners of her lips twitched almost imperceptibly. "And you don't think you could stop me?"

"I don't know anything about you other than that you're on my land without permission."

"Your men dragged me onto your land. You can't blame me for being here."

"They wouldn't have brought you here without good reason. Why don't you tell me what you were doing to attract their attention?"

She refused to back down an inch. "Why don't you give me my medication first?"

I could be just as stubborn. "Why don't you tell me what it's for?"

We held each other's gaze steadily, neither of us willing to back down, and the connection between us felt like an electric current running through me, making my whole body vibrate. It seemed impossible that she wouldn't be feeling it too.

Finally, she blinked first. "I have epilepsy. The medication keeps my seizures under control."

Shit. That made my chest constrict even further, the idea of her being in danger bringing out every protective instinct I had. Hunter or not, *mate* or not, I wouldn't mess with someone's health that way. "That was all you needed to say."

Opening the bag, I handed her one of the small vials. With the practiced hand of someone who had done it thousands of times before, she popped off the top and emptied the contents into her mouth. "Thanks."

"You're welcome."

That small exchange seemed to ease the tension somewhat, so I tried to build on that to get her talking.

"Let's start from the beginning, alright? I'm Alpha Vaughan Stevens. We're a peaceful pack and we've always cooperated with hunters when necessary. I understand some of your colleagues came to visit us earlier today and they were let onto the land and given a meeting with my Beta. We've acted entirely in good faith. There's no reason to resort to spying on us when you could simply ask us anything you want to know. I'd appreciate if you could explain to me what you were doing and why."

I thought the request was more than reasonable, but she ignored it to ask me a question of her own. "Where were you today?"

I was tempted to tell her to mind her own business, as she'd done with me, but that wouldn't get us anywhere. Maybe if I demonstrated some openness, she'd repay me in kind. "On pack business. I spent last night in Canada. You can check with Customs and Border Protection, they scanned my passport when I returned. I drove straight back here so you'll find I didn't have time to kill anyone, since that seems to be what you're implying."

"I didn't say anything about killing anyone. What were you doing in Canada?"

That *really* wasn't any of her business. "Listen, Calista, you're the one who's done something wrong here, not me. Stop avoiding the question."

"What have I done wrong? There's no law against flying a drone over the forest."

Her blue eyes blazed with indignation, challenging me, and damn it if I didn't get a little turned on by it. As much as her refusal to answer frustrated me, I could appreciate her strength of will.

When I spoke again, my voice had gone deeper, completely out of my control. "The only way this ends well for you is if you tell me exactly what you're after. Maybe we want the same thing. Maybe we can work together. But if you continue to defy me, I'll be perfectly happy to lock you back up. Like it or not, I'm in charge here, and the sooner you accept that, the better."

Chapter Twelve

~Calista~

Vaughan's patience wore thin as he addressed me, to the point that I wouldn't have been surprised if he started growling. His brown eyes darkened and his voice deepened, betraying the animal side of him that couldn't be far from the surface. A pissed-off man, I could deal with, but I would rather not go up against an angry wolf without a weapon in my hands.

No matter how much my body reacted to his firm demands, completely against my will, I had to defuse the situation.

Although I tried to keep it in check, my body seemed to have a mind of its own. I'd never felt such a primal, instinctive attraction to someone, and the circumstances really couldn't have been worse.

At least I'd gotten *some* information. He said he'd been out of the country which would be easy enough for us to verify. We had some hacker friends who could get into the border protection system. It wouldn't prove he had nothing to do with the murders, but it would tell me if he felt the need to lie to establish an alibi.

Overall, he came across as straightforward and upfront. He pointed out that they'd acted in good faith by meeting with my parents, and I had to agree with that. He even gave me my medication when I asked for it. Objectively, I couldn't fault him for anything other than for being what he was. Unfortunately, in my mind, that was a pretty big caveat.

No matter how civilized he might seem, the potential always existed for him to lose control, and his tone of voice when he threatened to lock me back up only proved my point.

I had no desire to go back to his cell. I wanted to get back to my parents, share what I learned and find out more about the new attack they investigated, so I would have to play nice, at least until he let me go.

"As my parents already told your Beta, we're investigating a murder that took place a few days ago. We have reason to believe werewolves were involved. You know as well as I do that we don't usually interfere with packs like yours unless there's a good reason, but our responsibility, first and foremost, is to protect humans."

"So, those were your parents." He didn't sound too surprised, so Felix must have noticed I used the word 'dad' when I answered my phone. "I guess they brainwashed you early, then."

The word made me bristle, my nostrils flaring in indignation. My parents always encouraged me to question everything and do my own research, the exact opposite of what he implied. "No one brainwashed me. I've seen the need for our work with my own eyes. I've seen things you can't imagine. If anyone is 'brainwashed', it's the members of your pack who blindly follow everything you say."

His eyebrows raised, heat flaring in his eyes even as he kept his next words level. "You don't know much about werewolves, do you?"

"I know enough." I spat the words out, my disgust coming through loud and clear. Apparently, I couldn't control my emotions as well as he did on this particular subject.

Vaughan's eyes narrowed as he leaned forward across his desk. "And you wonder why we're worried about you surveying our land. Clearly, you've made up your mind about us. You've already decided that we're guilty, haven't you? You're just trying to prove it. Why? So you can attack us in good conscience? So you don't have to feel bad about the innocent lives you take?"

"We *protect* the innocent from supernatural creatures like you. We're trying to prove who's behind these attacks to stop them from happening again."

"All humans are innocent and all supernatural beings are bad? No, it doesn't sound like you've been brainwashed at all."

He shook his head, looking almost disappointed, and my stomach twisted uncomfortably for no good reason at all. Why on earth should I care what he thought about me?

"I didn't say that. Don't put words in my mouth. I know some humans are monsters, and I've met plenty of supernatural creatures who weren't. Those ones aren't my focus."

"So, you're here because you decided my pack *are* monsters?"

"I haven't decided anything." He must have been trying to bait me, but I wouldn't be caught in his trap. "I've lived in this area my whole life and I've never bothered you before, have I?"

"I've never seen you before." For a second, it almost seemed like he regretted that fact, but he quickly moved on. "Felix seems to think he's seen you somewhere, though."

Of course he had. "We met a few weeks ago during a hunt."

Vaughan shook his head. "No, before that. You've never been involved with werewolves before?"

"Not intentionally. Other than…" I trailed off as I realized what I'd been about to share. If I told him what happened to my family, it would only back up his theory that I was predisposed to dislike him and his pack. It would be better not to bring it up. "Never mind."

To no one's surprise, he wouldn't let that go. "Other than what?"

"Nothing. It's not important."

"Clearly, it is, or you wouldn't have brought it up." He raised his eyebrows again, curiously this time. "I'm in no hurry, Calista. We can sit here as long as it takes for you to answer me."

My lips tightened as I thought over my options. Telling him might confirm my prejudice, in his mind, but it also might make it more clear to him why I didn't immediately trust every word out of his mouth. I experienced the worst of what werewolves could do. These murders *were* personal to me, and maybe if he knew that, he would better understand where I was coming from.

"Sixteen years ago, a series of murders took place, very similar to these ones. They were carried out by a werewolf pack."

Vaughan's jaw clenched, his nostrils flaring slightly. Those tells betrayed his agitation even if his voice remained steady.

"Allegedly. I'm familiar with the situation, but you must have been a baby then. You couldn't have been there."

"I was five when the wolves killed my family."

He didn't expect me to say *that*.

Emotions flitted through the expressive depths of his brown eyes, everything from surprise to concern to disbelief. He stared so long, my body began to heat beneath his gaze, but I didn't look away, determined for him to know every word was true.

"There were no survivors from those attacks," he finally said. "That's what I was told."

"Apparently, you were misinformed."

"And you remember it? You're sure werewolves were behind it?"

"My memory of that night is sketchy," I admitted. "But I *do* remember seeing wolves. It's one of the few memories I have of my childhood at all."

"I thought you said the hunters were your parents."

"They adopted me after I was orphaned that night. They weren't able to have children of their own thanks to a demonic possession that my mom endured. I told you: we've seen it all."

Vaughan didn't seem to know what to say to that, so I pressed forward, bringing us back to the topic at hand.

"I understand why the drones might seem aggressive to you, but my only goal here is to make sure that no other families go through what mine went through. What these new victims have just been through. If you're not involved, you have nothing to worry about. But if you are, if you or anyone in your pack has done this, we *will* find out, and we'll make sure it doesn't happen again, no matter what that takes."

Once again, our eyes locked into a battle of wills across the desk, and I held his gaze as steadily as I could, trying to let him feel the force of my conviction.

I expected him to argue, to try to say something to convince me, but instead, he surprised me by getting to his feet.

"Where are you going?"

He pushed his unruly hair away from his face, his arm muscles tensing beneath the fabric of his t-shirt as he did. The gesture had no right to be as sexy as it was. "I'm going to the scene of this new attack, and you're coming with me. We can take a look at the scene together and figure out what to do next. I didn't kill anyone, Calista, but I'll help you find out who did."

Chapter Thirteen

~**Vaughan**~

Calista stood up to follow me, looking uncertain as I handed her the bag with her phone and the rest of her medication in it. She might take off once we were off my land, but I didn't think so. Her investment in the situation seemed pretty clear to me, her pale blue eyes practically shining with it, and when she told me the reason why it meant so much, I couldn't blame her.

Her views on werewolves were misguided and short-sighted, but I could see why she held them, and having hunters around who honestly believed the worst of us would be dangerous for the whole pack.

For that reason, I offered to help her get to the bottom of these new attacks. *Only* for that reason, despite what Atlas suggested in my head.

You want to prove yourself to her. You want to impress your mate.

She can't be my mate, I replied tersely. *I mean: she is, but I can't act on it. What she thinks of me personally makes no difference. I just need her to leave the pack alone.*

He didn't reply, which I knew meant that he disagreed, but we could argue about it later. As I pulled my office door open, I had another problem to deal with: Leo.

"Are you finished, Alpha? Amanda should be ready by now, she's waiting for you to come and introduce her to your team."

Fuck. Why did this all have to be happening at the same time? "I have to go out for a while, off pack land. It's important. You can introduce her if you like."

His disapproval couldn't be plainer. "That wouldn't be appropriate."

"Well, then, tell her it'll have to wait until tomorrow. She'll understand that pack business takes precedence. Make sure she has anything she needs and tell her I'll see her in the morning."

A glance back over my shoulder showed me that Calista was right behind me, no doubt having heard every word of that. Not that it mattered, I quickly reminded myself. She had no idea we were mates or anything about Amanda. She didn't know what any of it meant.

We made it halfway down the hall before Felix appeared. "You're leaving?"

Leo must have linked him already. "Yes. We're going to check out the second murder site. I'll be back as soon as I can."

His eyes moved between me and Calista curiously. "Do you want me to come with you?"

Again, that would be smart, and again, I turned him down. "No, but could you do me a favour? Pull up everything we have about the attacks that the Deep Valley pack were blamed for, sixteen years ago. I'll take a look at it when I get back."

His eyes registered surprise but he quickly agreed. "Of course, Alpha." He turned to Calista with a bemused smile. "I guess this is goodbye."

"I guess so." She still seemed just as taken aback by the fact that we were leaving as everyone else did. "I don't suppose I could get my drones back? They're quite expensive."

Felix already had it covered, as I would have expected. "They're in your truck, along with the keys."

"Thanks." I could tell the consideration surprised her, in a good way. Hopefully, she'd see we really weren't that bad. "And thanks for dinner. Tell Savannah I said goodbye."

"You talked to Sav?" How the hell did my sister get involved? I tried to imagine what they would have talked about, but in the end, I couldn't. Instead, I shook my head, trying to stay focused. "No, never mind. I don't want to know. Let's go."

Outside, I pointed to my truck.

"This is me. You can lead the way, I'll follow you."

Calista got into her truck while I mind-linked with the border team, letting them know we'd be leaving and not to stop her. I had no idea where we were going or how long it would take to get there, but Calista drove at a steady pace, not making any effort to lose me, and I was grateful for the time alone to try to gather my thoughts.

Werewolf didn't often get mated to other species but it *did* happen. I had no reason to suspect outside interference. The Moon Goddess must have intended this match between us, strange as it seemed.

In some ways, Calista fulfilled every quality I could have asked for in a mate. Beautiful, of course. Anyone could see that. Clever, I could tell by the way she argued with me. Brave, undoubtedly. I might not agree with everything hunters did, but no one could call them cowards.

But therein lay the problem too: as a hunter, she had firmly-held beliefs which directly contradicted with my entire way of life. She didn't see me as being her equal. In her eyes, I was something to be controlled, to be contained, and, if necessary, to be eliminated. How could I take someone who saw me that way as my mate, even if I hadn't already entered into an agreement with Amanda?

And I *had* entered that agreement, I couldn't forget that either. The treaty would help to protect my pack, and I'd always been taught that, as Alpha, the pack's needs came before my own desires, especially when they were in direct contradiction to each other.

When I weighed the pros and cons, I really couldn't find any argument in support of spending more time with her, but there I was anyway, following the taillights of her truck in the fading light of the early evening as she turned off the highway into another farm, not all that different from the first one except that there were two houses, side-by-side, both front doors covered with police tape.

Shit.

The smell of blood hit me as soon as I opened the door, but Calista's caramel scent drowned it out as she walked over to me. "I spoke to my parents on the drive over here. They've filled me in on what they found out."

I supposed I should have expected that, and I had to wonder what she'd told them about me, but I refrained from asking to focus on the more immediate concern. "What did they say?"

"Two generations of the same family," she told me, pointing to one house and then the other. "Grandparents in one house, the younger family with two kids in the other one. All of them were killed, just like before. Fur on the scene. They're running tests on it now."

She didn't say that she expected it to turn up my pack's signature, but she didn't have to. I could tell by her tone.

"Where do you want to start?" I asked.

We went to the house on our left first, and I had to admit to being impressed as she picked the lock in a matter of seconds. Inside, the smell of blood grew even stronger, and I picked up our pack scent again too. *Damn it.* That shouldn't be possible.

"What do you smell?" Calista watched me warily, her eyes fixed on my nose.

"I can smell my pack," I told her honestly. Since the fur her parents found would probably confirm it, there didn't seem to be any point in hiding it. "It doesn't make any sense. I left orders for no one in the pack to leave our territory while I was away."

"And they can't disobey you?"

The question felt like a trap, but again, I answered truthfully. "They could. Their loyalty to me is partly ingrained, but it has to be earned too. Wolves can act against their Alpha. Mutinies happen. What I meant is that if someone went off pack land and no one informed me about it, it would mean not only were there people willing to act against my orders but people willing to cover for them too. It would mean widespread treason within the pack, and I just can't believe that's the case."

"So, if they did this, it would have to be with your permission." She gestured at the blood-stained carpets in front of us.

"I'd like to think that no one could do it without my permission," I had to agree. "But since no one had my permission, I have to believe there's another explanation. You know much more about other supernatural beings than I do. Is there anything that could mimic our scent? Shapeshifters of some kind, maybe? Witches?"

The question intrigued her, I could tell, and she took a moment to turn the possibility over in her head. "You think someone is trying to frame you?"

"It seems much more plausible to me than any of my pack members doing something like this."

"Do you have enemies who would go to these lengths?"

Honestly, I couldn't think of any, but telling her that probably wouldn't help. "We're a large pack with a lot of resources," I said instead. "Weakening us would open doors for a lot of other people."

"So, you have no actual leads." Her lips pursed as she continued to look around. "Let's go to the other house."

The scene inside the second home was much the same and again, our pack scent lingered in the air. In this house, as in the one from earlier in the week, the blood trailed into the kitchen.

"This seems to be a calling card of sorts," Calista said, bending down to snap some photos of the bloody paw prints on the floor. "Apparently, the pack that killed my family did the same thing, helping themselves to food after they killed everyone."

I'd never heard that detail before about the murders all those years ago. "That's very strange."

"I think so too," she admitted. "I wondered if it might be a copycat, someone trying to evoke the previous attacks."

"Or maybe it's the same people who carried out those attacks," I pointed out.

Her eyes snapped up to me. "Those wolves were stopped."

"Massacred, you mean." I didn't see a point in tiptoeing around it.

Calista stood up, slipping her phone back into her pocket. "Either way, the attacks ended with their deaths."

She said that as if it could only mean the Deep Valley wolves had been responsible, but I saw another possible explanation. "Maybe because whoever framed them got what they wanted? Maybe they couldn't destroy the pack on their own, so they staged the attacks to get hunters to do it for them, and when they did, there was no need to kill anyone else. And now, maybe they're trying to do the same with my pack?"

It made sense to me as I spoke the words out loud, but Calista looked far less certain. "There's no evidence of that."

"Maybe not, but you can't tell me it's impossible. I'm sure you've seen crazier things."

Her lips twitched, almost as if she wanted to smile, and she quickly tightened them again. "True. But I also know you might be trying to plant all these conspiracy theories in my head to distract me. You're still the only one we know for sure was away all day."

Atlas growled in my head and I almost did the same. Instead, I took a step towards her, getting closer to her than I'd ever been before. Her eyes widened in surprise but she didn't step back, as if she wanted to prove she wasn't afraid.

"Do you really think I'm a cold-blooded killer, Calista?" My voice had gone down to its lowest register, as it did when Atlas was close to the surface. "You want me to believe that you came here with me, alone, when you honestly believe I might have killed these people all by myself?"

Her blue eyes stared up at me defiantly, but I could see another emotion lurking behind them too. It didn't look like fear. I couldn't quite place it.

"I told my parents I'm here with you. If you kill me, they'll have all the proof they need of your guilt."

"Liar." That word *did* come out as a growl, and Calista's eyes went even wider. Behind her surprise, that other unknown emotion grew stronger. "You don't really think I did this. You wouldn't be here if you did."

We stared at each other a moment longer, locked in another battle of wills, but I'd made my point. I took a step back, turning away from her, and Calista surprised me by reaching out to touch my arm. "Vaughan, wait..."

As soon as our skin connected, a cascade of sparks rippled through my body, the physical embodiment of the mate bond I'd always dreamt of, and Calista drew her hand back quickly, as if she'd been burned.

"What was that?"

Chapter Fourteen

~Calista~

I thought the attraction I felt to Vaughan back in his office was bad enough, but when I touched him, my skin literally hummed with electricity. A wave of energy sizzled through me, from my fingertips that rested on his arm all the way to the top of my head and down to the tip of my toes, and everywhere in between. Especially, to be totally honest, between my legs. It didn't help that I'd already been a little turned on by the closeness between us and the sound of his growling, which should *not* have been sexy but absolutely was.

I jerked my hand back, trying to quell the sensation before it got any worse. Wolves could smell sexual arousal, I'd read, and it would be humiliating if he knew just how much he turned me on. "What was that?"

Vaughan's eyes widened for just a second, a brief flash of panic showing on his face before he laughed. "It's called static electricity. You shocked me."

No static shock I'd ever received or given before felt like that, but werewolf physiology differed from humans. Maybe that explained it. "Sorry."

"No problem. I can handle it."

His muscles flexed beneath his shirt, almost as a reflex, and I nearly lost focus again.

Come on, Calista. You're better than this.

"What were you going to say?" he asked.

"What?" I forced my eyes back to his face.

"You said 'wait' just before you tried to electrocute me. What were you going to say?"

It had completely gone out of my head, but I could just about remember when I thought back to the argument we just had. "I just wanted to say that my questions are nothing personal. I have to treat everyone as a suspect until I have more information, and you have to admit, to an impartial outsider, the evidence against you looks bad."

"And you've appointed yourself as judge, jury and executioner."

His lips pulled down in disapproval before he opened the door to step back outside. In the fresh air, he breathed in deeply and an unexpected pang of sympathy hit me. The metallic tang of the blood in the house had been strong for me; I couldn't really imagine how bad it would be for him with his enhanced sense of smell.

"You're missing one key thing, though: a motive. Why would I or anyone from my pack be doing this? We've got everything we need on our territory. You've seen that for yourself."

It did seem that way from the beautiful pack house and the meal they gave me, even as a prisoner. However, people didn't always kill for material gain.

"Sometimes, with supernatural creatures, there's no bigger motive," I pointed out. "It's simply bloodlust."

"We're not wendigos," he said, almost growling again. "We don't feed on humans, and we don't kill for fun."

"My family would disagree."

Logically, I knew he bore no personal responsibility for that attack, but I also didn't think werewolves were as peace-loving as he tried to make them out to be. I'd seen his pack training when I flew the drone over their land that afternoon. What would they be training for if they didn't intend to fight?

Vaughan sighed, running a weary hand through his disorderly hair. "I'm sorry about what happened to your family, but you should know that my pack never accepted that the Deep Valley wolves were behind it. Something else must have been at play, and maybe if we can figure out what's happening here, we'll find out the truth about what happened then too."

Deep Valley. He said that name before, back at his pack house when speaking to Felix, and it stuck out to me then, too. It felt almost familiar somehow, like I'd heard it before, but I couldn't place it. My parents never referred to werewolf packs by name since we had no way of knowing what they called themselves. I didn't know Vaughan's pack's name, and I resisted the urge to ask. It made no difference to me.

That wasn't entirely true. It *shouldn't* have made a difference to me, but I felt curious about it anyway. The idea of being part of a tight-knit community, one that gave themselves a common name and protected their own, appealed to me in a way I couldn't entirely define.

If they weren't werewolves, I would have found it even more appealing.

Vaughan continued speaking, unaware of my train of thought. "I'll talk to my team and try to put together a list of who might be interested in framing us. Maybe you could narrow down the types of beings who would be able to mimic a werewolf attack and our scent? For now, I need to get back to my pack."

I needed to go too. My parents would be waiting.

I lied to Vaughan earlier when I told him that my parents knew we were together. I *had* spoken to them, but I hadn't told them about my time in the werewolf pack or about meeting the Alpha. Something held me back from confiding the whole truth even though I didn't usually keep secrets from them, at least not related to a job.

Was it because I thought they wouldn't let me see him again if they knew? But why should that matter? I didn't *want* to see him again, other than in relation to the case.

My emotions rarely confused me so much. Normally, I kept them under tighter control, the way I'd been taught, but this case had stirred up things I didn't even know I'd buried. It didn't help that my body still hadn't forgotten that strange tingling sensation when I touched him.

"I guess I should take your number," I suggested. "I can let you know what I find out."

I held out my phone to him and he entered his number while I tried not to stare at his strong hands. When he handed it back to me, his fingers brushed mine, and again, a current seemed to flow between us, softer and warmer that time. Maybe humans and werewolves naturally had different electrical balances?

Vaughan didn't comment on it. He simply said goodnight and got back in his truck while I got in mine. Out on the highway, he turned back towards his pack land while I went south instead, heading home.

Although night had fallen by the time I arrived, my parents were still sitting up, waiting for me. They knew about the drone footage since it had already been uploaded to our files, but I lied to them to explain my long absence, saying that my truck broke down on the way home. I expected my dad, at least, to be annoyed with me, and he didn't let me down.

"You specifically heard me say I wanted to wait to send the drones in," my dad reminded me. "If they caught you..."

"They didn't catch her though," my mom interjected, taking my side since she wanted to send the drones in the first place. "And the images we got are excellent. We know a lot more about the pack now."

"We don't need to make enemies of such a big pack," he argued back. "This is completely different than the last one."

"Which is why we need even more detailed information if we need to act against them," my mom countered. "Obviously, we can't kill the entire pack, but there are other methods we could use and Calista's pictures could be vital."

The idea of attacking any of the people I met that day - Felix, Savannah, Vaughan, even Darius - knotted my stomach, but I did my best not to let it show. If they were responsible for the murders, we'd have no choice. "Have you got the results of the tests on the fur?"

My mom nodded. "It's a match for the last scene."

I expected as much, so I voiced Vaughan's concern out loud, wondering what my parents would make of it. "Do you think there's any chance this might be a set-up?"

Curious looks met me from both sides. "What do you mean?" my dad asked.

"Well, we know it's possible to find fur samples lying around. We found them ourselves when we went looking. What if this isn't werewolves at all, but some other kind of creature mimicking their attack style and leaving the fur behind to fool us?"

"Leaving it behind specifically for us?" my dad questioned, and I nodded in confirmation. "So that we'd think it was the wolves and attack them?"

The idea intrigued him, I could tell, but my mom seemed less convinced. "That seems unnecessarily complicated. Why go to the trouble? Why not just attack the werewolves themselves if the creatures are capable of such brutality in the first place?"

That was a good question and I dug into my reasoning for an answer. "Maybe there's a reason they can't? Are there any creatures who are naturally weak against werewolves?"

"Not that I can think of, but we could do some research." My dad looked over at mom since she would be the one doing it.

"We can't waste time on a wild goose chase. If the previous pattern holds, the attacks will get more frequent. We need to prepare to move."

"But we need to be sure we're stopping the right people," my dad countered. "And this pack has been open with us so far, unlike the other one."

He stopped speaking suddenly, looking almost queasy, and I stepped forward, placing my hand on his arm in concern. "Dad? What's wrong?"

"I just..." He swallowed hard, not meeting my eye. "I just hope we didn't make a mistake back then."

"Don't jump to any conclusions," my mom admonished him. "We did what we had to do and the attacks stopped."

That demonstrated the difference between my parents in a nutshell; my mom was endlessly practical while my dad, despite being the better tactician and more skilled hunter, had more natural empathy for the creatures we hunted. He even felt bad about killing the wendigos, since they were only doing what was in their nature.

"It's been a long day," my mom continued, standing up. "We should all get some rest. We need to be sharp tomorrow."

None of us could argue with that, and I said goodnight before heading to my room, my head filled with a million different thoughts. One of them, though, kept popping back to the front of my mind: a large, handsome one that I would much rather forget.

Chapter Fifteen

~Vaughan~

The drive back to my territory could hardly be called comfortable. No matter what else I tried to focus on, my thoughts kept straying to the sparks I felt when Calista touched me, and I couldn't stop myself from imagining what it would feel like to have her touch me more, to touch *her*, to give into what our bodies so clearly wanted even if we were both fighting it. My cock stiffened at the memory and remained rock-hard most of the trip, but I did nothing about it, almost revelling in the torture.

The night before, I could have had Amanda in my bed and hadn't been able to summon up the slightest bit of arousal, yet there I was, halfway to climax just from Calista's fingers brushing my arm.

You still think you can go through with it? Atlas asked me, suffering just as much from the encounter with our mate. Each syllable he spoke in my head ached with his longing.

Mating with Amanda? I asked to buy myself some time, even though I knew what he meant.

He didn't dignify my question with a response, so I carried on.

I have to. You know that. The pack comes first.

Those had been my father's final words to me. Not 'I love you', not 'I'm proud of you', even though I knew he did and he was. Instead, he used his final breath to remind me of my duty.

I promised him I understood. I thought I did. It took coming face-to-face with my fated mate to make me realize my dedication had never truly been tested before.

By the time I got back to the pack house, most people had gone to bed, including Amanda. As guilty as I felt about abandoning her as soon as we arrived, if duty came first, it had been the right call. If we could get the hunters working *with* us rather than against us, hopefully, we wouldn't have to worry about an unwarranted attack.

Felix seemed to have waited up for me. The light shining from beneath the door of his office told me he must still be working, so rather than heading upstairs, I knocked and let myself in. Smaller than mine, his office still had a large window with a great view into the forest, and he'd decorated the room with his own touches, including a vintage arcade game in the corner and his pinboard full of the different kinds of supernatural beings he'd met.

"So, you had a nice quiet day while I was gone?" I asked sarcastically, dropping into the seat across from him and running a hand through my hair to brush the curls away from my face. With his computer screen illuminating his face and a handful of papers spread out across his desk, he showed no signs of stopping for the night.

"About as stress-free as your day," he guessed, matching my tone. "What'd you find out?"

I filled him in on the murder scene and the theory I'd come up with that someone might be trying to frame us. "When Calista asked me who might want to get us in trouble, I blanked," I admitted. "Can you think of anyone who hates us that much? A rival pack, maybe?"

"Other wolf packs would be happy to get their hands on our lands, but they wouldn't be able to mimic our scent or mask their own. It must be something else."

My frown deepened. "What have we done to piss off any other species?"

One shoulder raised in a half-hearted shrug. "Sometimes, it doesn't take much. I'll reach out to my networks tomorrow and see if anyone has any suggestions. First, here's the info you asked for about the previous attacks."

He pushed the papers on his desk over to me and I quickly flipped through them. Copies of the official police reports from the attacks caught my attention, and buried within the details, it mentioned blood in the kitchen at each scene, just as Calista had told me. "It must be a species that can eat," I suggested, pointing out the consistencies between the reports and the current scenes. "That eliminates ghosts, right?"

"And a few other things," he agreed. "Vampires don't eat food, for instance."

It might not be much, but anything that helped us narrow down the suspects should be taken into account. "Did you see anything about any surviving family members who had been in the house?"

The reports all listed the information of the deceased but nothing about any additional members of the household, as far as I could see.

Felix shook his head. "Everything I read suggested there were no survivors. Why?"

"Calista says one of these was her family." I held up the papers in my hand as Felix's eyes widened.

"Shit. That would explain her hostility towards us, then."

"Yeah. She's not our biggest fan." My eyes dropped back to the papers, hoping that Felix wouldn't pick up on the way my voice tightened just talking about her.

He seemed to notice but misjudged the reason for it. "Is she a danger to us?" he pressed. "What were those vials she had with her?"

I answered the easier question of the two. "Epilepsy medication. She drank one in front of me so it definitely wasn't poison. I don't think we need to worry about it."

"Epilepsy?" he repeated, his brows puckering thoughtfully. "I've heard of it, but I don't know exactly what it is."

His interests had always leaned more towards the supernatural than humans.

"It's an overload of electrical activity in the brain that leads to seizures. It doesn't usually affect werewolves since our natural healing abilities keep the neurons in our brains under control. I assume the medication she takes is preventative, to stop seizures from happening."

He nodded as he processed that. "It's weird that the vials weren't labelled."

That thought had crossed my mind too, and I had a theory. "Hunters live on the edges of human society. She might not use a regular doctor or drug store."

The idea of her being ill and going through some kind of back-alley clinic made my skin itch with a protective need to care for her, so strong I could barely push it down. Gripping onto the arms of the chair I sat in, I brought the conversation back to the attacks.

"Anyway, she says she survived the attack on her family. She remembers seeing wolves, which makes me think we might be dealing with some kind of shapeshifter, since it doesn't seem likely to be another pack, as you said."

"What else does she remember?" Felix asked, leaning forward across his desk. "You sure got a lot more information out of her than I did."

A rather ridiculous amount of pride swelled my chest at the suggestion that Calista confided more in me than she told Felix. Although she'd been guarded, she *had* actually told me quite a lot now that I thought about it, and obviously, she felt the sparks between us too. That couldn't have been plainer from her reaction to them, though thankfully, she bought my explanation of it simply being static electricity.

It seemed that, despite being human, the bond still affected her at least a little.

As much as I wanted to ask Felix what he remembered about cases when humans were mated to werewolves, I had to bite my tongue. He would definitely figure out why I asked, and I didn't need to complicate things any further.

"The wolves are the only thing she remembers. She was pretty young, and it must have been traumatic. I'm not surprised she doesn't remember more."

"I understand," Felix assured me. "Memory's a funny thing. I still can't figure out why she looks so familiar to me."

Unfortunately, I knew exactly why *I* couldn't get her out of my head. "Let's get the whole team together in the morning, alright? I promised we'd try to come up with a list of suspects."

"Should I invite Amanda too?"

As the future Luna of the pack, she should be involved in anything that affected us as much as this did, and I couldn't think of a good reason not to include her. "Yeah, I guess so."

Felix laughed. "Don't sound *too* enthusiastic about it, Vaughan."

"I'm just tired," I tried to claim, though I knew he knew the truth. "I'll see you in the morning."

Lying in bed, my earlier arousal came roaring back as I let myself remember the feel of those sparks, Calista's sweet scent and her beautiful, pale blue eyes. In the darkness of my room, I gave into it, stroking myself until I came with her name upon my lips, knowing it would be the closest I'd ever get to being with my fated mate.

Chapter Sixteen

~Calista~

Beneath the full moon, a large crowd gathered in the forest, thousands of people strong. In air cold enough that we could see our breath, many of the children whimpered from the chill, wanting to be home in their beds. My heart beat fast, a feeling of urgency filling me as we moved from the dark shadows of the woods.

"How much further?" someone cried from the rear of the crowd, their voice carrying across the still, silent night air.

"We have to reach the caves," a deep voice from ahead of me answered. "We'll be safe there."

I knew that voice, and as I looked towards it, Vaughan's eyes met mine, full of worry, regret and... affection?

"I'll go to the rear to keep them calm," I could hear myself suggesting, though I hadn't consciously decided to say the words.

"No." Vaughan's refusal was firm and rough, but not threatening. It almost sounded desperate. "You're staying with me."

He urged everyone forward again, and others around me did the same. I recognized Felix and Savannah, though neither of them acknowledged me or seemed to think it strange that I would be there. They were too worried about whatever made the odyssey necessary in the first place.

Suddenly, a growling, gurgling noise came from somewhere in front of us, and Vaughan immediately stopped, holding up his hand to halt the rest of us. "It can't be," he whispered. I only heard him because I stood so close; no one else would have.

"They're in the caves?" I whispered back, though again, I didn't decide to speak the words. They simply came out of me.

"They must be. We'll have to go back and find shelter somewhere else…"

He glanced back with despair at the thousands of people behind him, but when he spoke to the group again, his voice had regained its usual authority, completely covering the feelings he'd just revealed to me.

"Change of plan. Everyone split into your designated evacuation groups. Follow your leader and don't look back, no matter what."

Felix and some of the other men shouted out names as the great group began to divide, heading in different directions. Vaughan stayed where he was, watching to make sure everyone knew where they should go. Finally, only he and I remained and he turned to me with that same look of familiarity and warmth mixed with apprehension.

"We'll have to…"

He didn't finish getting the words out. Something snatched him from behind, pulling him into the trees. All I saw were long, sharp claws curling around his body as I screamed out his name, my heart filled with panic and fear.

"Calista!" My mom's hand shook my shoulder roughly as I blinked my eyes open in the early morning light. She stood over me, still in her pajamas, her brows drawn together in concern. "Wake up. You're having a nightmare."

"Oh." I rubbed my face with my hands, trying to orient myself in surroundings so completely different from the ones I'd just been in, I could hardly make sense of it. "Sorry."

She left me to go get ready while I sat up in bed, trying to calm my racing heart, the terror still strong in my body. I'd never had nightmares before, not that I could remember. I never even really dreamed. It had been so vivid, I would have sworn I still felt the cold air on my skin, but why my mind would invent such a scenario, I couldn't imagine.

Even as I got up and got ready for the day, the dream lingered in my mind, throwing up new questions. Along with the obvious ones like why I would have been anywhere with the werewolf pack and what they were trying to escape from, I kept coming back to one question more than all the rest: if the pack had been in danger, why didn't they shift? The children couldn't, but all the adults should have been able to, yet in my dream, no one had, not even the Alpha. I'd always been told that dreams could be illogical, so maybe it didn't mean anything, but everything else had been so lifelike, that one detail stuck out as strange.

Focusing on that helped me to avoid the even bigger question lurking in the back of my mind with the lingering vestiges of the dream: why did it feel so good to be surrounded by all of those people, as if I belonged there with them? Why did it feel so *right*?

My parents were already on their computers when I got downstairs, my dad on the hunting boards and my mom reviewing the drone images I'd taken the day before.

"This looks like the power station, and perhaps a water treatment facility as well." She pointed to the building I'd also identified as a power station. "That could come in handy."

I thought I knew why the power station would be useful, in terms of cutting off their power and therefore weakening any electronic security or self-defense measures, but I didn't know what we would do with the water treatment plant. "What would you use the water for?"

My parents exchanged glances before my mom answered me. "As we already said, we can't kill the whole pack. There are far too many of them. However, I've been working on something that we could introduce into the water supply that would render them harmless."

I had no idea what she was talking about. "What kind of 'something'?"

"A medication to suppress the werewolf's wolf side."

"You can really do that?" She never mentioned anything about such a treatment before. Always experimenting, she had more ideas than I could keep track of, but this one sounded like a pretty big deal. I would have remembered if she told me. "How do you know it would work?"

"I've been working on it as a side project for a long, long time. I've run tests. It works."

"It works on an individual, in controlled doses," my dad corrected, his eyes not leaving his computer screen. "We don't know what it would do in the water supply. There could be side-effects."

"It would make them essentially human," my mom told me, ignoring my dad's interjection. "They'd be unable to shift into wolves, which would stop them from carrying out any more of these attacks."

Unable to shift. Those words immediately brought my dream back to the front of my mind. Was it just a coincidence I had that dream, and now we were talking about inhibiting the pack's shifting ability? Maybe it had actually been some kind of premonition, but that still didn't make sense, because what would I have been doing there, and why would Vaughan have been looking at me the way he did?

Besides, I'd never had any kind of gift of foresight before. There had to be some other explanation.

I forced my mind back to the present conversation. "Would the changes be permanent?"

"Only as long as they keep using the water. If they stopped or if they moved off the land, their wolves would eventually come back. It wouldn't remove or kill the wolf, only mute it, the same way your epilepsy medication stops your seizures. If you stopped taking it, your seizures would come back."

"We still need to determine whether the pack is behind these attacks, beyond a doubt," my dad reminded us. "I've been asking around about Calista's theory about the attacks being a set-up, and I've had some interesting feedback."

Taking credit for Vaughan's idea felt wrong, but since I couldn't tell them where it actually came from, I simply asked about his research instead. "What have you got?"

He gestured vaguely towards his computer screen. "Someone sent me a link to some old legends about ancient shapeshifters who lived in this area centuries ago. Apparently, they attacked some of the earliest settlers around the forest, thinking that they were stealing their land."

That sounded interesting, and Vaughan had particularly mentioned shapeshifters as a possibility. "What kind of shapeshifters?"

"The legends aren't clear, but it suggested they could transform into different wild animals, and that the settlers were killed in their beds. Sound familiar?"

"I could dig up similar stories from around the world," my mom pointed out. "It's a common myth, but no one's ever seen them around here."

"Or they just don't *know* they've seen them," my dad countered. "These are solitary creatures, usually living on their own or maybe with one or two others. They don't live in packs like werewolves, so if they stay in their human form, finding them would be tricky. But here's the interesting thing: shifting between forms apparently makes them very hungry, but they don't feed on human flesh. They might feed immediately after a shift out of necessity."

A shiver went down my spine as I remembered the bloody handprints in the kitchens of the houses we'd visited. It certainly sounded like we were on the right track. "Why haven't we ever heard of them before?"

There weren't a lot of creatures we hadn't come across, at least in passing. "Likely because they don't actually exist," my mom suggested. Clearly, she still needed some convincing.

My dad had a different theory. "They were thought to have died out, but maybe they haven't; maybe they just went into hibernation, like the wendigos do?"

"What would they have against the werewolves, though?" my mom wanted to know. "And why wouldn't they just attack them directly if they dislike them so much?"

In my head, I added another question: if these shapeshifters were to blame, how did they mimic the werewolves' scent? Leaving the fur at the scene would be one thing, but Vaughan actually smelled his pack scent.

Since I couldn't mention that to my parents without revealing that I'd been to the house with Vaughan, I left the question unasked.

Overall, the idea intrigued me, but we still had more questions than answers, with time working against us. To start, I needed to find out if Vaughan had made any progress with his own questions, and I needed to ignore the excitement that bubbled up in my stomach at the idea of talking to him again. My infatuation with him, or whatever I felt, was starting to annoy me; I even dreamed about him, for crying out loud.

The sooner we finished this job and I could move on with my life, the better.

Chapter Seventeen

~Vaughan~

From the moment I woke up, Atlas' restless energy filled my head. Usually the strong and silent type, his antsy behaviour had me on edge too, even more than I would have been on my own.

We've been over this, I reminded him. *I can't claim her. Even if I wanted to, it's too late.*

It's not too late until you mark Amanda and sever the bond, he argued. *It might be difficult or unpleasant to break the agreement, but not impossible.*

He had a point, but there were other obstacles too. *Calista doesn't even have a wolf, not to mention that she hates us.*

Of course I'd prefer if she had a wolf, but there must be a reason she was chosen for us. We can't just ignore that.

It went on that way all through my morning run. A light frost had gathered on the ground, signalling the changing of the seasons, but I welcomed the way the cold bit into Atlas' paws as he raced through the trees. Anything to distract us both from the war inside our heads made a welcome change.

Back at the pack house when my run finished, people had already started gathering for breakfast and I couldn't put speaking to Amanda off any longer. I asked Felix to gather my leadership team in our meeting room and bring some food with him, and after a quick shower and change, I knocked on the door of the room Amanda had been given, just down the hall from mine.

The door opened to reveal her dressed in a soft red sweater and black pants with high-heeled shoes, her hair and makeup perfectly done. She looked elegant but not overdressed, just right for a Luna, and ever-so-slightly impatient. Obviously, she'd been waiting for me.

"Good morning." I gave her what I hoped felt like a friendly smile. "I know Leo passed on my apologies for last night, but I'd like to offer them in person too."

"It's fine," she assured me, sounding sincere in her acceptance. "Business will come up, I understand that. Once we're bonded, you'll be able to keep me updated through our link."

The ability to communicate telepathically with each other gave werewolves an advantage over other species. Pack members could link each other whenever they wanted, like calling someone on the phone, and between mates, the bond went even deeper, sharing emotions and physical sensations as well as thoughts.

The idea of Amanda being in my head whenever she wanted didn't exactly fill me with joy, but I kept the smile on my face anyway. "In any case, I'd like to introduce you to my team. We're going to have a working breakfast meeting and I'll fill you all in on what's going on."

Gratification lit her smile as she stepped out into the hallway, closing her door behind her. "Please, lead the way."

Her turn of phrase reminded me that I hadn't even shown her around the house yet, so I took the opportunity to do a quick tour on our way to the meeting room, partly to give us something to talk about that would keep my mind off Calista. "This floor is the primary living space for me and my team, as you've probably guessed. Felix and Leo are down at the end of the hall, while Ethan, Darius, Matthias and Luke are on the other side of the staircase. We have a few guest rooms as well, and my room is just here."

I gestured to the closed door as we walked past it, but I didn't open it to show her, even though she slowed down as if she expected me to. It would be her room too, as soon as we were mated. When I didn't stop, she quickly caught up to me again.

"Upstairs, there are more rooms for the staff that live in the house, usually just the ones who are single. People who work in the house and have families generally live in the houses surrounding the pack house. On the main floor are the communal rooms for pack business."

I showed her the living rooms, the library, the games room, the ballroom, kitchen and dining room before heading to the business 'wing' of the house where the offices and meeting rooms were located.

"The whole pack has access to the house?" she asked, noting the people wandering in and out, many of whom stopped to stare at her as she walked by. I could see the appreciation in the eyes of the men and a touch of envy in some of the women. Objectively, I recognized her beauty, but her appearance didn't inspire any kind of lust in me, and Atlas was no help at all. Now that he'd seen his fated mate, he didn't even want to engage with Amanda. At least that meant he'd gone quiet inside my head; I would take the small blessings where I could get them.

"Yes, the ground floor of the house belongs to the entire pack. We have security to keep an eye on things, but people know which rooms are off limits. No one goes into the offices or upstairs without permission. At night, there are guards on patrol."

"You have a lot of faith in your pack." She said it mildly, but I could tell she had some concerns about that, and she quickly confirmed it. "Perhaps too much, given the new members you've taken on who you don't really know that well."

"I prefer to give people the benefit of the doubt until they give me a reason not to."

As I pushed open the door to the meeting room, the men inside all got to their feet, the conversation dying off as soon as we appeared.

"Good morning, everyone. I'd like you all to meet Amanda Wicklow, the daughter of Alpha Warren Wicklow of the Ravenstone pack, and your future Luna. Amanda, you've already met Leo, but this is the rest of my team."

I introduced them all one by one and Amanda shook hands with each of them, looking comfortable and confident as she made small talk and took a seat next to me at the table, the only one that had been left open for her. No doubt I had Leo to thank for that.

Congratulations, Vaughan.

Hey, you want to arrange a mate for me too? You've got the golden touch.

She doesn't have any sisters, does she?

My team's banter echoed in my head, all of them genuinely happy for me, but it only made me uncomfortable when I didn't feel any of the happiness they all seemed to think I should.

"Let's get down to business," I said out loud, cutting off any further conversation through mind-link or otherwise. "We've got a situation that needs all of our attention."

Before that morning, Felix and I had only shared the essential details about the first murders with the team, but after the second incident and the visits from the hunters, they needed the whole story. I laid it all out for them as clearly as I could, ending with the conversation that Calista and I had and the thought that had crossed my mind that someone or something might be trying to set us up.

"The hunters are going to check what kind of beings would be capable of creating such a convincing replication of our pack scent and signature, and I promised that we would try to think of anyone who might have it in for us. That's why we're here. Who would want to get us in trouble with hunters?"

Darius spoke up first, but rather than answering my question, he focused on a different part of my story instead. "Let me get this straight: we caught this hunter spying on us and you not only let her go, we're working with her now?"

I didn't appreciate the suspicion in his voice, but I couldn't blame him for it either. "What was I supposed to do? She hasn't actually done us any harm, and she's just doing her job. She wants to stop the murders and so do we. We're on the same side."

"Hunters can't be trusted," Matthias argued. "After what happened with Deep Valley, I don't want to have anything to do with them."

"Deep Valley?" Amanda repeated, not familiar with the reference. "What's that?"

Leo stepped in to explain. "They were a small pack who lived not far from here. Only about forty wolves in the pack, but they were friendly with us and good allies. Their pups even came to our school since they didn't have their own. About fifteen years ago, some humans got killed, a lot like these current attacks, and the hunters decided the Deep Valley wolves were behind it. They went in at night and slaughtered all of them, even the children and the pregnant Luna. They had long-range explosives so the pack wasn't alerted of their presence on the land until it was too late. It was brutal."

Amanda's wide eyes and pale cheeks looked appropriately horrified. "On what evidence?"

"The same evidence that's accruing against us now," I told her grimly. "That's why this is so urgent."

"Shit," Felix muttered beside me, and I nodded in agreement. "It's serious, so I need your best ideas."

"No, that's not what I meant." Felix shook his head, looking almost nervous and excited at the same time. "I know where I know the hunter from."

"Calista?" My voice hitched as I said her name out loud and Amanda gave me a curious look that I did my best to ignore. "Where?"

"Leo just reminded me. The Deep Valley Alpha had two sons at our school, do you remember them?"

I tried to picture the boys, but my search in my memory came up blank. "By name only. I remember when they died and how we were all told about it. Why?"

He looked surer of himself the more he spoke. "They were blond and blue-eyed, and they had a little sister who was supposed to be starting school soon too, if they hadn't been attacked."

I still didn't see the connection. "And?"

"Vaughan, she looks just like them. And her name... I'm pretty sure they called the little girl Callie."

Callie. Short for Calista?

It had to be a coincidence. It didn't make any sense. "They were all killed, though."

"We thought they were, but Calista told you she survived an attack, didn't she? Maybe she survived the *hunter's* attack."

I supposed that could be possible, but only if we ignored one big thing. "She's human."

On that point, he couldn't argue with me, but he didn't give up on his overall theory. "Maybe the event traumatized her so much, it did something to her wolf?"

Wouldn't she still smell like a werewolf, though? And given her attitude towards us, she certainly seemed to believe she was human. She believed everything she told me the night before, I would swear to it. Atlas, however, perked up in my head again, eager to grasp at this new hope, no matter how unlikely it seemed.

"Track down some pictures of the Deep Valley pack if you can," I suggested, wanting to see this resemblance for myself before anyone got carried away.

Felix nodded. "I'm on it. Maybe we could get some hair from her or something and do a DNA test. It might give us some answers."

"I can try to set up a meeting with her," I agreed, trying to ignore the way my heart leapt at the idea.

Almost immediately, though, it sank again as the woman next to me spoke up. "I'll come with you. She might open up more with another woman there, and it'll be easier for me to touch her without arousing suspicion."

Fuck. Having the two of them together in the same room felt like a recipe for trouble to me, but I couldn't think of a good reason to say no. As everyone else promised to get a list of any potential suspects to me within the hour, I returned to my office to do the same, and to wait for Calista to get in touch.

Chapter Eighteen

~Calista~

After spending a little more time with my dad, scouring our usual sources for any further mentions of shapeshifters or any other species which might be capable of mimicking the werewolf attack, I excused myself and sent a message to Vaughan.

We have one potential lead but not a lot to go on. What have you found?

His reply came back almost immediately. *Very little, but maybe our leads line up. Can you meet to discuss?*

Both his quick response and the suggestion to meet made me much happier than they should have. His eagerness had everything to do with wanting to get to the bottom of these attacks and nothing to do with me personally, I had to remind myself, just like I shouldn't care about seeing him. I only needed to finish the job.

I can be there in an hour.

Walking back through the kitchen, I tried to sound nonchalant. "I'm going to go to the archives in town and see if I can find any mention of these shapeshifters."

My dad nodded in approval while my mom pursed her lips. "I really think this is a waste of time, Calista."

"Well, you don't have to do it, then. I'll keep you updated. Bye."

Without giving her a chance to protest further, I headed out the door and to my truck.

Rather than taking the backroads like I did the day before, I stuck to the highways to get there faster. Since they would be expecting me,

I didn't need to sneak around, and sure enough, when I reached the security booth and gave my name, the man there waved me in after complimenting my music choice and wishing me a good day. To my surprise, no one accompanied me; it seemed he'd been instructed to let me in on my own.

He seemed nice, actually. They all did, and when I thought back to what my mother had proposed, a tiny twinge of guilt pulled at my stomach. How much would it affect them if they lost access to their wolf sides? Would it be that bad for them? I really had no idea.

I passed by a school on my way through the town, and it must have been recess time because hundreds of kids were outside playing. Their happy shrieks drifted through my closed window, reminding me of school days on my own at another new school where I was the new girl who quit trying to make close friends, knowing we wouldn't be staying for long. The kids at this school sounded happy and sure of their place in the world, and for a brief moment, I almost envied them.

Those kinds of feelings were exactly why my mom always said we shouldn't get too close to *any* supernatural creature. It could make the job that much harder if they stepped out of line.

When I reached the pack house, Savannah stepped out of the front door, dressed for fall in her scarf and boots over her skinny jeans, and her eyes lit up when she saw me. She immediately changed course, making a beeline over to me. "Hi, Calista! I heard they let you go. Those idiots can overreact sometimes. I'm glad Vaughan straightened them out. What brings you back here?"

It didn't sound like she knew exactly what had brought me there in the first place, so I kept my response vague. "I actually need to talk to your brother. What are you up to?"

She leaned closer to me with a mischievous smile. "With winter coming, the men will be out in the forest chopping wood. There's a lot of grunting and testosterone, and they like to show off for any of the women who come to watch. It's like an all-you-can-eat buffet of eye candy. You should come join me when you're done with Vaughan!"

Her enthusiasm made it sound appealing, even though I'd never done anything like it in my whole life, but even if I wanted to join her, I had far too much work to do. When I finished with Vaughan, depending on what he had to tell me, I should actually go to the town archives like I had told my parents I would. They had some early historical records from the earliest settlements of the region that might mention these shapeshifting creatures.

It was worth a shot.

"Maybe another time," I had to let her down. "Enjoy yourself, though."

"I definitely will." She gave me a wink before heading off into the trees while I made my way inside.

A man stood just inside the door and his nose twitched as soon as I walked in, no doubt picking up on the fact that I was human. "You're here to see the Alpha?" he asked, and when I nodded, he accompanied me down the hall to the same office where I had met with Vaughan the day before. The door stood open, and Vaughan himself sat at his desk, his head down as he reviewed some papers in front of him, his curly hair hanging down either side of his face.

My fingers itched at my sides, wanting to brush the hair back. I could almost imagine how it would feel to thread my fingers through it, and the roughness of his stubble against my palm as I ran my hand along his jaw. In his eyes, I could picture the same affection that he'd looked at me with in my dream, along with something harder and more needy, something that sent a pang of excitement straight to my core.

Where the hell did that come from?

It flashed through my mind and body before I could stop it, and I could only be grateful that werewolves didn't have the ability to read minds. It almost seemed they could, though, because before the man could announce my presence, Vaughan's head raised, his eyes connecting with mine.

When his nose twitched, though, I realized that he sensed my presence because of my scent, not because he could hear me thinking. Just how bad did I smell to these wolves, I had to wonder?

"Calista. Thanks for coming." He cleared his throat as he gestured to the seat across from him, addressed the man who'd been with me. "Thank you, Gerrard. Can you let Amanda know that our guest has arrived?"

Gerrard bowed his head and left the room, leaving the door open since, apparently, we were still expecting someone else. "Amanda?" I asked curiously as I took a seat in the chair Vaughan had indicated.

Vaughan grimaced, just for a moment. "Yes. She's asked to join this meeting. Apparently, she thought I might be too intimidating for you on my own."

My eyebrows shot up of their own accord. "Did I seem intimidated by you yesterday?"

Vaughan chuckled almost nervously, running his hand across the back of his neck. "No. I can't say that you did."

"And who's Amanda?" She must occupy a position of importance in the pack to be included in the meeting, and I wanted to understand the dynamics. All I really knew of werewolf pack hierarchy was that they were led by the Alpha.

"I am." A woman's voice spoke from behind me, and I immediately turned my head to see a beautiful, sophisticated-looking brunette closing the door behind her. She walked over to me with a smile, holding her hand out, and I shook it before she took a seat next to me. "You're Calista?"

"Right." She hadn't actually answered my question, though, so I rephrased it. "What's your title?"

She glanced over at Vaughan before her eyes returned to me, her smile still firmly in place. "I don't have an official one yet, but I'm Vaughan's fiancée. So I will be the Luna, just as soon as we're mated."

His fiancée. My eyes also darted to Vaughan, hoping, unreasonably, that he would deny it, but he didn't. He simply swallowed, looking slightly uncomfortable, without saying a word.

My throat closed up, a sharp stab of disappointment stinging in my chest, which made no sense. What did it matter to me if he was engaged?

What reason did I have to feel betrayed? He hadn't mentioned it, but why should he have? It wasn't any of my business.

It had absolutely nothing to do with me, and the feeling of loss that washed over me could only be called ridiculous. Was my crush really that strong? Did I somehow convince myself that the dream meant something, when it had only ever been in my head?

My feelings baffled me, and the very last thing I wanted was for either of them to guess what I felt, so I forced myself to respond normally. "Congratulations."

"Thank you." She smiled over at Vaughan, but I didn't look to see his reaction. I kept my eyes on her instead. "But you didn't come here to talk about that. What have you found out?"

Right. We needed to stick to business. "I'd like to hear what you found first, actually."

Her smile faltered for the first time, but Vaughan stepped in. "Of course. As I said in my text, it's not much. Darius, who looks after our security, told me that some strangers showed up about a month ago at our border, asking who owned the land and how long we'd been here, and a bunch of other questions about our right to be here at all. He said they smelled human and our men answered all their questions as well as they could. They left and haven't returned since. He didn't think much of it at the time, but maybe it means something? Maybe someone has an objection to us being here?"

He hadn't been kidding that it wasn't much, but on the other hand, it did line up with what my dad had said about the shapeshifters that morning, about them attacking early settlers for 'stealing' land. It felt like they might be two pieces of the same puzzle, but we were still missing a lot of pieces to make them fit.

I had my mouth open to share my own information, such as it was, but before I could get any words out, the door burst open again, and Felix rushed in, a piece of paper in his hands.

"Vaughan, I found this picture, you won't believe..."

He trailed off as his eyes fell on me, widening as they did so.

"I'm sorry, I didn't realize you'd started your meeting."

"Is it about the murders?" I asked eagerly, unable to guess what else would have him so worked up.

His eyes moved to Vaughan, looking for direction. I followed his gaze and so did Amanda, all of us watching Vaughan's lips tighten in obvious reluctance. What didn't he want me to know?

Chapter Nineteen

~Vaughan~

Only a couple of minutes into my meeting with Calista, it felt like I had completely lost control of the situation. First, Amanda identified herself as my 'fiancée', using the human word that Calista would understand. Though I couldn't argue with the truth of it, Atlas growled in my head anyway, especially when we saw the look of surprise that crossed Calista's face, followed by what almost looked like a tiny bit of disappointment.

Perhaps I just imagined that last part. Maybe I simply projected my own disappointment onto her, since seeing the two of them side-by-side only made the contrast clearer in my mind. The pull towards my fated mate was stronger than I ever could have imagined, so strong that simply sitting there and not claiming her took every ounce of self-control I had, even though none of the reasons why I shouldn't had changed.

And just when I managed to bring the topic back to what we needed to be talking about, Felix burst in, obviously having something to share with me about Calista, not realizing that she would be sitting right there. My Beta usually had more sense than that, so I had to guess he'd found something important.

Calista wasn't stupid. If I sent him away after an interruption like that, she would guess that we were hiding something from her, right when I needed her trust the most.

With that in mind, I held out my hand for the paper he carried. "Let me see it."

Felix stepped forward to hand it to me, mouthing 'sorry' at me when Calista couldn't see him.

The paper held a printed photo from a formal dinner at the pack house. My parents hosted dinner parties whenever leaders from other packs came to visit, and the photo came from one of those occasions, my father standing in his best suit and my mother in a beautiful blue dress next to him. Beside them stood another couple, a burly, bearded blond man, his suit straining to contain his width, and a woman…

A woman who looked like the spitting image of Calista.

My breath caught as I held the picture closer, taking in the details. The resemblance was almost uncanny. Aside from a narrower nose and a different hairstyle, they could have easily been twins. However, given how long ago the photo had been taken, another relationship seemed much more likely.

This is the Deep Valley Alpha and Luna? I asked Felix by mind-link.

About a year before the attack, he confirmed.

"What is it?" Calista asked, leaning forward in her seat to try to get a look at the paper in my hands. She still thought it must be about the investigation, and, in a way, it did have to do with that, just not in the way she thought.

I couldn't hide it from her but I also didn't want to jump to any conclusions until we had more information. Despite what it looked like, I still didn't understand how it would be possible for Calista to be from the Deep Valley pack. My nose didn't lie, and it told me she was human.

Wordlessly, I held the paper out to her as Felix took a step back. As Calista studied the photo the blood drained from her face, leaving her pale and more frail-looking than before. My hands tightened around the armrests of my chair as I forced myself to stay in my seat rather than going over to comfort her.

"What is this?" she whispered, looking up at me in confusion. "Are these my parents?"

"What do you know about your family?" I asked, asking a question of my own to avoid answering hers.

Her words rang with truth in spite of her uncertainty. "I don't know anything. I've never seen a picture before. I don't even know their names. How do you have this?"

Amanda stepped in, putting a comforting hand on Calista's arm as she peered at the photo over Calista's shoulder. "We *think* these might be your parents. There's certainly a resemblance; that woman is just as pretty as you. If you wouldn't mind giving us a few pieces of your hair, we can run a DNA test to find out for sure."

I hadn't expected her to simply ask outright, and Calista also looked up at her in surprise. "How do you have their DNA?"

"We don't," Felix answered. "But we know some of their relatives. It should be enough to get a match."

Calista's gaze dropped back down to the photo, clearly overwhelmed by this unexpected turn of events as her index finger brushed across the faces on the page. "Who are they? What are their names?"

"Let's wait until we get the results of the test," I suggested as gently as I could. I didn't want to raise her expectations any more than they'd already been. We still had a lot of blanks to fill in. "If you want to provide a sample, Felix can get started on it right away."

Without hesitation, she reached up and yanked out a few strands of her pretty blonde hair, wincing as she pulled them loose, and my grip tightened again at the idea of her being in any pain. My face tightened too when Amanda looked over at me curiously. My intended mate really didn't miss much, examining me as if I were under a microscope, trying to look normal when I felt anything but.

As Felix took the hair, his fingers brushing against Calista's causing Atlas to growl in my head, I tried to steer us back, once again, to the matter at hand. "You said that you had a possible lead for the attacks. What is it?"

Calista straightened up, clearing her throat as she also made a concerted effort to get back to business. "You might have been onto something when you suggested shapeshifters."

She told me the information she and her family had found which didn't amount to a whole lot, but could be the start of the right path for us to go down. She concluded by saying that she planned to scour the local archives for mentions of these creatures, but I had a better idea.

"I have a friend who's a history teacher, and he's part native-American. He's especially obsessed with old legends and beliefs among the local tribes. If there are stories about these beings from before the settlers came, he would know them."

Calista eyed me curiously. "You have non-werewolf friends?"

I raised my eyebrows back at her. "Why wouldn't I? I'm not completely uncivilized."

Her cheeks took on a faint pink hue, making her look even prettier as she glanced between me and Amanda. "I didn't mean it like that. I just thought you stayed on your pack land most of the time."

"Mostly, we do," Amanda agreed. "Usually for our own protection. Humans can be quick to judge what they don't understand."

I couldn't say whether Amanda meant that as an insult or not, but Calista clearly took it as one, her cheeks turning even redder as she tried to sound unaffected. "Well, it sounds like it might be worth talking with this man. I'd like to come along."

I had assumed as much, and I pulled out my phone. "I'll let him know we're coming."

Calista continued to examine the photo in her hands while I spoke to Brendan, explaining the gist of the information we wanted so he wouldn't be completely blindsided when we arrived. He didn't say he knew anything, but the enthusiasm in his voice suggested he might have some ideas, and I felt optimistic when we hung up.

"Alright, he's expecting us. Let's head out."

Calista got to her feet as I did, and so did Amanda, looking as though she intended to come too, though that hadn't been my plan. Quickly, I scrambled for an excuse to keep her on pack territory instead.

"Amanda, my sister is excited to meet you and introduce you to some of the other women in the pack. I don't want you to miss out on that. Calista and I can handle this trip on our own."

Truthfully, I had no idea if Sav had anything planned, but I could bribe her into spending the day with Amanda if I had to.

"If that's what you think is best," Amanda agreed, though I didn't miss the rather shrewd look she threw in Calista's direction.

I assured her it would make me happy, and as Calista excused herself to use the restroom before we left, I quickly linked with Sav and convinced her to spend the day with my 'fiancée'. Feeling the tightrope beneath my feet getting narrower all the time, I headed out the door with Calista to continue our investigation.

Chapter Twenty

~**Calista**~

Nobody asked for the photo back. It seemed to be a printed copy, not an original, so when no one said anything about returning it, I folded it carefully so my parents' faces weren't bent and slid it into my back pocket.

How did these werewolves have that photo in the first place? My adoptive parents always said my house burned down, leaving nothing behind. The pajamas I wore were my only belongings in the world when they took me in. That made sense I remembered flames; flames and wolves were the *only* things I could remember from that night.

Yet, when I laid eyes on the photo, another image suddenly sprang to mind.

Although the woman looked eerily similar to me, the man's face triggered the memory. In my mind, I could see him from below as I looked up at him. Above his head, stars danced with the moon, and a smell of earthy cedar filled the air. In his expression, I recognized patience and love, and it filled me with both warmth and sadness at the same time. The warmth of belonging and the emptiness that came from losing it.

No sooner had that memory faded than another one came, fuzzier than the first. I could remember fur, like a large dog nuzzled up against me, accompanied by that same scent of soil and cedar and the same feeling of belonging.

For fifteen years, I hadn't felt anything like it. Something had always been missing in my life but I'd never been able to put my finger on exactly what it could be. Suddenly, I felt closer to an answer than I ever had before.

The images were mere flashes, no more than a few seconds, but they were also the first memories I had ever had of my life before the attack. Seeing the photo seemed to have unlocked them, and I wanted to take it with me and study it more later, hoping it might trigger something else in my mind.

The picture distracted me so much that I almost forgot the uneasiness I'd felt at learning about Vaughan's engagement, until we headed out the door of the pack house together and he gestured over at his truck. "Do you mind if we just take one vehicle? We could talk things out together rather than wasting that time sitting alone."

The idea of being alone with him in such close quarters for any length of time immediately made my stomach flutter in anticipation, to my complete consternation. He didn't mean it that way, not when he had a fiancée, not to mention him being a werewolf. My body needed to calm right down.

"I'd rather take my own truck. I might need to leave at short notice if something comes up."

He didn't seem put off by that. "I'll go with you, then. If you need to leave, I can have someone come and pick me up."

I couldn't think of a good reason to say no without admitting that I simply didn't trust myself to be alone with him, and I had no intention of letting him know that. With a shrug, I headed towards my truck and Vaughan followed, getting in the passenger side while I hopped behind the wheel.

"How do you know this guy we're going to see?" I asked once he'd given me the address to put in my navigation system.

"We met on a forestry management course," Vaughan said, frowning as he looked down at my dash. "Do you mind if I turn the radio down? It's a little loud."

I'd forgotten that his hearing would be more sensitive than mine. "Of course, that's fine."

I went to reach for the volume at the same time he did, and when our fingers touched, that same electrical tingle shot through my body. What *was* that? I thought it might just be a werewolf thing, but when Felix took the hair sample from me earlier, his hand touched mine and nothing out of the ordinary happened. Amanda put her hand on my arm when I looked at the photo, and I hadn't felt anything then.

It only seemed to happen with Vaughan.

I pulled my hand back awkwardly as he turned the volume down to a more comfortable level for him.

"Forestry management?" I asked, trying to ignore the way my body continued to buzz even after we were no longer touching.

Vaughan cleared his throat, as if he felt slightly uncomfortable too. "Yeah. We own a good-sized piece of land here, and most of it's forest. I want to make sure we're taking care of it the best we can. Brendan took the course out of interest and to see how traditional, natural methods of managing forest growth could be used. He's got a pretty wide range of interests and he's very smart. If anyone can help us with this, he can."

"And he believes in supernatural creatures?"

Not everyone did. A lot of people preferred to think they didn't really exist.

"Yes," Vaughan assured me. "We can speak freely in front of him. He knows I'm a werewolf."

That would make things easier, though it surprised me that he went around telling people. "How long has your pack been on this land? You said these humans showed up asking questions about your ownership of the land. What did you tell them?"

"We've been here almost two hundred years. No one was living here then. The indigenous people in the region lived outside of the forest, on the plains. They might have hunted in the forest, but there were no settlements. We didn't take it from anyone."

He sounded a little defensive about that. "I never said you did. I'm just trying to understand why anyone would think you didn't have the right to be here. Do you know where your family came from before then?"

"Not exactly. I only know they came from somewhere further east. Werewolf settlement mimicked human expansion in a lot of ways. My ancestor who founded the pack got kicked out of his own pack for accepting his human mate. A few others followed him and they set up a new pack here."

"Accepting a human mate?" I repeated. I knew all those words, but they didn't make sense to me in that order. "What does that mean?"

Vaughan's expression turned even more guarded. "How much do you know about werewolf culture?"

He had a habit of doing that, I'd noticed. Whenever he didn't want to answer one of my questions, he would ask me a question in return. "Not much," I answered honestly. Other supernatural creatures, I studied in some detail, but I'd always avoided learning about werewolves. They were the villains in my story, the monsters who exposed me to the existence of monsters, and I preferred not thinking about them at all if I didn't have to.

Gradually, those feelings were fading. The werewolves I'd met in Vaughan's pack weren't monsters. They had good and bad qualities, as we all did.

In some ways, they were a lot like me.

"A mate is what it sounds like, I assume? Someone to reproduce with?" I tried to keep the words clinical, but even saying 'reproduce' in front of Vaughan sent a warm flush up my cheeks as my traitorous imagination conjured up the parts of him necessary for that to occur.

"Yes, but it's more than that," Vaughan explained. "Taking a mate is the equivalent of humans marrying. It's a lifetime commitment."

My mind immediately made the connection. "Amanda is your mate?"

His lips tightened as he looked away from me. I could see the firm set of his jaw when I glanced over at him before turning back to the road. "She will be, yes. There are two types of mates. One is fated, what humans would call a soulmate, but the connection is even stronger. Werewolves recognize their fated mates on sight. They've been joined together for a reason, but they need to accept that connection. If they don't, it will break."

I tried to put the pieces together. "You said your ancestor's soulmate was a human. Does that happen often?"

"It does happen." The ends of his words were clipped, as if the subject made him uncomfortable, so I didn't dwell on it despite my curiosity.

"What's the other type of mate? You said there are two."

"If a wolf's fated connection breaks or if they never find their fated mate, they have the option to take a chosen mate. It still forms a bond between them, though not quite the same as a fated bond."

I thought I understood, and I blurted out my conclusion before even wondering if I should. "Amanda is your chosen mate."

He nodded in confirmation, the movement causing his hair to fall over his face and shield his reaction from me, but I couldn't help thinking that he didn't seem overly happy about it. Maybe he wasn't, or maybe he just didn't show a lot of emotion in general. Either way, it really wasn't any of my business despite the pang of jealousy that ran through me at the idea of the two of them together, him looking at her the way he'd looked at me in my dream.

The feeling of belonging the picture of my parents conjured up, the one I felt in that dream with Vaughan, didn't exist for me in real life. The dream couldn't have been a premonition, not when Vaughan was already promised to someone else. I had to stay focused and stop letting my body and my imagination run away with me.

Hopefully, Brendan would have the answers we needed to move forward, and when this case was over, I would find my own way to move forward too.

Chapter Twenty-One

~Vaughan~

Talking to Calista about mates could only be described as excruciating. Atlas hounded me in my head, pointing out all the times it would naturally fit to mention to her that 'oh, and by the way, you're my fated mate', as if that wouldn't completely freak her out. Why would she believe me? And even if she did, did he expect her to embrace the idea? The possibility of her rejecting me hurt more than never telling her at all, so I kept my mouth shut, answering only the questions she asked and nothing more.

When she guessed that I'd taken Amanda as a chosen mate, I could have sworn that disappointment crossed her face again, the same as it had in my office when Amanda introduced herself as my fiancée, but it came and went so fleetingly, I might have imagined it. I probably had, given that she'd given me no other indication that she felt anything for me other than disapproval of my entire species.

And possibly *her* species too? That was still up for debate. I couldn't jump to any conclusions until I had more information.

Brendan lived on a quiet, hilly street, his house built into the hill so that the garage and entrance were at ground level but the main living space was upstairs. I'd been to his house once before and been impressed by the library he'd created for himself, not to mention the local history artifacts. It looked like a mini-museum, and when he gave Calista a quick tour before we settled down in the living room to talk, I could tell he'd impressed her too. Hopefully, he also had the information we came there for.

In his mid-40s and unmarried, Brendan looked every inch the book-worm, with thin, wire-framed glasses, corduroy pants and a patterned sweater that must have been knitted in the 1960s, before he was even born, making him look like he belonged to a different era. His copper skin and dark hair gave a hint to his mixed-race heritage.

"Can I dive right in or do you need any background info about the supernatural world?" Brendan asked after he offered us a drink and Calista and I both declined. We were eager to get down to business.

"Calista's a hunter," I told him bluntly. "She probably knows as much as you do, and definitely more than I do."

The corners of her mouth curled upward in appreciation, just for a second, before she pulled them back down. "I know Vaughan told you what we're looking for, but it might be helpful for you to understand why as well. We should all be on the same page."

With that, she brought him quickly up to date on the current attacks and the ones sixteen years earlier, the evidence we found at the scene and what her family found online that morning about shapeshifters.

"I've encountered several kinds of animal shifters who can go back and forth between two forms, but none that can take on any shape they like," Calista summed up. "Based on what you know and everything I just said, do you think that's what we're talking about?"

Brendan shook his head. "No, I don't. There are legends, certainly. You've probably heard of 'skinwalkers' that some indigenous tribes believe in."

We both nodded. Beings that could take on animal form, they'd appeared in movies and TV shows, despite the tribes that believed in them not wanting to talk about them. They believed that speaking of the beings could make them appear.

"Well, I don't think that's what we're talking about here," Brendan told us.

"Then why bring it up?" I had to ask. If we started listing all the beings that weren't involved, we'd be here all day.

He shrugged as if it should be obvious. "Because we have to eliminate the more obvious possibilities first. At first glance, it might seem obvious, but the long break between the attacks Calista's parents read about, the ones on the early settlers, to the more recent attacks suggests something else."

"So you have a different idea?" Calista asked.

"I do. I had a look at the same old stories your parents probably found and some ones that I've got in my records too. There are some key differences between those stories and the ones about skinwalkers. I do, however, have a different theory, one that I believe fits the circumstances better. It involves possession."

I hadn't been expecting that, but Calista leaned forward in her seat, something clearly clicking into place for her. "Possession that allows for shapeshifting?"

"Possession *of* a shapeshifter," he corrected.

Calista's lips pursed as she thought it over. "Spirits?"

"Yes."

"And witches?"

He nodded in approval. "You've got it."

They seemed to be speaking in their own shorthand, leaving me behind. "Wait, I *don't* have it. What are we talking about?"

"You can explain it," Brendan suggested to Calista, the look of appreciation he gave her making Atlas growl in my head yet again, though I would swear he was only attracted to her brain and nothing else. "I'll jump in if I think you've got it wrong."

Calista took up the challenge as she turned to face me, her pale blue eyes bright with understanding. "Possession usually involves demons, but sometimes, if a spirit is strong enough and they're summoned by a witch, they can take physical form through possession."

"And by spirit, you mean a ghost?" I wanted to make sure I had that part right. Felix knew much more about this kind of stuff than I did.

"Right. Someone that used to be alive and hasn't moved on afterwards. Usually, there's some kind of unfinished business that keeps them tethered. Witches can communicate with them using certain types of magic."

I understand that much, sort of, but it still felt like several pieces were missing. "The ghost possesses the witch?"

On that point, Calista shook her head. "No. The witch helps the process but he or she isn't the vessel. In this case, if the person being possessed is capable of shifting, they would have that ability before being possessed."

That made a little more sense. "So, a ghost is out there possessing a shapeshifter?"

"More specifically than that, I think it's possessing a werewolf, or maybe even more than one." She nodded to herself as she thought it over again. "It must be someone from your pack, whether you want to believe that or not. There's no need to mimic your scent because they already have it. However, I also think the person or people committing the murders could be completely unaware of it. Often, the vessel has no memory of being possessed or the actions they take while being controlled."

Well, that wasn't good news at all. Any of my pack would be horrified to know they'd been used in such a way. I sure as hell would be.

"Why would a witch want to frame us?" I didn't think I even knew any witches, and certainly not any who would have that much of a vendetta against us.

"It might be the spirit rather than the witch," Brendan interjected. "If what's happening now is the same as what happened during the early years of European settlement, two hundred years ago, it couldn't be the same witch but it could well be the same spirit."

"We've pissed off a ghost somehow?"

"Maybe someone with a connection to the land?" Calista suggested, and I had to concede that could be possible.

The Deep Valley land hadn't been far from ours. Maybe they'd angered the spirit the same way we had, without knowing it?

"Possession takes a lot of energy," Calista added. "Anyone who's possessed needs to eat much more than they normally would."

That might explain the food they took afterwards. It did all fit, I had to admit, but it still left me with one big question. "Assuming this is all true, what do we do now?"

Chapter Twenty-Two

~Calista~

This had always been the part of the job I enjoyed the most. The actual hunt could be satisfying when it went right but I didn't get the same gratification that some hunters did from the kill. Solving the puzzle and figuring out which creature lay behind it in the first place always felt the most fulfilling, especially when it involved something more out-of-the-ordinary than our usual work. Maybe, in a different life where my family hadn't been killed and I'd grown up 'normally', I would have been a detective instead.

If Brendan had it right, this case definitely qualified as unusual. I'd never investigated a spiritual possession before. Demonic possessions were relatively common and I knew how to deal with them. A vengeful spirit, especially one who might have been around for hundreds of years, would be something new.

Even so, I had a pretty clear picture of what would be required to prove the theory, so when Vaughan asked what came next, I had an answer ready.

"We go back to your pack and try to find any wolves who might have been a vessel for the spirit. You said no one was off the pack land besides you, but if this theory is right, someone must have been. We start with those who might be able to leave without their absence being noticed. Possession leaves traces of evidence behind. If we find out who the vessel was, we work backwards to figure out when they might have come into contact with the witch. Finding the witch is key to finding the spirit and it's the spirit we need to get rid of."

Brendan looked impressed. "Sounds like you know what you're doing. If it helps, I can try to dig into any local groups or online discussion boards for witches and spirit summoning. You never know, we might get lucky."

"That would be great, thank you." The more eyes we had on something like this, the better. The break we needed could come from anywhere. "I would actually start by looking at discussions from sixteen years ago. If it's the same witch who was involved then, he or she might have been looking for information back then rather than recently."

As soon as those words were out of my mouth, I remembered my dad's reaction that morning when we were talking about the potential of the werewolves being framed and how he hoped they hadn't made a mistake in eliminating the pack all those years ago. If Brendan's theory proved correct, his fear might actually have been justified. It seemed entirely possible that someone from that pack had been possessed to carry out the attacks rather than doing them intentionally, and while my mom would argue they'd acted on the information they had available at the time, my dad would take it harder if they'd killed an innocent pack.

To be honest, if I imagined that pack as being similar to Vaughan and the other werewolves I'd met over the last two days rather than as the monsters I'd always pictured them as before, the idea of killing them in error left my stomach feeling uncomfortably leaden too, even though I hadn't been personally involved.

Hunters made mistakes; we were human, after all, but that would be a pretty big one to have made. For that reason, I almost hoped Brendan was wrong, but either way, we needed to get to the bottom of it and find out for sure.

"This has been really helpful, Brendan, thank you," Vaughan said as I mulled all those thoughts over in my head. "Can I ask you one more quick question before we go?"

"Of course. What is it?"

Vaughan shot me an almost nervous look before clearing his throat. "I'm just wondering: have you ever heard of two werewolves having a human child?"

What on earth did that have to do with anything? I didn't see how it related to the job, but maybe he had another reason for asking. Maybe there had been a situation in his pack, or maybe... my stomach dropped again as it crossed my mind that Amanda might be pregnant, even though, once again, I had no reason to feel that way. She and Vaughan were engaged; of course they had sex. Why should it matter to me?

I'd slept with men before but never been in what I would call a relationship, and I hadn't felt any need to find one. It didn't fit into my life. For that reason, I'd never been jealous before either, and it made no sense that I should be feeling possessive over a man I barely knew and who hadn't shown the least bit of interest in me.

Brendan shook his head. "I've never heard of that. I suppose it's possible, theoretically, but it would be extraordinarily rare. Werewolf genes are inherited, and it's not just one gene that's different from humans, there are several. Those genes are dominant too, which is why when full-blooded werewolves and humans mate, the children are always werewolves."

"Okay. Thanks." Vaughan seemed both satisfied and dissatisfied with that answer, and I bit my tongue to stop from asking why he wanted to know. The immediate task in front of us still needed my full attention.

When we got back outside, Vaughan pulled out his phone. "I'll ask Felix to gather the people he thinks could have left pack land unnoticed. They'll be waiting when we get back."

"Good. We can't waste any time. My parents are afraid the pace of the attacks is going to increase..." As if I'd tempted fate simply by speaking those words, my own phone rang with my dad's ringtone, and I immediately feared the worst. "Hold on, let me get this."

Vaughan stepped around the other side of my truck to make his own call while I answered my phone.

"Hey, Dad."

"Hey, honey. I'm afraid you probably know why I'm calling."

Damn it. "Where was the attack?"

He gave me a few details of the incident and the address, not all that far out of the town we were currently in, telling me that he and my mom were already on the way there, and I promised to meet them there as soon as I could.

Vaughan came back over to me just as I hung up and I turned to him apologetically. "Change of plan. There's been another attack, a very recent one. The police were called because neighbours heard screaming. I'm going to go check it out with my parents so you'll have to get someone to come and pick you up. I'm sorry."

Vaughan's forehead creased in disagreement. "I should go with you. There might be clues I pick up on that you don't. I'll call Felix back and tell him to find out who's not on pack land right now. That should narrow things down a hell of a lot."

Everything he said made sense, but my parents would certainly have some questions if I turned up with the Alpha of the pack we were investigating, questions I didn't particularly want to answer just yet.

I tried to keep my explanation brief. "My parents will be there."

"And?"

Apparently, he was going to make me spell it out. "They don't know about you. They don't know that I've been working with you."

His eyebrows drew closer together, looking both confused and almost disappointed. "You said yesterday that you told them you were with me."

True, I had said that. "I lied."

"Why?" He stepped closer to me and my heart rate immediately increased, the air between us almost crackling with that electric buildup that seemed to exist between us for reasons I didn't understand. "Why don't you want them to know?"

That was a good question, one that I didn't have a full answer to. "It's not usually encouraged to spend a lot of time with the creatures we're investigating."

Vaughan didn't buy that. "They came to my territory and met with Felix, so it can't be that forbidden. Try again."

This assured, almost cocky side of him reminded me of our first interactions in his office, and it frustrated me how much it turned me on. Having him so close to me definitely didn't help. "They know how I feel about werewolves. They would find it strange that I agreed to work with you."

"Why did you, then?" He had somehow moved even closer. I could almost feel his breath as I looked up into his brown eyes, full of challenge. "If you hate me so much, why are you still here?"

He was actually going to make me say it. "I don't hate you," I admitted, my gaze dropping, for just a second and completely against my will, to his mouth before looking back up into his eyes. "It's complicated."

That seemed to be the first thing I'd said that he believed. "Yeah. It is."

He held my gaze, his deep brown eyes full of emotions I couldn't name, and just when I thought he would let it go and step back, he leaned down and kissed me instead.

Chapter Twenty-Three

Kissing Calista was a terrible idea. All I knew about her feelings for me was that she didn't hate me. She begrudgingly admitted that much, but it still left a wide gap between that and any kind of attraction. All the other obstacles between us still remained: her general dislike of werewolves, her humanity, and my 'engagement'. I knew all of those things as I stared down into her pale blue eyes, and yet, I did it anyway.

I could blame the chemistry I felt between us. I could blame Atlas and his almost overwhelming desire to be close to her. I could say that I wanted to kiss her once to know what it felt like with my fated mate, while I still had the chance, before our bond severed.

What it really came down to, though, was that I simply wanted to. And when our lips connected and the sparks of our bond flowed between us, I knew immediately that I'd made a huge mistake.

Once would never be enough.

Warm and soft, her lips tasted both salty and sweet, like the salted caramel scent that overwhelmed me every time we were close to each other. Deep satisfaction filled me, a feeling of coming home, familiar and comforting and exciting all at the same time. My body responded immediately, my heart beating faster and the blood pumping through my whole body but especially to my groin. If I had my way, I would have pushed her back against the truck and pressed my body against her to let her feel exactly what she did to me.

I didn't get a chance, though. Not even a few seconds after the kiss began, it ended. Calista pushed me back, her eyes blazing mostly in indignation but, unless I was very much mistaken, at least a little excitement too.

"What do you think you're doing? You're engaged! You can't…"

She stopped abruptly, wincing as her hands went to her head in tandem, her fingers pressing against her forehead.

"What's wrong?" My arousal instantly turned to concern at the thought of her in any kind of pain.

"My head," she said before wincing again. "I think a seizure might be coming."

Fuck. I'd almost forgotten about her epilepsy. The kiss couldn't have triggered it, could it? I should have done more research into exactly how it worked, but I pushed my self-recriminations aside to focus on her. "What do you need?"

"I should sit down in case I lose consciousness."

"Okay, come here." Taking her hand, I led her over to Brendan's lawn. I sat down first, my legs spread so she could rest her back against my chest with my arms supporting her. "What do I do if you pass out?"

She must have really been concerned because she didn't resist me. Her body melted into mine, moulding against my contours as if we had been designed to fit together. "Just make sure I'm in a safe position and can breathe. If I seize, I should come of it in a minute or two. If it lasts more than five minutes, there are rescue meds in the glove compartment of my truck. It's a syringe, just squirt the medication into the side of my mouth. It gets absorbed through my cheek."

I could handle that. "Got it. Just relax, okay? Breathe. You're safe." I could feel the breath she took, her chest expanding as she filled her lungs deeply, though all I could see from my current position was the top of her blonde head leaning against my shoulder. "Do you want me to be quiet or keep talking?"

"You can talk. Your voice sounds good."

Despite the situation, a smile quickly flashed across my face. That might be the nicest thing she'd said to me, and I knew what she meant.

Her voice sounded good to me too. Everything about her appealed to me.

Maybe I could take this opportunity to find out more about her condition directly from her. "How often does this happen?"

"Not often." Her words were soft, but clear. "My medication usually keeps it controlled."

"Have you always had epilepsy?"

Since epilepsy didn't affect werewolves, her condition seemed to support her being human, confirming what my nose told me, but it directly contradicted what Brendan just explained about werewolf genetics. If she were really the daughter of the Deep Valley Alpha and Luna, how could she be human? If she *wasn't* their daughter, how did she look so much like them? Something didn't add up.

"No, not always," Calista answered me, unaware of my train of thought. "It started about four years ago, when I was seventeen. I guess I had a couple of big seizures then, I don't really remember anything about them. I just woke up in bed and my parents told me what happened. I started taking my meds twice daily after that and the medication keeps it in check."

She didn't remember those incidents and she didn't remember much about the attack against her family either. It sounded like her mind put up barriers as a response to traumatic situations, but maybe, at least when it came to her family, remembering might help to unlock important information. Could there be a way to retrieve those memories that must still exist somewhere in her mind?

"Is there anything that brings your seizures on?" I asked next. If we were going to keep spending time together, at least for the length of this investigation, I wanted to do whatever I could to keep her safe.

Unfortunately, she didn't answer me. Her body began to twitch, her limbs jerking as her head rolled to the side.

Shit.

Do something! Atlas growled in my head.

There's nothing I can do, I replied, which, though true, frustrated me more than anything ever had. I couldn't remember ever feeling quite so helpless as I held her loosely, keeping her head as steady as I could and her airway open. I might have forgotten to breathe myself with all my attention focused on her.

In my head, I counted the seconds, ready to get the medication she'd told me about if she needed it, but not much more than a minute passed before her movements slowed, and stopped. As I took a deep breath in relief, a new scent lingered in the air, something mixing in with her usual delicious mate scent.

The scent of a wolf.

Do you smell that? I asked Atlas, unsure if my nose could be playing tricks on me.

He assured me I didn't imagine it. *I do. I feel something too, very faintly.*

Feel what?

Before he could answer me, Calista began to stir, and the scent disappeared. Everything returned to the way it had been before.

"Are you okay?" I asked, trying to shift her in my arms so I could see her face.

"Yeah." She mumbled the word, but at least she could speak. With a heavy blink, her pale blue eyes tried to focus on my face. "I should go."

She had to be kidding. "Calista, you can't drive like this. I'll take you."

"No. My parents..."

"Have no idea who I am," I reminded her. They hadn't met me when they visited the pack, and they wouldn't know by sight that I was a werewolf at all. "I'll come up with a cover story if you don't want to tell them the truth. Trust me, okay?"

She gave me a weak nod, and I stood up, lifting her in my arms and loading her gently into the passenger side of the truck. She kept her eyes closed as I got behind the wheel and took her phone. Sending a text to the last number that had called her, I asked for the address where she'd agreed to meet her parents, and it quickly came back.

We may have come to Brendan's for answers, but as we set out to the scene of the latest attack, I had even more questions than before.

Chapter Twenty-Four

~Calista~

The pain had dissipated but my head still felt foggy and my limbs heavy and tired, as though I had just done something physically exhausting. I knew I should consider myself lucky; many people took a lot longer to recover from seizures than I did, but I still hated the feeling of disorientation afterwards. Something always felt not-quite-right, and that feeling seemed amplified this time around, stronger than ever before.

It didn't help that I seemed to be hearing voices too.

Just before I began to seize, when Vaughan's chest vibrated against my back, his deep voice in my ear, I thought I heard another voice entirely, even though I knew no one else was around. A female voice, it definitely couldn't have come from Vaughan, and it sounded both nearby and far away at the same time. *Calista*, it called to me. *Help me. Help him.*

I lost consciousness before I could figure out who 'me' or 'him' were supposed to be, and sitting in my truck with my eyes closed as Vaughan drove us to meet my parents, I couldn't hear the voice anymore. It must have been an illusion, like the dream I had, but why would my mind suddenly be playing tricks on me like that? I'd never suffered from delusions before, and the only thing in my life that had changed lately was getting to know these werewolves.

Had they done something to me to mess with my mind? Maybe there had been something in the food they gave me the night before after all. I didn't want to believe that, though. Whether I wanted to or not, my instinct told me to trust Vaughan, and I'd learned a long time ago to trust my gut.

Even if he *was* the kind of guy who would kiss me while engaged to someone else.

Why the hell did he do that, anyway? And why the hell did I like it so much, at least for the few seconds until the logical part of my brain kicked in?

Every kiss I'd ever had before felt pretty much the same, but not this one. Not with Vaughan. When our lips touched, the same electricity that always seemed to spark between us caught fire again, stronger than ever before. It pulsed through me, taking on a life of its own, pulling me towards him and connecting us, like a secret shared between our bodies that I couldn't begin to understand.

Attraction was one thing, a thing I'd been suppressing successfully up to that point, but that pull was something entirely new.

Why would it happen? Why would it happen with *him*, an Alpha werewolf with a fiancée, the very last person in the world I should feel anything for?

My thoughts were all over the place as I tried to focus enough to open my eyes again. Through the fog in my head, I heard Vaughan on the phone, talking to Felix over the speaker. He told him to organize an immediate census to account for everyone on their pack land at that exact moment. They must have had a mechanism in place to do that because Felix didn't argue. He wished Vaughan luck and told him he'd sent my DNA for testing.

My parentage was a whole other issue, along with the photo still tucked into the back pocket of my jeans. With what felt like twenty different things happening at once, I didn't know which to focus on. Maybe that explained why my brain overloaded and seized out of nowhere. It made as much sense to me as anything else.

"How are you feeling?"

It took me a second to realize those words were directed at me, and I forced my eyes open, squinting against the brightness of the sun through the truck window. Vaughan had his eyes on the road, but they darted over to me, filled with concern. For a moment, I almost thought I could see a trace of affection in them too, the same as I had in my dream.

"I'm okay." I adjusted myself on the seat, sitting up straighter as I rubbed my hand over my face, trying to shake the shadows from my mind. "The recovery is usually worse than the seizure. At least I never remember that part."

"It scared me," he admitted. "I've never seen anyone having a seizure before."

The idea of a strong Alpha werewolf being scared by my seizure struck me as kind of funny, but I supposed it made sense. The scariest things in life were usually the ones out of our control. "Werewolves don't have seizures?"

I meant it as a joke, sort of, but Vaughan shook his head. "No. Not that I've ever heard of. We heal very fast, so a lot of human diseases don't affect us."

That must be nice. "Well, you don't have to worry. I'm fine. Are we almost there?"

"Yeah. It's just up here."

He pointed ahead to a farm just off the highway, just like the others. My parents' truck was already in the drive, along with an ambulance and a couple of police cars. We were early on this one if the ambulance hadn't left yet. The bodies must still be inside.

"Stay close to me," I warned Vaughan as he parked the truck. "Don't say anything unless you're asked a question. The police don't always like us hanging around, so we try to stay out of the way as much as possible."

"I'll be right beside you."

His deep voice made that sound more enticing than it should have.

A young police officer stood at the door, and he eyed Vaughan and I warily as we approached. "This is a crime scene, ma'am. You can't be here."

"I understand. I'm looking for Steve Haddon."

Though my dad hadn't used his name, I assumed Steve had been the one to call him about the attack. Still looking at me suspiciously, the man at the door used his radio to call for Steve, and soon, his familiar face appeared at the door.

"Hi, Calista. Your parents are in the kitchen." He gave me a grim smile before turning to Vaughan. "Who's this?"

"A friend. He's helping with some research into the case."

Vaughan simply nodded in agreement, keeping his mouth shut as I'd requested, and after hesitating for just a moment, Steve told the man at the door to let us both through, using the same line about us being animal experts that he used at the previous scene.

The scent of blood inside didn't seem as strong to me as in the other house Vaughan and I had visited together, probably because it hadn't had a chance to go stale yet, but Vaughan could clearly smell it better than I could. He immediately covered his mouth and nose with his hand, trying not to gag.

"The bodies are still upstairs," Steve whispered to me, confirming my earlier guess as he led us down the hall to the kitchen. "I'll try to get you up there before they're taken away."

"It happened just now, during the day?" That seemed strange to me. The other attacks had all happened at night.

"Yes, not much more than an hour ago, we think." We arrived at the kitchen where my parents whispered with each other by the counter. Blood stained the countertop and the fridge handle, just as in the other houses. "I'll leave you here while I check upstairs. Give me just a minute."

Steve left the room as my parents both looked over at Vaughan curiously, their eyes roaming his tall, broad frame with no shame. Since I had to say something, I gave them a story mostly based on truth. "Mom, Dad, this is Vaughan. I met him while doing some research on the case. He knows quite a lot about werewolves. I had a seizure just after you called and he drove me over here."

That should cover all the bases, and as I hoped, my mention of the seizure distracted them from Vaughan's presence.

"Are you okay?" my dad asked.

"What were you doing when it happened?" my mom questioned at almost the same time.

"I'm fine," I told them both, choosing to answer my dad's question rather than my mom's since I had no intention of telling them that Vaughan kissed me just before the seizure started. They really didn't need to know about that. "It didn't last long. What do we know here?"

My dad shrugged. "Not much that we didn't know already. The MO matches the other attacks exactly." He gestured to the bloody kitchen as proof of that.

"The pace is accelerating, just like we were afraid of," my mom pointed out. "We're up to four dead families now. We can't wait any longer."

I knew exactly what she meant even if Vaughan didn't, and my chest tightened. "Actually, we might have a different explanation. I'll explain it to you once we're done here."

Steve returned to invite us upstairs on the strict instructions not to touch anything. We all gave our word and the four of us followed him back up the stairs, my dad struggling with his prosthetic leg, but refusing to ask for help, as usual.

We found the first victim in the master bedroom. Missing his shirt, with the closet door open and a bloodied shirt on the floor next to him, I could only guess he'd been in the middle of changing when he'd been attacked. He must have had no warning at all. Chunks of flesh were torn from his skin, consistent with a wolf attack, and fur stuck to his body, glued there by his own blood. As my parents knelt down to take a closer look, I leaned over to Vaughan. "Anything?"

"Our scent again," he confirmed in a murmur. "But something else too. Smoke and... copper, maybe? I didn't smell it in the other houses."

That would absolutely be consistent with a spiritual possession. The scent must have faded in the other houses before we got there. I didn't smell it, but his sense of smell would be stronger than mine. I believed him when he said he could smell it, especially since copper wouldn't necessarily be a scent someone would associate with ghosts unless they'd studied them.

When my parents finished, we went down the hall to look at the other bodies: a woman and two children, their blood splattered across the playroom in total contrast to the bright, sunny colours of the walls and the toys.

"Fuck," Vaughan muttered under his breath, looking like he might be sick, and I knew how he felt. No matter how often I saw something like that, it still turned my stomach.

The mother must have been trying to protect her children, I would guess. Her body lay closer to the door and seemed to have sustained more damage. I knelt down next to her to examine her wounds, trying to fight down the joint feelings of guilt and nausea that bubbled up inside me. If we'd been quicker to find the creatures responsible, this wouldn't have happened. I knew that feeling lay behind my mom's eagerness to act, but the more I thought about it, the more convinced I became that the werewolves weren't to blame, at least not directly. There was so much fur on her body, it seemed unlikely to be entirely natural.

I looked back at Vaughan to get his attention and he immediately understood my request, squatting down next to me. "What is it?"

"Do wolves usually shed this much fur when attacking?"

He frowned as he looked down at the body. "No. These kinds of wounds are caused by claws, swiping like this." He made a sweeping gesture with his hand, his fingers spread and bent to mimic a wolf's paw. "The undersides of the paws have no fur and there's no reason for the top of the paw to touch the body."

I figured as much. "So, this fur must have been left behind intentionally."

"That makes more sense," he agreed.

After a quick look at the children's bodies, which Vaughan couldn't even bring himself to look at, we returned back downstairs and headed outside to speak to my parents more freely. A small copse of trees sat just behind the house and the four of us made our way over there to get some privacy.

I opened my mouth to tell them all about Brendan's theory, but my mom had something else on her mind as she held up a familiar-looking folded piece of paper. "Where did you get this?"

My hand immediately went to my back pocket and found it empty. The photo of my parents had somehow ended up in her hand instead. "How did you get that?"

My dad looked between the two of us curiously, obviously feeling out of the loop. "What is it?"

My mom ignored him, answering me instead. "It nearly fell out of your pocket upstairs when you bent over. Where did it come from?"

Another question, but I wanted mine answered first. "Those are my parents, aren't they?"

"Where did you get it?" she repeated.

"Why does that matter?" My question seemed like the more important one.

"Look out!"

The shout came from Vaughan a second before a bloodied wolf stepped out of the trees, just behind my dad.

My dad reached for his gun, but I could tell he wouldn't get to it in time as the wolf knelt down to pounce. Quicker than either of them, the man next to me shifted into a large, snarling, black wolf, leaping between the two of them to cut off the attack.

Chapter Twenty-Five

~Vaughan~

As soon as we got out of the house and headed over to the trees, the pack scent got stronger rather than weaker. That didn't make any sense; it should have dissipated in the open air. The only reason it would still be around and stronger would be if someone else was still nearby.

Who's there? Identify yourself.

I sent the message out by mind-link to my entire pack, which should have reached anyone within range. No one responded, but the scent continued to get stronger.

I said: identify yourself. Tell me who's there. I repeated the message, imbuing it with all of Atlas' authority as well as my own. No one from my pack should have been able to resist it, but still, no answer came.

Perhaps if the wolf were being controlled by someone or something else, they wouldn't be able to respond. Calista had said the person probably wouldn't remember the whole experience if they were under the spirit's influence, so maybe the part of their mind that should react to my Alpha authority had also been muted by the possession.

Calista and her parents were talking about something, but I didn't hear a word of it as my eyes, ears and nose strained to figure out exactly where the scent originated from. The tiniest flicker of movement caught my eye, much closer than I'd anticipated, and I had no time to deal with it unnoticed. After alerting Calista and her parents to the danger, and with no other choice since my Alpha authority didn't seem to be working and I had no other weapons, I shifted into my wolf to meet the attacker head-on.

Calista's father seemed to be the wolf's target, so I gave Atlas control as we leapt between the two to intercept him.

"Dad, get back!" Calista shouted as Atlas knocked the other wolf off-course, the two of us tumbling to the ground together.

I didn't recognize the wolf, but that didn't really surprise me. We had thousands of wolves in the pack and I'd never been great at remembering human faces, let alone wolf ones.

Stop this! Stand down! I tried again to get the wolf to respond to my authority, but it had no effect. In its eyes, I could only see anger and bloodlust, and its jaws clamped down on my front left leg, its teeth tearing through my skin as Atlas howled in pain. The scent of human blood in its fur stung my nose, leaving me in no doubt that this same wolf had been the one who murdered those innocent people inside. As its inhuman eyes turned towards Calista and her family, I knew I had no choice.

Whoever this wolf had been, that person was no longer in control, and it seemed the spirit inside wouldn't stop until it had killed every human in sight.

Calista's dad had his gun drawn but he couldn't get a clean shot as Atlas continued to wrestle with the other wolf, trying to hold him back. Above the snarls and growls, I could hear Calista urging him not to shoot since he might hit me instead. The fact that she wanted to protect me drew out my own protective instinct even more. No one threatened my mate and her family, not even one of my own wolves.

Stop them, no matter what, I told Atlas, giving him permission to go for the kill. Maybe if the spirit remained in possession of the wolf's body when it died, the spirit would die too? That would make things a hell of a lot easier.

Using all his strength against the possessed animal, Atlas sunk his teeth into the wolf's neck. Warm blood immediately pooled against his mouth as he paused, giving me one more chance to try to negotiate.

We don't want to kill you, I tried to tell the wolf. *Please, stand down.*

Its back claws dug into Atlas' stomach instead, and with a growl of pain and frustration, Atlas bit through his throat. The wolf whimpered as blood spurted over Atlas' fur, the scent of the wolf's blood mixing with the human blood already staining its fur as the wolf convulsed, twitched, and finally, went still.

Gulping for air and trying to rid himself of the taste of blood in his mouth, Atlas took a step back. Pain shot through the wounds in his front leg and stomach, and through my heart as well. I still didn't know who the wolf had been and wouldn't know until I got him or her back to the pack, but chances were they had a family and friends. They were a part of my pack, my extended family, and they were a victim of the spirit as much as the humans inside were. I hated that it had come to that kind of an end.

A moment later, what looked like steam began to seep through the open wound in the wolf's body, gathering into a small cloud before disappearing into the air, leaving a scent of smoke and copper behind it.

What the hell was that? Atlas growled in my head.

I had a feeling I knew, but I would need Calista to confirm it for certain. *I think that might have been the spirit. Unfortunately, I don't think it's dead.*

Fuck.

I couldn't have said it better myself.

I also wouldn't be able to ask any questions at all until I shifted back to my human form, which I wasn't looking forward to. First, Calista had wanted me to keep my werewolf identity a secret from her parents, but that ship had sailed. Second, when I shifted in the first place, my clothes had torn apart. When I shifted back, it would leave me completely naked in front of both Calista and her human parents. Not exactly the first impression I wanted to make.

Though I didn't have to worry about impressing her parents anyway, since we were never actually going to be mated, I tried to remind myself.

Perhaps I should be much more concerned that I'd just exposed myself as a werewolf in front of a family of hunters.

Since I didn't have any choice but to shift, I had Atlas turn around before taking control again, and staying crouched down with my back to the humans, I took my human form again.

"He 'knows a lot about werewolves', did you say?" Calista's mom deadpanned. I hadn't got a very friendly vibe off her in the first place, and if anything, her voice seemed to have cooled since then.

"He just saved our lives," Calista pointed out, sounding exasperated and almost short of breath herself. Fabric rustled from behind me and I could hear her stepping closer. "Here."

Her jacket appeared over my shoulder as she offered it to me. It wouldn't do much, but it would allow me to cover my midsection, at least, and I appreciated that she wanted to help. "Thank you."

Getting to my feet, I tied the jacket around my waist so that it hung over me like a loincloth. My ass was still almost completely exposed, but at least I had *some* modesty, and I turned back around to face the humans with as much dignity as I could.

"Was that the spirit that left the wolf at the end?" I asked, wanting to steer the conversation towards the bigger picture, and trying to act as normally as possible while standing there wearing next to nothing.

Calista immediately followed my lead. "I think so. Demonic possessions look like that, except the smoke is black."

"What are you talking about?" Calista's dad still had his gun out, his finger on the trigger, but he lowered it to his side. Apparently, he didn't see me as an immediate threat. I couldn't say the same for her mom, who glared at me with barely-concealed distaste.

"That's the theory we were going to tell you about, and it seems it's just been confirmed," Calista explained. "We think a spirit has been possessing the werewolves to make them carry out these attacks. You remember I mentioned someone might be trying to set them up? That someone might be this spirit."

"So, we need to find the witch who's controlling it," her dad suggested, immediately jumping on board with the idea. "Do you have any clues?"

"We should continue this conversation in private," her mom interjected, still glaring at me. "And away from here, before the police come across this."

She spread her hands to indicate me and the dead wolf behind me, and though I didn't like her tone, I had to agree with that conclusion. The longer we stood there, the more we'd open ourselves up to discovery by the human officers. Covered in blood, I didn't like my chances of trying to explain the situation to them.

Calista's lips pursed, but she nodded in agreement too. "Vaughan, I assume you want to take the wolf back to your pack. Are you okay to load it into the back of my truck?"

Her gaze dropped to my bloody arm and stomach, grimacing as she took in the damage, but the wounds weren't that bad. They would heal on their own, and I could handle the pain. "That's fine. I'll meet you there."

Bending down, I lifted the lifeless wolf in my arms and made my way to my mate's truck. Pebbles and twigs stung against my bare feet as I walked over the dirt ground, and my arm throbbed as the wound continued to heal, but I pushed through it to get the wolf into the truck and myself into the passenger seat before I attracted any further attention.

Only when I sat down did I realize that I'd left my phone behind when I shifted. Hopefully, Calista would see it and pick it up on her own. It didn't seem worth the risk to try to retrieve it myself, so I simply waited for her to return, my body and my heart both aching from the fight, and dread filling me as I contemplated what still lay ahead. Even once we found out who the wolf was, that didn't answer the bigger questions: why did this spirit have it out for us, and what could we do to stop it?

CHAPTER TWENTY-SIX

~**Calista**~

I had never seen a werewolf shift before, and I never thought it would affect me the way it did. One minute, Vaughan stood there beside me, solid and strong but respectful and restrained, and the next, his clothes tore from his body as he transformed into a literal beast, fur and claws and fangs and all. As accustomed as I was to supernatural creatures, it still seemed rather magical and, to be completely honest, a tiny bit sexy too.

That might just be Vaughan, though. I probably wouldn't feel that way about *every* werewolf.

The huge wolf's agility and power didn't surprise me, but the way he approached the fight did. It seemed measured and considered, or as much as two animals grappling with each other could. Several times, he paused, expressing dominance but appearing to give the other wolf a chance to back down. I always imagined werewolves in their wolf form to be little better than a wendigo, letting their animal instincts control them, but when I watched Vaughan as a wolf, he still seemed part-human.

"Shoot the rabid one," my mom urged as my dad aimed his gun at the struggling wolf pair. The bullets were lined with silver, ash, and oak, a multi-purpose design to take out multiple kinds of supernatural creatures. The idea of what it might do to Vaughan made my chest tighten so much, it became hard to breathe.

"There's no clean shot," I quickly countered. "Let him handle this. If he gets into trouble, you can shoot."

In the end, Vaughan didn't need our help. He killed the other wolf, his sharp teeth ripping through flesh and dripping with blood, but I couldn't help imagining I saw regret in his eyes as he did it. It certainly didn't look like he enjoyed it.

When he shifted back to his human form, completely naked, contrasting feelings of protectiveness and the now-familiar arousal I felt around him rose up inside me. After offering him my coat, I looked back to my parents to keep from staring at the firm muscles that begged to be touched, his strong back and shoulders and his rather perfect, rounded ass. If I'd ever seen such a perfect specimen of the male form before, I couldn't remember it.

He was engaged, I had to remind myself. Lusting after him would get me nowhere, even if he *had* kissed me earlier, which he still hadn't offered any explanation about.

As soon as Vaughan walked away, carrying the dead wolf on his own despite his own injuries, wearing only my jacket around his waist, my mom immediately started her rapid-fire questions. "Who is he? Why did you bring him here? Why are you with a werewolf? What's going on?"

The first three questions, I could answer easily enough; the last one would be trickier to explain. "His name is Vaughan, as I told you. He's the Alpha of the Crimsontooth pack, the one we're investigating."

My dad's mouth dropped open in surprise, and I didn't miss the uneasy look he and my mom shared. "What are you doing with their Alpha?"

"It's a long story, but we ran into each other during my investigation. He's trying to help. We've got a theory about what's actually going on here and I think we've just been proven right. You saw that spirit as well as I did. That wolf was possessed."

"It certainly looked like..." my dad started to say, but my mom cut him off before he could finish.

"This theory of yours came from the werewolf?"

From her tone, I could tell that lessened its worth in her eyes, and my back immediately stiffened. My instinct to defend Vaughan surprised me in its strength, but I limited my response to the facts. "He suggested someone might be trying to frame them. We worked together to put the details together, and possession made the most sense to me even before what we just witnessed."

"It could be a decoy." Her intransigence on the subject made me glad that Vaughan hadn't stuck around to hear all of this. With a sigh, she held up the piece of paper still in her hands. "Did he give you this picture as well?"

My frustration matched hers. "Why are you so convinced the werewolves are behind this? Why won't you even consider other possibilities, especially after what we just saw? I'm the one who has reason to hate them, not you. They didn't do anything to you."

My voice had raised against my will, and my dad threw a nervous glance over his shoulder towards the farmhouse where the police continued their work. "Let's all stay calm. Calista, there are some things you don't know. Maybe it's time you did. We should go home and talk about it there."

My mom and I both disagreed with that, for different reasons. Before I could voice my concerns, she spoke up first. "We don't have time. The next attack is coming soon so we have to act now. Even if it is possession, we can stop it by inhibiting their ability to shift. If they're possessed and can't shift, they're no more useful to the spirit than any human. At least we can stop any more innocent families from dying"

Almost surprisingly, I could see the validity of her suggestion. Maybe if we presented the option to Vaughan to temporarily inhibit the wolf side of his pack members, he might voluntarily agree to it in order to protect his pack.

My dad had his own reservations, however. "The treatment hasn't been tested on such a wide scale," he reminded us both. "We can't guarantee there wouldn't be side effects. It might even be toxic, especially for the younger ones. I think we should continue the hunt as usual now that we know what we're looking for: we need to find the witch who's enabling this spirit."

"And what if we can't?" my mom shot back. "What if it takes too long? More innocent people die. We can't take the risk."

"And innocent werewolves might die if you contaminate their water! Don't you see what this means? If a spirit was behind the previous attacks too, that wolf pack was innocent. They didn't deserve to die."

Guilt soaked through his words, his anguish at that possibility clear, and my mom's expression softened. She rarely gave in to my dad, but there were occasions where it became clear how much she loved and respected him. "Let's not jump to any conclusions. We'll go back home, like you said, and make a plan."

That still didn't work for me. "I need to take Vaughan back to his pack. He came with me; I'm his ride. Maybe there's some kind of lockdown they can implement now that we know what's happening. If we want to prevent any further attacks, we should work *with* the wolves. I honestly feel like we're on the same side."

My parents exchanged glances again before my dad nodded in agreement. "Fine. Your mom and I will go home and make a plan. Stay alert, and we'll let you know as soon as we have anything."

"And if you feel another seizure coming on, take your meds before it starts," my mom added.

Having wasted enough time, we returned to our vehicles. My parents got in their truck as I pulled open the door to mine, trying to ignore Vaughan's nakedness in the passenger seat. My jacket still covered his lap, but it really only hid the bare minimum.

He held up a hand to stop me from getting in the truck before I could pull myself up. "Wait. Before you get in, I dropped my phone during the shift when I lost my clothes. Could you grab it for me?"

"Sure." I waved goodbye to my parents as they drove away before returning to the spot where the wolf attack had taken place. Scraps of fabric lay scattered on the ground, but despite looking in and around all of them, I couldn't find any sign of a phone. Reluctantly, I had to concede defeat and returned to the truck empty-handed. "I'm sorry, I couldn't see it anywhere."

The corners of Vaughan's mouth pulled down in a grimace, but he shook his head in acceptance. "Alright, never mind. I wanted to give Felix a call but it can wait until we get back."

"Or you can use mine if you know the number," I offered.

Vaughan shook his head sheepishly. "I have no idea what it is."

I couldn't blame him; no one memorized phone numbers anymore. "We'll get there as fast as we can, then."

With a naked werewolf beside me and a dead one in the back, I turned my truck back towards the Crimsontooth pack land.

CHAPTER TWENTY-SEVEN

~Vaughan~

When Calista turned towards my pack's territory, I looked over at her in surprise. "I thought we needed to speak to your parents first."

She kept her eyes on the road, her hands gripping the steering wheel firmly. "I just spoke to them. They're going to keep working on things on their end while I take you back to your pack to see what we can find out there."

That probably would be best, though I wasn't looking forward to finding out the identity of the wolf in the back of the truck. Atlas had gone quiet in my head again, feeling the guilt and regret just as much as I did, if not more. We'd never killed one of our own pack before.

We'd never had reason to.

"Your parents seem to have pretty different ways of dealing with things," I pointed out, trying to keep my voice free of judgement. She hadn't officially introduced them to me, but I didn't blame her. Even during our brief interaction, her mom didn't seem to like me very much at all. "Are they always like that?"

A brief smile flashed across Calista's face though she still didn't look at me. "Yeah, that's just how they are. The job we do is tough and everyone deals with it in their own way. In the long run, they keep each other balanced."

Her eyes flitted to me for just a second before quickly returning to the road, and I couldn't help feeling a tiny bit of satisfaction. From the way her gaze dipped to my bare chest before looking away, it seemed that the reason she was so focused on the road had less to do with the non-existent traffic than it did with my nudity making her slightly uncomfortable, and I had a strong feeling that her uncomfortableness stemmed from attraction.

It shouldn't matter to me. I shouldn't want her to want me, but I threw my arm over the back of the seat anyway, giving her an even better view if she chose to take it.

"What... uh, what are you parents like?" she asked, still studiously studying the road ahead.

"They were the same, I guess, in that their personalities were quite different from each other. My mom can be secretive and quiet, whereas my dad never had an opinion he didn't share with the world."

"Were?"

I nodded, drawing Calista's eyes back to me for just a second before they darted away again. She'd correctly picked up on my use of the past tense. "My dad died four years ago. That's when I became Alpha."

"I'm sorry." Her words were simple and quiet. "I know the pain of losing a parent, but it's probably even worse when you've known them all your life."

"I don't know if it's worse. I don't think it's ever easy, but I'm grateful for the time I had with him."

"And you miss him?" Her eyes found mine again, ever-so-briefly, and this time, I only saw sympathy in them.

"Of course. He was a great man and a great Alpha. The pack meant everything to him and he made sure I understood my responsibility. I wouldn't be able to do this job if not for his guidance."

"It sounds like a lot of responsibility," she mused. "Do you ever get a day off?"

"Kind of?" I let out a rueful chuckle. "Physically, yes. Mentally, it's always there."

"I know what you mean. Hunting is like that for me. It's a job that never ends and people's lives are at stake. It doesn't leave a lot of time for anything else."

Once again, her eyes returned to me, and a moment of connection passed between us, an understanding that hadn't been there before.

Clearing her throat, she looked back at the road. "What about your mom? Is she still alive?"

"After my dad died, she needed a change of scene. Her way of dealing with it, I guess. She moved down to Arizona but she comes back to visit a few times a year."

"She must be coming for your wedding?" Calista guessed, and I almost smiled even though the reminder of my upcoming mating ceremony didn't bring me any joy. What made me smile was that Calista brought it up, as if she needed to remind herself of my engagement.

"Yeah, I'm sure she will. Leo will take care of all the arrangements."

We both fell silent for a minute or two, the mention of my engagement putting a damper on both our moods. Or mine, at least. I could only guess what Calista might be thinking. We really should have been focusing on more urgent matters, anyway, which Calista did when she finally looked over at me again.

"My mom actually has an idea about how to stop these attacks, but I don't know what you'll think of it. I'm not even supposed to be telling you about it but I think your opinion could be important."

That certainly got my attention, especially since she sounded more unsure about it than I'd ever heard her sounding before. Normally, she was pretty damn sure of herself. "What is it?"

Her hands tightened on the steering wheel, her knuckles turning white from the force of her grip, and she took a deep breath before speaking. "I don't know exactly how it works, but apparently, she has a way of suppressing a werewolf's wolf side. She thought if we did it to your entire pack, temporarily, it might discourage the spirit from using you to make any further attacks. If a possessed werewolf can't shift, it couldn't cause nearly as much damage. It would buy us more time to find the spirit before anyone else gets hurt."

The hairs on the back of my neck immediately stood up as the implication of what she just said sank in. *Her mom can suppress a wolf.* Would that affect the wolf's scent? Make them seem entirely human?

What if Calista had a wolf and didn't even know it?

She swallowed nervously, waiting for my response, but I couldn't even focus on why she'd brought it up. My thoughts were filled with what it could mean for her. She obviously hadn't made the connection, but she didn't know the things I did about her birth parents.

"How does she know it would work?" I asked, using all my strength to keep my voice level. If I had this right, I didn't want to just blurt it out. It would be better if she could figure it out for herself, if I could guide her towards the realization.

Calista shrugged. "Apparently, she's tested it before, but only on a single subject at a time. She's not sure what the effects would be of a pack-wide implementation. I don't want to sugarcoat it for you. There could be side effects, possibly even toxic ones, but with your agreement, we might be able to implement it in a safer way than if we had to do it without your permission."

Her mom had tested it on a single subject. That only reinforced my suspicion that Calista herself might have been that test subject. It made more sense than any other theory I'd been able to come up with so far. How would she have given it to her without Calista being aware of it, though?

She smelled like a wolf after her seizure, Atlas reminded me, the excitement in his voice clear. If she really was a werewolf, that changed things completely in his mind, but I tried not to get ahead of myself. We had to take this one step at a time.

It might have something to do with her seizures. My mind immediately flashed back to the medication she'd taken in my office, the unlabelled vial of liquid. Could that be it? Calista just told me the effects of any treatment would be temporary, so she must have to take regular doses of it to keep it working more permanently. That might be why she had the medication in the first place. Maybe her seizures were directly related to trying to keep her wolf in check. She'd told me the episodes had started when she was seventeen, just before the time a werewolf's wolf should be making its appearance.

It fit. All the pieces fit, and as I finally saw the whole picture, a loud growl rumbled in my chest. What the fuck gave these hunters the right to take her and raise her as human, lying to her about her origins and taking away half of herself? What had her poor wolf been through, being shut away in Calista's mind for years?

How would Calista feel when she found out about it?

Everything she believed about herself had been built on a lie. I had to help her find the truth, but I had no idea how she would react. Would she believe me? Would she resent me for shattering the illusions that she seemed perfectly content with?

Where the hell did we go from there?

Chapter Twenty-Eight

~**Calista**~

Vaughan's growl filled the cab of my truck, vibrating through me like the bass of a slow, sensual song, setting my whole body on edge, and my grip on the wheel tightened again as I tried to order my body not to respond. That shouldn't be sexy. Growling was *not* sexy. It definitely shouldn't make my heart beat faster or set off a steady pulse between my legs. Just because he sat there naked and bloody and virile didn't mean I should be attracted to him.

Maybe under the right circumstances, growling could be sexy, but he didn't mean it that way. His growl came from a place of anger, and I really, truly needed to stop objectifying someone else's fiancé.

"I understand your concerns," I assured him, chancing a glance over at him even though the sight of his naked body played havoc with my thoughts. "That's why I wanted to talk to you about it first. You must have your own doctors and scientists, right? If my mom can explain to you what the medication will do, your own people can test it so that you can make an informed decision."

Vaughan blinked back at me as if I were speaking a different language. "What?"

"I know you didn't want to kill that wolf," I elaborated. "I don't want to put you in a position where any other members of your pack are being possessed and you need to make that choice again. This might be a way to avoid that, but I know it's a big decision when it's never been tested on this scale before."

"I'm sorry, I think I'm lost." His body angled towards me as he gave me his full attention. Unfortunately, the movement made my jacket on his lap shift, exposing even more of his thigh and his naked hip, which of course led my thoughts to his naked ass and dragged my mind down into the gutter. "Back up a second. How would this treatment..."

He trailed off, not finishing his question, and I glanced back at him again to see what had distracted him. His brown eyes were fixed on me and his nose twitched as he inhaled deeply.

"Calista."

My name had never sounded as enticing as it did when it rumbled out of his mouth, low and deep and almost desperate-sounding.

"What?" The aching in my body only got worse at the sound of his voice and the feel of his eyes on me. The more I tried to tell myself to ignore it and think of something else, the more fixated on it I became.

"I can smell you." He rasped out the words as though they hurt him, as if the effort of speaking them caused him pain.

Unfortunately, I knew exactly what he meant: he could smell my body's reaction. He could tell just how turned on I was. Embarrassment flushed down my neck, the sensations only getting stronger as he called attention to them, the lust I'd been trying to hold back pushing even stronger against the walls that barely contained it.

Playing dumb seemed pointless, so I didn't bother. "You're sitting there completely naked, in case you've forgotten. If the tables were turned, if I were naked in front of you, you might respond to it too. It's not intentional."

The sound of his exhale sent another wave of longing through me that I did my best to ignore. We had to be getting close to the pack land, I hoped. I didn't know how much longer I could hold myself together.

"So, you *are* attracted to me?"

Why did he say it like that? And why did it matter, anyway? "You have a fiancée," I reminded him, though I really shouldn't have to. He should be able to remember that all by himself.

"I do, but our relationship is a business arrangement. We aren't in love. We've never even kissed. I barely know her."

If that were true, it would explain his behaviour with her in his office earlier, but him telling me that didn't make anything about the situation any better. "Whatever the background is, you still made a commitment to her."

"I did," he agreed again. "And you're avoiding the question. Fiancée or not, werewolf or not, do you feel something for me?"

He was doing his best to put me on the spot, but I couldn't just pretend those other things didn't exist. "What good does it do for me to answer the question? It doesn't change anything. It doesn't mean anything."

Another growl echoed from his throat, more out of frustration than anger, and my body immediately hummed in response. "It means something to me."

Biting my lip so hard I thought the skin might break, I stared at the open road ahead, trying to decide what answer I could possibly give that wouldn't lead to disaster. What would he do if I said yes? Would he act on it? Would he risk whatever arrangement he had with Amanda to satisfy the lust between us? I know how wrong that would be, but I'd never been so tempted to give in to something I knew objectively to be completely wrong.

Nothing had ever tempted me quite like him.

Vaughan exhaled again when I still didn't answer. "If it makes it easier for you, I can go first. I'm attracted to you, Calista. I have been since the moment I first saw you sitting in my cell, and everything I've learned about you since then, your skill, your determination, your intelligence, has only made you more appealing. That's why I kissed you earlier even though I knew I shouldn't. There's something between us and I think you feel it too. Tell me I'm wrong."

I could have said exactly the same thing. I could have told him how my first glimpse of him had imprinted itself into my memory, completely against my will. I could have explained how each minute we spent together had challenged all the things I thought I knew about werewolves, and how his careful, considered thoughtfulness combined with his authority and strength ticked every one of the boxes I never knew I had when it came to my ideal man. I could have said how his kiss hadn't left my mind since it happened, despite everything else going on and all the problems with it happening in the first place.

I didn't say any of that, though. "We're here," I said instead, pointing ahead to the checkpoint at the border of his pack's territory.

Vaughan's lips tightened, his jaw clenching at my deflection, but he nodded as he slipped back into his Alpha role, turning back to face forwards. "Go straight to the pack house. I'm going to link with Felix to catch up."

'Link' must refer to the way they had of communicating with each other, so I kept quiet for the rest of the drive, nodding at the men at the checkpoint who waved us through. The streets of the town were emptier than they'd been when I arrived that morning, but when we got to the pack house, a group of people gathered to meet us, including Felix and Amanda, and several others I didn't recognize.

As Vaughan got out of my truck, still wearing only my jacket around his waist, Amanda's eyes widened and her eyes darted over to me while I tried not to blush. Werewolves must be naked a lot when they shifted between their forms, so I tried to act like it hadn't been any big deal for me to see him that way either. Hopefully, she couldn't smell my state of arousal as easily as Vaughan had.

"The body's in the back," Vaughan explained, immediately jumping into action. "Please, be careful with him."

"Him?" I murmured under my breath curiously.

Vaughan nodded with that same regret I saw in his eyes when he killed the wolf in the first place. "He's been identified. He's the only wolf not accounted for. His name was Tim and he was only nineteen. He'd only had his wolf for a year."

Pain seeped through his words, anguish over the life he had to cut short, and I opened the tailgate to let the two men up so they could collect the wolf's body while the rest of the group all spoke to Vaughan at once, eager to find out what happened and what they could do to help.

"We'll meet in the boardroom in ten minutes," Vaughan announced to all of them. "First, I need to speak to Felix and Calista in my office."

Amanda opened her mouth to protest but Vaughan quickly shook his head.

"Alone."

Not waiting for anyone else to speak, Vaughan headed into the house while I followed with Felix behind me. When we reached the office, Vaughan went across the hall instead to the same bathroom I'd used earlier that day.

"There are some clothes for me in here," he explained. "Go with Felix and I'll be there as soon as I'm dressed."

Following the Beta into Vaughan's office, I couldn't help noticing there was no trace of his usual smile. He looked almost as serious as he had when he first questioned me. It might have to do with the death of their pack member, but I had a feeling there was more to it, especially considering his tight grip on the folder in his hands.

"What's that?" I asked bluntly, pointing at the folder as we both took a seat in front of Vaughan's desk.

"These are the initial results of your DNA test."

"Really? That was fast." I thought those tests took weeks, or at least days.

"It doesn't confirm who your parents are yet. That will take a little longer."

He'd lost me. What else would it show besides who my parents are? "What does it say, then?"

Felix glanced back over his shoulder at the door. "We should wait for Vaughan to get here."

I didn't see why. "You already told him what it says when you were 'linking' to each other, didn't you? That's why he wanted us to speak first."

It made sense, and Felix's grimace confirmed my guess. I leaned forward, my eyes fixed on him.

"It's my DNA, Felix, and I have a right to know: what does it say?"

Chapter Twenty-Nine

~**Vaughan**~

Fully dressed again, I grabbed Calista's jacket off the sink where I'd put it down, inhaling her salted caramel scent as I did. Maybe I would need to wash it before I gave it back to her since it had spent the last half hour covering my cock? It frustrated me that the thought turned me on as much as it did, that touching her jacket had been the closest I'd been to my fated mate.

She'd been close to admitting she felt something for me in the truck, I could have sworn. It had been rotten timing to get back to our land when we did, but if she felt nothing, she would have just said so. The fact that she fought me on it meant that she had something to hide, and based on the delicious scent coming from her in the enclosed space of her truck, I had a pretty good guess what that 'something' might be: she felt the mate pull between us too, whether she wanted to or not.

Pulling the door open, I only took half a step before I had to stop to avoid a collision with my Gamma who stood outside the door waiting for me, his arms crossed.

"Not now, Leo." My eyes were already on my office door, just over his shoulder, where Felix and Calista waited for me. Felix already told me what the results found, and Calista deserved to know too.

"Vaughan, what is wrong with you? You can't keep ignoring your mate!"

My *mate* sat just beyond those doors behind him, waiting to find out the truths that had been hidden from her for her whole life. I had no intention of ignoring her, but I knew that wasn't what he meant. "I asked you to arrange my mating ceremony, not to give me relationship advice. I just had to kill one of our pack members! You don't think that's more important?"

Though he couldn't argue with me, my answer didn't satisfy him. "Of course you need to deal with it, but let her help you. She's supposed to be your partner, and right now, she feels like a third wheel to you and this human woman, who I had to assure her I had never seen you with before."

So, Amanda had some suspicions about Calista. It didn't surprise me, not with how smart and observant she seemed to be. Leo had a point that I would have to deal with Amanda before long, but at that moment, Calista remained my priority and every second I stood there talking to him kept me from her.

"Leo, I say this with all the patience I can muster right now: *get the fuck out of my way.*"

My Alpha authority bled through each word and my Gamma immediately stepped to the side, his head bowed in submission. I would have to apologize to him later; I'd asked him to look after Amanda and he was simply trying to follow my orders, but I pushed him and Amanda and everything else to the back of my mind as I stepped across the hall and opened my office door...

... only to find Calista and Felix wrestling with each on the floor, him on his back while she straddled him.

The growl that burst out of me instantly froze them in place, both of them looking up at me with startled expressions. Atlas clawed against our boundary in my mind, furious with my Beta for touching my mate, while I tried to regain my composure. "What the hell is this?"

Calista got to her feet first, looking chagrined. "Sorry. We got carried away."

She held out her hand to Felix as a peace offering, and he took it, pulling himself up as Calista's arm shook beneath his weight.

"Carried away with what?" I slammed the door behind me, still on edge both from Leo's intervention and from the scene I'd just walked in on. Atlas didn't stop growling until they were no longer touching. "People are dying and you're fighting like children?"

Calista blushed in embarrassment and even Felix looked ashamed, unusually for him. "We didn't mean for it to get that far," she told me, glancing over at Felix while I took a seat behind my desk. "I wanted the results he has and he wouldn't give them to me until you got here. I tried to grab them and... well, one thing led to another."

Taking a deep breath, I tried to calm myself back down. Knowing both of them, it seemed plausible. The results were the important thing, and I wanted to be able to support her when she got the news. I couldn't do that if I were stewing in jealousy. "Go ahead, Felix."

We'd discussed through mind-link that he should give her the results so it didn't look like I had tried to manipulate anything. I would be there to answer questions and help her through it, but he would be the bearer of the news.

The folder in his hands had been bent during their struggle, so he ran a hand over it to try to smooth it out again as he pulled out the piece of paper inside. "As I said before, Calista, these results don't prove that the people in the photograph are your parents. Those answers will come later, but we tested your DNA for a few specific markers and those results are the ones we have."

"Markers? For what?" She leaned forward, trying to look at the paper, but unless she had studied genetics, the codes on it wouldn't mean much.

"For variations in the DNA code between humans and other species."

Her eyes immediately snapped up from the paper, staring at Felix for a second before they darted over to me. "Is this a joke?"

With her eyes on me, I answered her question despite it going against what Felix and I had discussed. "It's not a joke. The other couple in the photograph, the ones standing beside the couple we think might be your parents, are *my* parents. They're werewolves, and the couple with them in that photo are too."

"That isn't possible." The words came out of her mouth as a knee-jerk response, but I could see the doubt in her eyes. She wanted to hear more, even if her words suggested otherwise, so I continued my explanation.

"They were the Alpha and Luna of the Deep Valley pack. They had three children: two boys and a girl. The girl would have been about five years old when they died, and her name was Callie."

Her lips formed the name but no sound came out. After waiting a beat to see if she would say anything else, I carried on.

"We always thought the whole family died that night, but since the pack house burned down, we never knew for certain. My guess, based on everything we've learned in the last few days, is that somehow, that little girl survived the attack."

Though I could have said more, I stopped there to let her fill in the blanks for herself. She needed to reach her own conclusion, no matter how much it made my heart ache to see her looking so confused, her eyes darting from side to side as she put the pieces together in her head, just as I already had.

"I saw wolves that night," she whispered under her breath. If it weren't for my werewolf hearing, I might have missed them. "They ran past me but they didn't hurt me."

Because they were trying to protect you, I thought, but I kept the words inside. She knew it too; I knew she did.

"The hunters took me in. They raised me as their daughter. But if I were a werewolf, wouldn't I..."

Wouldn't she have a wolf? Clenching my teeth to keep from speaking, I waited for her to figure that part out too. All the information was there, she just needed to rearrange it, and I saw the moment it hit her: the realization, the dismay, and the horror. No other word would do it justice, and I honestly couldn't imagine how she felt.

"They know the treatment works." Those words were clear, spoken out strong and loud as she focused back on me, looking like she might be sick. Every part of me yearned to go to her and take her in my arms to try to ease the distress she felt.

"Felix, leave us."

My Beta looked over at me in surprise. He must have been expecting more of a fight from her, and definitely a lot more questions. However, he didn't know about the wolf suppression treatment, so he didn't know that we already had most of the answers. Almost all of them, in fact, except the big one: *why?*

"Are you sure?"

I nodded, my eyes still on Calista. "Go."

Without any further protest, he got to his feet, placed the test results on my desk and walked out, closing the door behind him, and as soon as he had, Calista's control broke. She got to her feet, her eyes blazing in both indignation and pain. "When did you figure it out?"

"Only when you mentioned the treatment. I had my suspicions about your parents, but I didn't know how you could be a werewolf until you told me about the treatment."

"How could they...? Why would they...?" She paced back and forth in front of my desk, not able to adequately sum up her outrage in any one question until she settled on one simple word. "How?"

I immediately understood what she meant. Focusing on the practical, she wanted to know how they'd given her the treatment. Again, I suspected somewhere inside her, she already knew, so I simply fed her the one clue I had. "After your seizure this afternoon, just for a moment, your scent changed. You smelled like a wolf to me."

She put it together just as quickly as I expected her to. "The seizures..." The colour drained from her face as the full extent that her 'parents' had betrayed her began to solidify in her mind. "They're not really seizures, are they?"

"I think there's more to them," I had to agree. "Calista, I don't know any of this for certain. All we know for sure right now is that you are genetically a werewolf. Your test results confirm it. As for the rest, I think we'll only know for sure if you stop taking your medication. If it's suppressing your wolf and you need to keep taking it so that it keeps working..."

"... then if I stop, it should stop working," she concluded, understanding me perfectly. "I'll try it, then. I have to know if they..."

Her knees buckled beneath her as the weight of the lies and deception hit her, her hands grabbing onto my desk for support, and though she managed to keep her balance, I leapt to my feet anyway, unable to hold myself back any longer. In a matter of seconds, I'd rounded the desk and gathered her in my arms with Atlas humming in approval, especially when she didn't push me away.

"I'll help you get to the bottom of this. We'll find out the truth together, okay? Whatever you need, I'm here for you, I promise."

CHAPTER THIRTY

~Calista~

Vaughan's embrace soothed me in a way that made no sense, and rather than pushing him away as I had when he kissed me, I leaned into it instead. It didn't take away all the hurt and confusion I felt; that would be impossible when my whole world had just been turned upside down, but at least it made me feel anchored again. It gave me some small point of reference from which to try to make sense of the swirling sea of chaos that surrounded me.

If those test results were true, and I really didn't see what Vaughan would have to gain by faking them, my entire life had been built on a lie, or at the very least an omission. If I thought hard about it, I couldn't remember my parents ever actually telling me that werewolves had killed my family, and with the information I'd just been given, I had to wonder if that had been intentional. Did they think that they were protecting themselves somehow by never explicitly lying?

They told me about the attacks, about how werewolves were behind them and how they'd hunted them. They made it sound as if they saved me from the werewolves, not from themselves. The implication had certainly been there even if they never said the words. They knew what I thought and they never corrected me.

And what about my wolf? If Vaughan's theory about me having a wolf and it being suppressed by my medication was correct, that went far beyond a simple omission of the facts. They experimented on me. They changed a fundamental part of my being in order to make me who they wanted me to be rather than accepting me as I was. Had I ever been anything more to them than a test subject?

My thoughts spiralled, the pain of betrayal stabbing at me again and again, but Vaughan's arms around me kept me from spinning out with them. His warm embrace, the solidity of his body and his comforting scent all helped to ground me so I could focus on making a plan.

"I'm due to take my next dose of the medication in about an hour. Can I stay here to see what happens if I don't? Do you have a doctor who could help me in case we're wrong and I actually start to seize?"

"Of course," Vaughan quickly agreed. "You can stay here as long as you need to. I'll arrange to have a doctor on call."

Nothing seemed like too much trouble for him, and though I didn't really understand why he would go to so much trouble for me, I was grateful for it. As much as I wanted to confront my parents, I needed to know exactly what they'd done first, and if I were being completely honest, I didn't feel safe going back to them. If they had been drugging me for years, what else were they capable of? If I turned into a wolf, would they hunt me as we had so many others?

In some ways, it didn't even shock me that my mom could do such a thing. She'd always been able to separate her scientific curiosity from her emotions, but the idea that my dad knew all about it and had approved of it or at least let it happen ripped a hole into my stomach that made me nearly double over with pain. Only Vaughan's strong arms kept me upright.

"I have to go and meet with my team," Vaughan murmured in my ear after another moment or two. "Do you want to come with me or do you need a few minutes?"

"You want me to come to your meeting?" It hadn't occurred to me that I would be invited. Meeting with Vaughan and Felix was one thing, but a whole room of werewolves felt different. I didn't belong there.

Or maybe I did. Maybe I always had.

"You know a lot more about possession than we do," he pointed out. "We could use your input."

My other option seemed to be sitting alone in his office and wallowing in the revelations Vaughan had just shared with me, and I would much rather do something productive. Keeping my mind occupied would help me to avoid falling any further into the turmoil I felt inside.

"I'm ready. We can go."

Giving me one last squeeze of support, Vaughan let me go slowly, as if checking that I could stand on my own two feet before he pulled back entirely. The room felt a lot colder without his touch. "It's this way."

Opening the door for me, he led me down the hall to a board-room-style meeting room with a large, rectangular table in the centre. Large windows looked out over the forest, as they did from Vaughan's office, and the light of the setting sun cast a golden hue over the table and its occupants. Almost a dozen people already sat around it, including a few familiar faces: Felix, Darius, Savannah and Amanda. Only one seat remained empty, between Felix and Amanda, clearly meant for Vaughan.

"Felix, we need another chair." Vaughan stated it so matter-of-factly that no one could argue, and the Beta jumped up to take care of it while Vaughan directed me to Felix's empty seat. I gave Savannah as much of a smile as I could muster while avoiding Amanda's piercing gaze. How good was a werewolf's sense of smell? Could she tell that Vaughan had just been holding me? Would she get the wrong idea? *Was* it the wrong idea? I couldn't bring myself to deal with those thoughts too, not with everything else going around my head.

Felix returned a moment later with another chair which he took to the other side of the table, sitting across from Vaughan who had me on one side of him and Amanda on the other.

"For everyone who hasn't already met her, this is Calista," Vaughan introduced me as nearly a dozen pairs of eyes all stared in my direction. "She's going to help us figure out how to stop these possessions as soon as possible. She's on our side."

He stated that so simply, putting his full trust in me, that despite the disorientation I still felt, a small sense of belonging managed to creep in as well. Somehow, in just a few days, I felt more a part of this community than I ever had anywhere else before, and I blinked rapidly to keep my emotions from overwhelming the tenuous control I had over them.

"Don't worry about remembering all the names, but I'll introduce you anyway." Vaughan gave me a supportive smile before pointing around the table, going clockwise from the seat next to me. "This is Ethan and Matthias. You already know Savannah. You've met Darius and Felix. That's Luke, Grant, Jason, and my Gamma, Leo. And of course, you know Amanda."

He was right that I wouldn't remember all of that, but I appreciated the attempt to include me anyway, and I gave them all a friendly nod, making eye contact with each one as Vaughan introduced them until he got to Amanda. She continued to stare at me while I let my eyes drop.

Vaughan gave everyone a quick update on what happened that day and the reasons that we settled on spiritual possession as the most likely explanation. "The spirit needs to be stopped," Vaughan stated firmly, "but first, we need to make sure that it can't do any more damage by using our pack. Calista, you said there would be signs that someone had been possessed, even if they had no memory of it. What are those signs?"

Everyone's eyes moved to me, which could have intimidated me, but when it came to talking about the supernatural, I had greater confidence. "Vaughan noticed the scent of copper and smoke at the scene of the last attack. Those are typical scents associated with spirits, and they would linger even after the possession for a short time. Most notably, the person who had been possessed would notice a metallic taste in their mouth and be able to smell smoke in the air, even when no one else smells it."

"We should get that information out to the pack and ask anyone who might have experienced that to come forward," Amanda suggested from Vaughan's other side.

Vaughan nodded in agreement, and an unexpected and completely unreasonable stab of jealousy shot through me as he turned his attention to her. "Felix told me that Tim had been on shift patrolling the border when he went missing, and I wonder if that's significant. Maybe we should start with the other members of the patrol force to see if there's some kind of pattern."

"I'm on it," Darius promised, and it made sense to me that the border patrol would fall into his area since he had been the one to apprehend me outside their territory.

"Identifying anyone who might have been possessed doesn't stop it from happening again," another man pointed out. Vaughan might have called him Matthias. "How do we protect ourselves going forward?"

Again, everyone looked at me, and again, I had an answer. "Onyx is the best protection. It causes the spirit pain, just as silver does to you. They'll almost always look for another host instead."

Would silver cause me pain too? It never had before, but perhaps only because my wolf had been suppressed.

"We should ask the pack to pool any onyx jewellery, so we can distribute it to those most at risk, like the border guards," Amanda suggested.

"I can do that," Leo volunteered.

"It's a place to start," Vaughan agreed. "If we don't have enough, we can contact one of our human allies and ask them to bring us more. I don't want anyone going off pack land until we have this under control."

The conversation continued for a few more minutes with various ideas being thrown around for some kind of buddy system so that no one would be left alone like Tim obviously had been.

"Spirits are able to possess more than one person at a time," I interjected before they got too carried away. "Pairing up wouldn't make much difference. It could just possess both of them."

"Is there a limit to how many people they can possess?" Savannah asked, which was a good question.

"There's no hard and fast rule, but the most I've personally ever heard of at one time is four."

"We'll set up groups of ten, then," Vaughan told the group. "If anyone thinks someone in their group is acting strangely, they alert one of us."

A few more plans were made before Vaughan frowned and turned to me, whispering under his breath again. "I just got a link from the security guys on the road. Your parents are here."

The storm inside me that had briefly calmed while dealing with the practicalities of the meeting immediately surged to life again. They must have come because they had some news about the case. They didn't know that I knew what I knew. Should I tell them? Could I stop myself from saying anything if we were all in the same room?

"Do you want me to let them in?" Vaughan asked, examining my expression carefully.

No matter how much I wanted to hide away, the job took priority, always. "Let them in. Let's see what they have to say."

Chapter Thirty-One

~Vaughan~

As Alpha, having different people clamouring for my attention wasn't new to me but I'd never felt pulled in quite so many directions at once.

On the one hand, my pack needed me. In times of crisis, they looked to me for leadership, as they should. I'd sworn to serve and protect them when I accepted the position, putting their needs above my own, but that had never been put to the test quite so pointedly. No matter how I tried to give the precautions against possession my undivided attention, my mind kept returning to Calista and her situation, and what might happen when her wolf surfaced.

I didn't even think of it as an 'if'. It felt completely certain to me, and I wanted to be there to support her in whatever form that took. I also knew that as soon as her wolf appeared, she would likely recognize me as her mate, so I needed to be prepared for that too, which meant not being worried about hiding the situation from my other 'mate'.

Amanda and I needed to talk.

I'd been putting it off for too long already, but how I could manage to do all those things simultaneously seemed impossible. When Calista's parents arrived at our territory, it gave me an opportunity to at least combine watching out for Calista with getting the information I needed for the pack.

Do you want one of us to accompany them to the pack house? Toby at the border asked me through our mind-link when I told him to let the hunters through.

Normally, that would have been our protocol, but after what we'd just discussed in the meeting, that would mean leaving only one pack member alone at the entry point to our land, which didn't seem like a great idea. I would have placed money on the fact that anyone else possessed by the spirit had also been patrolling the outer reaches of our territory where it would be easier to get to them. *No, it's okay. They've been here before, they know where they're going. Just let them in.*

After reviewing our plans for a few more minutes, I summarized the immediate actions for everyone to take: "Felix and Amanda, you'll be in charge of dividing the pack into groups of ten. Leo and Sav, gather as much onyx as you can find." I had no idea how common onyx was or how much might exist in the pack; jewels weren't exactly my area of expertise. "Darius and Matt, check in with everyone who's been on border duty over the last week to see if they've experienced any of the symptoms Calista mentioned. I'm going to meet with the hunters to see if there's anything else we can do. Is everyone clear?"

They all promised they were, and while they left to get started, Calista and I returned to my office to wait for her parents to arrive.

"How do you want to handle this?" I asked her as soon as we were alone. "Are you going to tell them what you know?"

She shook her head immediately, as I expected. "No. For now, we focus on the spirit. I'll make up an excuse about why I'm staying here with you. I want to know if they really have been drugging me before I say anything."

Since I would have done exactly the same, I didn't argue with her, though I knew it wouldn't be easy for her to be in the same room with them with those doubts hanging over her head. Hell, it wouldn't be easy for me either. Just the thought of how they had abused her over the years, if our theory proved true, made me want to have them locked up in my cells for the next twenty years or so, the way they'd deprived her wolf of freedom. It would be the least they deserved for manipulating and lying to a person they claimed to love.

When they were shown into my office a few minutes later, I stood up to greet them but Calista remained sitting in front of my desk, her legs crossed and her hands clasped on her lap. I could practically feel the tension pouring off her, but beyond saying hello, her parents didn't say anything to her as they sat down in the empty chairs next to her, facing me. Her dad had a large, zippered canvas bag with him that I eyed curiously. The wolves at the border would have checked it so I didn't worry about it being dangerous, but I also couldn't guess what might be in it.

"I'm hoping that you have some news for us," I began. "We've started taking some precautions, with Calista's input, but we'd like to see this spirit stopped completely."

"That's why we're here," Calista's dad assured me, reaching down to unzip the bag. From inside, he pulled out pieces of wood and demonstrated how they fit together. "These are wrist cuffs made of ash. If anyone does get possessed and you manage to get one of these cuffs on them, it will trap the spirit inside them. It won't be able to leave."

I glanced over at Calista for confirmation, and she nodded at me. "If the wolf you killed earlier had been wearing one, the spirit would have died with him. Unfortunately, we didn't have any with us then."

"I don't intend to kill any more of my pack members," I pointed out, though it shouldn't have been necessary. The guilt over Tim's death would be with me for a very long time to come.

"You don't have to," Calista quickly assured me. "By trapping it inside the human, or werewolf in this case, it buys us time. We find the witch and we do an exorcism on both the witch and the spirit. That will get rid of it permanently."

"And what happens to the witch?" I wondered.

"It depends on how deeply they've bound themselves to the spirit," Calista's mom explained. "If the connection is strong enough, they die too. If not, then we judge how evil their intentions were and make the decision about whether to let them live or not."

My nostrils flared at the certainty in her voice that it would be her call to make. "And you have no problem playing judge and executioner, just as you did with the Deep Valley pack."

Calista's dad flinched beneath the accusation, but her mom held my gaze steadily. "Someone has to do it. We save lives, we keep the world safe, and yes, occasionally, we get it wrong. Sometimes, there's collateral damage, and while it's regrettable, it doesn't change the value of what we do. Our job isn't for the faint-hearted but it's necessary."

Did that apply to what she'd done to my mate too? Did she find that 'necessary'? We stared each other down for a moment longer until Calista cleared her throat.

"Do we have any leads on the witch?"

"No, we're still working on that," her dad answered, also sounding eager to move on. "I'm going to be making a few visits to some of our regular sources to see if they've noticed any unusual buying behaviour over the last few weeks, anything to indicate an increase in occult activity. Calista, I thought we could do that together while your mom works on other preventative measures."

The way Calista tensed at those words reminded me of what we'd been discussing in her truck before we got sidetracked. She had mentioned that her parents had suggested temporarily disabling the wolves of my whole pack; that had been the catalyst for me realizing what must have happened to her. In light of the revelation as it pertained to her, I hadn't had a chance to ask her for more details about how they would get it to work on a pack-wide basis. Surely, they wouldn't be able to convince us to all take medication unwittingly the way they had with Calista.

Calista's response focused on her dad's request that she accompany him. "Actually, I'm going to stay here and help Vaughan and the others with the measures they're already putting in place. They should make any other precautions unnecessary."

Her mom's steel-edged gaze moved to Calista instead and the two of them seemed to have an entire conversation with their eyes, both daring the other to speak aloud first.

"We're grateful for Calista's help, and for yours," I interjected, trying to diffuse the tension. "She can stay here tonight as our guest."

"You can call me if you get any more information," Calista added, making it clear she'd made up her mind. "I'll do the same."

Reluctantly, her parents seemed to accept that, though thanks to my exceptional hearing, I heard Calista's mother mutter under her breath, "You've certainly changed your opinion on werewolves awfully quickly."

Sitting a lot closer to her, Calista heard her too, and her glare turned even more heated. "If we're right about all of this, I never had a reason to be upset with them in the first place."

"We should go," Calista's dad said, getting to his feet, obviously eager to avoid a fight. "Thank you for your hospitality, Alpha Vaughan. I hope we can take care of this without anyone else getting hurt."

"I hope so too." I had one of the other staff members escort them back to their truck and back to the border while Calista and I were left alone once again. "You did well keeping it together."

She gave me a rueful smile. "So did you. What's your plan now?"

I glanced down at my watch. The time Calista should be taking her medication had just passed, so if her wolf was going to surface, it could happen at any time. "I'm going to ask my sister to show you to your room, if that's okay? She can get you both something to eat. I need to take care of something and then I'll come and join you. The doctor's already on call, if necessary."

Taking a deep breath, Calista nodded. "I guess we'll know the truth soon, one way or the other."

I hoped so, which was why I needed to have one more conversation before I joined her. Before things went any further, I needed to talk to Amanda. It wouldn't be fair to lead her on any longer when deep down, I'd already made up my mind. When Calista's wolf appeared, I intended to claim my true mate, if she'd have me, and I didn't want to be thinking about Amanda when it happened.

I needed my mate, and for the first time in my life, I planned to put my own needs first.

Chapter Thirty-Two

~**Calista**~

It felt like I should be doing something more productive than taking a break to eat, but Vaughan insisted he had everything under control and that I needed to take care of myself first.

"If you do have a wolf, she's probably going to want to shift. My wolf says he'd be going crazy if he'd been cooped up for years. Shifting takes energy, so you need to eat,"

He said that as if the fact that I might physically turn into an animal later that evening would be perfectly normal. To him, I supposed it would be, but for me, it would be very strange indeed. I really couldn't imagine it, but worrying about it didn't do me any good. It might happen; it might not. Maybe we were wrong about all of it. Maybe my parents hadn't been using and controlling me my whole life. We would have to wait and see.

Savannah came to meet us at the door of Vaughan's office, as bubbly and full of energy as she'd been the first time I met her. Standing side-by-side with her brother, her resemblance to Vaughan became even more pronounced. They had the same colouring, the same brown eyes and the same slightly wild, curly hair, but where the contours of his face were hard and defined, hers were softer and smoother.

"I heard you're staying with us tonight," she announced, looking genuinely pleased at the prospect. "Come on, I'll take you to your room. The staff has already taken some food up there for us. You have to tell me your secret. Whenever I ask to have supper brought to my room, the answer is: 'Get your ass down to the dining room, Sav.'"

Vaughan rolled his eyes. "If you were asking for any reason other than being lazy, the answer might be different." In their interaction, I could see how comfortable they were with each other, and the affection that lay behind their words. "Sav, let me know right away if you need me, okay? I'll be there as soon as I can."

Leaving me wondering just how much he'd told his sister about what she was supposed to be looking out for, he shot me an encouraging smile before he headed back into the meeting room we were in before. Savannah led me to the large staircase in the entrance hall.

"How many people live here?" I asked as we reached the landing of the second floor. It looked like a hotel with corridors stretching out in both directions, multiple doors leading off of each one.

"Most of the pack's leadership team," Savannah told me, reeling off a list of names as she pointed vaguely to the doors. Most of them, I recognized from the meeting we'd just been in, including Darius and Felix. "This is my room, and Vaughan's is over there."

My eyes darted to the door of his room as my mind conjured images it created much too easily, images of him in bed with that firm body I had gotten such a good look at in my truck earlier, and my cheeks immediately began to flush. No matter what else might be going on, he was still engaged, and I needed to concentrate on the job, not to mention my potential pending metamorphosis, rather than the half-animal, half-man who made my pulse race.

Unfortunately, Savannah didn't get that memo. As soon as she showed me into the very nice guest room with a large queen-sized bed, a TV, a bookshelf, and its own private bathroom, nicer than any bedroom of my own I'd ever had in my life, she grabbed the two plates of food that had been left for us and headed for the bed, waiting for me to join her before she handed me one and leaned forward expectantly, her brown eyes fixed curiously on mine.

"What's the deal with you and my brother?"

"What?" I did my best to look innocent even as my heart beat faster. Could she hear that? Just how good was a werewolf's hearing?

Would I soon get to find out for myself?

The plate she handed me had a toasted BLT sandwich and some fries on it, the smell making my mouth water, and I popped a couple of fries in my mouth. Did they honestly eat this well every day? Had my life once been like this, with a comfortable bedroom, a warm and well-decorated house, delicious food and a pack that felt like a big, welcoming family?

Savannah took a bite of her own sandwich, putting her hand in front of her mouth as she answered me while chewing. "Don't get me wrong: I love my brother, but he's not the easiest guy to get to know. He doesn't warm up to people right away, but he's hardly left your side all day."

"He's focused on the situation and we're trying to solve it together," I explained, though I found her characterization of Vaughan interesting. I wouldn't have called him stand-offish at all. In just a single day, I felt I knew him better than almost anyone I'd ever met. It sounded crazy when phrased that way, but it didn't make it any less true. "We seem to understand each other. We're just on the same level, I guess."

Savannah nodded in acceptance, though she still had more to say on the subject. "He doesn't find many people on his level, then. Amanda asked me about his friends today, and it made me realize just how few he actually has. It's sad, really."

The mention of Amanda sent another wave of guilt through me as I remembered the feel of Vaughan's lips on mine and his admission to me that he felt something for me but wasn't in love with his fiancée. If I were smart, I would change the subject, but I couldn't help asking for more information instead. "He mentioned that they chose each other as mates. Is that common among werewolves?"

A loud snort was her answer. "No, not at all. Fated mates are what everyone wants. And why wouldn't you? Someone who naturally completes you, with fantastic sex thrown in? Sign me up!"

Her enthusiasm made me smile, and her response piqued my curiosity. "What makes it better than regular sex?"

I expected her to say something about how it would be better because they loved each other, or something equally sentimental, but her explanation turned out to be a lot blunter. "One word: sparks. Your skin literally lights up at their touch, and that means *everywhere* they touch you. With any part of their body."

The fingers of her right hand formed a circle as she poked her left index finger through it, leaving me in absolutely no doubt what she meant, but I could barely concentrate on that as the words she'd said echoed in my head and reverberated through my whole body.

Sparks.

Did she mean that strange electrical energy that seemed to flow between me and Vaughan whenever we touched?

"That only happens between fated mates?" I asked, trying to keep my voice level as I took a bite of my sandwich.

"Yup. I mean, I've met some guys who made me see stars, but it's not the same thing. The sparks only occur with your fated mate."

What did that mean? Was there something more between me and Vaughan than simply being on the same wavelength? If there was, did he know it? And if he did, why wouldn't he tell me?

Exactly how many people were hiding things from me?

My imagination had started to run away with me again, I admonished myself. Maybe somewhere deep down, I *liked* the idea of Vaughan being meant to be with me rather than Amanda, but that didn't make it true.

"So, your fated mate isn't here in the pack?" I asked, trying to put the focus back on Savannah.

"Nope," she confirmed, taking another big bite. "If he were, I would have found him by now. It's not that big a town. Unless he hasn't turned eighteen yet, but I hope that's not the case. Older men are better."

She stated that like everyone agreed on it, and I couldn't argue as the memory of Vaughan's body flashed across my mind yet again.

"How old is too old?" I asked jokingly, but before she could answer, pain flashed across my head. I recognized the feeling immediately, the first sign that a seizure might be approaching, and Savannah instantly picked up on it too.

"Is something wrong?"

"Not... yet," I managed to say, breathing deeply to try to ease the aching in my head. "But it's coming."

"Okay. Shit. Hang on. I'll get Vaughan here."

Having his soothing presence would help, as both pain and fear spread throughout my body. Was this a sign my wolf was trying to break through, or was I simply going to seize because I hadn't taken my medication? The answer should be clear soon enough, and I honestly didn't know what I wanted that answer to be.

Chapter Thirty-Three

~**Vaughan**~

As I expected, when I linked to Leo to tell him I wanted to see Amanda, he jumped into action. *Of course, Alpha. I'll bring her to you now. Just a second.*

At least one of us was eager. I had no idea how to say what I had to say without coming off as a complete asshole. I signed the agreement, I went and took her from her home and brought her all the way to my pack, and now, I intended to tell her I found my fated mate.

If our roles were reversed, I would be annoyed, certainly, but I might be relieved too. Was it too much to hope that Amanda might feel the same? We hadn't gotten attached to each other yet. Maybe she would appreciate being given more time to find her own fated mate. I thought mine didn't exist, but I only needed to wait a little bit longer to find her and perhaps, Amanda would be the same.

Not sure whether it would be better to be sitting or standing for the conversation, I hovered near the table as the door opened and Amanda walked in. Leo gave me a nod from the door before closing the door behind her, leaving the two of us alone.

"Hi." I gave her an awkward smile as I gripped onto the back of the chair in front of me. She looked just as polished and put-together as she had that morning, not showing any signs of fatigue from what must have been a tiring day. "Thank you for pitching in today. I'm sure you didn't expect to be dealing with something like this as soon as you got here."

With an elegant shrug, she stepped closer to me. "It's definitely an introduction I won't forget, but I'm happy to help however I can. I know you're used to doing things on your own, but if you need to bounce ideas off someone or just rant about things and get some frustration out, that's what I'm here for. You can count on me, Vaughan. What do you need right now?"

Her helpful attitude didn't make what I had to say any easier. "I just need to talk to you. Why don't we sit down?"

Since my hands were already on one of the chairs, I pulled it out and offered it to her. With a smile at the rather old-fashioned gesture, Amanda took a seat while I sat in the chair next to her.

That smile only made me feel worse, and I didn't want to string her along for a second longer than I had to. Looking her square in the face, I came clean. "There's no easy way to say this so I'm just going to get it out. I've met my fated mate."

Although she hadn't really been moving much in the first place, I could still see the way she froze in place as the words left my mouth, the colour draining from her face. Guilt flowed through me even though I knew neither I nor Calista could be blamed for it. Nobody had planned this or tried to hurt anyone. Sometimes, life just happened regardless of what plans people made.

"I see." The words from her mouth were clipped and strained as she blinked quickly, making me feel even worse. "The blonde hunter?"

It wouldn't have been hard for her to guess based on how much she seemed to pay attention to everything. "Calista. Yes. We only met for the first time last night. I didn't know before I brought you here."

She gave a short nod, her jaw tight. "Does she know?"

Her deduction and observation skills were very impressive. "No. Not yet. It's possible that she's actually a werewolf, despite her scent, so I want to give her wolf a chance to surface and tell her directly rather than me telling her."

"And you intend to accept her?" Her lips were so tightly drawn, I could barely see them anymore. Everything in her bearing felt tense and unhappy. Perhaps I should have been relieved she hadn't lashed out at me, as she would have every right too, but this controlled restraint almost felt more painful. I never wanted to hurt her.

Again, I kept my answer as honest and straightforward as possible. "That depends on her, but if she wants me, then yes. I want to accept her."

Saying it out loud made it even more real to me. In all the stress of the past 24 hours, I hadn't really let that amazing fact sink in: *I found my fated mate.* Everything I ever thought I wanted in a mate and more, the idea of being with her almost made me feel I could fly. Just as clearly, I knew I would never feel that with Amanda, no matter how good a Luna she would be, and entering into an agreement that denied both of us that feeling suddenly felt completely unthinkable.

So, when she asked me a follow-up question, I knew my answer immediately. "And if she doesn't accept you? Do you still want to go through with our agreement?"

"No." I grimaced as she flinched, but I tried my best to explain myself to her. "The mate pull is stronger than I ever imagined it would be. It's all-encompassing. It literally feels like I've found a missing piece of myself, and I think we both have a right to experience that. If Calista rejects me, I'll wait for a second chance. Now that I know what's possible, really *know* it rather than just hearing about it, I know it's worth it. If I'd known before, I wouldn't have entered into the agreement in the first place, because you deserve that too. You deserve someone who would be stupid enough to mess up an alliance with a powerful pack because he wants to be with you so badly."

I tried to lighten the mood with that last sentence, but to my dismay, tears filled her eyes for the first time. She did her best to blink them away, her voice sharper than before when she spoke again. "I would have preferred if you told me last night, as soon as you found out, before I spent the whole day with your pack who are all now going to know you've rejected me."

She had a point, and I could only wince. "It came as a complete shock to me and I didn't know for sure what I wanted to do. That's not much of an excuse, I know, but I did take our agreement seriously. I didn't want to simply throw it away, especially when she might not accept me, but the more time I've spent with her, the more I realize I don't really have much of a say in it at all. I can't change how I feel. It's destiny."

I didn't know if that would satisfy her, and I didn't have a chance to find out. Savannah's mind-link burst through my thoughts before she replied. *Vaughan, Calista's head is hurting. You said you'd come?*

I will. I'm on my way. That might be the sign we'd been waiting for, and I had to go. "Amanda, I'm sorry. I'm needed somewhere else. We can talk about this more later if you want to."

"Is there really anything else to say?" Her deep brown eyes, previously open and hopeful, had closed off entirely. "Go. I can look after myself."

As bad as I felt about leaving her there, my need to be with Calista was stronger. "I'm sorry," I repeated awkwardly as I got to my feet and headed out the door. Bounding up the stairs three at a time, I made it to the guest room in record time, and quickly dismissed Sav. "Go and keep Amanda company. If she needs anything, make sure she has it."

"I'm not your personal assistant. You can't order me around," my sister retorted, but I could see the concern in her eyes as she looked over at Calista. They've been eating their dinner on the bed but the plates remained half-eaten as Calista held her head in her hands.

I made an effort to soften my tone as I rephrased my request. "I could really use your help, Sav. I just broke things off with Amanda and she could use a friend."

Savannah's eyes widened in surprise. "Why the fuck would you do that?"

She didn't know about Calista, obviously, and I couldn't go into all of that in front of her. "I'll explain later. Please."

Exhaling loudly, Savannah left the room, and I immediately sat down next to Calista on the bed.

"How are you feeling?"

"It feels like I'm about to seize again." Her breath sounded short, letting me know how much pain she must be in even if she wouldn't say so.

"The doctor's on call," I reminded her. "If it goes on for more than five minutes, I'll get her in here. I'm right beside you, okay? No matter what happens, I'm here."

She nodded only once before her head dropped completely and her body began to jerk just as it had earlier that afternoon. That time, it felt like her wolf had been on the edge of appearing, strong enough that her scent changed. Without the medication to hold her back, would she break through fully this time? The air around us felt electric with possibility. In a matter of seconds, Calista's whole life might be about to change, and mine right along with her.

CHAPTER THIRTY-FOUR

~**Calista**~

Normally, when a seizure came on, I blacked out and couldn't remember anything afterwards. The excess electrical energy in my brain made everything stop working, including my memory. Essential functions of living such as breathing and swallowing continued, but nothing happened on a conscious level. Since the textbook definition of seizures lined up with that description, I never questioned it.

In the guest room of the Crimsontooth pack house, however, something different happened.

The pain in my head and the narrowing of my vision started the same as usual. I described it once to my dad as a feeling of falling into myself, losing the ability to control my speech and body movements, the world getting farther away until I fell into the blackness of unconsciousness.

That evening, though, the place I fell wasn't entirely black. Shades of gray clouded the edges of my mind, and eventually, brighter patches of light, dancing above my head. Though I still couldn't see anything, it felt warm and safe. A deep, masculine scent filtered through the dim light, and soon, a voice accompanied it.

"Your brothers are just teasing you, Callie. They're trying to be funny. I'll tell them that they're not."

A soft mattress took shape beneath me and a pillow beneath my head, the sheets smelling of lavender and more comfortable than anything I could recall. In the fog, a shape appeared, coalescing into the form of a man, the man whom the voice belonged to. Tall and wide, he looked humongous to me. Large, rough hands rested on his lap while hairy arms gave way to a tattooed shoulder and chest. He should have looked intimidating, but the softness in his eyes reassured me.

Was this a dream? A memory? The man seemed to be talking to me and he called me Callie, which Vaughan had said my parents called me. He also looked like the man in the photo, though a little older and more tired-looking, as if he'd just been dragged out of bed.

Could this be my father?

"They said I have to do whatever the Alpha's son says." The sniffling, tentative voice echoed in my ears in a way that made it clear it had come from me, though it didn't sound like me. The voice belonged to a little girl, one who felt comfortable telling this big man her deepest fears.

His lips curled into an indulgent smile. "Technically, you'll be on their pack land while you're at school, so you should follow their Alpha's rules as much as you can. His son isn't any different from you, though. As an Alpha's daughter, you're his equal. His pack might be bigger, but ours is just as important. Never forget that."

He sounded so certain of that fact that the tension in my body began to relax, though I barely knew what I feared in the first place.

"Besides, Vaughan is in sixth grade, older than your brothers. He's not going to be worried about bossing you around. Maybe you can be friends with his sister since she's about your age. That will be fun."

His encouraging smile soothed me even further, even as the mention of Vaughan's name sent a jolt through my body. Our families had known each other; I knew that from the photo. If my family hadn't been attacked, would I have known him all my life? Would I have always been drawn to him the way I had been since we met?

The man who must have been my father leaned forward, kissing my forehead. "Time to sleep now, Callie."

"But the dream..." The feeling of uneasiness that had just been banished came roaring back. In my mind, I could see snippets of memory: a fire, screams, and a flying creature that exploded in a flash of light and pain.

My father, though, was already on his feet. "The dream is just a dream. Just like the last time. There's nothing to worry about. Go back to sleep and the morning will be here before you know it."

Against my will, my eyes began to close, taking me back into darkness, but I didn't fall asleep or lose consciousness. In the blackness, I floated, restless and uneasy, until another voice began to speak to me.

Calista?

Soft and weak, it sounded almost like a whisper of wind or an echo of a song that lingered in the air rather than a real word.

I answered it anyway. *Yes?*

You can hear me? The voice got a little stronger, sounding both surprised and excited that I replied.

Yes. Who are you? I already had an idea but I needed to hear the words. I needed to know my mind hadn't simply invented all of this.

Her answer immediately confirmed what I suspected. *I'm your wolf. My name is Skye. I've been waiting so long to meet you.*

I felt no surprise as I moved on to the more pressing question: *Why haven't you spoken to me before?*

There's usually a wall between us. I can't get through it. When I try to go over, I'm pushed back down.

The wall metaphor interested me, but did it actually confirm anything? Based on the theory Vaughan and I came up with, I expected her to say something along those lines. For all I knew, everything that had happened since my seizure started, the scene with my father and now this conversation with my 'wolf', took place only in my head, and I conjured up this voice out of nothing. How could I prove to myself that she actually existed? I needed her to tell me something I didn't already know.

What happened the first time you tried to speak to me?

Her voice seemed to get louder the longer we spoke. I no longer had to strain to hear her. *We actually spoke then. I came to you earlier than planned because you dreamed of danger.*

I had no memory of that. If I'd heard someone speaking inside my head before, surely I would have remembered it.

You dreamed that you would be tied down and injected to stop your first shift. That's the night the wolf is strongest. I tried to prevent the events of the dream by coming to you early, with the Goddess' blessing, but you didn't believe me. You thought you were going crazy when you heard me speak and you told your parents, who made your nightmare come true. They restrained you and upped the dose on the injections until I couldn't get through anymore. Since then, the medication has made it impossible for me to break free, no matter how hard I try.

Although I couldn't remember any such dreams or being tied up, I did remember the days spent in bed when I had my first seizures. Could that be the same time? *Why don't I remember any of this?*

The medication also affects your memory. It's the same reason you don't remember your family. They've been giving it to you in small doses your whole life, ever since the night of the attack. When I tried to appear, they experimented until they got the dose just right.

Though I couldn't feel my body, a feeling of cold dread washed over me anyway, as if the dark place I floated had suddenly turned several degrees cooler. *Are you sure?*

Positive. I've been watching the whole time, Calista, I just couldn't tell you. If you can let me out, I can help you remember all of it too. You just need to set me free.

She said that as if it would be simple, but I had no idea what she meant. *How do I do that?*

First, you need to open your eyes.

That was easier said than done when I couldn't feel my eyes anymore. My mind remained stubbornly detached from my body.

You can do it, she encouraged me. *Focus on our mate. His scent, his touch, his voice: all of it will help to ground you.*

Our... what?

Did she actually just say that? Hope that Vaughan might be my mate crossed my mind when Savannah mentioned the sparks, but I figured it must be wishful thinking. He couldn't be... could he? I didn't even really know exactly what it entailed to be mates, but if it involved him and I being together, it already sounded too good to be true.

Skye's hum of satisfaction filled me with warmth, erasing the cold that had taken hold. *Of course Vaughan is our mate. You felt it the moment you met him, even if you didn't recognize what it was. He's waiting for you. For **us**. Open your eyes, Calista, and show him who we really are.*

Chapter Thirty-Five

~Vaughan~

Atlas' growling in my head didn't make it any easier to sit there and watch Calista as her body jerked uncontrollably. From my experience that afternoon, I knew holding her didn't make any difference, and since we were on a bed rather than the ground, I laid her down gently, making sure she could still breathe and couldn't hurt herself. Every fibre of my being and every instinct I had, along with the wolf in my head, urged me to 'fix' it, but I knew I could do nothing but wait. If her wolf was fighting to get through, I had to let it happen.

With one eye on my watch and the other on her convulsing body, my eyes and ears and nose all tuned to take in the smallest changes, I watched and I waited.

Until Amanda asked me flat out what I would do if Calista rejected me, I hadn't known the answer myself, but as soon as the words were out of my mouth, I knew they were true: I couldn't settle for anything less than what I felt for the woman on that bed. In just 24 hours, she'd completely turned my world upside down. Having watched other wolves in the pack go from confirmed bachelors to lovesick mates overnight, unable to function without their other half, I never truly believed it would happen to me, but at last, I understood just how they felt. Now that it had happened, I wouldn't trade it for the world.

Those other wolves didn't have to deal with their mates having been raised to hunt and distrust our kind. They didn't have to break it to them that they might not be the species they'd always believed themselves to be. Nothing about the time Calista and I had spent together could be called simple, and yet, I wouldn't trade it for anything either. The night before, I had been convinced I could resist her. After spending just one full day together, I knew that had never truly been an option.

I just had to hope that she felt the same once she fully accepted her true identity.

As my watch ticked past four minutes, my heart thudded against my chest even harder. Had we been wrong about her wolf? I couldn't see how; all the signs were there. Maybe it would simply take longer than I hoped? Maybe she would have to go through multiple seizures, maybe days of them, before her wolf felt strong enough to appear? I hoped that having me near and feeling the mate bond would help, but it might just be wishful thinking. If she didn't wake up in the next half a minute, I would have to get the doctor. Already on standby in another guest room down the hall, she could be with us in a matter of seconds if needed.

Twenty seconds... ten seconds...

Just as I went to open my link to the doctor, Calista's seizing stopped. A moment later, her eyelids began to flutter, and I immediately knelt down on the floor next to the bed so I would be eye level with her as soon as she woke up, though not so close that I would scare the hell out of her.

As I breathed in, waiting for her to come back around, her salted caramel scent made my mouth water, but I could smell something behind it too, the same as I had that afternoon.

I could smell her wolf.

Did it work? Atlas panted in anticipation as we both held our breath.

With a groggy blink, and another, Calista's blue eyes tried to open, but she couldn't seem to keep them that way. As her fingers on her right hand twitched, Atlas growled at me.

She's reaching for you. Touch her!

I'm getting there, hang on. When did he get so bossy? My hand covered hers, the sparks between us feeling even stronger than before, and a moment later, her eyes blinked fully open.

"Vaughan."

My name came out of her mouth as a croak, but the soft smile that accompanied it filled my whole body with warmth. "Hey. I told you I'd be here. How do you feel?"

"Strange. I don't know if I just had a really weird dream or..."

Her eyes widened as she trailed off, and instantly, I leaned closer. "What? Is it happening again?"

"That depends what you mean by 'it'." Her lips hesitantly curled into a disbelieving smile. "There's someone talking in my head."

Atlas howled in approval while I burst into my own grin. "Your wolf? You're talking to her?"

Calista nodded, her eyes still wide with wonder. "She says her name is Skye. Vaughan, this is... I don't know..."

She trailed off again, obviously overwhelmed, while Atlas spun in delirious circles of delight in my mind. Squeezing her hand, I tried to give her all the encouragement I could. "It's a lot to take in. I can't imagine. It was strange enough for me when Atlas appeared, and I'd been expecting him my whole life."

"Atlas." Calista repeated the name softly, her blue eyes shining. "It suits him. Skye approves."

The pride Atlas felt flowed through me, and in that moment, everything felt absolutely perfect: my mate and her wolf connecting with me and my wolf, just as it should be. Could she feel it too?

"Did she... uh, did she tell you anything else?"

If her wolf was strong enough to make contact, she must be strong enough to recognize our mate bond too. As much as I wanted to gather Calista in my arms, I needed to know she understood why first. I wanted her to feel it just as much as I did.

As usual, Calista understood me perfectly, completely on my wavelength. "She says you're my mate, if that's what you mean."

"That's exactly what I mean." Leaning forward again, my face rested only inches away from hers as I looked straight into those beautiful blue eyes of hers. "Do you know what that involves?"

"Not exactly," she admitted in a whisper, and I knew how much she hated not having all the answers. We'd only known each other for a day, and already, I knew that about her. "But what about Amanda?"

She must have been in too much pain earlier to have heard what I told Savannah. "I've ended things with Amanda. I never felt anything for her, and after you and I kissed earlier and the things I told you in the truck, the idea of mating with her made no sense to me. I couldn't pretend I wanted to go through with it anymore."

As I mentioned our kiss, my gaze dipped to her mouth, so close to me and so incredibly enticing, but rather than closing the short distance between us, Calista pulled back, abruptly sitting up.

"You knew from the first time you saw me that we were mates?"

Pushing myself up, I sat down on the bed beside her, resisting the almost overwhelming urge to take her in my arms. Now that our bond had been acknowledged, it pulled at me more than ever. How could she resist it? "I knew from the second I saw you sitting there in my cell, probably plotting about how you were going to get out."

I hoped to make her smile, but she didn't take the bait. Instead, her arms crossed defensively. "How long were you planning on withholding that rather important piece of information from me?"

Atlas growled again in my head. *I told you we shouldn't have ignored the bond.*

Not now. I didn't need to be getting grief from both of them at the same time. "I wouldn't say withholding..." I tried, but Calista cut me off before I could finish.

"No? Would you prefer we call it lying, then? You thought that, just like my parents, you had a right to decide what I should and shouldn't know?"

Shit. The parallels hadn't occurred to me before, but I winced as she drew attention to them. She had a point. When I decided not to tell her, I had been putting myself first, at least partly.

Since I couldn't deny it, I offered an explanation instead. "You were here to investigate me and my pack. Without a wolf of your own, I knew you didn't feel the bond the way I did. Would you have even believed me if I told you, or would you have thought I said it to distract you from the murders?"

She couldn't argue with that, but I still owed her an apology anyway.

"You're right, though: I shouldn't have kept it to myself as long as I did, and I'm sorry. Part of it was not wanting to screw things up politically with Amanda's pack and to be honest, I still don't know what's going to happen there. Part of it was a good old-fashioned fear of rejection. I'm still a man, after all. And another part... well, it sounds kind of stupid, but I wanted you to want me on your own, without me telling you that you should. In my own clumsy way, I was trying to let you make the choice rather than making it for you."

Calista thought that over, chewing on her bottom lip as she considered not only my words but all the interactions we'd had over the last 24 hours. I could practically see her mind working through it all, and I appreciated it more than I could say that she let me explain and gave weight to my explanations.

"You did try to get me to admit how I felt in the truck," she conceded. "Would you have told me about us being mates then if I'd said I had feelings for you?"

"I might have." I didn't want to lie and say I would have for sure, but it had certainly felt like a possibility. "Is that what you would have said, if you answered me?"

I raised an eyebrow at her and at last, she smiled, her cheeks colouring as she glanced down. When she spoke again, the words were all I could have hoped for. "I felt something the first time I saw you too. I didn't know what to call it, but it felt like something stronger than attraction. And the more time we've spent together, the more it feels like there's an energy between us that I haven't felt before. It's intangible and changing, but it's there. I didn't know how to explain it, and to be totally honest, it scares me."

Without me consciously guiding it, my hand found its way to her face, cupping the side of it, my thumb on her cheek and my fingers curling around her neck. "It scares me too, Calista, in the best way."

When she leaned into my touch, not pulling away at all, I couldn't hold back any longer. My lips were on hers a second later, and unlike the first time we kissed, she didn't seem to have any intention of stopping me.

Chapter Thirty-Six

~Calista~

My mind had raced before, but never like it did in the moments after I opened my eyes and found that the voice in my head, the voice that claimed to be my wolf, was still with me. People talked about a train of thought, but it felt like someone had cut the brakes on my train and pushed it off the side of a cliff. Skye kept talking to me while I spoke to Vaughan, interjecting her own thoughts into the proceedings while I struggled to accept what her existence meant, not only for my future but for my past.

My 'parents' really had lied to me. They manipulated me into thinking I needed the medication while using it to hide who I really was. They let me believe my family had been killed by werewolves when my family *were* the wolves who had died at the hunters' hands. That would be bad enough, but now it seemed that my wolf family had been innocent in the attacks in the first place.

Those thoughts formed a whirlpool in the centre of my mind, deep and dark. It would have been easy to fall into them completely, but I didn't want that. With all my might, I pushed the feelings of pain and betrayal away to try to focus on the conversation with Vaughan about us being mates. I focused on how he broke things off with Amanda even before knowing for sure that I was actually a werewolf. He chose me, but he left the choice about whether or not I wanted him in my hands.

When his lips pressed against mine, one thing among all the swirling thoughts in my head came through crystal clear: I *did* want him. I wanted him in a way I'd never wanted another man before.

Thoroughly.

Possessively.

Desperately.

With his kiss, the storm inside me calmed. Although he stole my breath away, the kiss also made me feel I could breathe again. He always smelled good to me, but since I woke back up, he smelled even better, like the fresh sheets I had smelled in my dream. My memory? Whatever that had been, smelling it on Vaughan made me feel just as I had then: safe and warm and protected. In an indefinable way, it smelled like belonging.

The sparks where our skin touched felt stronger than before too; less shocking but even more stimulating. They spread through my body, waking and igniting every inch of me, making me more aware of my body than ever before and especially of the effect he had on it.

"I know we still have a lot more work to do," he whispered, barely lifting his lips from mine to get the words out. "But the rest of my team is on top of things. Nothing can happen tonight without them being aware of it. If they need us, they'll let me know, but right now, the most important thing to me is you."

He truly meant that. I could hear it in the possessive, growling undertone to his words that mirrored the way I felt inside. I could feel it in the way he held me, as if it might kill him to let me go. He was a man who took his duty seriously, but he needed me more. And though I knew he had a point, that the danger hadn't passed and that eventually, I would have to deal with my parents and everything else, at that moment, I wanted to leave all of it outside the door. My whole life, as much of it as I could remember, I had put the needs of everyone else above my own.

For once, I wanted to be selfish.

"Do you feel this electricity the same way I do?" I asked him, running my fingers down the side of his handsome, chiselled face. His eyes closed as he inhaled, savouring the sensation and answering my question before he even said the words.

"Fuck, yes." The words rumbled out of him so deeply that my whole body vibrated in response. "It feels incredible. I can't wait to feel it everywhere."

Everywhere. Just the idea had my heart pounding and my body throbbing. "It really happens everywhere?"

His lips curled into a mischievous smile that made my stomach flip. "Should we find out?"

Lifting the back of my shirt, his fingers slid beneath it, brushing across my back and sending a new wave of shivers through me. In a matter of seconds, he had me more turned on than I could ever remember being, and he'd still hardly touched me.

Foreplay had never been my thing before. The times I'd had sex, it had been all about scratching an itch rather than any kind of emotional connection, so I did what I normally did in these situations: I reached down myself and pulled my shirt over my head, exposing much more of my skin to him in an attempt to move things along.

Vaughan's eyes widened in surprise and undisguised desire as he took in the sight of me in my bra. "You're going to drive me crazy. You're so fucking gorgeous."

No one had ever called me that before and I glanced down at my body, trying to see what he saw. Hunting kept me in shape, the utilitarian diet and long hours of activity giving me a firm stomach that contrasted with the soft swell of my breasts. My underwear, like all my clothing, favoured function over style. "You find plain white underwear sexy?"

A smile lit Vaughan's face again, somehow making him even more handsome than the thoughtful, more brooding expression I'd become accustomed to seeing on him. "On you, I like it all, but I think I'd like it even better *off* of you."

One big, strong hand reached up to cover my right breast, cupping it in his palm and squeezing as a sigh of satisfaction slipped out of my mouth. It felt damn good, but not quite as good as it could.

"There are no sparks," I mumbled, not meaning to say the words out loud. Usually, I had much better self-control, but at that moment, my guard felt lower than it had ever been before.

Taking the hint, Vaughan pulled the fabric down, letting me spill out of it, but rather than grabbing my bare breast with his hand, he leaned down and sucked my nipple into his mouth instead.

"Oh, God." Tingling warmth spread out from where his lips and tongue touched me, making my body throb even more. Completely out of my control, my back arched, pushing my chest towards him so he could shower it with even more attention. In a flash, he had my bra fully off as he switched his attention from one breast to the other, his fingers flicking across the one his mouth had just left.

Maybe foreplay wasn't so bad after all.

My thighs clenched, my hips tilting towards him as his tongue circled my nipple before he sucked it firmly into his mouth. Somehow, my hands ended up in his hair, though I didn't recall putting them there. My fists clenched as he pinched one nipple with his fingers and gently bit down on the other one.

Skye had gone quiet in my head though I could feel her satisfaction just as much as I could my own. It almost felt like I could feel Vaughan's too. The air was thick with it, our desire for each other, the enjoyment we currently shared, and the anticipation of what was still to come.

"So, you feel it there, I guess," Vaughan teased me, lifting his eyes to mine even as his head remained at chest-level. "What about lower?"

He began to kiss his way down my stomach as my heart beat even faster. Though I wasn't a virgin, I'd never let anyone go down on me before. It felt more intimate, somehow, than simply fucking. My previous sexual encounters had only ever been after a quick release for both of us, but obviously, Vaughan wanted more, and rather than turning me off, the idea excited me even further.

Laying down on the bed, I quickly undid my jeans while Vaughan growled in approval. In a matter of seconds, he had them pulled down, underwear, sock and all, leaving me completely naked on the bed while he was still fully clothed. He didn't seem at all concerned about his own situation. His focus was entirely on me.

Positioning himself between my legs, Vaughan inhaled deeply before letting out a deep, satisfied growl. "I wish I could explain to you how fucking good you smell. Your mate scent is tantalizing enough on its own, but when you're turned on...*fuck*. It's like all my favourite scents at once. Salty, sweet, and rich. If you taste as good as you smell, I'm never going to want to eat anything else."

From anyone else, those words would have sounded ridiculous, but in the heat of that moment, imbued with all of his rugged sexiness and animal magnetism, they were the hottest thing I'd ever heard. "I guess you better find out, then," I invited, and his eyes somehow both lit up and grew darker at the same time.

Without any further delay, his head dipped to my waiting pussy, and from the very first contact of his tongue against me, my whole scale of what felt good had to be rewritten. Nobody came close to what Vaughan did to me. The sparks shouldn't have come as a surprise by that point, but they did anyway. While his tongue moved, tasting me, those sparks vibrated and tingled straight into my core, driving my need higher and pulling a strangled noise from my throat that I would swear I'd never made before. Time ceased to exist, as did my awareness of anything in the world outside of me and him, and the feel of his mouth on me.

"Vaughan." I choked his name out as his tongue slid across my skin, over and over, faster and faster, exploring every inch, dipping into every available empty space, until he reached my clit and my brain ceased to function. Just like when I seized, I couldn't control the convulsions of my body, but unlike then, I remembered each and every second of it. The pleasure that had been building suddenly released, and I clung onto him as the wave washed over me, bathing me in a deep fulfillment unlike anything I'd ever felt before.

In more ways than one, he made me feel like a brand-new woman, and in that moment, I knew one thing for certain.

I wanted more.

Chapter Thirty-Seven

~**Vaughan**~

Atlas' howl of approval when Calista came nearly made me laugh, which wouldn't have been the best reaction to have with my face still buried between her legs. Luckily, she seemed too distracted by her orgasm to notice.

I don't need a cheering section, I told my wolf drily. *I know what I'm doing here.*

He'd never offered his opinion during sex before. Not that I had a lot of it, and never within my own pack, but when it did happen, he usually stayed quiet. I didn't go around giving him pointers when he got lucky either.

This is different, he argued. *It's our mate. It has to be good.*

It never crossed my mind that it wouldn't be. Calista and I seemed to understand each other on a deeper level than anyone I'd met before, not to mention the way she turned me on. We would work well together, I simply knew it, but apparently, my wolf had less faith in me.

I didn't expect Calista to be a virgin, and the way she undressed for me seemed to confirm she had some experience. She didn't show any signs of nervousness or uncertainty, so I didn't feel any either. We both wanted this and we both expected it to be good; I didn't see how we could fail.

Making her come had only been the beginning, though. I'd told her I couldn't wait to feel the sparks of our bond all over my body, and I meant it. Just imagining what it might feel like to have that connection with my cock buried inside her took my breath away. Since she seemed perfectly willing to help me find out, I didn't see any reason to put it off any longer.

Calista watched with hazy, satisfied eyes as I stood up off the bed to remove my own clothes. My shirt went first, one hand grabbing the back of it and pulling it over my head. Calista's eyes immediately lowered to my chest, sending the blood rushing even more urgently to my cock. In her truck, she'd done her best to avoid looking at my naked body, but that reticence had completely vanished, letting me know it had never been shyness. She only avoided looking because of how it affected her, and now that I had admitted to being hers, she had no reason to hide. As I unzipped my jeans and pulled them down, sighing in relief as the pressure on my cock eased, my mate wasted no time in checking me out. Based on the colour in her cheeks and the widening of her eyes, it looked like she liked what she saw.

That made two of us, then, since I'd never seen anything more captivating than the sight of her naked, satisfied, and eager for me.

"Do you have a condom?"

Her words stopped me in my tracks as I pulled my jeans off, and I glanced up at her in surprise. I had to admit the request slightly disappointed me since I didn't know if I'd still feel the sparks the same way without the skin-to-skin contact, but if she wanted it, I respected that. "Would you like to use one?"

"I'm not on birth control, so I think we better."

"Okay, let me just check…"

I pulled open the drawers of the night stands and the dressers in the guest room, looking for one of the little foil packets. My search came up empty, which didn't really surprise me. It had been a long shot to find anything there. Werewolves had a strong sex drive and a high fertility rate, and most female wolves went on birth control as soon as they considered becoming sexually active. Our high-functioning immune systems also spared us from the STDs that affected humans. All of that meant that condoms in a werewolf pack were almost rarer than silver, but I knew one place I could get one in a pinch.

Dr Wilson? I mind-linked to the doctor on standby to help with Calista's seizures.

I'm here. Do you need me, Alpha?

Yes, but not for Calista. I need... do you have a condom?

A few seconds ticked by in a silence that would have embarrassed me if I weren't so hungry for my mate in any way I could have her.

Of course, she finally replied. *I'll bring one to you.*

Closing the link, I turned back to Calista with a sheepish smile. "It'll just take a moment to get one. Why aren't you on birth control?"

The question came from simple curiosity, not as any kind of accusation or complaint, and she took it that way, not taking any offense. "My mom said the hormones would interfere with my epilepsy medication."

The reminder of her parents' manipulation put an instant damper on the whole situation and I could have cursed myself for bringing it up, however inadvertently. Since I couldn't ignore it, though, I tried my best to lean into it and make her smile. "And what do you think she'd say if she knew you were about to fuck your Alpha werewolf mate?"

As I hoped, she let out a snorted laugh that struck me as the most adorable thing I'd ever heard. "It might actually make her speechless for once. I'm almost tempted to call her and let her know." Lying there with her blonde hair spread out over the pillow beneath her, she looked like an angel, innocent and sweet, but I'd had enough of a glimpse of the smart, sexy side of her to know there was so much more to her than that.

The doctor's knock on the door came none too soon, and I opened it as narrowly as I could to take the condom from her, ignoring the amused smile that tugged at the corners of her lips. Luckily, I knew I could count on her to be discreet and not mention to anyone else that I'd asked for one. "Thank you."

The door had barely closed and I already had the package open, rolling the condom onto my stiff, ready cock. As I stepped closer to the bed, Calista sat up, looking like she wanted to reach out and touch me, but I pushed her back down, firmly but tenderly. I didn't want her to have to worry about anything but enjoying herself. We'd have time to do much more later, to truly enjoy and explore each other. At that moment, I simply wanted to give us both a taste of how good it could be, just enough to hold us over while we dealt with all the other things that needed our attention.

My fingers slid between her legs again, making sure she still felt ready for me, and Calista's sigh gave me exactly the answer I hoped for. Positioning my cock against her pussy, I held it there for a second, smiling as her hips tilted towards me, trying to draw me in, letting me know just how much she wanted it too. Without wasting another second, I pushed into her, slowly, firmly, and deeply, and nothing in my entire life had ever felt so incredibly perfect.

The sparks were still there through the condom; maybe a little bit muted, but that only gave me something to look forward to later. At that moment, it felt perfect, especially when Calista moaned out my name. Fuck, nothing ever sounded so good.

All the self-denial I'd subjected myself to since we met poured out of me, every tense moment and longing glance released in the thrust of my hips into her warm, welcoming body. The faster I moved, the more she seemed to like it, spurring me on.

"Harder?" I asked, wanting to learn exactly what turned her on, and when she nodded, her legs tightening around my waist, I let out a growl of approval. Adjusting my angle to give myself better leverage, I drove into her again, getting even deeper than before.

The back of Calista's head pressed into the pillow, her eyes closing as her lips parted. "Yes. Vaughan, yes. Just like that."

My lips could barely form the words to respond, my mind surrendering to the needs of my body, but I managed to grunt out a promise to her between stuttered breaths. "However you want it. Whenever you want it. I'm yours, Calista. I always was."

She peered up at me in wonder and desire, panting through each thrust of my hard cock. "I didn't know... it could... be like this."

Neither did I. We were learning together, and I'd be there through whatever other discoveries she still had ahead of her.

Could people really fall in love in a day? It seemed impossible, counter-intuitive, but as I moved inside my mate, rocking us both in perfect harmony and watching her beautiful face as she revelled in the pleasure we shared, it felt like so much more than merely lust. Her taking me inside her showed how she trusted me, though she had every reason in the world not to trust anyone. Deep in my heart, I knew I would never be truly happy again unless she was right there with me, feeling valued and treasured.

Did all mates feel that way? Did knowing her background and what she'd been through make me even more protective?

How was it possible that I wanted to put her on a pedestal and fuck her senseless all at the same time?

When she came again, I followed right behind her, finding fulfillment in her fulfillment and pleasure in her pleasure, just as I wanted and better than I ever dreamed.

My mate.

Chapter Thirty-Eight

~Calista~

The expression in Vaughan's eyes changed immediately after he came. Where before, he'd been looking down at me with desire and something close to affection, afterwards, the look grew harder and more possessive. Hungry, even. Hell, he even licked his lips.

With my body still flush with the pleasure of my own orgasm, the second one he'd given me, seeing him look at me that way both frightened me and turned me on at the same time. I barely recognized the way my body reacted, but I loved it too.

"Vaughan?" I tried saying his name to snap him out of whatever that look meant, and it worked. He blinked a couple of times, as if waking from a daydream, before pulling out of me and lowering himself onto the bed beside me, looking up at the ceiling and taking a deep breath.

"That was amazing," he murmured in a deep, satisfied tone that sent another small wave of pleasure through me. I'd never found anyone as inherently attractive as I found him. Everything he did was sexy.

And the sex *had* been amazing, he had that right, but that didn't explain the look he gave me. "What happened just now?"

He didn't pretend not to know what I meant. That was one of my favourite things about him, at least so far. He never avoided my questions, not like my parents did at times. Of course, now I knew why they sometimes pretended they didn't hear me when I asked about things they didn't want to talk about.

He turned his head to face me, those warm brown eyes of his even more startlingly sexy so close up. "Two days ago, I never thought I'd find my fated mate. Yesterday, I met you but I thought we would never have a chance to be together. Tonight, I got to be inside you, and when we finished, I had an instinctive need to mark you. It hit me hard, a lot stronger than I expected. Atlas wanted me to do it as well, so I had to fight against it."

"Mark me?" The word obviously meant something specific to him, but I didn't know what that might be in this context.

He started to answer me at the same time that Skye began giving me an explanation in my head, making it impossible for me to understand either of them.

"Wait! Hold on. One at a time."

Vaughan smiled, thankfully understanding what I meant rather than assuming I was losing my mind. "Skye can tell you if she wants to."

My wolf sighed happily at the sound of Vaughan saying her name. *No, he can explain. I'm curious what he'll say.*

"She says to go ahead," I told Vaughan, though it felt strange to be the go-between for the man in front of me and the voice inside my head. "Are you ever able to talk to her directly?"

Vaughan shook his head, causing a few strands of his thick hair to fall down across his face. He reached up to brush them back as he answered me. "The only human a wolf can communicate with is its own counterpart. Your wolf will be able to speak to the other wolves in the pack once you're officially part of the pack, and once we're fully mated, Atlas and Skye will have a special connection, just like we will. She can give me a message through Atlas or through you, but I'll never speak to her myself, and you'll never speak to Atlas."

I didn't necessarily like the sound of that. "So, there's a whole part of you that I'll never really know?"

"Yes and no." Vaughan's fingers trailed down my arm as he looked into my eyes, answering my questions calmly and patiently. "Atlas is part of me, yes, but he's not *me*. Just like Skye, as wonderful as I'm sure she is, isn't you. You're a whole complete person on your own; with Skye, you're even more. The dichotomy is what makes werewolves special. We're a two-for-one deal."

He arched his eyebrows at the last bit, obviously teasing, and it made me smile. "Alright, I think I understand. Let's go back to the mark you were talking about. What is it?"

His fingers continued to brush against my skin, both soothing and distracting me at the same time. "I guess you could say it's the werewolf equivalent of a wedding ring. It's a visible sign to every other wolf that you have a mate. It changes a wolf's scent, so we can tell the difference between mated and unmated wolves, and it opens that special connection I mentioned between mates. Once we mark each other, we'll be bonded. We'll be able to communicate telepathically, we'll be able to sense each other's emotions and we'll know if the other is in trouble or injured."

That all sounded rather overwhelming, and Vaughan seemed to realize that, hurrying to add a disclaimer.

"It's not something to be entered into lightly, which is why I fought against the instinct to do it before you fully understood what it meant. Just because you slept with me doesn't mean you've decided to be with me forever."

No, it certainly didn't, and I appreciated that he recognized that. Even if it felt natural to him, my frame of reference was completely different. So much had changed for me in such a short amount of time, and the idea of making any kind of lifelong commitment, even to someone as well suited to me as Vaughan seemed to be, had never been on my radar before.

"I'm still getting used to all of this, but it doesn't mean I don't want to be with you. I just need some time."

"I know," he assured me. "I'll be as patient as I can."

"You're doing a great job."

I leaned forward so my forehead pressed against his, the sparks flowing between us again as we shared a moment of connection. Even with everything else still up in the air, it felt so right to be beside him. It felt like I *belonged* there.

When I pulled back a minute later, I returned to more practical matters. "Are we talking about a literal mark? How is it made?"

A mischievous smile pulled at Vaughan's lips. "With a bite. Right here."

His fingers left my arm and brushed against my neck instead, sending a shiver through my whole body. How could I seriously be getting turned on *again*? That couldn't be normal.

Actually, it is, Skye piped up in my head. *Werewolves have a higher sex drive than humans, in both human and wolf form.*

Each new revelation made my head spin even more. When I studied supernatural creatures before, it had always been academic, but now that things actually applied to my own life, they seemed more and more unbelievable. *So, you're saying your wolf is going to have sex with his wolf?*

Of course. She said it like I should have known that already. *We're mates the same as you and Vaughan are. That arousal you're feeling now is partly from me. I've been cooped up in here for a long time, Calista. I could hear and see everything since I first came to you at seventeen, but I couldn't say or do anything. I know you've been through a lot today, but I need to shift soon. As soon as you're ready.*

When would I ever feel ready for that? *I have no idea how that works.*

I know, but I'm here to help you. So is Vaughan.

"Is everything okay?"

Vaughan's question made me realize that, to him, it probably just looked like I'd been staring into space for a minute since he couldn't hear the conversation in my head. Figuring out how to handle two different planes of conversation would definitely take some getting used to. "Skye says she wants to shift."

Needs to, she corrected me.

"*Needs* to," I repeated out loud, the emphasis making Vaughan smile. "Is that possible? Does it just happen? Do I need to do any kind of preparation first?"

His smile widened, indulgent and kind. "It doesn't just happen, but your wolf will know what to do. If you want to, I'll walk you through it. We should go outside, though: generally, we don't allow shifting inside the house."

The thought of the forest outside, dark now that the sun had gone down, made me shiver, calling to mind the dream I'd had and our frantic attempted evacuation. So many things about that dream made more sense to me now: the way Vaughan had looked at me and the fact that I was there at all, for a start. Could there have been more to it than a simple dream?

In the dream, Vaughan hadn't been able to shift, and as far as I knew, that part hadn't come true. It seemed there would be one easy way to find out: if we went outside to shift, he could do it too, and we could find out if there was a problem. If so, I would tell him the rest of it immediately and we could try to figure out what it meant.

"Let's go and try," I decided. The day had been absolutely insane already; why not turn into a wolf to cap it all off?

Chapter Thirty-Nine

~**Vaughan**~

As much as I wanted to hold Calista's hand as we made our way downstairs, I had to be practical. Very few people knew yet that she was my mate. Most people in the pack still thought Amanda and I were going to be mated, and I owed it to Amanda to make a formal announcement and explanation before I started showing off my true mate, no matter how much I wanted to.

So, when Leo showed up to block our path out the back door, it took all my strength not to groan. If he'd come to lecture me again about not spending time with Amanda, I truly didn't have the patience.

"What is it, Gamma?" Spitting out the word, I used his title to let him know not to push his luck.

His reply might have been stiff, but at least it didn't concern Amanda. "You're part of my group, Alpha. I can't let you leave the house on your own."

It took me a moment to realize what he meant: I'd ordered the whole pack split up into groups of ten to watch out for signs of possession, and of course, that meant me as well. Even though Calista would probably know better than anyone if something happened to me, I couldn't flout my own rules. A true leader didn't behave that way.

"Well, I'm going out, so the group has to come with me, then." As Leo linked with the others to pass on that message, I turned to Calista with an apology. "I'm sorry, it looks like we're going to have some company."

She shrugged, trying to look nonchalant even if she didn't feel that way. "I understand. I'm glad everyone's taking the precautions seriously."

A small group soon gathered by the back door: along with Leo, there were three of the kitchen staff, two of the men who worked security for the house, Felix, Savannah, and Amanda.

Of course Amanda had to be there. Just my luck.

Avoiding her gaze, I explained the situation to the group: "As I'm sure you can all smell, Calista is a werewolf. Her wolf has been suppressed for a long time and she's eager to shift. I'm going to help her through it. The rest of you can set up a perimeter around us in the forest, at a distance to give us some privacy. You all remember that your first shift can be a little awkward."

No one could argue with that, but Felix had some additional conditions. "Everyone check in with me every thirty seconds so I know it's still you. Amanda, since you don't have a link to any of us, you can stay with me."

With everyone agreed, we headed out into the nighttime forest. The temperature must have been close to freezing as our breath hung in the air around us while we walked. The hoot of a distant owl made my ears prick up, tuned in to any sign of anything unusual, but besides the crunch of the brittle leaves beneath our feet, everything else seemed normal.

When the others had gone to set up their circle, I turned to Calista. "We'll need to undress first. If we don't, our clothes will be destroyed, just like mine were earlier today."

Competing feelings of uncertainty and a hint of desire flashed through her pale blue eyes. "Won't we be cold?"

"Only until we shift. Your wolf's body temperature is warmer than yours, and if she's as eager as you say, it shouldn't take long."

To make her more comfortable, I went first, pulling off the clothes I had only recently put back on and leaving them in a neat pile at my feet on the forest floor. Not one to back down from a challenge, Calista followed suit, wrapping her arms around her naked body to keep out the chill. Even though we'd just finished satisfying each other, the sight of her immediately got blood flowing back to my cock, and I cleared my throat before my reaction got out of hand.

"Skye will know how to make the shift. It's an instinct that all werewolves are born with on their wolf side. You just have to let her take control."

"How do I do that?" Calista shivered as she asked the question, maybe from the cold or perhaps just out of nerves.

"Relax your mind and body as much as you can. Clear your mind of all thoughts."

She huffed in frustration. "That's a little difficult right now."

I could only imagine, but it would be necessary. "Picture the most soothing environment you can think of. Imagine yourself calm and relaxed there."

Her eyes closed as she tried to follow my instructions. "Can you keep talking? Your voice helps."

A warm flush of appreciation spread through my body at the idea that she found my presence relaxing. I felt just the same; a lot of people put me on edge, but I'd felt comfortable around Calista right from the start, even taking into account the tension between us. With that in mind, I did my best to make her feel comfortable while also appealing to Skye to push her way forward.

"This forest has always been part of you. Your own pack lived on the southern edge of it and you would have played there as a little girl. The scent of the pine trees, the earth beneath your feet, the stars above you, it's all welcoming you home. Imagine how good it will feel to run through it as you were always meant to."

Calista's head dropped, and for a heart-stopping second, I thought she might be seizing again. Immediately, I stepped towards her to catch her if she was going to pass out, but instead, her body dropped forward, onto her hands, in preparation for her shift. Skye had obviously taken control.

As fur began to sprout across her naked back, I shifted too, letting Atlas take over so he could be there for his mate, and I had never felt him as happy as he was at that moment. We watched together as Calista slowly and painfully took on her wolf's form for the first time, her bones cracking as they shifted into their new position, leaving a breathtakingly light-furred wolf in her place. Her wolf wasn't white, but almost golden-looking, her fur the same colour as Calista's hair.

She's beautiful, Atlas panted in awe, and though I had no firm opinion one way or the other, it made me glad that he thought so since I certainly felt the same about her human counterpart.

As she pawed at the ground, stretching out her limbs, I knew we wouldn't be able to stay in the small circle we'd created for ourselves.

Quickly, I mind-linked my Beta. *Felix, we need to go for a run. The rest of you can follow. We'll stay away from the border.*

Yes, Alpha, came his obedient reply.

Since I couldn't yet link with Calista or Atlas with Skye, he gestured with his head instead, inviting her to run alongside him, and after a few hesitant steps, she began to trot, and then, in a burst of joy, to sprint, while Atlas howled excitedly and followed in close behind as they raced through the trees. The cool air rustled through their fur and the moon shone down on them almost as if it were offering them a blessing.

In the excitement of my mate's first shift and the run, I could almost forget about everything else going on, at least until we got deeper into our territory and a new and unusual scent reached my nose. It was faint, but distinct, and I noticed Skye's nose twitching too. Suddenly, without warning and still mid-stride, she shifted back to Calista's form, stumbling over her feet and hitting the ground hard as she rolled to a painful stop.

Instantly, I pulled up beside her and shifted back to my human form too. "Are you alright?"

"That... hurt," Calista admitted, grimacing in pain. "I guess I should have stopped running first."

"You'll get used to it," I promised, tempted to smile at her blunt assessment of her mistake, but aware of her pain. "Why did you stop?"

"That smell... do you smell it too?"

"Yes. Do you recognize it? What is it?"

Her grim expression gave me a hint I wouldn't like her answer but her words were still about the last thing I would have expected her to say. "It's a sasquatch. We should get everyone back inside, right away."

Chapter Forty

~**Calista**~

"A sasquatch?"

Savannah stared at me in disbelief while the others around her exchanged uneasy looks. We'd just returned to the pack house after our run, thankfully without running into the creature in question, and gathered back in the meeting room for me to share my theory with the rest of Vaughan's team. Vaughan handed me a glass of water, which I gulped down gratefully after the exertion of the shift and our run together. He seemed so tuned in to what I needed, anticipating things before I could ask for them. I'd never experienced that kind of connection with anyone so quickly.

"Do sasquatches really exist?" Savannah asked.

A lot of people mistakenly believed that humans invented the sasquatch. Also known as 'bigfoot', the large, ape-like creatures could bear a resemblance to a tall, hairy human, but their instincts were purely animal.

"They do," Amanda replied before I had a chance to. She sat across the table from me and Vaughan, between Leo and Savannah. "We had one on our pack land when I was young."

"They're more common farther north," I added. "Around here, they're much rarer, but I've hunted them before. That's how I recognized the scent. It's unlikely to be only one, they almost always travel in small groups."

"If they're on our land, wouldn't we sense it?" Darius asked from the far end of the table. "A spirit is one thing, I can understand why we wouldn't feel it, but a sasquatch is a corporeal, living thing."

"A living *animal*," Felix corrected, completely accurately. "We wouldn't feel it just like we wouldn't feel a deer wander into our territory."

"What do they want?" Leo wondered. "Are they dangerous?"

I could answer that one. "They won't go out of their way to attack people, but if they feel provoked in any way, they're very dangerous. They're strong and they're..."

A sudden, sharp pain seared across my forehead, stopping me in mid-sentence, and Vaughan immediately reached out to put his hand on my arm. "What is it?" he asked, letting his concern bleed through in front of everyone.

"It almost feels like another seizure coming on, but that shouldn't be possible..."

The pain flashed again as I grabbed my head, trying to hold it in. My fingers pressed into my temples, providing little relief against the throbbing sting.

Skye? Is something wrong?

Although I spoke to my wolf in my head just like I had before, no answer came, and though the pain showed no signs of easing, something else concerned me far more. Several things suddenly came into sharp focus, things that had seemed disparate until that moment, but put together, they formed a complete picture that I didn't like the look of at all.

"Vaughan, is your wolf okay? Can you still speak to Atlas?"

Everyone's eyes moved to him as he frowned. "Of course I can, why do you..."

He didn't even get the sentence out before Leo gasped from across the table, his hands flying to his head. "Shit. Ow. What the hell?"

I quickly turned my attention from Vaughan to him. "Leo, can you speak to your wolf?"

His eyes darted back and forth a couple of times before widening in disbelief. "No. He's not there. I can't feel him. What's going on?"

A large, almost empty glass of water sat in front of him too, and as much as I didn't want to believe it, I had to. Nothing else made sense.

"Nobody else drink the water! Vaughan, get the word out to the rest of the pack. It's been contaminated."

"I'm on it," Felix volunteered as Vaughan turned to me in confusion. "Contaminated? With what?"

I could barely bring myself to say the words. "With the same 'medication' that my parents used to suppress my wolf."

"Your parents..." He put it together even quicker than I had. "They did something to our water?"

It shamed me to admit but I had to be honest. "I'm afraid so. They talked about it as a possibility before and they were on the pack land earlier."

His expression grew more outraged with each passing second. "How could they..."

Felix interrupted before I could find out if Vaughan literally wanted to know how they'd done it, or if he was just ranting about the callousness of the action in general. "Alpha, I'm getting reports of headaches and missing wolves from across the pack. Luckily, most of the groups we created have at least one person who's unaffected, but a couple of groups, I can't reach at all."

Damn it. It sounded like things had spread already, though at least Vaughan and the others around the table seemed unaffected.

Almost all the others, at least. Savannah must have drunk the water too because she soon cried out as the pattern repeated itself yet again.

"You knew about this?" Amanda spoke up from across the table, eyeing me suspiciously. "You knew this might happen and you didn't say anything?"

Guilt shot through me, but I tried my best to give an honest explanation. "I told Vaughan they'd discussed silencing your wolves, but I didn't mention the water specifically. I didn't think they were actually going to go ahead with it."

At that moment, I couldn't remember exactly why I hadn't mentioned it. So many things had been going on that we would start talking about one thing and get distracted before I could share everything I knew.

"You told Vaughan to let them in," she reminded everyone else at the table. We had been sitting right there when Vaughan got the call that my parents had arrived and he asked me if I should let them in. I said yes.

Felix spoke up again, still linking with other members of the pack while the conversation carried on around him. "Alpha, I'm speaking with the guard at the water treatment plant. He says he let the humans in earlier today on your orders."

"My orders?" Vaughan repeated in utter disbelief. "What orders?"

"He says you sent a text authorizing the humans to take a look at the treatment room. They were only there for a couple of minutes."

"I never sent any..." Vaughan trailed off as the realization hit him the same moment it hit me. "I didn't send any texts because my phone was lost. Or at least, that's what I was told."

The doubt I could see in his eyes as he turned to me nearly took my breath away. It looked bad, I could see that. He sent me to look for his phone, and I returned and told him I couldn't find it. My parents must have taken his phone, sent the text on his behalf, and gone to the water treatment plant when they arrived at the territory, when I told Vaughan to let them in. He had no proof I didn't have anything to do with it except my word.

"I have to wonder if anything she's told you is true." Amanda's sharp tone stabbed at the already fraying trust between us. "If they can take our wolves away, what else can they do? Fake a mate bond, maybe? Isn't it remarkably convenient that she turned up right as all of this began?"

"Mate bond?" several of the people around the table repeated in a whisper, not having had any idea that Vaughan and I were mates until that moment.

"Vaughan, I didn't..."

I tried to offer an explanation, but he turned away from me, his jaw set.

"We're not safe here. Gather everyone together, go door-to-door if you can't reach them by mind-link. We need to evacuate. Right now."

Chapter Forty-One

~Vaughan~

Everything seemed to be spinning out of control. Someone wanted to hurt my pack and was using a vengeful spirit to do it. Or perhaps, the spirit had targeted us and used a witch to do it? I couldn't be certain. What did I know? Our best defense, our ability to shift and protect ourselves, had been taken away from many of us, and to top it all off, sasquatches were roaming our territory. I didn't see how things could get a lot worse.

At least I still had Atlas.

I'm only here because you didn't drink the water, he pointed out in my head. *You would have eventually if Calista hadn't told you not to. If she were behind all of this, why would she stop you?*

He had a point, and the longer I thought about it, the more I realized that Amanda's suggestion about Calista's involvement didn't make much sense. Calista *had* told me her parents were considering suppressing our wolves, I'd just been too caught up in what that meant for *her* to probe her on it as much as I should have.

More than that, I trusted my gut. I trusted the part of me that told me she was on our side right from the start. If she wanted to take us down, she didn't need to go to the lengths Amanda suggested. Even if she could fake a mate bond, which I'd never heard of before, why go to all the trouble? It seemed like a lot of work just to gain access to our land. She couldn't have known that I would let her parents in unaccompanied. Obviously, I regretted that decision in hindsight, but she hadn't influenced me in any way to make it.

"Should she really be here while we're discussing this?" Leo asked, eyeing Calista suspiciously. "If she's working with the hunters..."

"We have no proof of that," I quickly interrupted before that kind of speculation could get out of hand. "Yes, Calista showed up when these attacks started, but so did Amanda. They both arrived on the same day. We wouldn't have known anything about the water being contaminated if she hadn't just told us, and we can't blame her for what her parents have done. How many of you would like to be held accountable for everything your family does?"

No one spoke up, as I expected.

"Let's concentrate on what's important. We need to prepare to move. You all know the protocol."

"Where will we go?" Savannah asked. My bold, brash sister looked uncharacteristically uncertain without her wolf to back her up.

"I have a plan for this kind of situation. Not that I ever expected *exactly* this situation, but close enough. We've got a place that's safe."

"Vaughan." Calista said my name softly beside me, and when I turned to her, I could see the appreciation in her eyes, the gratitude that I hadn't jumped to any conclusions, but genuine concern there as well. "Your plan isn't the caves, is it?"

Once again, she managed to surprise me. How the hell did she know that? The caves were a closely guarded secret; most of the pack didn't even know they existed. A natural series of subterranean caverns that stretched into the hills on the west side of our land, Felix and I had literally stumbled upon them as young boys, along with a small group of other kids from our school. I couldn't remember exactly who else had been with us, but Felix probably could. In any case, we told my dad, the Alpha at the time, and he ordered them to be closed off again to prevent any accidents if other kids decided to explore them on their own.

They stayed that way, the entrance blocked and their existence generally unknown, until just a few weeks earlier when Felix and I had gone back to them to evaluate their usefulness as a sort of pack-wide 'panic room'. With only one entrance and exit, a natural source of water if we dug down, and large enough to accommodate the entire pack, they would be easy to defend and virtually impossible to detect for anyone who didn't know they were there.

I'd never imagined having to use them so quickly and I couldn't begin to guess how Calista knew about them.

"What caves?" I asked her, playing dumb. With my whole team listening, I needed to appear to be as impartial as possible.

"I'm not sure." Aware that everyone else could hear us, Calista's eyes darted cautiously around the room before returning to me. "I had a dream about it."

Several of the men exchanged uncertain glances, which I could understand. It sounded pretty far-fetched, but so did everything else that had happened. If we accepted the rest, why should we dismiss Calista's dream? "What happened in your dream?"

Calista filled us all in on the details that she could remember about how we had been evacuating the pack through the forest in the night and how none of us seemed to be able to shift. Apparently, I had been planning on taking everyone to the caves but it backfired and something attacked me.

"The creature I saw take you could have been a sasquatch," Calista suggested. "Maybe the spirit got frustrated with the precautions you were taking and possessed the sasquatches in order to attack you."

"So there's a group of sasquatches out there, possessed by an evil spirit who wants to kill us, while half the pack is unable to shift because the hunters poisoned our water supply," Darius summed up in frustration. "That's perfect. We're sitting ducks."

"On the plus side, not *all* the pack are unable to shift," Savannah pointed out. "And we know to avoid the caves, thanks to Calista."

I shot Sav a grateful smile for throwing her support behind my mate. Amanda hadn't said another word yet, but she still didn't look pleased.

I kept my attention focused on Calista. "Have you had dreams like this before that turned out to be true?"

Her pale blue eyes looked up at me, open and trusting. "Before today, I would have said no, but when Skye made her appearance, she told me that just before she was originally meant to come to me, I had a dream about being restrained and drugged. She says it came true when my parents first gave me the drug, though I don't remember. And I think..."

She trailed off, her brow furrowing as she searched her memory.

"I think I dreamed about the attack on my pack before it happened. Several times, and each time was slightly different. I think... I think I was able to survive because I knew what might happen and I could try to avoid it. If that's the case, then nothing about what I saw is set in stone. We can still change it, and I think avoiding the caves is the best plan."

"That's a lot of 'I thinks,'" Amanda pointed out, not angrily, but not in a particularly friendly tone either. "What are the alternatives?"

None seemed as good to me as the caves, but if Calista said to stay away from them, I would take her word for it. I also wanted to bring Amanda on board, though, especially since she seemed to know something about sasquatches too, so I answered her directly. "Since a few of us are able to shift, I'd like to go and locate the sasquatches before they can find us. If they really are possessed by this spirit, we have special restraints we need to get on at least one of them. Do you have any ideas how we might do that?"

Her back straightened and her chin tipped a little higher, as if she were pleased I had asked. "Yes, actually. Like I said, my pack has dealt with them before and we had a plan in place to trap and release them. We don't kill other creatures just because we don't like their species."

Those words seemed directed at Calista, but I ignored them to focus on the practical. "Good. You and Calista can compare notes and come up with a plan. Felix, you and I will gather a team to carry it out. Everyone else can make sure the entire pack is accounted for, stays in their groups, and gets themselves somewhere safe and secure. The school and the hospital both have siege plans in place, so you can start there. Are we all clear?"

A look passed between Calista and Amanda that I couldn't decipher, but they both gave their agreement, and with our plan in place, we set to work.

Chapter Forty-Two

~Calista~

Although I'd only known Skye for a few hours, the sudden silence in my head without her felt strangely unnatural. What would it be like for the others who had lived with their wolves all of their adult lives? I didn't blame them for being afraid and upset, and I understood why some of that anger would be directed at me, given what my parents had done.

Not everyone blamed me, though. Hearing Vaughan and Savannah stick up for me in the meeting, even though they had only known me a little more than a day and had every reason to be suspicious given the uncertainty around the whole situation, gave me a sense of acceptance and belonging I'd never really known before, or at least not since my own family died.

Deep down, I'd never truly felt I belonged in the life I'd been living for the past sixteen years, and after all the revelations of the day, I finally knew why. My adoptive parents never accepted me for me. They wanted their own version of me, the version that *wasn't* a werewolf. I'd always admired my parents for the selfless way they put the needs of other people before themselves, but apparently, that didn't carry over to me. My needs had been subverted to theirs, without my knowledge, and they'd done the same thing to Vaughan's pack, putting them all in danger.

Maybe they weren't planning their own attack as they'd attacked my pack, but by sabotaging them and doing their best to leave the werewolves defenseless, they put them in harm's way just as surely as if they had pulled the trigger themselves.

We were going to have a lot to talk about when I saw them again.

First, though, we still had the small matter of the sasquatches to deal with. Vaughan's suggestion that we try to capture one using the ash wrist cuffs that my dad had brought earlier made complete sense to me. If the spirit possessed all of them, capturing just one should be sufficient. The spirit would be trapped inside the body and an exorcism would destroy it. Maybe we wouldn't be able to track down the witch involved, but without the vengeful spirit, the witch's power would be diminished anyway. The pack would be safe. It seemed a reasonable, logical plan.

The only flaw was that he'd asked me to work with Amanda, who had just accused me, in front of the whole group, of plotting against them, lying to their faces, and tricking Vaughan into thinking we were mates. Vaughan told me there were no feelings between them but it didn't seem to be quite as simple as he'd made it sound. Still, if she knew how to trap a sasquatch and get the cuffs on, we should probably take her advice on board. My training focused on killing, not capturing, so despite my misgivings, I would have to put any hurt feelings I had aside and see what she had to say, for the good of Vaughan's pack.

"You two can use my office," Vaughan murmured to me as everyone stood up, the meeting having drawn to a close. "Felix and I will go into his."

"Thank you, Vaughan." The affection in his eyes and his faith in me were the only things standing between me and feeling completely adrift. He was my anchor in the new world opening up for me, and I truly appreciated it.

He squeezed my hand quickly before walking away just as Amanda came around the table to join me. Without a word, I headed down the hall to Vaughan's office, and we both took a seat in front of his desk, facing each other. Though it must have been a long day for her just as it had been for me, not a hair looked out of place, her face still fresh and her clothes far more stylish than anything I owned. She looked exactly like a politician's wife, which, in some ways, made complete sense for the role she had been about to take on. Vaughan was a leader, if not an elected one, and his partner would be in the public eye as well. In the short time I'd been there, I'd seen how the others deferred to him and sought him out, and I hadn't even begun to consider yet what that part of being with him would mean for me.

"Look, I know you don't trust me," I told her bluntly. We might as well acknowledge it instead of dancing around the issue. "I think we can both agree, though, that capturing these creatures takes precedence over anything else."

"That's why I'm here," she agreed, her words crisp and brittle but her jaw set with determination. "The Alpha trusts you, so what I think really doesn't matter. You'll learn that about werewolf packs soon enough."

Though I didn't know exactly what she meant by that, I meant what I said about where our priorities lay and I didn't intend to let myself get distracted. "What plan did your pack have in place for trapping a sasquatch?"

She followed my lead, sticking to the problem at hand. "Generally, they would only come onto our territory if they were hungry. Even if they aren't starving, they usually stop to eat if the opportunity presents itself. Food is the obvious bait, then, so we'd kill a deer or elk and leave it where they would be likely to stumble upon it. From there, we'd either use a sedative that would be absorbed through their hands when they picked up the carcass to feed on it, or we'd have someone wait nearby with a dart gun. Once sedated, we could transport them back out of our territory."

And they'd probably end up attacking human hikers before being hunted by people like me, I couldn't help thinking, but I kept those thoughts to myself. Antagonizing her any further would be counter-productive. "Would most packs have those kinds of sedatives? Would Vaughan's?"

"They should have something that would work. Most packs who live in the wilderness stock sedatives so they can deal with wild animals coming on their land. However, I'm not sure if food will motivate them this time around. If they're possessed, will they behave normally or will they be fixated on what the spirit wants them to do?"

I had just been thinking the same thing, and I talked through my thoughts out loud. "Possession makes the victim hungry as it takes a lot of energy, but in the cases we've seen with this spirit so far, the possessed creatures carried out their assigned tasks first before helping themselves to food; namely, killing the human occupants of the houses. So, I agree with you: using food as the bait before they've accomplished their goal might not work. Though they might be tempted by it, the spirit's commands would probably overpower those natural instincts."

Amanda nodded in agreement. "We'd need something else as bait, then. Something the spirit wants."

I pointed out the obvious, even though the thought of it made my throat close up with fear. "If my dream was accurate, it seemed to want Vaughan."

As those words came out of my mouth, I could hear how they might sound to her: she'd accused me of sabotaging the pack, and I just suggested we use the Alpha as bait. I braced myself for her disbelief or indignance, but instead, after staring at me in surprise for a moment, she actually began to smile.

"I can't decide if you're some kind of evil mastermind or a bit of an idiot."

That fit in so well with how out of control I felt that I found myself smiling back, despite the insult. "I'd like to think I'm not either. I'm just a woman in a situation I never expected to find myself in, trying to make sense of it."

Though her smile stayed on, something else flashed through her eyes. "Aren't we all?"

A twinge of guilt pricked at my stomach as I took in her words. However unintentional it had been, I *had* just stolen her fiancé. Vaughan had no feelings for her, but I didn't know for certain if she felt anything for him. Though I had no idea what to say, her rhetorical, somewhat ironic question gave me an opening to try to connect with her, and I tried to make the most of it.

"You might not believe me, but I really didn't plan any of this. I didn't even know what a mate was before today. I certainly never wanted to cause you any kind of trouble, since I had no idea you existed either. What's happening between me and Vaughan is completely unexpected and a little overwhelming, but in the end, it's his decision to make. I truly am sorry that you got caught in the middle of it."

Amanda's lips tightened as I spoke, but not necessarily in anger. She looked away from me, down at the floor, as she considered my words, the silence stretching out between us heavily as each second ticked by until she finally replied.

"I appreciate that he would do anything to be with his fated mate. That's what any werewolf *should* do. The timing is awfully coincidental, but perhaps that's just the way life goes sometimes. As I said, Vaughan trusts you, and as long as I'm here in this pack, I'll respect the Alpha's decisions. You don't have to worry about me."

It felt like there must be something more behind her reaction than what she said, but I knew from my own experience that sometimes, it could be easier to keep it inside. We didn't really have time for a full heart-to-heart, not that I had any experience with that sort of thing anyway. At least she seemed to have accepted I didn't want to actively hurt the pack, so for the time being, I would have to consider that a victory. "We should speak to Darius and find out what kind of sedation methods they have available and where on the territory would be the best place to lure the creatures."

Amanda nodded, getting to her feet. "I know where he'll be. Just a word of advice, though: maybe you could stop referring to supernatural beings as 'creatures', now that you are one."

She had a point, and my neck flushed with embarrassment. "I'll try."

Having settled into a tentative truce, we headed down the hall to the Delta's office to work out the rest of the plan.

CHAPTER FORTY-THREE

~**Vaughan**~

Any worry I might have had about sending Calista and Amanda off together got pushed to the background when Felix and I got to his office. As soon as the door closed behind us, he pushed past me, his eyes blazing.

"She's your mate?" His words were clipped and almost angry-sounding. "Why were you keeping it a secret?"

With everything else that happened in the meeting, Amanda's revelation to the group about Calista being my mate had been brushed over, but obviously, Felix had been stewing on it, waiting for a moment alone with me to ask me about it. "You know exactly why. She was a human hunter, so we thought, and I had just brought my chosen mate here. What could I do?"

He flopped down into the chair behind his desk, his jaw set. "You could have told your best friend what was going on."

Shit. It had been hurt rather than anger I heard in his voice. I seemed to be doing a great job of alienating just about everyone.

With a sigh, I lowered myself into the chair across from him. "And what would you have said if I told you?"

Practically, he couldn't have done anything, but he didn't focus on that. "I would have talked it through with you, helped you figure it out; you know, the things that a friend and a Beta is supposed to do. You might remember that the Alpha finding his mate is kind of a big deal for the whole pack, especially since it sounds like you tore up the agreement with Amanda?"

"I've already talked to her, yes. I know it'll screw things up, and I know it'll mean more work for you. I'm sorry about that, honestly, but Felix, what am I supposed to do? She's my mate. You're the one who told me to go with my gut back when I signed the contract in the first place. I didn't listen to you then, but I'm following your advice now, because my gut, my heart, my wolf, and every other part of my body is telling me that Calista is the one I'm meant to be with. I thought I could resist it but I can't. The bond is too strong. I need her, and I made my choice. There's no going back now."

I grew more impassioned as I spoke, leaning forward in my chair to try to impress upon him the earnestness of my feelings, and some of the tension went out of his shoulders as he sighed. "Fuck. You've got it bad."

It sure seemed that way, so I didn't bother to deny it. "I do. You remember how our dads used to shake their heads at us when we made fun of all the lovesick, newly-mated wolves, and tell us we'd understand when we found our mates? I get it now, and even though I know how annoying it is to hear it, I'm going to say it anyway: you'll understand when you find your mate."

Felix's eyes rolled almost to the back of his head but a smile had started on his face, letting me know my apology had been accepted, at least temporarily. "What's the plan now?"

"With Amanda or Calista?"

His smile grew wider. "Actually, I thought we might deal with the murderous Bigfoot family wandering our territory first before we focus on your love life any further, Alpha."

I threw him my dirtiest look. "You're the one who brought it up in the first place."

"True, but let's get down to business." He leaned forward, his elbows on the desk and his expression completely serious again. "Who's going to take these on the sasquatches?"

Ever since I said Felix and I would sort out a team, I'd been asking myself the same question. "You and me, obviously. Darius and his two lieutenants. Matthias, if he's still got his wolf."

He hadn't been in the meeting, and Felix shook his head. "I can't reach him by link, so I think he's a no."

Damn it. Leo and Savannah were out too since they'd also lost their wolves temporarily, and so had Calista. Even if Skye hadn't been silenced, I wouldn't have wanted her involved so soon after getting her wolf in the first place. As I'd already seen when she shifted mid-stride, she still had a few things to figure out.

"We need at least one more," Felix mused. "Maybe Amanda, since she's dealt with them before?"

The idea made me uneasy, probably because of the way she'd accused Calista of manipulating me in the meeting. "We don't have a mind-link to her, which makes it more difficult if we need to change things on the fly."

Felix didn't seem fazed by that. "We worked together pretty well in our wolf forms when we went out with you earlier. I think we could handle it."

He sounded certain, and I didn't have a better idea. Hopefully, her experience really would benefit us. "Alright. That's our core team, then. Someone will have to carry the ash cuffs and shift to their human form in order to put them on the sasquatch. I think that should be me."

Immediately, Felix shook his head. "I'll do it. You don't know the first thing about sasquatches."

"And you do?"

He gestured up to his pinboard of different supernatural beings on the wall. "I've met a hell of a lot more species than you have. You get to learn some of the similarities. Ask Calista, she'll tell you the same."

The thought of my mate immediately sent a warm, contented feeling through my chest, distracting me once again. "You like her, don't you, Felix?"

I'd never realized how important it would be to me that my Beta and my mate got along. They would be the two most significant people in my life, and life would be a lot easier if they could work together and genuinely enjoyed each other's company.

Felix snorted in reply. "Why? Are you going to change your mind about her if I don't?"

"Not a fucking chance."

He grinned at me again, his earlier hurt completely dissipated. "Good. And for the record, I do like her. Once she develops a sense of humour, we'll get along great."

She could be a little serious, but then, so could I. Maybe she wouldn't be a perfect match for Felix, but in the end, that didn't matter. She was a perfect match for me.

"Let's go find her and Amanda and see what they've come up with."

The women were already talking to Darius when we caught up to them, and quickly, they filled us in on what they'd decided about luring the sasquatches out.

"We thought you should be the bait," Calista told me apologetically. "In my dream, they went for you first. Maybe they can sense your authority. I know it's a lot to ask but..."

"Of course I'll do it." Using any of my pack members as live bait would have been hard for me to swallow, so I would much rather do it myself. "Felix is going to cuff the sasquatch while the other members of the team protect him and me. We can do this, and once we get him, you'll perform the exorcism, right?"

Calista's lips tightened in a way I already recognized. It meant she had something to tell me that she either didn't like or didn't think I would like. Maybe both. "Actually, I've never done one myself. I think it would be better if we had some backup."

"You don't mean..."

She couldn't possibly be saying what I thought, but she quickly confirmed I had it exactly right. "We need to get my parents here to help."

Chapter Forty-Four

~Calista~

Vaughan looked just about as thrilled with the idea of asking for my parents' help as I felt, but I had to be realistic. I knew my skills and strengths, and exorcism had never been one of them. My mom had the most experience and my dad could do them in a pinch, but I'd never done one on my own. With a spirit as powerful as this one seemed to be, it didn't seem like the best time to try to learn on the job.

"The hunters might not come back," Vaughan pointed out, not even able to bring himself to call them my parents. "They might think it's a trap and we want revenge for what they did."

That didn't seem very likely to me. "If they ask, I'll tell them I haven't told you they're behind the loss of your wolves. Even if they have some suspicions, I don't think it'll be a problem, though; they'll put aside any fear for their own safety in order to deal with the spirit."

The job came first, always. My parents might have surprised and disappointed me in other ways, but when it came to hunting, I felt certain I could predict what they'd do.

"I don't like it," Vaughan told me bluntly. "But I trust you. If you think it's necessary, then make the call."

Giving me a nod, he strode off to deal with the next thing on his list while I pulled out my phone. Vaughan's support meant a great deal to me and made me feel stronger than I would have on my own, but my fingers still hovered over the call button a few seconds longer than necessary while I steeled myself to try to pretend I didn't know exactly what my parents had done.

My dad answered on the second ring. "Any news?"

Straight to business, as I expected. "You mean besides the fact that you poisoned the werewolves' water supply?"

I hissed the words as if I didn't want to be overheard, so he wouldn't know the werewolves already knew about it.

A touch of guilt coloured my dad's reply. "I know you wanted to wait but we had the opportunity and your mom convinced me we couldn't put it off. It worked, I guess?"

"Their wolves are gone, if that's what you mean."

I could almost picture the way he would have winced on the other end. "Are the children okay?"

Now he cared about the children? Thankfully, they didn't seem to have done any damage to the pack's younger members, but that had been far from certain, as his question made clear. "I haven't heard about any severe side effects yet, but you didn't need to be so underhanded about it. They would have worked with us if you gave them the chance. Now, they've got sasquatches on the loose on their land and no way for them to defend themselves."

"Sasquatches?" My dad sounded almost as confused by that as the werewolves had.

I gave him the short version, knowing he would put it together as quickly as I had. "I think they're possessed by the spirit. We're going to try to capture one of them and put the ash cuffs on, at which point we'll need to do an exorcism. I don't have enough experience to do it. That's why I'm calling."

He immediately focused on the practical. "Have you got some kind of sedative?"

"They're working on it now. I'll handle this side, just get here as soon as you can. Hopefully, we'll have a possessed sasquatch waiting for you."

"We're on our way," he promised, hanging up before I could reply, and in the silence, a painful pang of betrayal hit me. He sounded just the same as he always did, ready to have my back, but I no longer trusted his intentions as I once had. That hurt almost as much as if I'd lost him entirely.

Shoving my phone back in my pocket, I headed down the hall to the entrance where Vaughan and the others had gathered. Just before I reached them, though, a smaller group of them suddenly headed to the door, including Vaughan and Felix, taking off at a sprint.

"What's going on?" I asked Savannah, who had stayed behind.

"They just got an alert that a sasquatch is attacking a house on the edge of town, close to the forest. They're going to protect the people inside."

It seemed we had no more time for planning. My eyes flitted over to the door that Vaughan had just gone through as I tried not to remember the image from my dream of him being dragged into the forest by the possessed creatures. Fear gripped my chest, squeezing at my heart that had been empty for so long until Vaughan woke it up again and filled it with the promise of something new. A new home. A new life. A new love.

He had to survive this. He *had* to, and since fixating on it or worrying about him wouldn't help me at all, I needed to do something practical. Focusing on the job had always calmed me before, and I dug deep to do it again. "Where did we get with a sedative? Did you find one?"

"Sedative?" Her furrowed brow made it clear she had no idea what I meant.

"Amanda said she would ask if your pack had any kind of sedatives to help subdue the sasquatch so they could be cuffed."

"And she did." Leo came over to join our conversation, holding a case in his hands. Like the other men in the pack, he was tall and fairly broad, his dark hair cut short and his lips a deep, natural shade of red, but he didn't look either as serious as Vaughan or as friendly as Felix, falling somewhere in between. "I just went to get it from our armoury."

I didn't know too many people who had their own armoury, but I appreciated that they were prepared. "Let's have a look."

A side table stood along the wall in the entrance hall with a large wood carving of a wolf on it. Savannah moved the statue onto the floor as Leo put the case on the table and flipped the locks open. Inside the case sat a dart gun with four vials, carefully packed.

"I'm not sure what's in the vials, and I don't know how to use the gun," Leo admitted. "I take care of inventory, not defense."

"That's fine. I have a good idea what it is, and I can definitely use it." Reaching into the case, I pulled out the dart gun, spun the chamber open and loaded one of the darts into it, clicking it back into place all in a matter of seconds.

Savannah's eyes were wide when I looked back up. "That was so cool."

No one had ever thought of me as cool before and I didn't really know how to respond to it, so I didn't say anything, focusing on what we needed to do next instead. "Let's go find the others, they might need our help."

"Wait, please." Leo put out his hand to stop me. "We haven't had a chance to talk yet. I'm the pack Gamma."

I didn't know exactly what that meant, and we really didn't have time for small talk, not when my mate might be in danger. Everything else paled next to the thought of losing him. "Nice to meet you. Let's go."

I tried again to step away, and again, he stopped me. "I owe you an apology, Calista. I've been trying to keep Vaughan away from you but I didn't realize you were his mate. None of us did."

Despite my urge to get to Vaughan, his words piqued my curiosity and I allowed myself one question. "Why did you want to keep him away from me?"

"As Gamma, it's my duty to serve and protect the Luna. I thought that was going to be Amanda so I've been trying to look out for her, but I never meant it personally against you. I know it might take a while to earn your trust now, but I'll do my best to make it up to you."

He looked so contrite that, even though I still barely understood a word he said, I accepted his apology. "It's fine, Leo. You can make it up to me by helping me get to Vaughan now. We need to help them trap the sasquatch and I need you to help me find them. Alright?"

"Yes. Absolutely." He gave me a tentative smile and Savannah nodded at me from beside him. "Let's get to work."

Chapter Forty-Five

~Vaughan~

The panicked call for help came to both me and Felix at the same time. I didn't recognize the voice, but I imagined Felix would.

Alpha, Beta! There's something at the door, trying to get in. It's big and hairy, with giant claws.

That sounded like a sasquatch all right. So much for our plan to bait the sasquatches out and set a trap. *Where are you?* I asked first. When the man gave us his address, I quickly followed up with another question. *How many of you can shift?*

Only two. The rest have lost their wolves and we've got some children with us too. We need help.

We're on our way, Felix assured him before connecting with the small team we'd put together. *Change of plan: we're heading out now!*

Since Amanda still had no link to us, standing there next to Savannah completely oblivious to what had just gone on inside our heads, I gave her the news in person. "The sasquatches are on the move. We have to go."

The three of us raced out the door, shifting as soon as we got outside, and headed straight for the house on the edge of the town. Darius and his two lieutenants met us along the way, making us a pack of six. As we drew closer, a foreign scent reached us, the same smell I'd noticed in the forest earlier with Calista, which she'd identified as the scent of a sasquatch. With all those clues, I shouldn't have been surprised when the house came into view and I caught my first glimpse of the beings in question, but it still managed to shock me anyway.

I supposed I'd been picturing the cheesy Bigfoot from low-budget TV shows, but the reality that greeted us couldn't be much more different. Three of them had gathered in front of the humble home at the edge of town, and my heart sank at the sight of them. These were no humans covered in fake fur. Well over eight feet tall and looking like a cross between a mountain gorilla and a bear, they were wide, solid, and, to be honest, rather terrifying. Long claws sprouted from their humanoid hands and feet. Their faces were devoid of hair, with large eyes, flat noses, and mouths full of sharp teeth we could see as they let out a roar that wouldn't have sounded out of place coming from a mountain lion. My heart pounded with adrenaline, the need to protect my pack so strong that it drowned out any fear.

As quickly as possible, I surveyed the situation to come up with a plan, linking to the others in my small group. *We need to separate them and get them away from the house. Divide and conquer. There's three of them and six of us so we'll split into pairs. Felix, you take Amanda.*

Everyone gave their assent and Sam, one of Darius' men, came with me as we led the way, running straight towards the house to get the sasquatches' attention. Our paws pounded the cold forest floor, the chill biting into the pads of our feet and our breath coming out in puffs in the cool night air.

As Atlas let out a howl, all three of the beasts turned towards us. In their eyes, I could see the same blank, single-minded purpose that had been in Tim's eyes when he attacked me that afternoon. Clearly, they weren't acting under their own volition, just as Calista theorized, and as they turned from the house to give chase to us, they seemed to have just one thing on their mind.

Destruction.

Sam and I went for the largest one, running around him just out of reach, and he quickly gave chase, his movements surprisingly nimble for a being of his size. Large claws swiped at me, only missing by inches as we tried to lead him back into the forest. My fur ruffled with the wind created by his movement. A sound somewhere between a roar and a growl rumbled out of him and shrieks of terror answered from inside the house behind us as we did our best to lead him away from it.

I'm calling for more backup, Felix's voice said in my head. *They're faster than I thought.*

I had to agree. The six of us against one of them might have worked, but at two-to-one, we felt significantly outnumbered. *Let's lead them back towards the pack house. Leo should have the sedative by now.*

Leo had gone to retrieve what we had after Amanda asked about it, but since he couldn't shift, he wouldn't be able to move as fast as we could. Bringing the sasquatches to him made more sense than making him try to track us down through the forest.

Sam, can you head him off on the left...

I had just started to share my plan with my teammate when the sasquatch made another wide, forceful swipe with its paw, and made contact with Sam as he tried to cross in front of the beast's feet. The sasquatch's sharp, long claws went straight through his side, impaling Sam's wolf and bringing him to his mouth. Through horror-filled eyes, I watched as the sasquatch bit the wolf's head clean off.

No!

Nausea and fury bubbled up inside me as Atlas let out a howl of pain at the loss of our second pack member in the same day. It physically hurt, cutting straight to my heart and fuelling both my anger and the desire to bring all of this madness to an end.

The spirit had a lot to fucking answer for.

Swallowing down the bile that had risen in my throat, I pressed on. *Sam's gone,* I let Felix know as Atlas cut back behind the sasquatch, trying to throw him off balance.

Shit. Felix sounded just as shell-shocked as I felt. *Darius is down too. Puncture wound from a claw but hopefully he'll be okay. I've called for medical help. Everyone at the pack house who can still shift is heading to us now.*

I set off in that direction even faster than before, the sasquatch coming after me on all fours in the darkness, gaining on me with its superior size. When I caught sight of the wolves approaching ahead of me, I called out a general warning through my pack-wide link. *Watch its claws. Stay out of reach, attack only from behind. Like this.*

In their view, Atlas ducked back behind the creature and attacked the back of its leg, causing the sasquatch to roar in frustration. As he tried to swipe behind his back to reach us, Atlas jumped out of the way, and the beast's claws dug into his own skin, making him cry out again.

Taking my lead, the three wolves in front of me began circling the sasquatch, keeping a wide berth in the front and darting in around the back to attack. The beast swung its claws wildly, trying to hold us off, and soon, I saw my chance. As he turned to the side to try to see behind him, Atlas leapt up, climbing up the sasquatch's body like a tree, his claws digging into the beast's hairy hide, and bit down onto his neck.

The roar the sasquatch let out made his whole body vibrate, and Atlas rumbled along with it as he clung onto the creature for dear life. Sensing their opportunity, the other wolves all attacked at the same time, and soon, three of us were hanging off of him as the sasquatch stumbled around wildly, his arms flailing as he tried to shake us off. Atlas' teeth remained embedded in the beast's neck, blood pooling in the holes his teeth had made, until he was able to get leverage with all four paws.

One of the other wolves was thrown off and stepped on as the sasquatch continued to stumble around, but finally, Atlas got his positioning just right. *This is for Sam,* he told me as he bit in deeper, and pulled back, ripping out the creature's throat. The sasquatch stumbled forward for a few more steps before veering dangerously to one side and, finally, he toppled over on the forest floor, bringing a tree down with him as he fell. The crash thundered through the forest, sending birds scattering up into the night sky above the trees.

Just the same as when Tim died, a steamy cloud gathered above the sasquatch's lifeless body before disappearing.

Covered in blood and panting from the exertion, Atlas disentangled himself while I mentally checked in with the others. *Are you all okay?*

Bonnie needs help, one of the wolves told me, gesturing with his head to the one who'd been stepped on. *I've just linked to the medical team.*

Good. Stay here with her for now, I instructed before reaching out to Felix. *This one is dead. Where are you?*

Around the rear of the house. We could use your help.

Immediately, I took off in that direction with a new bolt of energy, and as soon as I rounded the house, I could see Felix, Amanda and a couple of other wolves doing their best to keep the sasquatch at bay. At the same time, Leo, Savannah and Calista appeared from inside, Calista holding onto a weapon with steady, practiced hands.

That had to be the sedative. We just needed to get her a clear shot, so I raced out into the open space of the back lawn, howling to draw the sasquatch's attention.

Once again, it worked. They seemed to respond to my howl, perhaps recognizing somehow that I must be the Alpha. The sasquatch broke free of the wolves around it, charging towards me like an angry bull while I held my ground, hoping Calista's aim lived up to Felix's description from the night he first met her.

Closer and closer the beast came, its flat nostrils flaring and drool stringing down from its snarled, bared teeth, its eyes fixed on me and nothing else. My wolf's heavy breaths evaporated in puffs of cloud above us in the cold night air.

Steady, I reassured Atlas as his paws twitched beneath us, wanting to move out of the way for the sake of self-preservation. *Just three more seconds. Three... two...*

The dart from Calista's gun hit the sasquatch directly in the side of the neck, but it didn't seem to slow it down any.

One! Move! I shouted at my wolf as he darted out of the way at the very last second.

The sasquatch spun around, trying to grab me, and as the sedative began to kick in, it lost its balance. A dark shadow blotted out the light of the moon above me as several hundred pounds of hairy beast came tumbling down directly on top of me.

CHAPTER FORTY-SIX

~Calista~

My heart seemed to stop as the newly-sedated sasquatch stumbled and fell directly onto Vaughan's wolf. Shock sucked all the air out of my lungs and my vision narrowed until all I could see was the huge, hairy form of the creature laying on the ground with one of Atlas' paws sticking out from beneath it.

Would I feel it if he were gone? Did we change my dream only enough to change the *way* he died, not the fact that he did?

"Vaughan!" Savannah screamed her brother's name as she ran forward, dragging me along with her. My feet seemed to have forgotten how to move on their own, but with her help, we reached the scene just as Felix and the other wolves shifted back.

"Get him out," Felix ordered, looking more serious than I'd ever seen him. "Everyone, lift!"

Placing the dart gun I still held down on the ground, I grabbed onto the sasquatch's side, with Savannah next to me and Amanda on my other side. A completely naked Amanda. All the wolves who had just shifted back were naked, but no one seemed to care, not when we were all focused on getting Vaughan out.

"Now!" Felix commanded, and with all my strength, amplified by fear and adrenaline, I lifted. The sasquatch must have weighed five hundred pounds easily, and on my own, I never would have had a chance. Working as a team, though, we got his body off the ground, and Felix and one of the other men managed to grab Atlas from beneath him, pulling him gently to safety before giving us the all-clear.

With a mighty thud, the sasquatch's limp body fell back to the ground as everyone abandoned it to crowd around Vaughan instead.

"Is he okay?" Sav called out, squeezing her way through to the front.

"Alpha?" someone else said, sounding almost lost.

I couldn't even get through, only getting glimpses of the motionless wolf's body lying on the ground. My feet had frozen to the ground again, my chest filled with the ice as the space that Vaughan had so recently warmed turned cold again.

"Everyone, step back," Amanda called out, surprising everyone by taking charge. "Leo, get the cuffs on the sasquatch. Anyone who can still shift should go help with the third sasquatch, it's still on the loose. Calista and Savannah can take care of Vaughan. Felix, I assume you've already called for medical attention?"

"I'll do it right now," he promised, also looking a little stunned at Amanda's forcefulness but deferring to her suggestions anyway. "Everyone move out, do what she said."

As they all moved out of the way, a path finally opened in front of me and my heart sank even further. Atlas was covered in blood, his fur matted and dripping with it, especially around his face, and my knees buckled beneath me.

No. Please don't let him die. Don't let me lose him too.

I didn't even know who or what I was pleading with, the words rushing through my mind without any clear direction. Savannah immediately grabbed hold of me, helping me to find my balance as we both got down onto our knees.

"He's still alive," she whispered to me, and the fact that she even had to state it reinforced just how much it looked like he might not be. "The whole pack would feel it if the Alpha died."

I gulped in a deep breath, taking some comfort from that thought. So many hunters died solitary deaths, with no one knowing for sure what happened to them or if they had even died at all. Being connected to others on such a primal, physiological level appealed to me in a way I didn't realize it would.

Once we were bonded, I would feel it too. *Please let me have that chance.*

As I reached out to touch Atlas' neck, looking for a pulse, pain ripped through my head again.

"Your wolf is trying to get through," Savannah guessed as I winced. "She wants to help her mate."

Atlas took a big breath as my hand finally connected with his skin. Even if his wolf form, I could feel the sparks between us, and the pain in my head grew even stronger as Skye fought against the medication holding her down.

A moment later, a group of people came running out of the pack house towards us. "We'll take the Alpha inside," one of them said. "The doctor will be here soon, she's just checking on someone else."

"Is it safe to move him?" He'd just been crushed beneath the sasquatch's girth; what if the impact broke his back? All my first aid training suggested that movement could be dangerous.

Werewolves might be different, though, and Savannah quickly confirmed I didn't need to worry. "Because of our shifting ability, our bones are more flexible, and able to heal better than humans. Broken bones aren't a big deal. We should get him comfortable."

Taking her word for it, I got back to my feet, still holding onto Savannah for support as the others gently lifted Atlas and carried him back inside the house. They took him straight upstairs to Vaughan's room, and I followed behind, barely giving a glance to the chunky, masculine furniture in shades of black and grey. Extra sheets had already been laid across the king-sized bed, and the men carrying Atlas lay him down gently before respectfully withdrawing, leaving me and Savannah alone with him.

Despite my head still aching, I reached for him again, and as soon as my fingers brushed against his skin, Atlas stirred again, letting out a soft whimper that drew an answering ache in my head.

"I'm here," I whispered, hoping Vaughan might be able to hear me from inside Atlas' mind. "Whatever you need, I'm right here."

It didn't take long for the doctor to arrive, and when I went to move back to let her examine him, she told me to stay close. "A wolf's mate is often the best medicine of all. He'll feel you nearby and it will give him strength."

My eyes widened in surprise as I gaped up at her. "How did you know I'm his mate?" We'd never met before.

She and Savannah exchanged knowing smiles. "Word travels fast in a werewolf pack, even when half of them can't mind-link. Now, let's check his vitals."

Her calm, professional presence helped to soothe my worry. My heart rate began to slow, making me realize just how fast it had been beating in the first place, and when she finished her assessment, she confirmed things weren't as bad as they seemed. "The blood doesn't seem to be his. He had the air knocked out of him and a few bones broken, but he'll heal from all that quickly. The biggest problem is that he must have hit his head. He should be conscious in a matter of minutes, but if he's not, call me and I'll come back." Obviously, she had other places to be, and as she got to her feet, she asked Savannah to go with her. "I could use an assistant right now. Are you available?"

"Go," I confirmed when Sav looked to me for permission. "I'll stay with him." I thought she might protest, or that someone would. After all, not that long ago, I'd been accused of poisoning the pack on purpose, and there I was, asking them to leave me alone with the injured Alpha. However, no one said a word about it, and that simple act of trust meant more to me than any words could.

"Talk to him," the doctor advised. "Let him feel your bond. That can only help."

With that, they both left, closing the door behind them so that Vaughan and I were alone. Or, Atlas and I were alone, at least. I couldn't be sure if Vaughan was even aware of me or anything else that was happening.

He knows you're here. He can sense it, even if he's not consciously aware of it.

Skye! My wolf's voice in my head sounded weak, as it had been when she first came to me, but I could hear her and instantly, I didn't feel so alone anymore. The medication in the water must not have been as strong as when I drank it directly from the vials. My parents must have been counting on the fact that the wolves would continue to ingest it over time. Or maybe it had to do with what the doctor said about the mate bond helping to heal; maybe Atlas; despite his weakened state, helped Skye to be strong enough to break through again. *We need to help Atlas and Vaughan. What should I do?*

Touch him. Talk to him. You remember how safe you felt when your dad came to comfort you after a nightmare? That's how it feels to Vaughan to have you nearby.

Obviously, she meant my real dad, my werewolf father, and I *could* remember that feeling, just barely. Trying to hold onto it, I ran my hands through Atlas' fur, ignoring the blood as I gently stroked his face.

"I'm here, Vaughan. We got the sasquatch. *You* got him. You were so brave out there. We just need to do the exorcism and we can put an end to this. My parents are on the way here and I need you there with me. I need you to help me figure out how to be a werewolf and what I'm supposed to do about everything. I need... you."

The last word came out almost as a sob, startling me as the thought of not having him pressed down on my chest, making it harder to breathe.

Though his eyes remained closed, Atlas' body began to change. The fur disappeared back into his skin, his nose flattened and his legs grew longer, slow at first and growing faster, until instead of a bloody wolf, a blood-stained naked man lay there, his brown hair matted just as his wolf's fur had been.

"Okay." The word was far weaker than Vaughan usually sounded, but the sound of him saying anything at all made my heart leap. "Just give me a minute."

A laugh of relief and surprise spilled out of me. The injuries didn't seem to have affected his dry sense of humour. "Of course. What can I do?"

One brown eye opened, peering over at me with a mischievousness that made my stomach flip and my heart soar. "I don't think I can stand up just yet, but I need to get cleaned. How about a sponge bath?"

Chapter Forty-Seven

~Vaughan~

Calista's eyebrows shot up when I suggested that she help me get cleaned up. Her gaze dropped to my blood-smeared skin before returning to my face, and I had no clue if she took my request seriously or not.

As soon as I regained consciousness and realized where I was, just before I shifted back, I linked with Felix for an update. He told me that the third sasquatch had just been killed. The sedated one had been chained to a nearby tree to keep him in one place until the hunters arrived to perform the exorcism, and it would still be a while before they arrived. He told me to take my time recovering and he'd let me know if anyone needed me urgently.

Therefore, we had a bit of time before we had to be anywhere, so if she wanted to help me clean up, I certainly wouldn't complain. When I made the suggestion, I meant it partly tongue-in-cheek, but partly not; I *did* need to get cleaned up and I didn't have the strength yet to get up. It would be more efficient with her assistance, and far more fun.

"You scared me." Calista's quiet admission took me by surprise, and it startled me even more to see tears pooling in the corners of her eyes. She hadn't out-and-out said she cared for me yet, but that felt pretty close, especially as she looked away after she said it, like she couldn't handle looking directly at me. "I'm no stranger to dangerous situations and people getting hurt or worse, but I've never felt as afraid as I did just now."

She didn't need to explain any further. As protective as I might be of my entire pack, what I felt for her already, in the short time I'd known her, hit even stronger. "That's because of the bond. We're linked, you and I. Losing you would be like losing a part of myself."

"And I almost lost you, when I only just found you."

Her lips pressed together tightly, trying to keep her emotions in. She always seemed so in control that I could tell the idea of letting that control slip scared her, but I never wanted her to feel she had to keep a guard up with me.

I opened my arms to her. "I'm fine, Calista. Come here."

Despite the blood and dirt caked onto my body, she came straight into my arms, lying down and nestling herself into the space at my side. My arms encircled her, letting her feel the sparks of our bond everywhere our skin connected, letting it soothe her the same as it did for me. Her breathing evened out, the tears retreating from her eyes as she felt for herself that I would be just fine.

"I've never felt anything like this bond," she admitted, her voice coming out muffled against my side. "I'm not usually so emotional. Is it a good idea to be so attached to just one person?"

"Everything I've been told suggests that the benefits hugely outweigh the negatives. And as for your emotions, it might be because of the bond, and it might be reconnecting with your wolf too. Finding the other half of yourself. It's a big change."

"You can say that again." We lay there in silence for a couple more minutes before she sat up again, her vulnerability put back in its place and her determined side in control again. "Where can I find a wash-cloth?"

A satisfied smile spread across my face as I realized her question meant she intended to wash me after all. "In my bathroom. There's a bowl beneath the sink. Towels and cloths are in the cabinet."

As she got up and went into the adjoining room to find what she needed, it struck me how natural it felt to have her there with me. My room had always been my private sanctuary, the one place on pack land that belonged to only me, but when it came to Calista, I wouldn't mind sharing at all. She simply belonged there.

"That was a great shot, by the way, when you hit the sasquatch," I called out loud enough that she could hear me.

"Thanks." I could just hear her reply over the sounds of rattling and doors opening and closing in the other room. A second later, the water taps turned on. "It's a female, by the way."

"What is?"

"The sasquatch. I noticed when we lifted her off of you."

I definitely hadn't noticed, and I wasn't sure why she brought it up. Before I could ask, she reappeared in the bathroom doorway holding a metal bowl full of water, a washcloth and a towel. My cock instantly twitched to life, blood pumping to it at the mere thought of Calista touching me.

When it came to her, it didn't take much to get me turned on.

"Sasquatches mate for life too," she explained as she came back to the bed and took a seat next to me. Dipping the washcloth into the water, she squeezed it firmly to wring the water out, her hands sure and steady, and every single movement far sexier than it had any right to be. "There's a good chance that one of the other ones you killed was her mate, and it's not their fault that they attacked you. They didn't do it any more intentionally than your pack members attacked those humans, and now, even if she survives the exorcism, she'll be alone."

I didn't feel great about that, but I also didn't see what other choice we had. "It would be easier if they were purely bad, but most beings aren't, not even supernatural ones. They don't deserve to die and neither did the humans. We have to defend ourselves and sometimes, there's collateral damage."

"You sound like my mom. My hunter mom, I mean." Calista's expression was thoughtful as she wiped the cloth across my chest, scrubbing at the stained blood there. Even through the cloth, I could feel a low hum of electricity where she pressed down against my skin.

"That doesn't sound like a compliment." Based on what her parents had done, any kind of comparison felt like a double-edged sword at best.

"I didn't mean it as an insult." Her brow furrowed as she scrubbed my neck clean, making sure she got all of the blood. As she pressed down on the spot that would bear her mark if she accepted me, a shiver trailed through my whole body, diverting the blood south again. "I've just always found the dichotomy between my parents interesting. My dad always sympathizes with the creatures we hunt, no matter what they've done, while my mom is more black-and-white. Despite my werewolf family's innocence, she doesn't feel any regret about killing them because they made the best choice they could have at the time. Sometimes, I envy her that certainty, even if I don't always agree with it. I think I probably fall somewhere between those two extremes."

"I guess I probably fall somewhere in the middle too. As Alpha, I have to make the tough choices sometimes, but it doesn't mean I don't feel regret about them." My eyes closed as she ran the cloth over my face. The water in the bowl turned pink with blood as she rinsed the cloth out again. "I don't enjoy killing but the world we live in can be brutal. You know that better than anyone."

Calista nodded in agreement as she scrubbed the last blood from my face, and her blue eyes looked down into mine with understanding. "I guess being in the middle makes more sense, and at least we can be there together."

That sounded pretty damn good to me. I would have sat up and pulled her into a kiss right then, but with my body still healing, I couldn't manage it.

Rinsing out the washcloth again, Calista began to move lower down my body. When she reached my semi-erect cock, she gave it a wide berth, wiping the cloth down one hip, across my thighs, and up the other side.

When she repeated the motion for a third time, I couldn't hold back my chuckle. "You didn't seem so afraid of touching me earlier."

Her blue eyes shot up to mine, indignant and a little embarrassed. "I'm not afraid."

"Then clean me everywhere," I challenged.

"Fine."

The cloth brushed over my cock so lightly, I barely felt it, and I laughed again. "You can scrub a little harder. You're not going to hurt me."

"I know that." A blush crept up her cheeks, making her look even prettier than before. "I'm just not used to... I don't even know what to call it. Casual touching?"

My eyes searched her face as she turned back to her tasks, scrubbing down my shins and to my feet. "What do you mean? You've had sex before."

Though she hadn't out-and-out told me that, I felt certain of it from her reactions to me.

Calista kept her gaze down, her eyes focused on my legs. "Yes, but it's always been... functional, I guess. Not a lot of foreplay or intimacy that didn't lead directly to sex."

That didn't sound like a lot of fun. "Well, if you agree to be my mate, I'm going to be touching you a lot, I'll give you fair warning right now. And I'd love it if you touched me too. Maybe you should give it a try."

Finally, she looked back over at me, her eyebrows raised and a hesitant smile pulling at her lips. "Right now?"

"Felix has things under control downstairs. We're not going to have sex, especially since my body is still healing, but you can touch me. As much or as little as you like."

The hesitation on her face fell away as her eyes returned to my cock and she set her mouth into the determined expression I'd come to recognize from her.

When her fingers connected with my shaft, lifting my cock to wrap her hand fully around it, any lingering pain disappeared as pleasure filled me from head to toe. "Fuck," I breathed, struggling to keep my eyes open, torn between surrendering to the sensations and watching her as she explored me.

The washcloth dropped into the bowl as Calista turned all her attention to me. Slowly, her fingers traced down my entire length, running over the ridge of my head and the veins crossing my shaft until she reached my balls. A hiss escaped my lips as she cupped them in her hand, gently rolling them around in her fingers before her hand drifted even lower, pressing against the spot between my balls and ass that made me groan. If I were a cat shifter rather than a wolf, I would have been purring.

With her hand on me, just like when we were together earlier, the rest of the world disappeared. I didn't have to be the Alpha, I didn't have to think about the pack and their needs. With her, I could simply *be*.

Her boldness grew with every sound she drew from me, the pressure of her hand getting stronger and her pace going faster. She spit into her palm to add some lubrication and the rough and dirty action sent another rush of blood straight to my cock. It pulsed beneath her touch, every stroke like heaven until I couldn't keep my eyes open longer. My head fell back, my eyes closing as every part of me focused on the sparks she ignited inside me.

"Fuck, Callie." I groaned out her name as I came, my warm cum spurting all over my stomach while her movements slowed, milking every drop from me until my cock stopped jerking in her hand.

"That was fun." My mate sounded almost surprised, with a touch of pride in her voice as she grabbed the washcloth again and wiped away the evidence of what she'd just done to me.

"Very fun," I agreed, grinning up at her when she leaned down to give me a soft kiss on the lips before going into the bathroom to wash out the bowl and cloth.

Only when my heart rate had returned to normal, my thoughts clearing after my orgasm, did I realize what I just called her.

I used her childhood nickname, and as I thought about it, a memory stirred deep inside me, a memory I didn't realize I had of the day that Felix and I first discovered the caves on our land. Whenever I thought about it before, the other boys that had been with us were fuzzy and undefined, but as I lay on my bed, my body relaxed and my soul happy, I could hear one of them clearly.

"This looks like a cave for monsters to live in," one of the boys exclaimed gleefully before turning to the one next to him. "We should bring Callie here."

"Dad said not to tease her anymore," the other one reminded him. "He said there's no such thing as monsters."

Obviously, he'd been wrong, and as the memory faded, a wave of understanding washed over me. Those boys in the cave must have been Calista's brothers, and that memory must have taken place shortly before they died along with the rest of the pack. After that, the caves were resealed, and not long after we reopened them, the danger to our own pack had started.

It couldn't be a coincidence. It had to mean something, and by the time Calista returned from the bathroom, I had already gotten to my feet.

"Are you feeling well enough to get up?" she asked in concern as I stretched out my sore limbs.

"I'm good enough, and we need to go and talk to Felix. I think I might know why the spirit is after us."

Chapter Forty-Eight

~**Calista**~

When I went into the bathroom to clean up from Vaughan's sponge bath and hand job, I left him lying on the bed, looking weak but completely satisfied. The power I had to bring him pleasure gave me a heady feeling, and seeing how turned on he got turned me on too. Foreplay with him would be very different than with anyone else, I could already tell, and if what just happened gave me a small taste of it, I already wanted more.

However, when I returned to the bedroom no more than a couple of minutes later, I found Vaughan on his feet and starting to get dressed, looking full of purpose.

"I think I might know why the spirit is after us," he said, but he refused to elaborate until we could speak to Felix. As soon as he had some new clothes on, he headed to the door, his balance not quite back to normal but his determination making up for it.

The Beta met us at the bottom of the stairs, having been summoned through Vaughan's mind-link. His relief at seeing his friend and Alpha relatively unharmed warmed my heart, but in his focused state, Vaughan didn't even seem to notice. He led both of us to his office where we could speak uninterrupted. The dark sky outside transformed the large window into a mirror, reflecting back the sight of the three of us sitting down in front of Vaughan's desk, forming a circle that made me feel like an equal, when just the night before, I had been their prisoner. So much had changed since then, I could hardly make sense of it all.

"I just heard from our border team," Felix told us before Vaughan could say anything. "Calista's parents are here. They're being accompanied to the house."

I didn't miss the fact that he specified they would be accompanied, unlike the last time. Understandably, no one trusted them anymore.

"We don't have much time, then," Vaughan pointed out. "But something occurred to me that I think might be important. Felix, do you remember the first time we found the caves, when we were kids?"

Though I didn't know what he meant, Felix obviously did. "Of course. Why?"

Vaughan answered the question with another. "Do you remember who else was with us?"

A frown stole across Felix's face as he searched his memory, looking out of character for him even from the short time I'd known him. Hopefully, it wouldn't be long before he'd have a reason to smile again. "There were six of us: you, me, Billy, Alex and..." He trailed off for a moment, his eyes widening in surprise before he completed his sentence. "Calista's brothers."

"My brothers?" I repeated. In all the other revelations of the day, I'd barely registered the fact that I once had brothers, and I had no idea what they had to do with our current predicament.

Vaughan clearly expected that answer since he nodded in confirmation. "I think that's important. They were with us when we found the caves, and in a matter of weeks, they and their whole pack, other than Calista, were dead. The caves were sealed back up, and only reopened a few weeks ago."

A shiver ran down my spine as I quickly grasped onto the implication of his words. "You think the spirit is connected to the caves."

Appreciation shone in Vaughan's eyes at my conclusion, along with concern. "I do. I don't know how spirits work, if they're tied to people or places, but it seems possible to me that by opening the caves, we disturbed something. Some supernatural being, some kind of force who didn't like having their space invaded."

It made total sense to me, and it frustrated me that I hadn't considered something similar before then. Of course, I hadn't known about my brothers finding the cave, which completed a rather large piece of the puzzle. It suggested a common motive for the two incidents, and it made sense with the other information I had. "When my dad did some research into the murders, he came across some local legends about shapeshifters who attacked early settlers. Perhaps the same spirit was at work then; maybe those early settlers also found the caves and paid for it with their lives."

"It could be some kind of ancient burial site," Felix added eagerly, looking just as excited about the potential breakthrough as I felt. "The spirit might be cursebound to an item or even some of the bones inside through some kind of ancient magic."

"Felix is a bit of a supernatural enthusiast," Vaughan explained to me, giving his friend an indulgent smile. "That's why you ran into him when you were out tracking the wendigo."

The idea of a werewolf studying other species for fun struck me as a little strange, but I supposed that, in the end, there was no reason they couldn't have an interest in the supernatural. In the end, they were just like anyone else. Just like *me*.

More than that, I had to agree that Felix could be on to something. "In the past, the spirit possessed some kind of shifter to carry out the attacks. This time around, both against my pack and yours, instead of attacking the packs directly, it possessed the werewolves to attack humans, resulting in attacks against the wolves by hunters."

"Why wouldn't it just attack us directly?" Vaughan wondered.

"You've just shown why tonight. You're too strong. Even when he sent sasquatches against you, you were able to defeat them. I'm surprised it even tried. Maybe it only did because it knew…"

I trailed off as one more piece slotted into the puzzle taking shape in my mind, one that made my stomach sink even more than it already had. Just when I thought things had gotten as bad as they could, they got a little bit worse.

"It knew what?" Felix asked, he and Vaughan hanging on my every word, so I forced the rest of my statement out.

"They must have known my parents would be working to silence your wolves. My parents are pretty private about their hunting techniques, though. I don't think they would have told anybody else about that."

Vaughan and Felix exchanged confused, curious looks. "What does that mean?" Vaughan asked.

"It means that the spirit is somehow involved with my parents."

As I thought back over everything that had happened: the attack on my own pack and the way my mom had shown no remorse over it, how she had pushed us towards attacking Vaughan's pack, not wanting to consider any other potential solutions, and how she *had* gone ahead and spiked their water supply even after my dad and I argued against it, I could only come to one conclusion, no matter how much it upset and sickened me.

"I think my mother is the witch."

Chapter Forty-Nine

~Vaughan~

It felt like I'd missed something. Felix's suggestion that the spirit could be linked to artifacts or bones in the cave made sense to me, and I could follow along with Calista's reasoning about why the spirit tried to set us up rather than attacking us directly, but when she suggested that her mother might be behind all of it, she lost me.

"How can your mother be a witch? Isn't that a completely separate species?"

Felix and Calista shook their heads in unison, and Felix answered for both of them. "There are people born with a predisposition to magic, but that's not what she means by witch. In hunting circles, a witch is a human who deals with spirits or demons. They can use those entities to work their own spells, but often, the spirit or demon ends up taking control because the witch underestimates its power. It takes a very strong witch to be able to fully tame any spirit, and especially one as strong as this one seems to be."

"It doesn't fully make sense to me," Calista admitted, her face pinched and her blue eyes troubled as she thought it over. "My mom is always the first one to condemn anyone hurting humans. She has no sympathy for any creature who steps outside the accepted rules. I don't understand how she could justify doing something like this, but maybe she didn't fully know what she was getting into? Spirits can be manipulative sometimes, but there's always something there in the human that they can exploit."

The hunters are here, Alpha, Darius announced in my head. *Should we bring them to you?*

No, not yet. Stay with them, I answered him through our mind-link. Out loud, I addressed Calista with the biggest question I still had. "If your mom is the witch, why would she agree to do the exorcism?"

Her face paled yet again, though I wouldn't have thought it could go any whiter. "I don't know. I don't even know if she could, because ideally, the exorcism would be done on both the witch and the spirit at the same time. Even if it works, if they're bound together strongly enough, she'd be endangering herself. Often, the witch dies with the spirit. Maybe she had something else in mind when she agreed to do it."

Shit. What were we supposed to do? People who knew how to perform the kind of exorcism we needed couldn't be found on every street corner and Calista had already said she didn't think she could do it herself.

Thankfully, she had a different suggestion. "My dad can do it if he has to. For the sake of your pack's safety, I think you should restrain my mother. Maybe I'm wrong; in fact, I hope I am, but it doesn't seem like a risk worth taking. Bind and gag her so she can't do anything else before the exorcism is complete."

Despite her firm tone, I could see that it pained Calista to make the suggestion. Whatever else the hunters had done, they had also raised her for most of her life, and accepting that her mother might be responsible for all of the deaths and destruction and might need to die herself couldn't be easy. Calista's strength and her willingness to put the needs of my pack first were qualities that would make her a wonderful Luna, if she agreed to accept me.

First, though, we needed to take care of the spirit, once and for all.

"Felix, I'm putting you in charge of the woman." Calling her Calista's mother left a bad taste in my mouth, so I didn't do it. "Call whatever backup you need, and when they bring the hunters in here, you can restrain her."

My Beta nodded in agreement, as I expected, and I turned to my mate next.

"You don't have to be here if you don't want to be. You can wait for us outside with the sasquatch, once we have things under control."

Every fibre of my being urged me to shield her from anything that would be painful for her, but also as I expected, Calista refused the offer. "No. I need to face her. I have to deal with it, like it or not."

With a curt nod, I linked Darius to bring the hunters to my office while Felix made his own arrangements. Calista and I both stood up, ready to face her parents when they arrived, and though I would have liked to hold her hand or otherwise give her some kind of physical support, that would only raise more questions. As difficult as I found it, and no matter how much Atlas whined at me in my head, I kept my hands by my side, letting her face her parents on her own.

When they arrived a few moments later, a couple of members of our security team were right behind them. "Where's the sasquatch?" Calista's mother demanded as soon as she walked in the door. "We don't have time to waste. We need to complete the exorcism while it's still sedated…"

She didn't have a chance to finish whatever she'd been about to say as Felix grabbed her arm and pulled her away from his husband. While Darius stepped between them, Felix and the others tied the woman's hands behind her back and gagged her mouth, rendering her harmless in a matter of seconds.

"What are you doing?" Calista's father cried out, his eyes darting between me, his daughter, and his struggling wife, while Darius did his best to hold him back without needing to restrain him too. "We came here to help. We're not armed. Calista, what is this?"

Everyone in the room turned to my mate, and standing next to her, I could practically feel the tension coming off of her. It radiated from her crossed arms and her tight shoulders, and the firm set of her jaw as she gave her reply. "You're not armed *now*, but you already spiked the water supply. You left them defenseless and vulnerable to the spirit.

You tried to kill them just like you slaughtered the Deep Valley pack all those years ago."

Muffled protest came from beneath her mother's gag, but I couldn't make out any words. From her father, the response was more muted, full of concern as he continued to look nervously between me and the other stone-faced members of my pack, and his equally grim daughter. "Obviously, you've made friends here and you're sympathetic to these werewolves. I understand that, but your mother and I aren't the enemy. We never have been."

Calista threw that back in his face bitterly, holding nothing back. "Never? Not even when you tied me to my bed and shot me full of an experimental treatment to silence my own wolf? Obviously, you don't consider me or any of the people here equal to yourselves or you wouldn't treat us the way you have."

The colour drained from his face so fast that I thought he might pass out. His mouth opened and closed a few times as he tried to decide what to say. For a moment, I thought he might try to deny it, but when his answer finally came, it acted as a confirmation to everything she had remembered. "We did what we thought was best for you."

Although I knew this was Calista's argument, I couldn't help stepping in. "Denying her a part of herself and hiding her past was 'best' for her? Letting her think that her real family were evil when in reality, they were innocent and you murdered them?"

"We thought they were behind the attacks," he reminded me meekly. "Would it have been better for her to think she came from a pack of murderers? To be a rogue wolf without a pack? She had a home and a life with us."

Perhaps he believed that, I couldn't say for certain, but I had a feeling from the angry glare her mother gave me that it went deeper than that.

Calista spoke up again, her voice cold and hard. "It doesn't matter now. All of that isn't why we've restrained your wife. It's because of what she's done with the spirit."

I could see how the words 'your wife' affected both of the hunters. Calista couldn't have taken sides any more clearly than that, clearly repudiating her link to her 'mother'.

"What are you talking about?" her dad asked, his voice quieter than it had been.

As efficiently as possible, Calista shared the conclusion we'd reached about the spirit being connected to the caves on our land, and how it had been responsible for both the attacks sixteen years earlier, and the ones now.

"There's only one other connection to both of those events besides the Crimsontooth pack, and that's us," she summed up. "You taught me to be logical and look for the coincidences that aren't really coincidences at all. That's what I've done, and the one thing I see in common, the driving force behind all of these events, is her."

Calista's 'mother' had stopped struggling during Calista's explanation, listening closely to everything being said while my men held her, but at Calista's conclusion, she tried again to speak, even more forcefully than before. Once again, we couldn't make out a word she tried to say.

My mate ignored her, her attention still focused completely on her father, and her tone softening just a touch. "I know you love her, but you also know this is wrong. The spirit has to die, and I don't trust her to do it. I'll help you. We can do it together."

"Even if it kills her?" he asked, his eyes searching Calista's desperately. Despite everything, a pang of sympathy tugged at my heart. We were putting him in an impossible position, that couldn't be denied, but the situation couldn't be allowed to go on. My entire pack's safety was at stake.

"What would she do in your place?" Calista challenged him in reply, and his eyes lowered, obviously knowing as well as she did that his wife wouldn't hesitate to do what needed to be done, just as she always had.

"Let's go outside then," he finally conceded, his voice shaking as his wife renewed her protests, squirming within my men's grasp as she tried to break free. They held her steady, and on my order, dragged her along with us, her feet barely touching the ground as we all headed for the back door, towards the sasquatch, and hopefully, towards a resolution for this whole terrible situation.

Chapter Fifty

~Calista~

Distancing myself from the job that needed to be done hadn't come naturally to me when I first started hunting. My mom worked hard to prepare me for it, teaching me meditation techniques to improve my focus and reduce susceptibility to distractions. Even so, the emotional toll had been something I had to learn to deal with on my own.

On the very first job I worked with my parents, shortly after turning sixteen, we encountered a gremlin who had taken up residence inside a bus maintenance station. Gremlins were mischievous and often fascinated by mechanical engineering. The particular one I hunted had messed with the engines and brakes on several vehicles, leading to multiple crashes and several fatalities. We split up to try and find it, and I'd been the one to finally track it down. I couldn't wait for anyone else to get there, as gremlins could be notoriously slippery. Instead, I did what I'd been trained to do; everyone knew suffocation was the most effective method of dealing with a gremlin, but later that night, my mom found me crying in my room.

"I hope those tears are for the people who died in the accidents," she admonished, her voice cold as she stood by the door, her arms crossed.

In both shame and sadness, I smudged my tears into my cheeks. "I didn't kill those people. I didn't have to look in their eyes as the light went out of them. That gremlin was a living thing and now it's not, because of me."

"And you wouldn't have had to kill it if it hadn't broken the rules first. He brought it on himself, Calista. You were simply bringing balance back to the universe. You didn't take a life; you saved others."

That had always been her philosophy: we were the executioners, the bringers of justice, never directly responsible for the deaths we caused. We looked at things logically and impartially, meting out punishments for the beings that strayed outside the invisible lines that divided the supernatural world and human society.

Every word she'd ever said to me on the subject could be used against her now that she'd been the one to cross that line, and so I did what she'd always taught me to: I put my own personal feelings aside and focused on the job that needed to be done.

Even so, a chill went through my body as we stepped outside the pack house into the night and made our way across the lawn to the forest's edge. My dad's limp on his artificial leg seemed more pronounced than ever but he kept moving grimly forward anyway. The sasquatch still lay on the forest floor, tied to a nearby tree, fast asleep. Her snores rumbled through the stillness of the night air and the moonlight fell on her hairy body, making her look like a shaggy rug spread out on the frosty dirt.

"You're sure the spirit is still inside her?" my dad asked as we approached. Several werewolves stood guard but Vaughan quickly dismissed them and they withdrew far enough that they were out of earshot but close enough to be called back if needed. The only people remaining around the sasquatch were me, Vaughan, my dad, Felix, and my mom who was still being held by two of the other werewolves. Her protests hadn't stopped since we left the house, but no one paid any attention to her.

"Witnesses saw the spirit leaving the other two sasquatches when they died," Vaughan confirmed. "But no one saw anything from this one between the time Calista hit her with the dart gun and when they put the cuffs you gave us on her."

That sounded fairy conclusive to me, and my dad seemed to agree. Reaching into his pocket, he pulled out a small iron cross.

"What's that?" Vaughan asked, leaning forward to get a closer look at it in the dim moonlight.

"It's a common tool for spirit exorcisms," my dad explained, ever the teacher even as his voice shook. His hand also trembled as he held the cross up for Vaughan to see. "The shape is less important than the metal. Not all spirits are Christian, but they all respond to iron. It weakens them, which will be important because it will try to fight back. They don't go quietly once they realize what's happening."

"The spirit will sense weakness in the person doing the exorcism if they don't fully commit to it," I added. "They'll try to overwhelm them. That's why I can't do it on my own; I don't know that I could hold it off."

"We should get started," my dad said, nodding to Vaughan. "As long as those chains are secure, everyone else should take a few steps back. Leave this to me and Calista."

Vaughan passed the order on to his men, and as they pulled my mother away, I saw my dad whisper 'I'm sorry' to her. No matter how hard she struggled and strained against the men holding her, she couldn't break away or say anything in return.

"Do you want me to stay?" Vaughan murmured in my ear, his warm breath sending another kind of shiver down my spine. He sounded reluctant to leave me there, but I didn't want to have to worry about him along with my dad. It would be easier with him at a safe distance with the others.

"No. We've got this. Just make sure everyone else is safe, okay?"

With a nod, he squeezed my hand once and stepped back with the others, leaving me and my dad alone in front of the possessed sasquatch.

"You know what to do," my dad said to me, his eyes fixed on the snoring beast who wouldn't stay still for long once he began the exorcism. "The spirit will try everything it can to sway me, but it can't possess me so long as it's trapped inside the sasquatch. I need you to keep me going if I start to waver. If I can't finish for any reason, then you have to finish it for me."

"I understand. I'm ready." No other job had ever been so personal for me, but I tried to approach it just like I had any other.

Gripping the cross in both hands in front of his chest, my father began the incantation. "Exorcizamus te, omnis immundus spiritus."

The Latin incantation had been used by hunters for centuries, and as it always did, the first few words warned the spirit of what was to come. Despite the sedative still flowing through its veins, the sasquatch suddenly sat up, its chains rattling in the quiet night, its eyes springing open but its gaze vacant. What we were looking at wasn't the sasquatch at all; only the spirit was present.

"You can't do this." The voice that came out of the sasquatch's mouth sent another chill through my body that had nothing to do with the cold night air. It sounded hoarse and pained, using vocal cords that had never been designed for speech. "We made a deal."

A deal? That was an odd thing for the spirit to say. Demons made deals, not spirits, at least not as far as I'd ever heard.

My father carried on as if nothing had been said at all. "Omnis satanica potestas, omnis incursio."

"You promised to help me." The voice grew shriller, more panicked and more angry with each word out of my dad's mouth. A low growl followed and the beast lumbered back to its feet, unsteadily, still fully under the spirit's control as the chains pulled at the trunk of the tree they were attached to. The sasquatch herself was still unconscious, her body being used against her will by the spirit. "I helped you and you said you'd help me."

Again, the spirit's tactic confused me. Usually, the entity being exorcized would threaten harm to the one performing the ritual or threaten to harm those they cared about. They would flail and destroy things and cause chaos. They didn't usually claim the person owed them anything.

"Infernalis adversarii, omnis legio." Though my dad continued speaking, his hands shook even worse than before, but I didn't notice how badly they trembled until a moment too late. The cross slipped from his hands, and without the iron deterrent, the sasquatch immediately lurched forwards with its unseeing eyes, its chain pulling loose from the tree and its hand swiping at my dad. Though I reached for him, I was too late. The hairy arm encircled my father, pulling him close to the sasquatch, out of my grasp.

"Stay back," my dad called out to me and the others. "Don't hurt it. If the sasquatch dies, we can't kill the spirit."

"If you kill me, you die too," the spirit in the sasquatch rasped. "We're bound together. Forever."

Bound together? That didn't make any sense, unless...

Unless...

Unless my *dad* was the witch?

The blood in my veins seemed to freeze as cold disbelief washed over me. How could that be possible? *Why* would he do that? My dad never wanted to hurt anyone. Why would he help the spirit to cause so much death and destruction?

"Calista, finish it." Each word came out as a gasp, all the air in my dad's lungs being squeezed out by the beast's sturdy grip. "Hurry."

My body seemed to be moving on auto-pilot as I bent down and picked up the cross that had fallen to the ground. Holding the cool metal in my palm, I looked back over my shoulder at my mom, still bound and gagged, and suddenly, her unintelligible protests made sense. She hadn't been trying to stop my dad because it would hurt her. She'd simply figured it out sooner than I had that my dad must be the one behind it.

"Why would you help it?" I asked, turning back to my dad and the sasquatch. "How could you?"

"There's... no... time." His voice grew fainter, his face buried in the creature's thick hair. "End this. Please."

"Callie?" Vaughan's voice behind me, using my old nickname, reminded me of exactly what was at stake. The pack remained in danger as long as the spirit stayed alive. "Are you alright? What do you need?"

He hadn't put it together yet why I hesitated. Why would he? Even I could barely make sense of it, but I knew one thing for certain: one way or another, this had to end.

"Omnis congregatio et secta diabolica."

As I picked up the incantation where my father had left off, the sasquatch let out a high-pitched scream that made me wince. Dropping my dad, it tried to grab me instead, but its movements were uncoordinated and slow. It used up most of its strength against my father, and I easily stepped back, out of the way.

"Ergo draco maledicte et omnis legio diabolica adjuramus te."

From the corner of my eye, I could see my father's limp body, unmoving, his artificial leg bent at an unnatural angle. I couldn't tell if he was still alive or not, and even if he was, he might not be for long if he and the spirit were truly bound together as the spirit said.

I couldn't stop, though. We'd come that far, and one more sentence would banish the spirit from our realm, sending it on to wherever it should have gone in the first place, breaking the ties that bound it to our plane and stopping it from harming anyone else, human or werewolf.

"Cessa decipere humanas creaturas, eisque aeternae Perditionis venenum propinare."

As the final words left my lips, the sasquatch stumbled back, falling back onto the ground with a thud that seemed to shake the ground beneath my feet. From its lips, a white, steamy cloud began to form, the essence of the spirit, but unlike before where it dissipated into the air, the cloud grew smaller and tighter before, with a bright flash, so bright against the night sky that we all had to shield our eyes from it, the light vanished, leaving only silence and emptiness in its place.

At last, the spirit had moved on.

Chapter Fifty-One

~Vaughan~

I kept one eye on Calista's mom as Calista and her dad worked together to complete the exorcism, waiting for the moment when she would start to show some kind of effect from it. Based on what Calista and Felix told me, the spirit's defeat would impact on her strongly, potentially fatally, so at some point, I expected her to stop struggling against my men, growing weaker as the spirit's power waned. However, the only time she stopped at all was when Calista turned around to look at her. In her eyes, I could see desperation as she shouted at her daughter through her gag. Desperation, but no sign of weakness at all.

Even when the procedure seemed complete, when the spirit left the sasquatch's body and vanished in a bright flash of light that I took for a good thing since that had never happened before, Calista's mom stayed standing. Her protests ceased but she didn't seem to lose any strength.

What did that mean? Maybe she hadn't been the witch after all?

As soon as the spirit had gone, Calista ran over to where her father lay on the ground, shouting orders back at me. "Let my mom go! Get a doctor for my dad. Check the sasquatch, see if she's still alive."

I didn't question any of it, trusting that my mate had a reason for everything she asked for, and I nodded at my men to confirm they could release the hunter. Free of their grasp, she ran to her husband, pulling at the gag in her mouth. After confirming that Felix would look after the medical side of things, I hurried over to join Calista and her parents.

"Is he dead?" I heard Calista's mom ask, arriving just before I did.

Calista's reply came out clipped and restrained as she knelt next to her father's body, her fingers on his wrist to check his pulse. "No. Not yet, anyway."

"Good. Then he can tell us what the hell he was thinking." She dropped to her knees next to her husband's body, lifting his head to cradle it in her lap.

"What's going on?" Yet again, I felt like I'd missed something important, and I didn't know how to support Calista through it until I understood the situation.

"My dad is the one who enabled the spirit," Calista told me, her eyes still on him rather than me. "He's responsible for all of it."

I definitely hadn't expected that response, and I took a step back, feeling the shock of it just as she must have. "What? Why?"

"That's what we want to know." Calista's mom sounded so angry that if I were her husband, I might prefer death to facing her.

However, the man on the ground opened his eyes, slowly and painfully, looking up at his wife in apology. "It said... it wouldn't... hurt anyone."

That response earned him no mercy. "And you believed it? Spirits lie! You know that."

He winced at her tone, or perhaps just from the pain he must have been in. Having recently been flattened by a sasquatch myself, I knew how it felt, but humans didn't have the benefit of quick healing that werewolves did. If he was bleeding internally, his body wouldn't heal in time to save him like mine did.

"What happened, Dad?" Calista's voice came out quieter than her mom's but full of just as much hurt and confusion.

His eyes moved over to her, full of regret. "Your mom was... possessed. Before you came to us."

I remembered Calista mentioning that. She said the hunters couldn't have children of their own because her mom had been possessed by a demon. After everything that happened that night, I had a better understanding of what that meant than I did before, but I didn't know what it had to do with the spirit, and neither did Calista, apparently.

"And?" she prompted.

"I couldn't... save her... on my own." Each word he uttered took effort, each phrase gasped between painful breaths. "Exorcism... would have... killed her. The spirit... came to me. Said it could help. Asked me to... help it in return."

"You idiot!" Calista's mom cried, not holding back despite her husband's fragile state. "You should have let me die. What's our number one rule? Never, ever make a deal."

Her husband kept his gaze focused on Calista, telling her the story. "It promised... it only wanted to protect... its resting place. It said it wouldn't... hurt anyone."

He'd already said that, and as his voice grew weaker, it felt like our time to get more answers might be running short. I tried to move the explanation forward. "That was when the first attacks happened? The ones that Calista's family were killed over?"

His eyes closing in shame, he nodded. "I didn't... put it together. I didn't know... the spirit... was involved."

"And this time?" Calista asked. "Why did you help it again?"

"It came back... a few weeks ago. Asked for my help again. I felt bad for it... and no one got hurt the first time... I thought. I didn't know... I swear, I didn't know until... tonight. When you told me... the caves..."

His ability to form complete sentences faded, and the doctor arrived as he uttered those final words. His wife stayed on the ground with him as the doctor began to check him over, but Calista stood up, taking a step back, and immediately, I moved over to her, putting my arms around her supportively.

"He always empathized with the creatures we hunt," she said softly, watching as the doctor worked to try to save her father. His eyes had closed and his skin looked paler than before. Though I was no doctor, even I could tell it didn't look good. "The spirit must have taken advantage of that and how desperate he must have been to save my mom. It used him, and he allowed himself to be used. So many deaths that didn't have to happen. I don't think he's fully allowed himself to take it in yet. The guilt will destroy him."

Guilt swam in her words too, though she wasn't to blame for any of it. Her father bore some responsibility, and so did we for opening the caves, though we'd had no idea what it would unleash. Between our actions in disrupting the spirit, her father's help in bringing it forward, and her mother's ruthless efficiency in hunting the scapegoat were-wolves, everything collided in a perfect storm of destruction that took out Calista's pack and could have done the same to mine too, if she hadn't been there to figure it out with me before it was too late.

"He loves his wife, and I think he loves you too." I'd been thinking about what he said in my office, about how he thought suppressing Calista's wolf was the best thing for her. Though I certainly didn't agree, I had a feeling he meant it sincerely. "I think he convinced himself he was doing the right thing for you, no matter how misguided his actions might have been. Love makes people behave illogically sometimes."

"I can't believe you're defending him after what might have happened to your pack." Although her body remained tense, she rested against me, making no attempt to move away.

"He didn't hurt my pack on purpose. What he did was foolish and reckless but not malicious. I'm much more upset about what they did to you, but it's your place to decide what to do about that." No sooner had I gotten those words out of my mouth than the doctor turned back to me and shook her head ever-so-slightly. I got the message: her patient wasn't going to make it. "This could be your last chance to say anything you want to say to him. You don't have to forgive him, but you should make your peace, whatever that looks like to you."

I treasured the last moments I spent with my father before his death and molded my life on the advice he gave me then. Until that day, I'd always put my pack first, as he told me to, but with Calista at my side, I might be able to compromise a little more going forward. Hopefully, she could find a similar compromise with her past, something she could live with.

Taking a deep breath, Calista stepped forward again as the doctor moved back, and I watched as she knelt down next to her adoptive father for the last time. A look passed between her and her mother, an acknowledgement that they both understood the end had come, and Calista leaned down to speak directly into her father's ear. Though his eyes remained closed and he made no reply, a single tear slipped from the corner of his eye.

A moment later, all movement stopped, and by the time Calista raised her head again, he was gone. There was no grand exit like there had been for the spirit, just a simple absence, a silence that hung heavily over all of us.

Felix came up to me as the two women knelt beside his body, united in their loss but divided in so many other ways. He spoke to me quietly so as not to disturb them. "The sasquatch didn't make it either. The damage to her body was too great."

One more death we could add to a week that had been full of it, but at last, it had come to an end. "Tell everyone to get some rest. In the morning, we'll take the sasquatch bodies to the caves and seal them up again. Even if the spirit's gone, I don't want to have anything to do with those caves anymore."

"I understand." Felix's hand patted my shoulder sympathetically. "Will she be alright?"

He meant my mate, and as I watched her try to come to terms with the loss of the second father in her life, I gave him the only answer I could: "I'll do everything I can to make sure she is."

Chapter Fifty-Two

~Calista~

Numbness spread through my body as my father went still. Despite the cold air around me and the unyielding ground beneath my knees, I felt curiously detached from everything but a floating emptiness, as if everything around me were not quite real.

The man next to me may not have been my biological father. He might have even killed my actual family. Yet, for sixteen years, he raised me and taught me everything he knew. He cared for me as best as he knew how, he saved my life more than once while hunting, including the time he lost his leg to the wendigo, and even if he'd made mistakes, losing his steady presence in my life made me feel like an anchor had been cut, like something that gave me a steady base from which to make sense of the world around me had been taken away from me.

That was what I tried to convey with the words I whispered to him when I said goodbye: "You always saw the good in everyone. I'll remember the good in you."

Although he didn't reply, I knew he heard me. Something deep in my heart told me so.

"I suppose you'll punish me now. Throw me to the literal wolves." My mom's voice cut through the haze surrounding me, bringing me crashing back down to earth. Suddenly, my knees hurt again and I shivered against the cold.

I raised my eyes to her, bristling at her tone. "Do you even understand what you did wrong? By robbing them of their wolves, you could have been responsible for the death of this entire pack. Thousands of people!

Maybe Dad was naive to trust the spirit, but you always believe the worst of every supernatural being, and you put them all in danger. Not to mention what you did to me."

"All I did was cure you." She couldn't have sounded any more unrepentant. "I've seen over and over again how these creatures give in to their animal side. I tried to spare you from that and give you a normal life."

"Normal?" She seemed to have a very different definition of that word than most people did. "You raised me to hunt monsters! How is that 'normal'?"

Though he didn't say a word, I could feel Vaughan's presence behind me as he stepped closer, supporting me but not interfering, waiting there in case I needed him.

From her spot on the other side of my dad's body, my mom must have seen him but she didn't look at him either. She kept her eyes on me. "Exactly. You hunt *monsters*, and you might have become one if we didn't stop it."

She truly didn't get it. "My family weren't monsters! Neither are Vaughan and his pack. Just because they're different from you doesn't make them evil."

If my time with Vaughan and his pack had taught me anything, that would be it. Werewolves could be evil, but they could also be good. They were utterly human in that regard.

My mom ignored my point about Vaughan's pack to focus on what happened sixteen years earlier. "If your family were so innocent, why didn't they agree to speak with us? If they had, maybe we wouldn't have had to kill them."

Again, she wanted to blame the victims, and although I didn't know the answer to her question, I also didn't believe her conclusion. "Vaughan and Felix *did* talk to you and you still drugged their water supply. Even if you didn't kill them directly, you still would have been responsible for their deaths if the spirit had wiped them out."

"She was pregnant."

Vaughan's interjection took both me and my mom by surprise, and we both looked up at him in confusion.

"Who was?" I asked just before she got a chance to.

"Your mom. Your biological mom. She was heavily pregnant at the time of the attack, and the Alpha's instinct would have been to protect his mate at her most vulnerable time. That must be why they refused to let the hunters onto their land. He wasn't hiding anything, he just wanted to keep his family safe, and he never knew what it would cost them."

His words drew a picture that matched so exactly with the big, strong, loving man I was just beginning to remember that the loss of my family hit me all over again. Not only my parents had been taken from me, but my older brothers and a younger brother or sister who had never even been born too. I could barely even imagine it.

The life I might have had and the one I ended up with couldn't have seemed more at odds with each other as I looked down again at my dad's lifeless form.

"The spirit must have fed off of Dad's hunting knowledge," I guessed, addressing my mom as I put things together in my mind. "It knew exactly what kind of evidence would convince you of the werewolves' guilt, so it planted it there."

"I think you're right," Vaughan agreed. "When we visited the murder scene, the amount of fur on the human bodies wasn't natural. It looked like it had been left there on purpose."

That sounded right, but I thought it went even further than that, and I kept speaking directly to my mom. "It knew Dad, and it knew you through him, so it played into your prejudices. It used you just as much as it used him. If you had been willing to consider for even a moment that the wolves had nothing to gain from the attacks, you might have seen the truth. You could have saved them and maybe saved Dad too. To the wolves from my pack, and to the ones who died here tonight, *you're* the monster."

I fully expected her to argue with me again, to stick to her guns and defend herself as she always had, but instead, her shoulders slumped as she looked down at her husband, realizing, perhaps for the first time, that she had lost everything. My dad was gone and I wouldn't be going home with her. Vaughan had made it clear that I would be welcome to stay with him, and though I'd only been there just over a day, it already felt more like home to me than the house she would be returning to.

When my mom made no reply, Vaughan spoke again. "How long will the medication in our water supply last?"

"Three or four days," came her quiet response, her head still down as she waited for the other shoe to drop.

"And the wolves who were affected? How long will it last?"

"No more than a day or two if they don't drink any more."

"You'll give the details of what you put in there to my team so they can test the water before we allow anyone to drink from it. Answer any questions our scientists have."

She nodded silently in agreement, still waiting. Vaughan had every right to punish her or to demand retribution and she obviously expected he would. However, his next words took us both by surprise.

"You're free to go."

My mom's head snapped up, her eyes full of confusion and suspicion. "Why?"

Vaughan's warm brown eyes looked down at my dad's body with far more compassion than my mom had ever shown him or his pack. "Losing your mate is the worst thing I can imagine. You've already been punished enough."

When he glanced over at me, heat flowed through my body, warming me against the night's chill. How he had the power to affect me so much with just a glance would definitely take some getting used to.

"It goes without saying that this amnesty is a one-time thing," he added, looking back at my mom. "If you act against my pack again, I won't be so generous a second time. You'll leave my land now and not come back, not unless Calista chooses to invite you back. That's entirely in her hands."

His generosity only made the difference between her rigidity and his empathy clearer, and to my shock, something close to embarrassment crossed my mom's face. I hadn't been sure she even knew what it meant to feel regret over something.

Vaughan called over a couple of his men who helped to take my dad's body back to my parents' truck, and when my mom got behind the steering wheel, Felix got into the car next to her, making sure she left their land without causing any further trouble. Her eyes met mine for a moment just before she pulled away, with no apology, per se, but perhaps just a tiny bit of understanding.

Or maybe I just imagined it. I honestly couldn't say.

"It's time to get some rest," Vaughan murmured in my ear, and as soon as we reached the foot of the staircase, he picked me up to carry me upstairs. I should have resisted, should have insisted I could walk myself, but the solid warmth of his body took away the cold and the pain, soothing my aching heart so much that I simply closed my eyes instead, my head resting against his shoulder, and sleep claimed me before he even reached the final step.

CHAPTER FIFTY-THREE

~Vaughan~

My heart melted as I lay Calista down in my bed, fast asleep. I never really knew what that phrase meant before, but when I took a step back to look at her, my chest felt like liquid, the emotions too strong to be contained. They flowed through my whole body, trickling into every part of me: affection, protectiveness, respect and need, filling every inch and nearly overwhelming me.

She's perfect, Atlas murmured in my head, mirroring my own thoughts. *How can anyone be so strong and so fragile at the same time?*

That, I didn't have an answer for, and as much as I wanted to stay there with her and try to figure it out, I still had a pack to run. Since Calista showed no signs of waking anytime soon, I took the opportunity to slip back downstairs to make sure everything else was under control.

At the foot of the stairs, directing the people still moving in and out of the house, Amanda looked completely in her element, and since I no longer had to face the prospect of being bound to her rather than my fated mate, I could objectively appreciate how naturally being a leader seemed to come to her. She would make an amazing Luna for someone. Just not for me.

"You should get some rest," I said as I came up behind her, making her jump. She'd been so caught up in looking after everyone else, she hadn't noticed me approaching.

When she did see me, a look of guilt flashed across her face. "I'm sorry, I didn't mean to overstep. Felix isn't back yet and I thought you'd be looking after your mate."

My words obviously didn't come across as I meant them to, since I hadn't meant to make her feel bad. I was simply thinking about her wellbeing. "You're not overstepping. I appreciate your help, but you've had a difficult day too."

A lot of that was down to me, I knew, and aside from accusing Calista of sabotaging us in the meeting, she'd handled it all incredibly well. Even that accusation had been in the spirit of protecting my pack, so I couldn't hold it against her, especially since she had worked with Calista afterwards when I made it clear my mate still had my trust.

All in all, I couldn't find much fault with anything Amanda had done, so when she answered me in a soft voice, looking down at her hands, a pang of regret went through me. "I don't mind keeping busy. It's better than sitting by myself with only my thoughts for company."

"Amanda, I..."

My hand reached for her shoulder, wanting to offer some kind of support, but she stepped back, out of my reach, shaking her head. The brief glimpse of vulnerability immediately disappeared, and when she spoke again, her voice had regained its previous strength.

"You don't owe me any further explanation, Vaughan. I'll make arrangements to return to my own pack as soon as possible."

She stepped further away, heading for the stairs, and I tried once again to hold out an olive branch. "You don't need to go right away. You're welcome to stay here as long as you like."

Amanda's lips formed a small, pained smile. "Tomorrow," she repeated softly. "Good night, Vaughan."

She strode up the stairs with firm, determined steps, not looking back as I watched her disappear around the corner at the top of the staircase.

"Vaughan."

Leo's voice from beside me rang with disapproval, the same as it had for the last two days, and my eyes closed in both guilt and sheer exhaustion. "I know, I made a mess of everything. Amanda deserved better."

My Gamma put his hand on my shoulder. "Amanda will be okay. You should be looking after your mate. That's your place right now."

As I turned to him in surprise, Leo offered me a smile that looked both apologetic and supportive.

"It's my job to serve my Luna. I thought that's what I was doing when I pushed you towards Amanda, when I was actually keeping you away from your true mate. Now that I know who she is, I'll always be looking out for her. Tell me what you need done and I'll look after it so you can go back to Calista."

When he ordered me to spend time with my mate earlier, I resented it, but now that his orders aligned with my own desires, I only felt relief. "We're going to need fresh water for the next week at least. It should be distributed to every house with extra supplies kept here at the pack house. No one should use the water from the taps until we know it's safe."

"Got it. What else?"

"Make a list of anyone still missing their wolves. Check up on them in the morning and have them visit the doctor if they're not back yet."

I gave him a few more instructions, and when he had it all, he ordered me once again to return to my mate, and I gratefully conceded, heading back up the stairs to my own room.

I'd left the room dark to help Calista sleep, but enough moonlight slipped in through the curtains that I could make my way to the bathroom without disturbing her. In the shower, I scrubbed off the remains of the sasquatch's blood and the dirt from the forest floor, getting myself as clean as possible before putting on a loose pair of cotton pants and crawling into the bed next to my mate. Dawn wouldn't be too far away, but while the night lasted, I intended to spend the rest of it there beside her, letting her feel our bond just as much as I felt it. I'd never felt more comfortable as I drifted off to sleep next to her.

"No! Stop! Please!"

Only seconds after my eyes closed, so it seemed, they were forced back open by the sound of my mate's cries beside me. In my sleep-hazed confusion, it took me a moment to realize what was happening, but when I did, I immediately took Calista in my arms. Some time had obviously passed since I joined her, since brighter light filtered in through the window, but she seemed to still be asleep, her eyes squeezed shut painfully tight as her face contorted in pain.

"Callie, wake up. You're dreaming. You're safe."

Her body wriggled in my arms, trying to get away from whatever haunted her subconscious, but I held her steady, whispering softly to her until her eyes blinked open. The panicked look I could see in those pale blue eyes in the early morning light nearly broke my heart, but as she realized where she was and who I was, her whole body relaxed, and the fact that she felt safe with me filled me with warmth. I couldn't remember feeling so many highs and lows in such a short amount of time before. My emotions had certainly been getting a workout ever since I met her.

"What were you dreaming about?" I asked gently, still holding her close so she knew I was there for her. "Another premonition?"

I hoped the danger had passed, but if she'd had a new vision, I would give it all the weight it deserved.

Thankfully, though, she shook her head. "No. Nothing new, just memories from the night my family died. I saw my mom there... my hunter mom. I remembered meeting her for the first time and her drugging me."

She drugged a five-year-old? I hadn't known that detail before. Maybe I shouldn't have let her go after all, but I kept quiet as Calista kept talking.

"Skye says I have more memories that will come back, memories that the medication suppressed, both painful ones and happy ones. But even the happy ones aren't really happy, knowing how everything ended."

Even though I held her right there in my arms, she sounded far away and lost, and I pulled her even tighter. Not an inch of space remained between us, my body pressed firmly against hers. "It's not the end yet. We can't erase what's gone before, but your life is far from over. I'm here to help you through it, we'll get you whatever help you need, and we can write a whole new ending together."

As the words came out of my mouth, I couldn't be sure they were the right thing to say, but the smile Calista gave me seemed to confirm she understood the sentiment behind them even if the phrasing could've been better. One of her hands reached up to touch my face, her fingers trailing gently down my cheek, sending a shiver of sparks through me. "I can't believe I thought you were the enemy."

"I still can't quite believe I'm mated to a hunter," I teased her, and as I hoped, her smile grew wider and bolder, the pain of her dream fading just a little in the promise of what lay ahead of us.

"Maybe we should double check that we really are mates. For science." Her hand drifted down from my face, down my bare back and slipped confidently beneath the waist of my pants. I loved how comfortable she felt with asking for what she wanted when it came to sex, and it seemed like we were once again on the same page.

"I think we should. For science," I agreed, catching just a glimpse of the way her beautiful eyes lit up before I claimed her mouth in a searing kiss.

Chapter Fifty-Four

~Calista~

Vaughan's kiss felt like a dream, especially compared to the nightmare I'd just had. Finding him right when I needed him the most seemed too good to be true. It felt like wandering through a storm and stumbling into the first open door I could find, only to find the most perfect man I could imagine waiting for me on the other side. How he should be meant for me, I still didn't entirely understand, so when I suggested to him that we confirm we were still mates, I meant it partly as a joke and partly not. After the extreme highs and lows of the previous day, I wanted to check that in the cold light of morning, nothing had changed.

It certainly didn't feel like he'd changed his mind as his lips moved against mine, sending those delicious tingles through my body, waking up every inch of me in anticipation. I still had my clothes on from the day before, which I found rather sweet. Despite having seen me naked the day before, he didn't assume I'd be okay with him undressing me in my sleep. On the other hand, he only wore a thin pair of cotton pants which did little to hide his growing erection.

Despite all the danger we'd been through and everything that had been revealed, I could lose myself in his kiss, and so I gave into it eagerly. All my problems would still be waiting for me when we left his room, so why not enjoy ourselves while we could and celebrate the incredible connection we shared that I could still barely comprehend.

As everything else around me fell apart, Vaughan and I came together, and I would cling to that until I found my balance again.

"You're so beautiful." Vaughan nearly growled the words, his eyes dark with lust as his hands threaded through my hair. "The night Felix met you, he told me about you. He said you were just my type and he was right."

"You talked about me?" I meant the words to sound teasing, but they came out so breathlessly that neither of us laughed. The electricity between us flowed too strongly.

"I had no idea then who you were or what you were to me. If I had, I'd have come and found you that same night."

"A werewolf showing up at my door to drag me away? I might have shot you." That time, I did manage to make it sound like a joke, and though Vaughan smiled, his eyes didn't lose any of their heat.

"I've waited a long time for you, Callie." His hips pressed against me, the length of his cock firm and defined against my thigh. "And it was worth every second."

No one had called me Callie before, no one besides my werewolf family that I barely remembered, but I liked the way it sounded on his lips. I liked the idea of it being something that only he called me, something special just between us. It felt natural, just like everything else about being with him.

He started to push me onto my back, his lips still pressed against mine, but that wasn't what I wanted. At that moment, I wanted to feel in control, at least in one part of my life if nothing else. So, I pushed back and he immediately gave way, letting me push him down until his back hit the mattress, his brown eyes looking up at me in surprise that grew even deeper as I sat up on top of him and pulled off my shirt.

"Is this okay?" I asked as I reached behind my back for the strap of my bra. He looked so stunned, I worried I'd done something wrong.

He blinked as if coming out of a trance, his eyes somehow turning even darker as they moved between my chest and my face. "It's so much better than okay."

As soon as my bra fell off, Vaughan's hands were on me. They trailed up my bare back, leaving a pathway of sparks behind them that went straight to my core, making me shiver as my hips ground into him. His cock felt even bigger between my legs, even with my jeans still on. The pressure of it against me had me rocking back and forth as his hands moved to my front, his thumbs flicking across my nipples as he cupped my breasts in his large, strong hands.

As good as that felt, I soon needed more. My whole body ached for him, craving him as if it needed him to survive. Though it almost killed me to step away, I had to hop off of him to take the rest of my clothes off, and as my jeans hit the floor, Vaughan pulled his pants down too, tossing them to the side. The sight of his firm cock lying flat across his stomach sent a pang of need through me so strong that my knees almost buckled.

"There's a condom in the top dresser drawer," he told me, his voice thick with desire, and I appreciated that he brought it up before I had to ask. My mom told me that my epilepsy medication would interfere with birth control, but that had probably been another lie; maybe the hormones would have stopped her wolf suppression treatment from being fully effective. With a deep breath, I pushed those thoughts away as I grabbed the foil packet from Vaughan's dresser. My priority right then remained Vaughan's cock and getting it inside me; everything else could wait.

He lifted his shaft for me when I got back to the bed, holding it upright from the base so I could slide the condom onto him, and when I climbed back onto him, nothing had ever felt as right as sinking down onto him did. Nothing compared to the way he filled me, physically *and* emotionally.

"Fuck," Vaughan breathed out, looking just as satisfied as I felt. "You feel even better than you look, and that shouldn't be possible."

Longing filled his eyes as he held my gaze, both of us taking a moment to appreciate the connection we shared and the way our bodies fit together. The unique scent I got from him, like freshly-cleaned bedsheets, mingled with something muskier and more masculine and utterly arousing. The smell comforted and excited me all at the same time.

It felt like home.

When he reached for me again, I intercepted his hands with my own, entwining my fingers with his. "Let me take the lead, okay?"

His hands hit the mattress as I leaned forward, my hair hanging down and creating a blonde curtain around us, blocking out most of the sun's rays. "Anytime you want, Callie," Vaughan promised just before I kissed him.

Sparks lit up my body everywhere we touched: our lips that moved hungrily against each other, our hands, still intertwined, and his hard cock inside me as I lifted and lowered my hips to ride him slowly. Every stroke sent another shot of desire through me, every time he bottomed out inside me both completely fulfilling me and making me eager for more.

You belong here, his body told me as I sank down onto him.

You deserve more than to simply survive.

You deserve to be happy.

My orgasm began to build as his tongue played with mine, as my handsome, powerful Alpha mate lay back and let me use him for our mutual pleasure. As I requested, he made no attempt to take over. Occasionally, his hips lifted from the bed, driving into me harder, but I didn't think he did it on purpose. His body has a mind of its own, as did mine when it started to move faster and faster, the need for release reaching a fever pitch inside me. Our eyes met again, only inches apart, and the need I saw reflected back at me made me feel both weak and powerful. Pressing my lips to his, I moaned into our kiss as Vaughan's hands tightened their grip around mine, his kiss growing harder and his hips thrusting up even more firmly until I reached my peak. Satisfaction washed over me, my body shuddering as I came, and Vaughan groaned from beneath me, his cock pumping with his own orgasm.

You belong here.

As our lips parted, both of us breathing heavier than before, Vaughan grinned up at me, his eyes hazy with happiness. "I think this position might be my favourite, but we'll need to experiment more before I know for sure."

That sounded just fine to me. "I've got time," I promised him. "I'm not going anywhere."

His strong arms wrapped around me, pulling me down so that my head rested on his chest, his cock still inside me. "I'd like to introduce you to the pack properly today. They'll all be eager to get to know you. If you're ready to accept the bond..."

He trailed off there, and I raised my head curiously to see why he'd stopped. His eyes had gone hazy again, in a different way, and when they cleared, he explained why.

"Sorry, Felix just mind-linked me. Apparently, Alpha Warren of the Ravenstone pack is on the phone, waiting to speak to me."

Although I had no idea who that was, I understood that he needed to go, so I slid off of him and onto the bed while Vaughan got to his feet, pulling off the condom and heading into the bathroom to clean up.

"Who's Alpha Warren?" I asked, looking down at my own discarded clothes on the floor. I didn't really want to put them back on again, but I had no other clothes with me. I supposed I would have to go back to my house to pick up my things, although the thought of seeing my mom again sat like a lump in my stomach.

Vaughan reappeared in the doorway, a pair of jeans covering his lower half and a grim look on his face. "Amanda's father. She must have let him know she'd be coming home, which means our agreement is void. I'm guessing he's not happy about it."

"Is there anything I can do?" I would rather think about his problems than my own, but Vaughan shook his head.

"I'll handle it. Why don't you have a bath or shower and relax a little? I'll have Sav bring you some clothes to wear and something to eat, and the doctor's going to come check on you too, just as a precaution after everything that happened with your wolf. I'll be back as soon as I can."

He'd thought of everything, it seemed, though I didn't want him to get the wrong idea. "I'm willing to work here, Vaughan. I don't need to be pampered."

His eyes softened with affection as he pulled on a sweater. "I promise I'll put you to work when you're ready. For now, let me look after you just a little bit. For Atlas' sake, if nothing else. He'd like to wrap you up in bubble wrap and keep you safe forever."

At the sound of Vaughan's wolf's name, Skye hummed happily in my head, reminding me that she'd been there the whole time. I had to consider her needs now too, just as Vaughan had to please his wolf, so I gave in. "Alright. I'll wait here for you, then."

"Thank you." He leaned down and kissed me, his eyes filling with heat once again as they drifted down over my still-naked body. "Maybe we'll have time to try out another position later on. For science."

I swatted him away playfully, smiling to myself long after he'd gone. No matter what else happened, I knew that working together, we would find a way through it. Although I hadn't said the words to him yet, I knew the truth deep in my heart. I would accept him as my mate. How could I not?

Chapter Fifty-Five

~**Vaughan**~

Felix's look of apology greeted me when I walked into my office. My Beta stood next to my desk and with a grimace, he gestured down at the desk phone with its blinking red light that indicated a waiting call. "I'm sorry I had to disturb you. I know you were with your mate, but he wouldn't take no for an answer."

I could imagine. "It's fine. I have to get this over with. Stick around, though: I want an update on the water situation and the sasquatches as soon as I'm done."

I'd stopped at my sister's room and linked to the pack doctor on the way downstairs, so between the two of them, Calista should be looked after for a while. That would give me time to get caught up on everything else.

With a nod of agreement, Felix took a seat in front of my desk while I went behind it, steeling myself for whatever reaction might be waiting for me on the other end of the line. Letting out a deep exhale, I pressed the button to answer the phone, leaving it on speaker.

"Alpha Warren, it's Alpha Vaughan here."

I figured I wouldn't need to say any more than that, and I didn't. My once nearly-father-in-law wasted no time in getting to the point, his voice gruff and simmering with anger. "Are you declaring war on my pack, Alpha Vaughan?"

Felix's eyebrows raised while I tried not to wince, directing my gaze down at the phone. "Of course not. I assume you've spoken to your daughter this morning."

"I certainly have, and I can't think of any other reasonable explanation for you coming to see us, accepting our hospitality and taking her all the way back there with you only to reject and humiliate her."

Put that way, it really did sound bad, but surely, Amanda told him the reason why I'd called our arrangement off. "I met my fated mate, Alpha Warren. I understand the timing couldn't be much worse, but I didn't plan it this way. I never meant to hurt or embarrass your daughter. She's a wonderful woman, and I hope we can work together in the future, whether she's in your pack or elsewhere. She handled the whole situation with incredible grace."

Felix gave me a nod of encouragement, letting me know my explanation sounded alright to him, but Alpha Warren didn't sound nearly as satisfied.

"You made a promise to me and to Amanda, a promise that you're breaking. How can we trust you to hold up any of the other conditions of our agreement? How can we trust anything you say at all?"

That didn't seem fair to me, and I told him so. "This is an exceptional circumstance. A wolf meets his mate once in his life, and nothing less would have made me go back on our deal. I thought I might be able to resist it. I tried, but I couldn't. You must know how strong the bond is, Alpha."

Actually, I had no idea of his own personal situation, but I hoped that appealing to the strength of the mate bond would help to convince him. However, he quickly refuted my assumption. "Sometimes, an Alpha has to put the needs of his pack above his own desires. It seems that's a lesson you haven't learned yet, even though you're old enough to know better."

His admonishment made me bristle, especially since it so closely mirrored my own father's instructions, but I refused to back down. "I won't apologize for accepting my mate. I never meant it as an insult towards you or Amanda, so if you choose to take it that way, that's on you. On my side, my pack still values your friendship and our agreement, and I hope we can preserve the remaining terms of it."

Alpha Warren's silence stretched out for several long seconds while Felix and I exchanged nervous glances. Animosity with the strong northern pack was the last thing we needed, but I knew that Felix had my back completely, and so would the rest of my pack, if it came to that. When it came to Calista, I couldn't compromise.

"Without you and Amanda mating, the agreement is unbalanced," the Alpha finally said. "We'll require an additional concession before we agree to honour it."

That sounded reasonable enough, considering I *had* broken the terms, however unintentionally. "Do you have something in mind?"

I expected him to ask for supplies, money, or perhaps even land, but the words that he spoke next took me completely by surprise.

"You have a sister, don't you?"

Felix's eyes widened in the same way mine must have. "Yes," I agreed cautiously. "Why?"

"A mating bond is the strongest bond between two packs. Since you refuse to form one with my daughter, perhaps your sister could take your place. There are several high-ranking wolves in my pack who are unmated. She could have her pick."

Immediately, I shook my head even though he couldn't see me. Signing away my own freedom was one thing, but I could never ask Savannah to sacrifice her own fated mate for the sake of a treaty. "I'm afraid that's not possible."

He seriously wants you to pimp out your own sister? Felix asked in my head, sounding just as outraged as I felt. Sav was like a little sister to him too, he felt just as protective of her as I did.

"Why not?" Alpha Warren demanded. "She's not mated, is she?"

"No, but..."

"Then there's no reason for you not to agree. She won't be forced into anything, Alpha, no matter what you might think of my pack. She can come here and meet my men. If none of them are to her satisfaction, she can return to you. It's a reasonable request, and if you refuse it, I'll have no choice but to assume that you aren't as committed to this alliance as you claim to be."

Fuck. What was I supposed to say to that? It did sound reasonable, but who could say what might happen if Sav actually went there? What kind of pressure would she be put under?

Despite the finality of his condition, I tried to counter anyway. "There must be something else we can offer, Alpha Warren. Besides my mate and my sister, nothing else is off the table. What do you need?"

"I need nothing, Alpha Vaughan, except the proof of your commitment. These are my terms: take them or leave them."

I looked to Felix for help, but he could shrug helplessly back at me.

When I didn't immediately respond, the Alpha spoke again. "You can take some time to think it over. Amanda told me she'll be leaving there today to return home. She can bring your answer with her."

"That's not very much time," I pointed out through clenched teeth. Amanda had made it clear to me she wanted to leave as soon as possible, and to get home in one day, she'd need to leave soon.

"Then you'll need to decide quickly just how much you want to remain our friend, Alpha."

With that, he hung up, the line going dead. In frustration, I picked up the receiver and slammed it down, though that accomplished nothing. "Now what?" I asked my Beta, who gave me another pitying look, not unlike the one he'd worn when I got down there in the first place.

"I guess you're going to have to talk to Sav. It's her life; she should be involved in making the decision."

I didn't want her to know it had even been suggested, but Felix had a point: if Savannah point-blank refused, that would be my answer. In a way, it took the decision out of my hands, and the pack would understand that. And she *would* refuse, I felt certain of that, so as soon as Felix and I went through the other things we needed to discuss, I would have to go and talk to my sister, and then figure out what the hell to tell Amanda to take as a message back to her father.

Chapter Fifty-Six

~**Calista**~

The doctor snapped her small briefcase shut as she finished her examination. "I'll give you a full physical and an EEG in the next few days just to make sure we haven't missed anything, but you look fine to me. You might feel a little more tired than usual for a while, but that's normal when your wolf first appears. Your body will get used to it soon enough. If you have any concerns in the meantime, just let me know."

"I will. Thank you." I couldn't remember the last time I'd been examined by a real doctor. My mom always treated me at home; just another thing that made more sense to me now that I knew the whole truth about myself. While I had the doctor there, I made one additional request. "Would you be able to prescribe me some birth control too?"

Savannah gasped in the corner, where she had been sitting and trying to mind her own business during my checkup, and she quickly clamped a hand over her mouth to stop the noise as the doctor and I both turned to look at her.

"I can have some sent over to you today," the doctor promised. "With your werewolf metabolism, it'll kick in pretty quickly, but even so, it will take a few days before it's fully effective. If you want to avoid pregnancy, you should continue to use an alternate method until then."

A few more days of condoms with Vaughan, then. Logically, I knew a few days wasn't all that long, but it felt like ages at that particular moment. I couldn't wait to be with him without one.

As soon as the doctor left the room, Savannah bounced over to sit on the bed next to me. "So, you and Vaughan don't want kids right away?"

"I'm not sure," I admitted. Before meeting Vaughan, the idea of having a family of my own seemed completely out of reach, something that only happened to other people and not to me. It would take a little while for my ideas for the future to catch up to how profoundly everything had changed. "Not today, anyway."

"The whole pack will be eager for you guys to have a kid," she warned me frankly. "But I say screw 'em. Enjoy each other for a while first. And who knows? Maybe now that he's getting laid, he'll finally back off and give me some breathing room so I can do the same!"

Just like that, she put me at ease again, and we talked and laughed and nibbled on the food Savannah had brought with her for a few more minutes until there was a knock at the door. "Callie? Are you decent?"

That had to be Vaughan, since no one else called me Callie, but I didn't know why he would care about me being dressed when I'd been naked on top of him not even an hour ago until I told him to come in and the door opened to reveal both him and Felix.

"I know that look. Let me guess: you want me to leave so you can talk about pack business." With a sigh, Savannah got to her feet, but Vaughan quickly shook his head.

"Actually, we're here to talk to you, but Calista should know what's going on too."

In short, clipped tones, he relayed his phone call with the Ravenstone pack Alpha and the suggestion Amanda's father had made regarding Savannah. I could tell by the tension in his shoulders that he hated the idea, and Felix didn't look much happier.

"Are these kinds of arranged marriages common among werewolves?" I asked.

"No," Vaughan quickly assured me. "He has no right to ask it. Sav, just say the word and I'll turn him down."

Obviously, he expected her to balk at the idea just as he had, but I had my suspicions even before she spoke that Savannah might take a different view of it. "Just to be clear: I get to go and date a bunch of different men, without you around, and decide if I want to take any of them as my mate? And I could decide to choose none of them?"

"That's what the Alpha said," Vaughan agreed reluctantly. "But that's assuming he doesn't have some trick up his sleeve. He really wasn't happy when I spoke to him. I'll tell him we're not interested..."

"I'll do it."

Savannah's words stopped Vaughan in his tracks as Felix's mouth dropped open.

"Savannah, I don't think you understand." Vaughan's voice grew deeper, like it always seemed to when he was especially serious. So many things about him were familiar to me already.

His younger sister crossed her arms at him. "Don't talk to me like I'm a little kid. Of course I understand: if I don't go, we lose the alliance, or worse. Maybe it even starts a war. Am I right?"

Grudgingly, Vaughan nodded. "He could be bluffing, though."

"Or he might not be," Savannah countered. "Is it worth the risk to find out? Especially when it's not a huge deal in the first place. I can go on a few dates. Send a chaperone with me, someone you trust. They can keep an eye out and make sure nothing shady's going on. Who knows? Maybe I'll even meet my mate there. We already know he's not here."

Vaughan's lips pressed firmly together, letting me know he still didn't like the idea, but he didn't seem to be able to find a flaw in his sister's logic. Eventually, he turned to me for help. "What do you think, Callie?"

Savannah's brown eyes darted over to me with a pleading expression, hoping for my support. From even the brief time we'd spent together, I understood how much she felt restricted by her position as the Alpha's sister and how enticing a bit of freedom must seem to her. Selfishly, I didn't want her to go, since we'd just started to get to know each other and I would have appreciated her guidance as I got settled into the pack, but I had to put Savannah's needs, and those of the pack at large, before my own. "I think Savannah can handle it. If she wants to go and you think it's safe, then I think you should let her go."

Savannah's grateful grin made me smile in return, even as I felt a pang of loss. For a moment, it almost felt like we could be good friends, and if she decided to stay with one of the men in the Ravenstone pack, we might never get the chance to be as close as we might have been. As much as I hoped it went well for her and that she had fun, I couldn't help wishing she'd come back to us at the end of it.

"I need Leo here to help with Calista's transition to pack life," Vaughan said, speaking half to himself and half to Felix. "Darius will be busy with the fallout from the last couple of days. I could send Luke or Ethan, I guess…"

"I'll go," Felix quickly volunteered, and from the way the tension in Vaughan's shoulders eased, he must have been hoping for that response. "I'll look out for her just like you would. I'll make sure nothing happens to her."

"Nothing *bad*," Savannah corrected, barely able to contain her excitement. "I hope to the goddess that *something* happens. Should I go and pack?"

Vaughan seemed just as incapable of saying no to his sister's puppy-dog eyes as I had been, and as soon as he gave his assent, she darted out into the hall gleefully, tossing me a quick wave over her shoulder.

"They're not going to know what hit them when Sav shows up," Felix tried to joke, but I could tell that he and Vaughan were both still worried.

"Go and pack your things," Vaughan ordered his Beta. "I'll speak to Amanda and let her know what's happening."

His expression turned more tender as he looked back at me.

"After all that, I'd like to call a pack assembly and introduce them to you properly. Would that be okay?"

I understood the question behind the question he asked: was I ready to stand up in front of the whole pack and be introduced as Vaughan's mate?

It was fast, that couldn't be denied. A week ago, my life had a structure and routine that I didn't expect to change. I thought I knew who I was and what my life would be. In a matter of days, everything had been turned upside down, and though I still didn't understand everything about being mates, I knew I would never find anyone better suited to me than Vaughan.

With more certainty than I'd felt in a long time, I echoed back the words Vaughan had said to me in bed earlier, knowing he'd understand the reference even if Felix didn't. "It's so much better than okay."

The smile that lit up his handsome face was all the more beautiful for its rarity. In an instant, he had me in his arms, sitting beside me on the bed as his body and his lips pressed against mine in a searing, passion-filled kiss.

As Skye howled happily inside my head, I could almost feel the love and acceptance of my biological family and pack, and how proud and happy they would have been to see me find my mate, one who suited me so perfectly.

Finally, I'd found where I truly belonged.

Chapter Fifty-Seven

~**Vaughan**~

Four days later

Sitting at the boardroom table as my team wrapped up their updates, my eyes kept being drawn to the two empty chairs at the table, one on either side of me.

Felix had gone to the Ravenstone pack with Savannah, their departure delayed by a day because it took Savannah so long to figure out what clothes to take. I'd received short, coded messages from him to say that things seemed on the level so far, but he didn't go into much detail since he couldn't be certain his messages were secure. Sav was safe and enjoying being the centre of attention, I got that much, but how the whole situation might end still felt very up in the air. I'd feel a lot better when they were both back where they belonged.

The other empty chair belonged to Calista. As my future Luna, she had jumped right in to pack management, wanting to learn as much as she could as quickly as she could. Seriously and methodically, she set about studying werewolves and my pack in particular. Normally, she would have been there with me at the meeting, but that day, she had an appointment with her psychiatrist. As difficult as it might be, she was working through the effects of losing her family, having her past hidden from her, and her father's death. It wouldn't be a quick process but she'd committed to it and I supported her fully. Her strength awed me, and the pack responded very positively to her when I made the introduction. Having her stand next to me at the funerals for the pack members we lost had made that whole difficult experience much more bearable.

All that remained was for us to mark each other and set a date for our mating ceremony, but no matter how eager I felt to move forward, I had been doing my best to take things at her pace and not push her to go faster than she felt comfortable with. In my mind, I had no doubts at all: I wanted her to be mine, officially and permanently. I wanted us to run the pack together and I wanted to give her the kind of home she'd never known. Eventually, I wanted a family of our own, but more than anything, I wanted her to be happy, and if that meant waiting until she felt ready, I would wait.

"The analysis on the water at the plant indicates it's clear of the toxin," Darius said, holding up a glass of tap water to illustrate his point. "Who wants to be the first to try it?"

Since I would never ask any of my pack members to do something that I didn't feel comfortable doing myself, I raised my hand. "I'll do it."

The glass slid down the table, person to person until it reached me, and I drank the whole thing down in front of everyone, hoping that Calista's mom had been telling the truth and that our analysis was correct. We should know for sure pretty quickly.

"How are things going on your commission, Leo?" I asked my Gamma as we waited to see if the water affected Atlas in any way. I'd given him a special assignment in anticipation of my mating ceremony, whenever it might happen.

"I've approved the design and the team will start construction this weekend. It should be ready on time."

Everyone else gave me their reports as we dealt with the usual day-to-day running of the pack. Things seemed pretty much back to normal. With the caves sealed back up, there hadn't been any further sign of trouble, and the human murders had stopped too, just as abruptly as they began. By the time the meeting ended, Atlas was still strong in my head and I gave the go-ahead to alert the pack they could once again drink the water.

Things could go back to the way there were, except that now, I had my mate to go through it all with.

Once the meeting adjourned, Leo and I chatted a little longer until a text came in on my phone. From its special chime, I knew it came from Calista, and Leo quickly excused himself. "Have a good night, Alpha."

As long as it involved Calista, I definitely would, and her message only drove my anticipation higher. *I've asked the kitchen to send dinner up to our room. I'll see you there as soon as you're free.*

Thankfully, I had nothing else urgent to do. If she'd sent that while I was still in the middle of a meeting, my concentration would have been completely shot. As it was, I could bound straight upstairs, throwing open the door so fast that Calista jumped in surprise.

"Did you teleport here? I just sent that message!"

Her teasing tone made me smile, but the sight of her distracted me from any thoughts of laughter. She sat at the dressing table I'd bought for her, combing out her long, blonde hair, and I stepped over to her immediately, running my hands through her hair after the brush and tilting her head back so I could kiss her. "With an invitation like that, you can't expect me to wait."

"What invitation? I just said I'd see you..."

My mouth was on hers before she could finish, and she didn't seem to mind in the least. Nor did she protest when I lifted her off her seat, carrying her over the few feet to our bed. In just a few days, I'd stopped thinking of anything in the room as 'mine', other than Calista herself. Everything else, I happily shared with her, and I knew that would have never been the case with Amanda, not in the same easy, natural way it came with my fated mate.

"Supper will be here any minute," she laughed breathlessly as I kissed my way down her neck, stopping to nuzzle at the spot where I would mark her. "It'll get cold if you don't stop."

"Let it get cold. I'm much hungrier for you."

When my kiss made it clear I meant it, Calista gave up any hope of convincing me otherwise. Instead, she pulled my shirt off, looking just as eager as I felt. That first moment of skin-to-skin contact, our bodies sparking against each other, still felt just as magical as it had the very first time she touched me, when I tried to convince her the sensation she felt had simply been static electricity.

It didn't take long for our clothes to end up on the floor and our naked bodies to be pressed together from head to toe. We'd explored multiple positions over the previous few days, but I still preferred when I got to look straight into her beautiful blue eyes, the way I did then, lying on top of her as my fingers slipped between her legs. A low growl of approval came out of me, partly from me and partly from Atlas, as I felt just how ready she was for me.

When I reached over to the bedside drawer for a condom, though, Calista stopped me, her hand sliding down my arm to pull it back. "It's okay. You don't need to use one."

My hand still in mid-air, I looked down at her in surprise. "What do you mean?"

"I'm not ready to get pregnant yet," she quickly clarified. "But I started on birth control, and the doctor says it should be safe now to give up the condoms. If you want to."

If I wanted to? Just the thought of it had the blood rushing to my already stiff cock even harder than before. It almost made me feel lightheaded.

"So, when you say you're not ready to get pregnant *yet*, does that mean you see us having children at some point?" Despite letting me introduce her to the pack as my mate, Calista had been tightlipped about our future in general. Since she brought it up, I couldn't help asking for a bit of clarification.

Her blue eyes shone as she looked back up at me, her cheeks flushed and her blonde hair spread out beneath her on the pillow, making her look like some kind of beautiful siren. "It means I'm ready to say I want to build a life with you, Vaughan. It's still a bit crazy to me after only a week, but I know this is where I'm meant to be. Life with you feels right, and I trust you to help me figure the rest out."

Every word out of her mouth sounded incredible to me, but I wanted to be completely sure I understood. "Does that mean..."

As my fingers brushed against her neck, she anticipated my question before I could ask it. "Yes. I think so. I'm ready for us to mark each other and to make this all official."

I could hear the tremble in her voice, letting me know that she might not have conquered all her uncertainties just yet, but she was willing to move forward anyway. I'd never met anyone braver.

"Well, the good news is, marking usually goes hand-in-hand with sex, so we're halfway there already." I pressed my naked body down onto hers again, pressing her further into the mattress to prove my point. "So if you're really sure..."

"I'm sure." She was the one to cut me off that time, pulling my head back down until my lips were on hers again.

As our tongues tangled, she reached down between us, grabbing my cock firmly and sending sparks of pleasure through me as she guided me to her entrance. When I pushed into her with nothing between us, the feeling was so intense, I had to stop and catch my breath once I got all the way in.

"Fuck, you feel amazing."

"So do you." Calista's eyes were closed as she let out a soft moan. "It's so good, I'm half afraid I'm going to wake up and all of this will be a dream."

I knew what she meant, but I also never wanted her to doubt my devotion, or my reality, for that matter. "Your dreams only show the bad things that will happen," I reminded her. "Never the good ones. Maybe that's why you never saw me coming."

As I hoped, that made her smile, her blue eyes lighting up with a mischievous twinkle. "Well, I can definitely see you coming now."

To emphasize her point, she shifted her hips against me, sending another shiver of electricity through my body. If she kept doing that, it wouldn't take long for me to come at all, so I had better make sure I satisfied her first.

My fingers moved down to her clit as I began to thrust into her, finding a rhythm that worked for both of us. It had always felt wonderful with her, but that time, feeling her directly on my bare cock, knowing that she accepted the bond between us just as I did, it felt better than ever. The world outside of our room ceased to exist in that moment with no thoughts in my head but the pleasure I could give her and the pleasure she gave me.

And when Calista's legs began to tremble around me, her climax approaching, I thrust into her hard one last time, burying my cock all the way to the hilt as I bent down and found the marking spot on her neck. Instinct took over, with Atlas' guidance, and my wolf teeth came out to pierce her skin, marking her as mine, once and for all.

That shouldn't feel so good, a soft voice murmured in my head. My mate's voice, for the first time through mind-link, confirming our connection.

Gently, I pulled my teeth out, lapping at the wound to help it heal. "Show me how good it feels," I whispered to her. "Make me yours."

All I had to do was offer my neck to her and Calista did the rest, no doubt guided by Skye as I had been by Atlas. As her teeth sliced through my skin, I came immediately, pleasure and pain combining perfectly to give me the strongest orgasm I'd ever had. I might have even blacked out for a second, but when I opened my eyes again, Calista smiled up at me in satisfaction, my mark fresh on her neck.

"I guess no one can call us enemies anymore."

"We never were," I reminded her, kissing her lips softly. "We were always meant to be like this, and we always will be."

Epilogue

~**Calista**~

The night before my mating ceremony with Vaughan, I had a dream. In it, we stood side by side at the front of a huge auditorium with each seat filled. My mate looked incredibly handsome in his suit, my mark on proud display on his neck, his long, curly hair tamed and his brown eyes shining with happiness as he took my hands in front of his pack to make his vows. Leo had picked out my dress since fashion had never been my strong suit, and I had to admit he'd done an incredible job. It suited me perfectly, the gold colour working with my blonde hair without washing out my skin.

When the time came for me to say the words back to Vaughan, I glanced out into the crowd just for a moment, and that was when I saw them: my werewolf family, sitting in the third or fourth row. They looked just as I remembered them from the memories I'd started to have, which came to me in flashes the more I delved into my past with the pack psychiatrist. The look of pride in my father's eyes softened his otherwise gruff appearance, and my mother brushed away tears as one hand cradled her swollen, pregnant stomach. My brothers were still boys, fidgeting in their seats in their suits, but they both smiled at me too when they saw me looking.

"Callie?"

Vaughan's voice sounded far away as he said my name curiously. I tried to look back at him, but my eyes were drawn to another man sitting right in the front with both his legs intact: my other father, the hunter who'd raised me. He also wore a look of pride on his face, accompanied by an apology, and when our eyes met, he nodded at me as if to say he accepted the choice I'd made, even if he didn't fully understand it.

"Callie?" Vaughan spoke again, and when I blinked, I found myself back in our bed with my mate's hand cupping my face gently. The sun had just started to filter through the large window, brightening the room enough that I could see the look of concern and affection on his face. "Are you okay? You were talking in your sleep."

I blinked again, trying to orient myself. "Sorry. What did I say?"

"You said, 'thank you for coming'. Since it's been a few hours since I did, I didn't think you were talking to me."

My lips curled into a smile at his bad joke before I could stop them, making him laugh.

"What were you dreaming about?" he asked, his thumb stroking my cheek. "Nothing bad, I hope?"

"No. Nothing bad." I left it at that, and he didn't press me. Instead, his lips found mine, and we got to satisfy each other one more time before we had to start getting ready for the day.

When the real mating ceremony came around that afternoon, it looked just as it had in my dream, right down to the look in Vaughan's eyes. When the elder called on me to recite the words I'd practiced, I glanced out into the crowd, just as I'd done in my sleep, but in the spot where I'd seen my family, other werewolves sat, members of my new pack who smiled at me in encouragement, their faces filled with delight at finally seeing their Alpha mated. In the front row sat Vaughan's mother who'd made the trip from Arizona for the ceremony. I didn't know her well yet, but the warm hug she gave me when we were introduced let me know she would be very different from the woman who raised me.

"Callie?" Vaughan whispered my name curiously, just as he'd done in my dream. "Is everything okay? Do you remember the words?"

I turned my head back to him, giving him a firm nod. "It's okay. I remember."

Just because I couldn't see them didn't mean my family wasn't there. Maybe that had been the point of the dream: to remind me that they were always with me and would always be part of my life as I set out on this new phase of it.

At the end of the ceremony, Vaughan kissed me so passionately that my body immediately flared with desire for him. I almost forgot that we were in front of thousands of people until the cheering started and I pulled back from him, blushing furiously as my mate laughed, his arms around me possessively.

A huge banquet had been set up in the pack house ballroom, so I expected us to head back there as soon as we finished in the town hall, but instead, Vaughan turned his truck towards the park in the middle of the town where a small crowd had already gathered.

"What's this?" I asked curiously, peering out the window.

"A gift to mark the day," was all my mate would say as he parked the truck and ran around to my side to open my door for me, helping me get down in my dress.

Hand-in-hand, we walked into the park as the crowd parted to make way for us, a sea of smiling faces on both sides. As we reached the centre of the gathered group, a beautiful fountain came into view that definitely hadn't been there when Vaughan first gave me a tour of the town. Against a carved three-dimensional background depicting the Montana forest, two rivers flowed down through the trees, meeting in the middle just before they emptied into the pool below. The water flowed gently, making the sound of it splashing into the pool soothing and almost musical. It felt calm and tranquil beneath the clear blue sky.

"Look at the inscription," Vaughan whispered, pointing to the carving at the base of the fountain.

Tearing my eyes away from the beautiful display, I looked down, and my chest immediately tightened as I read the words there:

In memory of the Deep Valley pack, forever linked with ours.

With new understanding, I looked back up at the rivers, one representing Deep Valley and the other, the Crimsontooth pack. The point where they met symbolized that very day, the day our packs joined together in my mating with Vaughan. The pool below was our future: vast and beautiful and undefined.

"Do you like it?"

Only when Vaughan asked the question did I realize I must have been staring for a while, too stunned to say anything, so I turned to him with tears in my eyes. "It's beautiful. Overwhelming. Thank you."

"Leo did most of the work," he admitted, always eager to give credit where it was due.

Though that might be true, I knew the idea had come from my thoughtful mate, and I reached up to run my hand down his handsome face. "Thank you," I repeated before pulling him down for another kiss, right there in front of everyone.

We were interrupted that time not by a cheer, but by a spray of water that hit us square in the face, making us both jump.

"Where did that come from?" Vaughan grumbled good-naturedly, looking down at the waters of the fountain, rippling as though something had just disturbed them.

Over his shoulder, I could just make out the mischievous smiles of two little boys, my brothers as they'd appeared in my dream, wearing their suits as they splashed in the water before the image faded.

"I think that was my family saying hello."

Vaughan gave me a curious look as the crowd around us began to applaud. I would tell him about the dream later, but in that moment, I simply took his hand, feeling his steady support beside me, the acceptance of my new pack in the faces around me, and the love of those I had lost, urging me on to the new life that lay ahead of me with my mate beside me.

At long last, I'd come home.

THE STORY CONTINUES...

If you enjoyed the book, please take a moment to leave a review. Thank you!

See what happens during Savannah's time at the Ravenstone pack in the second book of the *Rocky Mountain Wolves* series, Honour Among Rogues. Coming soon!

KEEP IN TOUCH

For more about my other books and to keep up-to-date with new releases, find all the links here:
https://linktr.ee/melodytyden